Gabrielle Donnelly was born and brought up in London, where she worked as a journalist on women's magazines before moving to Los Angeles to specialize in show-business journalism. She lives in Los Angeles with her husband, Owen Bjørnstad, and has been an ardent fan of Louisa May Alcott since she was a small girl.

THE *LITTLE WOMEN* LETTERS

When the great-great-granddaughter of Josephine March finds a batch of letters, the words of the Little Women shed a light on a new generation of sisters. The Atwaters are a loving family and Fee's three daughters, Emma, Lulu and Sophie, couldn't be less alike. Emma is planning her wedding, Sophie is an up-and-coming actress, and Lulu — the clever one — is stuck in a series of dead-end jobs. But when she gets her hands on Grandma Jo's letters, gathering dust in the attic, everything seems to change and different worlds begin to open up. And even though dark family secrets emerge, Jo's words offer comfort and guidance across the centuries. Sometimes family is all that matters. And sisters are the closest friends you can find.

GABRIELLE DONNELLY

THE
LITTLE WOMEN
LETTERS

Complete and Unabridged

CHARNWOOD
Leicester

First published in Great Britain in 2011 by
Penguin Books Ltd.
London

First Charnwood Edition
published 2012
by arrangement with
Penguin Books Ltd.
London

British Library CIP Data

Donnelly, Gabrielle.
  The Little Women letters.
  1. Sisters- -Fiction. 2. March, Jo (Fictitious character)- -
  Fiction. 3. Great-grandmothers- -Correspondence- -
  Fiction. 4. Large type books.
  I. Title
  823.9'2–dc23

  ISBN 978–1–4448–1118–6

Published by
F. A. Thorpe (Publishing)
Anstey, Leicestershire
Set by Words & Graphics Ltd.
Anstey, Leicestershire
Printed and bound in Great Britain by
T. J. International Ltd., Padstow, Cornwall

This book is printed on acid-free paper

For Lydia Newhouse who had the idea,
and for Harriet Barber who helped
make it happen

Author's Note

In dating Jo March's letters and the events in the March family, I have taken as a starting point the only specific date mentioned in *Little Women* — that of Amy's drawing up and signing of her will, stated to be 20 November 1861. However, this means that the opening of the book took place in December 1860, with Father off ministering to the men in the army 'where the fighting was', almost four months before the American Civil War had actually started. In respect and affection for Louisa May Alcott, I have chosen to follow her chronology rather than that of strict historical accuracy.

1

Plumfield, October 1888.

Dearest Amy,
My daughter has arrived in this world, and bless the infant, she is the reddest and the squallingest baby you ever did see! We both had a hard time of her birthing, but she came through like a trump, and when they laid her upon my breast she looked up at me with her little sharp gray eyes, and nodded with a decided air, as if to say, 'There now! I don't think we'll be doing *that* again, Mamma, and I for one rejoice to know it.'

Fritz and the boys are already in thrall for when she's not roaring she's a merry soul and keeps us all entertained most mightily. Meg broods over her like a lace-capped mother hen, ignoring the squawks but greeting each crow and coo as if they were the songs of Herr Wagner and the oratory of President Lincoln himself. Daisy and Josie pay obeisance at her throne, and, all in all, she looks set to be petted and spoilt *almost* as much as a certain little yellow-haired girl I once knew back in Concord. But upon consideration, if she grows into one tenth of the woman that same little girl grew into at last, then I shan't have cause for complaint — about that or about anything else. If only Marmee and my Beth were still here with us, I believe I shouldn't have a wish left in the world.

I must say, dear, that it is perfectly capital to have a daughter! Of course I love my tall boys and am proud as Punch of them, but it had always been a secret little disappointment to me not to have had a girl, too, as you have your Bess, and as Meg — happy woman! — has Josie *and* Daisy. And now, just when I had thought that part of my life was done, comes the most precious little gift that I had ever dared to dream of. I shall raise my girl to be good, and industrious, and useful to the community, and also to run and play and be jolly, and to build up a strong body as well as a lively mind. I shall teach her to have all the good and womanly impulses, but I shall teach her, too, that girls *are* as valuable as boys, and every bit as clever, given the education. I long to see the times she will grow up into — for times *are* changing for girls, blessedly. Perhaps when she is old enough she shall even be allowed to vote in the Elections, as the women in England are hoping to — and when that joyous day arrives shan't I just toss my old woman's bonnet into the air, ruffles and ribbons and all, just see if I don't, and scandalize the town, the way I used to when I was a girl!

Dear Amy, I want to say a word to you about how we shall name her. I know you've been concerned that if the baby were a girl I should want to name her for Beth, and to tell you the truth, if we hadn't your Bess already in the family, I *should* want that, for you know that Beth is in my heart always. But your Princess Goldilocks is the bearer of the name now, and such a dear and precious name as it is, it must have the one proprietor only. So my girl shall be plain Josephine like her mother — it pleases Fritz, Josie says she don't mind, and we'll call her Cissie, so there shan't be two names too much the same — and, dear, you don't mind very much, do you, if I give her Elizabeth as a second name? I should like to feel that Beth is watching over her, too, from heaven, as she watches over us all and always will.

Thank you for your letter, and I can't tell you how much I relished the parcel collected from your travels — little Cissie Bhaer shall have quite the Parisian air to her when I take her into town! I'm glad to hear that Teddy is behaving himself among the fine lords and ladies of Europe, and that Bess continues to improve at her mud pies (now don't frown, dear, for it don't become you, and you know I never *will* learn to refer respectfully to your sculptures, however artistic they may be). Come safely home from Rome, dearie, and come as quickly as you can, for I long with all my heart to present to all three of you this completely captivating, newest and littlest — although very far from the quietest, as her ma's poor head can attest — of little women.

Ever your topsy-turvy sister,
Jo.

3

Nearly a century and a quarter later, and more than three thousand miles away, Fee Atwater sat in the kitchen of a tall, narrow house in Islington on a rainy Sunday in early spring and ate brunch with two of her daughters while awaiting the arrival of her third. Fee was American-born and raised, and although she had lived in London, and most happily so, for the majority of her adult life, there still remained parts of America that would be with her until the day she died. One of these was the habit of Sunday brunch, for Fee and her family a cheerfully haphazard occasion centring around the table of the friendly, untidy kitchen, abundant with well-thumbed cookery books, photographs in frames and random bunches of flowers stuck into jam jars and milk bottles, during which family members and friends would come and go, helping themselves as they passed to bagels and cream cheese, smoked salmon and scrambled eggs, and lately — since Fee had recently succumbed to the charms of Ottolenghi on Upper Street — a variety of ready-made salads and side dishes to round out the feast. These last caused her husband, when he was at home, to examine the prices on the containers and complain that she was driving them all into bankruptcy; in response to which Fee would point out that she made sufficient money of her own as a family therapist to indulge her family in treats once a week, and that, by the way, she did not notice him exactly turning in horror from those same extravagant side dishes when they were offered to him.

4

Fee and David Atwater were a happy couple. David Atwater owned a small publishing company specializing in travel books, which took him away from England often, and sometimes for several weeks at a time. Fee was independent by nature, the product of a long line of strong-minded Yankee women from Massachusetts, and both agreed that the space his travels put between them did their marriage good. Whatever the cause, their marriage was a strong one. They both respected each other and made each other laugh, fought sometimes but always made up, and after nearly thirty years of marriage, still reached, almost unconsciously, for each other's hand when they walked down the street.

'I wonder what Matthew and I'll be like,' said Fee's eldest daughter, Emma, now, dreamily, to her mother — she had recently announced her engagement, to no one's surprise and everyone's pleasure, to Matthew, her boyfriend of three years, 'when we've been married as long as you and Dad have. It seems funny now to think that even three years ago we didn't know each other — I wonder what we'll be like when we've been together for another twenty-five years.'

'I should think *he'll* be a wreck,' remarked her younger sister Lulu, who at twenty-four had still not yet grown out of the habit of insulting her siblings. 'He's a brave, brave man, and I told him so only last week.'

'Well, that must be the reason he's called the wedding off,' said Emma. 'Thanks for the explanation, Lu, I'd been wondering. Mom, do you know how many calories there are in this aubergine salad? It looks sort of suspiciously delicious to me.'

'Only one way to find out,' said Lulu. She reached across her sister to grab the container, helped herself to a portion and immediately puffed out her cheeks into a fat ball. 'Ooh, I've gained half a stone! I'm enormous!'

Fee poured coffee into her mug, and looked across the table at her daughters, wondering, not for the first time, how she had managed to give birth to two creatures so comprehensively different each from the other. Emma was her model daughter, so perfectly behaved that Fee and David had sometimes worried that she was due for an eruption of repressed misconduct. But the eruption never happened — pleasing people came naturally to Emma, it seemed. She had slept through the night as a baby, had sailed through adolescence with neither spots nor tantrums, had graduated from London University with a good degree in social policy and now worked in the administration department of a private organization that investigated satisfaction in medical patients.

Three years ago, she had met, through friends, a pleasant-faced young computer consultant called Matthew Hudson; a year later she had moved into his meticulously tidy flat in a narrow street just behind the Angel Tube station, and they planned to marry early in the following year; she had confided to Fee that three years after that, when he would be thirty-two and she thirty, they would start trying for children.

6

Emma had brown shiny hair that no one ever saw unkempt, big blue-grey eyes and an old-fashioned pink and white complexion. She wore well-cut trousers for work, and for leisure jeans in the winter or flowery skirts in the summer, which she topped with shirts from Zara or Whistles. She kept her nails short but impeccably manicured, and was careful never to gain weight. She would, her mother thought almost wistfully, make the most beautiful bride imaginable.

If Emma was peaches and cream, then Lulu, her mother often thought, was some sort of peppery curry, full of spices and unexpected flavours. A sturdy, untidy girl, with watchful brown eyes and a mane of wild chestnut hair that overwhelmed her features and which she refused to have cut, she stalked through the world where her sister glided, glowered where her sister smiled, and from the beginning, it seemed, had made it a point to challenge convention and confound expectations. At school she had been several times the topic of worried consultations between her parents and her teachers until, suddenly tiring of mischief-making, she had surprised everyone by proving to be unusually clever, had gained a First Class degree in biochemistry from St Andrew's, and promptly afterwards declared that she had not the faintest intention of embarking upon a scientific career.

Now, eighteen months later, she still had not decided what it was she really did want to do with her life, and so was working through a series of temporary jobs, each one, it seemed, more unsuitable than the last, while living with her best friend Charlie, to whom she paid rent mostly by cooking their meals and doing odd jobs around the home. Alfreda Alessandra Maria Fitzcharles — known to her friends as Charlie — and Lulu had shared a flat at university. Charlie was darkly beautiful, rather rich and, in the eyes of the Atwaters, a little exotic, the daughter of an Irish hotelier who travelled extensively and an Italian model who had died in a plane crash when Charlie was small. The family owned a flat in Belsize Park to which Charlie had generously invited Lulu to stay until such time as she was earning enough money for a place of her own.

Fee did not on principle approve of any of her daughters getting something for nothing, but consoled herself with the reflection that Lulu, a good handyman and an excellent cook, made a point of making herself useful around the flat, and it was obvious to her, besides, that Charlie enjoyed Lulu's company. Fee worried a little about Charlie, who had little family of her own and sometimes seemed lonely to her. Charlie was here at brunch now, smiling quietly at Lulu's clowning while liberally spreading a bagel with cream cheese which she then topped with strawberry jam — Charlie had never needed to worry about a calorie in her life.

'That is so unfair,' said Emma enviously, watching the progress of the bagel from Charlie's plate to Charlie's mouth. 'If I ate even a quarter of that, I would be the size of a baby elephant.'

'Sorry,' said Charlie. 'I've inherited my

mother's metabolism, it seems. It's very irritating, I know.'

'Don't apologize to *her*,' said Lulu. 'She'd eat your arm to get to it if she really wanted it, wouldn't she, Toby?' She reached down to scratch the marmalade-coloured cat that sprawled on the chair next to her, blinking benignly at the proceedings. 'When's Dad coming home, Mom? Speaking of elephants.'

'Thursday, around midday,' said Fee, 'depending on Air Peru. I hope he arrives quietly this time. Last autumn we converted Sophie's old bedroom into my office, Charlie, and he still sometimes forgets that when he comes home in the daytime. Two weeks ago, I was seeing a woman who was telling me the most terribly sad story about her divorce; she was crying, I was listening and handing her tissues, and, right at the very saddest point, the front door crashed shut and we heard a bellow from the hall: 'Fee-Fee, my little bundle of naughtiness! Big Sugar Candy Daddy's home!' which he always thinks is hilarious. I nearly killed him.'

'You should put a note on the front door for when he arrives,' said Emma.

'That's an idea, Emma, I might do that.' Fee smiled at her sensible eldest. 'Lulu, honey, did you get my message about Professor Hamilton?'

Lulu sighed. 'Yes, Mom, I got your message about Professor Hamilton,' she said. 'Are you ever going to get *my* message that I don't want to spend my life locked away behind a test tube like a half-blind, obsessive-compulsive-disorder-ridden lab rat?'

'Well, sweetie, I can't think you want to spend your life looking after the office files in a second-hand shop, either, do you?'

'It's not a second-hand shop,' said Lulu. 'It's an arts and antique-goods importership, and believe it or not I'm quite happy there. It's close to the flat, Mr Goncharoff is really sweet to work for and he never minds it if I . . . '

Too late, she stopped.

'If you kind of sort of don't get around to coming into work when you don't feel like it,' her mother concluded. 'Oh, Lulu, what are we going to do with you?'

'I'm not asking you to do anything with me,' said Lulu. 'I'm a grown woman, I'm not expecting you to give me money, and what I do with my life is up to me to decide when I decide to decide it, not anyone else.'

'I don't understand you,' said Emma. 'Just flitting around jobs like that. There are women who'd kill for a brain like yours.'

'Well, it wouldn't do them much good on Death Row, would it?' And that was enough, Lulu decided, of discussion of her professional prospects. 'Anyway, *Mom*, I don't know that you're in a position to lecture me here. When you were my age, you were living in a Women's Collective outside Boston, reading Gloria Steinem, and ritually burning your bra every Saturday night.'

Lulu was tactless but not artless: the topic of burning bras was one that Fee was rarely able to resist.

'We never burned them,' she said now, firmly.

10

'That was an outright lie put about by the male establishment, who were so terrified of us it was pitiful. We just gave ourselves permission not to torture ourselves by squeezing into those terrible corsets and girdles the way our poor mothers had, and we were much happier for it, which drove them crazy.'

'You lived in a Collective?' said Charlie. 'What was it like?'

'It was mad,' said Lulu. 'They raised chickens and lived on eggs and earwiggy apples, and went out every weekend in gangs beating the bushes for male chauvinist piggery, wearing dungarees and huge round badges that said things like 'A woman needs a man like a fish needs a bicycle'. And then they were surprised when men didn't like them.'

'It was wonderful,' said Fee. 'We were young and idealistic, and, yes, Lulu's right, we took ourselves far too seriously. But we didn't have the luxury of making jokes about equality back then. We had a task to do and by God we worked at it, and by God we opened the world up for the next generation of women. You girls wouldn't have anything like the lives you have now if it hadn't been for us. Have you had some couscous, Charlie? It's quite good.'

'Shouldn't we save some for Sophie?' said Charlie, looking down the table at the dwindling feast.

'Sophie?' Lulu wrinkled her brow in pretend puzzlement at the mention of her younger sister. 'Who's Sophie?'

'The one who always arrives last,' Emma

11

reminded her. 'Sort of loud, sort of blonde, sort of all over the place, really.'

'Oh, that Sophie,' said Lulu. She flung her arms wide and beamed around the company. '*Hi*, Mom, hi, guys, *sorry* I'm late, you'll never *guess* what happened on my way over here, I'm an *actress*, I'm absolutely *lovely* and I *love* you all. That one?'

'You'll need a blonde wig,' said Emma. 'And the arms sort of go up a bit instead of straight out. But otherwise you'll do.'

'You mean I've got the part?' Lulu clasped her hands to her breast ecstatically. 'I *love* you!'

'It's very kind of you to think of her, Charlie,' said Fee. 'But she knows we were starting at twelve and it's now nearly two. If she can't be here in time to eat with the rest of us, she can take what we leave over.' But she rose anyway to start a fresh pot of coffee.

As she did so, the heavy front door slammed open and then shut, bringing with it a brief gust of wet wind and Sophie herself, taller than either of her sisters and slim as a greyhound, with butter-yellow hair cut in a pixie bob around delicate features and huge, expressive blue eyes that currently were blazing with indignant fury. She marched into the room, not troubling herself with a greeting, and dropped into a chair.

'You'll never guess what's happened!' she announced.

Emma and Lulu exchanged glances, tried and, at last, failed to repress their laughter.

'What?' said Sophie, staring at them. 'Hi, Charlie,

like the jumper. What's up with the two ugly sisters there?'

'They're being very silly,' said Fee, coming to kiss her youngest, and sending a warning frown at the others over the top of her head. 'What's up, baby girl? Did something bad happen?'

'Bad!' said Sophie. 'It's terrible! Tragic. Disastrous. You'll never believe it! Get this.' She sat up and swept a miserable gaze around the table. 'Ruby is getting married,' she said.

There was a silence.

'If we knew who Ruby was,' said Lulu at last, 'we might be able to raise just a little more interest here.'

'Ruby is Esme's sister,' said Sophie. 'Her elder sister, and, honestly, she's horrible. She has one of those long sour lemony faces and she doesn't like anyone and she doesn't approve of anyone, and she's vegan and she goes on at us when we even eat eggs, never mind meat, and she's big into recycling and she goes on that we don't recycle enough, although I'm actually quite good at it if you want to know, and if you try to make a joke she looks disgusted, and if you go out for a meal with her, which God knows I try not to, she'll count up what her food cost and not pay a penny more even when everyone else is splitting the bill, and she's just generally so horrible that even I don't like her, and I do like most people, don't I, Mom? Is that fresh coffee? Thanks, Mom, I'm starving, what have you left me to eat?'

'So let's get this straight,' said Lulu, watching her sister make healthy inroads into the remains of the brunch. 'Your flatmate's sister is not very nice, but she's getting married . . . '

'Can you believe it?' Sophie swallowed a quarter of a bagel and waved the rest incredulously. 'She met him at a rally for peace in Outer North-East Bora Bora or somewhere, which is actually heavy on the dramatic irony because she's the least peaceful person I know, and love bloomed and it's this big whirlwind romance and they're gadding off next week to pull out all the stops at Waltham Cross Registry Office with half a glass of shandy and a jacket potato afterwards. And he's nice! At least, he seems nice, but all I can say is he must be mad, because she's really, really, and I mean *really* — '

'We don't all find everyone easy to be with, sweetie,' said Fee. 'But even difficult people do find partners.'

'I'm still waiting,' remarked Emma mildly, 'to find out exactly how this affects you.'

'How it *affects* me?' said Sophie. She took another bite of bagel and shook her head in disbelief at her sisters' slowness of uptake. 'Don't either of you get it? When she moves in with him, she'll be moving out of her flat. And the deal's always been that if or when she moved out of her flat, then Esme would move in to take her place. Which means that Esme will be moving out of *our* flat, which means that I'm out on the street.'

'But can't you get another roommate?' said Fee. 'It's a small place, but at that rent surely someone would want it.'

'Well . . . kind of a problem there, Mom,' said Sophie. 'The flat was sort of a private arrangement between Esme and me.'

'Private arrangement?' Emma hooked her chair into the table and rested an interested chin on her hand. 'What might that mean exactly?'

Sophie sighed and looked with disfavour on her sisters.

'Do you two have to be here for this part?' she said. 'Don't you have a cauldron that needs stirring or something?'

'Oh, no, no,' said Emma. 'We've got all day for this one, haven't we, Lulu?'

'I'm all ears,' said Lulu.

'OK.' Sophie sighed again. 'Well, we didn't do anything *bad* or anything. It's just that the landlady is a friend of Esme's parents, and when Esme moved in she did say that she could have friends to stay, and I am a very good friend of Esme's, so, well, I just stayed there a lot.'

'Although it was officially only a flat for one person,' said Fee. 'Oh, Sophie, you know that was wrong.'

'We didn't do anything illegal, Mom,' said Sophie. 'And I was a model tenant — I kept the place in much better shape than Esme did, actually. And Mrs Powell really liked me. We met a couple of times when she came to visit. She thought I was Esme's friend down to stay from the North.'

'The North,' mused Lulu. 'It gets better, doesn't it, Emma?'

'Islington is north of Battersea,' Sophie informed her with dignity. 'And I do a really good Yorkshire accent, actually, Uncle Jim taught me.'

'Sophie, that's not right,' said Fee. 'If this Mrs Powell only wanted one tenant, she had every right to say so, and you should have respected that.'

'I know.' Sophie hung her head in penitence. 'I'm a very bad girl, and a disgrace to my parents who tried to teach me good values in spite of myself.' She brightened. 'But you'll be able to have another go on me now, won't you, when I move back in.'

'Move back in?' said Fee. 'Sweetie, there's nowhere for you to move back into.'

'Course there is,' said Sophie. 'I know my room's gone, but what's wrong with the top floor?'

'Don't you remember? Lulu's room hasn't been safe to sleep in since the storm. The ceiling's about to fall down at any moment, and we're just hoping that Kevin can find time to come and repair it before it goes completely. He's a busy man these days, but he's so good we don't want to ask anyone else.'

'Good, then I'll take Emma's room. I always wanted it anyway.'

'Honey,' said Fee. 'We have a lodger.'

There was a pause.

'Have we?' said Sophie.

'Man called Tom?' said Lulu. 'American scholar? Tall and sort of quiet, keeps himself to himself?'

'Him?' said Sophie. 'Is he still here? I thought he went back to America.'

'No, he's here,' said Fee. 'He *is* very quiet, mind.'

'Oh,' said Sophie.

There was a silence around the table.

'Maybe we could pull out the sofa bed in the living room,' said Fee.

'You'd hate that,' said Sophie. 'I'll think of something.'

'Well, it's there if you need it,' said Fee.

'It's OK,' said Sophie. 'I'll think of something.'

There was more silence.

'You could live with us for a while,' said Charlie.

'Charlie!' said Lulu. 'I will kill you. Of course she can't.'

'Well, if she's got nowhere else to go. And we do have the spare bedroom.'

'You don't know her. She's awful. She leaves her stuff everywhere and borrows your clothes without asking.'

'I don't borrow *your* clothes,' said Sophie quickly. 'They're just sad. Charlie has some nice stuff, though.'

'You see! She hasn't even moved in yet.'

'But I'd ask her first, because she's a nice person, not a horrible sister.'

'Charlie, you can't do this.' Lulu looked at Charlie, and shook her head, firmly. 'You're my friend, not some one-woman flophouse for poverty-stricken Atwater women. She can't afford to pay you any rent, you know.'

'*You* don't pay rent,' said Sophie.

'Number One, Charlie is *my* friend, not yours. Number Two, I pay what I can. And Number Three, I do all the cooking, which is my contribution to the household.'

'I can cook,' said Sophie, causing much merriment to her sisters.

'I *can*,' said Sophie. 'I've learned this last year. Mom, make them stop being so mean to me.'

'It seems that Lulu already has the cooking under control, sweetie,' said Fee. 'But if Charlie is serious, maybe you could find some other way to be useful? This is very kind indeed of you, Charlie, if you're sure it's OK?'

'Don't do it, Charlie,' said Lulu. 'You'll regret it. We'll both regret it.'

'The spare room's just sitting there,' said Charlie. 'Let's let her move in, Lulu. We can be the Haverstock Hill branch of the Women's Collective.'

'Charlie! I love you!' cried Sophie. She ran to Charlie and flung her arms around her neck, peppering her with kisses.

'Ew.' Charlie, who was rarely tactile, distanced herself with a stern arm. 'Get off me or you can't come to live with us.'

'Good,' said Lulu. 'Keep kissing her, Sophie.'

Sophie withdrew, disappointed. 'Call yourself Italian?' she grumbled. 'You're supposed to be Mediterranean and affectionate.'

'I don't call myself anything,' said Charlie. 'I just don't have any sisters. Women with sisters are always kissing each other at home and then when they go out in public they can't control themselves and become a menace to society.'

'I don't kiss my sisters,' said Lulu. 'I'm not even sure I like them, let alone want to go smooching over them.'

'Yes, you do,' said Charlie. 'You do it all the

18

time and you don't even know you're doing it.'

'What, like this?' Lulu cast a dramatic head onto Emma's breast, seized her hand and kissed it noisily. 'Yum, smoked salmon.'

'You see,' said Charlie. 'You're doing it right now.'

'No I'm not, I'm showing you what I don't do. Pass me a bagel, Mom, she's made me want seconds.'

'They're lucky to have sisters, aren't they, Charlie?' said Fee. She poured more coffee into her mug and passed the pot hospitably to their guest. 'I always wanted one, but I was an only.'

'I wanted a brother,' said Sophie, casting a reproachful glance at Emma and Lulu. 'He'd have brought all his friends home for me to meet.'

'Instead of having to put up with your sister's boring friends offering you free bedrooms in Belsize Park,' said Lulu. 'Thanks very much.'

'You wouldn't want to meet *my* brother's friends,' said Charlie. 'They're serious weirdoes.'

'You have a brother?' said Sophie hopefully.

'He lives in San Francisco,' Lulu told her. 'Maybe you should go and join him — she just said he likes weirdoes.'

'Mom! She's being mean to me again.'

'Be nice to each other, girls,' said Fee. 'Remember what Grandma Jo used to say. A happy family makes a happy life.'

The effect of the name on her two younger daughters was instant. Lulu groaned and slumped across the table, her tongue lolling in a

19

mimicry of anguished death; Sophie hunched down in her chair, squinted her eyes, drew her lips across her gums and puffed at an imaginary corn cob pipe. 'Dag-nabbit it, Ma, I done shot me a nice fat possum for my tea but them thar pesky raccoons done ate him up first, so I done ate them instead and they's bitter-tastin'.'

'You're awful about Grandma Jo,' said Emma. 'I think she sounds really cool.'

'Who's Grandma Jo?' asked Charlie.

'I've told you about her,' said Lulu.

'Apparently you haven't,' said Charlie. 'Or I wouldn't be asking.'

'I can't believe I haven't told you about Grandma Jo,' said Lulu. 'We hear of no one else. Night and day, winter and summer, year after year after year. We beg on our bended knees, we implore her through gnashing teeth, Mother, we say, enough about Grandma Jo. But does Mom listen? Noooo.'

'Grandma Jo was my great-grandmother,' said Fee. 'She lived to be a hundred, although I never knew her, unfortunately. They say she was quite a personality.'

'She had three sisters,' said Lulu. 'There was Margaret, who was A Perfect Gentlewoman. There was Bethie or Betsey, who was An Angel who died young. And there was Amy, who slept with a clothes peg on her nose to try to change the shape.'

'Did it work?' said Charlie.

'No,' said Sophie, firmly. 'It just hurt. A lot.'

'I tried an experiment,' said Lulu. 'On her. Mom was *not* amused.'

'Neither was I,' said Sophie. 'It really hurt.'

'Amy married a rich man and Meg married a poor man . . . ' began Lulu.

'But they were both the richest women in America in the wealth that really counted . . . ' continued Sophie.

' . . . a busy and useful life and a home full of love,' they both finished in chorus.

'There's nothing wrong with those things,' said Emma. 'Not that you two seem interested in either of them.'

'Who did Grandma Jo marry?' asked Charlie.

'A German professor!' snorted Lulu, laughing — the idea had always amused her.

'*Kommen Sie hier, mein liebe* little dumpling,' said Sophie, 'and I vill show *Sie* how ve do sings back in old Bavaria.'

'They had a school for boys, which went bust in the Depression,' said Lulu.

'L'arned them little varmints to skin a squirr'l right 'bout as fine as ol' Ma Jo herself,' added Sophie.

'She wasn't just some old hillbilly,' said Emma. 'She wrote books.'

'So Mom says,' said Lulu. 'But conveniently none of them have survived, so we have no way of knowing what sort of books they were.'

'*A Hundred Ways to Make Moonshine*,' said Sophie. '*Spittoons: A User's Guide.*'

'She had a daughter called Cissie,' said Lulu, 'who was arrested three times for being a suffragist, who had a daughter called Jojo, who flew planes in the Second World War, who had Mom, whose full name is Josephine again, who

21

had Emma, who's really called Josephine too, only I couldn't pronounce it when I was little so we use her middle name. They're all the most horrible old bags; it's a family tradition.'

'You'll be sorry one day,' said Fee, 'when I'm dead and gone and your daughters come to you the way normal, nice daughters do, wanting to hear stories of the family, and you'll have been so busy making fun that you won't be able to remember any of them.'

'I'll send them to Auntie Emma,' said Sophie. 'Since she's so fond of Grandma Jo, she can tell them all about her.'

'No, I won't,' said Emma. 'I'll tell my own children everything I know, but I'll make them swear not to breathe a word to your horrid brats. If you want to know anything, you'll have to go to Aunt Amy.'

'Ooh.' Sophie shuddered.

'Aunt Amy is Mom's umpteenth cousin twice removed,' Lulu told Charlie. 'She's a terrifying old thing who lives in Boston and keeps going on about The Faaam'ly.'

'She's very kind to you girls,' said Fee. 'She doesn't have children of her own and you're more important to her than you might think.'

'She sends us money on our birthdays,' said Lulu. 'All wrapped up in weird little lectures about spending it sensibly and not frittering it away, and every so often she descends on London and wants to see what we've bought with it.'

'She'll be pleased to see this,' said Sophie. She drew one knee to her chest and displayed a trim ankle adorned with a small, vividly coloured butterfly.

'You didn't!' said Emma. 'Mom, did you know about that?'

'She's over twenty-one and it's her body,' said Fee. 'It wouldn't be my choice, but she's not asking me to do it.'

'I've wanted one for ages, haven't I, Mom?' said Sophie. 'I'd really like to have a huge one going all the way down my arm, but it's no good for my work. A small one's OK, though — Helen Mirren has one.'

'She also has a career,' said Lulu.

She had spoken in fun, but Lulu had yet to discover the line between teasing and unkindness.

'Lulu!' said Sophie, her blue eyes clouding in hurt.

Lulu had an unfortunate tendency, when she knew she was in the wrong, to say things that only made matters worse.

'Oh, please,' she said now, wearily. 'I was only joking! Don't be so sensitive, it's really annoying.'

'I don't think it was a very funny joke, sweetie,' said Fee. 'Why don't you apologize to your sister and tell her you didn't mean it.'

But Lulu, finding herself now set on a course of cruelty towards her sister, did not yet possess the personal skill to turn it around.

'Who says I don't mean it?' she demanded. 'How come it's OK for all of you to go on and on at me about *my* career, but I'm not even allowed to comment on hers, even though she hasn't had an acting job since October?'

'I have!' said Sophie. 'I worked all the end of last year, remember?'

'Third helper from the right at Selfridge's Christmas Grotto doesn't count as acting work, Soph.'

'I was the chief elf, actually,' said Sophie. 'And of course it counts as acting work, unless you think I actually became an elf for four weeks, which, knowing you, you just might. Anyway, at least I know what I want to do with my life, not like some.'

'Well, if that's all it takes,' said Lulu, 'I'd like to be the Sugar Plum Fairy, please. It's about as likely to happen.'

'Lulu! Mom! Emma!'

'For heaven's sake, Lulu,' said Emma, 'can't you make the smallest bit of effort to grow up a little? You're twenty-four now, not fourteen.'

'And I'm *so* sorry I'm not prematurely middle-aged like you. 'Can't you make the smallest bit of effort to grow up?' What on earth are you going to sound like when you really are forty-five instead of just pretending to be?'

'That's enough,' said Fee. 'This conversation is going downhill and I am going to change it now. Lulu, honey, I'd like you to be very kind, please, and do me a favour.'

'Great,' mumbled Lulu. 'The old distraction technique.' But there was that in her mother's voice which was not to be dismissed.

'I'd like you to go into the attic, please,' said Fee, 'and find something for me.'

'Oh, Mom!' said Lulu. 'I hate the attic. It's

dark and dusty and there's a ghost up there, Emma gave me nightmares about it for years.'

'Well, your father's out of town and there's no way I'm balancing on that ladder at my age, so I'm going to have to ask one of you lithe young girls, and the one I'm asking is you.'

'Why me, though? Why not Helen Mirren?'

'Spiders,' said Sophie. 'I have arachnophobia, remember?'

'I'd like to see you remember it if someone offered you a part in the next Spiderman movie.'

'Mom says if it ever became a hindrance to my career, she knows a hypnotherapist, don't you, Mom?'

'So it's OK to have it as long as it only stops you from doing favours for other people? Nice one.'

'You could always ask Emma,' said Fee, innocently.

'Go ahead,' said Emma. 'Ask me. I wonder what I'll say?'

Lulu sighed. 'OK,' she said. 'Since I'm the only one stupid enough to do it. What is it you want, Mom?'

'Oddly enough, it's your Aunt Amy who wants it,' said Fee. 'There's an exhibition coming up at the Massachusetts Historical Society, and she wants to offer a collection of recipes my Grandma Cissie put together and had privately printed back in the 1920s. It's somewhere among my collection of papers from home, in the far corner under the eaves.'

'Oh, fine,' said Lulu. 'Great idea, Mom. There are enough *papers* in there to sink a ship — with a bit of luck you won't see me again till next Christmas.'

'Yes!' Sophie balled her fist in triumph. 'Score, Mom.'

'I don't think you'll need to go through all of them,' said Fee. 'There's the big trunk with all of the papers in it, and then there's that little bookcase next to it, and I'm pretty sure it's in there. It's not very big and it has a red cover — if you'd just be an angel and take a quick look for me, then I can tell Aunt Amy that at least we tried.'

'Want me to come and help you?' said Charlie.

'There really isn't room for two up there, sweetie,' said Fee. 'Why don't you stay down here with us instead, and tell Sophie more about the flat.'

'Yes, do that,' said Lulu. 'Tell her all about the flat. Don't forget the rule that anyone with blonde hair has to clean the toilet every Saturday morning.'

It was all very well, she thought, trudging up the creaking stairs of the old house that led to the attic, for Mom to sing the joys of sisterhood from afar — Fee had no idea what it was really like to have sisters. Lulu was a middle child, and there were times when she felt the burden of this keenly. For all her childhood, it had seemed, whatever she had achieved, Emma had achieved earlier and, usually, accomplished better; and when Lulu herself had been only three years old, along had come Sophie, always younger, always more charming, helping herself without thought or question to everything from Lulu's dolls, to her clothes (because, whatever Sophie might say now, there had been many years when she had been less scornful of her sister's dress sense), to their mother's attention. And even now that they had all reached adulthood, the pattern seemed to continue. Emma's life, with career and marriage plans so neatly settled into place, stood in constant reproachful contrast to Lulu's day-to-day scrabbled existence; meanwhile, here was Sophie quite literally moving in on Lulu's life, invited, no less, by Lulu's best friend. Fee should try living with real sisters instead of weaving pretty ideas about them, Lulu thought, not for the first time, and see how she liked it.

The truth was that now, two years out of college, Lulu was finding adulthood more than a little difficult. For one thing, there was the issue of her career. She was sure — and had remained sure in the face of suggestions from many of her professors at university — that the world of scientific research was not for her, but the question now remained of just what sort of professional world was. Too quirky and outspoken to fit into the conventional office set-up which suited Emma so well, and yet without the burning propulsion towards one particular goal that inflamed Sophie, she found herself, at nearly twenty-five, a little alarmingly lacking in professional direction. In vain had her parents suggested one further qualification after another — she lacked the patience for teaching, she said, or the administrative ability for social work, and law would be yet another series of the dry facts of which she had had sufficient while studying biochemistry. (To Emma's suggestion of public relations, and Sophie's of fashion modelling, she had returned every ounce of the disdain she felt each had merited.) Yet she could not drift aimlessly forever, nor could she stay forever in Charlie's flat, making herself useful by cooking meals and changing light bulbs. It was time to settle seriously into adult life — but how or where she was supposed to find a life to settle into, Lulu had no idea.

She climbed past her parents' bedroom and Fee's consulting room, standing across from each other on the first landing, and up to the top landing of the house, where Tom the lodger's room stood opposite her own old bedroom. She retrieved the rickety ladder from the corner of the landing, pulled down the attic door and scrambled up to the small, dusty space, crammed with the paraphernalia of nearly three decades of family life, boxes of baby clothes laid by for a generation that was yet to come, once-loved toys that no one had had the heart to throw away, piles of college textbooks that might yet be referred to, broken tennis rackets that maybe one day someone would take the time to restring.

Carefully, she picked her way through the narrow path between the piles to the corner, where, under a small window with raindrops drumming thunderously on the old warped pane, there sat a large trunk containing the family papers that Fee had had shipped from

Boston when her own mother, Grandma Jojo, had died. Next to it was the bookcase, which Fee had been less than ingenuous in describing as small, because it came up to Lulu's shoulders and held four shelves packed to overflowing with books, papers and storage boxes of various sizes.

'Thanks, Mom,' Lulu muttered to herself. She switched on the electric light, thin and yellow, to augment the watery grey light from outside, dragged out a broken-down stool to sit herself on, and set to the task.

The top shelf of the bookcase held piles of photographs, some in albums, some not, ranging from old-fashioned sepia to the faded, once-bright colours of thirty years ago. Lulu rooted through those briefly, tracing the long Massachusetts faces of her mother's family as they moved through the last century and more, stopping to inspect an old woman with a sweet expression, wearing a lace-edged cap and holding a baby in a large lace collar, a glamorous younger woman with permed hair and dark lipstick, smoking a cigarette and looking haughtily to the side, a couple of young men in American naval uniforms, and finally, delightedly, happening on one of a younger, thinner Fee, with wild curly hair and a stern expression, waving a banner that read THE PERSONAL IS POLITICAL.

The second shelf held books, piles of them, as the family had been readers for generations, crammed higgledy-piggledy into the space until the shelf buckled beneath their weight. Poetry jumbled against Victorian romances, books of sermons jostled with The Pickwick Papers,

29

Ralph Waldo Emerson with Raymond Chandler, and also, a little to Lulu's surprise, with a series of penny dreadfuls from the 1860s, their covers illustrated with scenes of bandits, nuns and fainting women. Nowhere among them, however, was a collection of recipes — Grandma Jojo, who had been a practical woman, must have packed it away into one of the storage boxes for protection.

The boxes filled most of the rest of the bookcase. There were a dozen or more of them, in canvas or cardboard, of differing sizes, and with their contents clearly labelled in Grandma Jojo's square, firm hand. Lulu squatted on the floor, brushed aside a couple of the spiders which so alarmed Sophie and set to examining them. The box marked JEWELRY she thought she could ignore, also the box marked MAPS. A shoe-box labelled RECEIPTS looked promising but proved to hold a collection of financial documents on thin white paper, the numbers stamped out with an old-fashioned typewriter ribbon. An elegant container finished in cream-coloured vellum and marked CISSIE raised her hopes, but on inspection contained only a series of battered journals scrawled in an all but illegible cramped hand — if this were Grandma Cissie's handwriting, thought Lulu, it was no wonder that she had decided to have her recipes printed professionally. There was a box marked TRANSCENDENTALISM, which apparently had once interested someone in the family, and another box marked CONCORD. Nowhere either in any of the boxes or stacked between them was the book Lulu sought.

Lulu rose from the floor, dusting her knees in disgust. As she bent to do so, she noticed, half-hidden in the shadow, a small leather case sitting on the floor between the shelf and the trunks. It was larger than the storage boxes, the sort of case that used to be carried by doctors, with a sturdy handle and an old, dulled brass clasp; unlike the boxes, it bore neither label nor description. Curious despite herself, Lulu picked it up, took it to the stool under the window and opened it while the raindrops beat a tattoo above her head.

This case contained not only papers, but other objects, too, a collection of a family's souvenirs, most of them seemingly from Victorian times. There was a carved fan and a pair of kid gloves; several sheets of music, some of them unopened, for old-fashioned songs that no one had sung for a century and more; a small nightcap, now yellow with age, and some abandoned needle-work; a leather box containing a little gold ring set with turquoise stones; and a black enamel brooch, with a lock of brown hair in the centre arranged into the shape of a weeping willow. Hidden away in a corner, Lulu caught a glimpse of a small book with a red cover, and reached for it hopefully; but it was not recipes, only a much-worn copy of *The Pilgrim's Progress*, battered and dog-eared from reading, its spine quite cracked away. Beneath the objects was a collection of paintings and drawings that had clearly been done by the same hand — whoever the family had been, someone among them must have once been artistic. There was a pencil drawing of a plump, smiling woman in a crinoline, and another of a pretty girl with the front of her hair tied up in what looked like a series of small paper parcels. There were some paintings of scroll work in bright colours, a rough sketch of a teenage boy on a horse, and another, more polished, of a young man lying lazily in a field smoking a cigar. At the very bottom of the box was a pile of letters, all written on thin, fragile paper, in the same large, energetic hand. Lulu drew out the topmost letter — the writing was extremely untidy, but also, unlike Grandma Cissie's, easily legible — and began to read.

Concord, July 1869.

Dearest Meg,
    Will we ever learn to bear it, do you think? A world without our Beth, a family with only three sisters where there once were four? A family of cripples, in fact — for we are not whole without her, we sisters who remain, and never again shall be. We are maimed like those soldiers wounded in the War we see now-a-days limping through Concord, one without an arm or an eye, one with but a stump where once there was a stout useful leg. But, oh, my dearest Meg, how very much more badly wounded are we than even those poor unfortunates, more badly damaged than even poor blind Billy who sits with his bowl outside the Soldiers' Home with neither arms nor legs

nor eyes, for we have lost a part that was more precious than any ordinary limb. If it meant I could have my Beth back again for only a week or a day, I'd trade places with Billy for life, and think myself the richer for it.

I think sometimes that I can bear the pain for *today* and sometimes I even think I can bear it for a month, but the thought of a lifetime without her is too hard, Meg. Father talks of God's will and of happier times to come, and tells me that I *will* see Beth again when I, too, cross the river to the Celestial City that awaits us all. But, Meg, I'm *not* a saint, as father is, I *can't* bear the thought of such a separation, and there are times when my heart aches so I think it will burst my breast with grief.

The days are tolerable, mostly. The rain has stopped — mercifully — and I'm able to busy myself about the household tasks and make myself useful if nothing else — you know I'm always better when there's work at hand. But the nights are hard, and do not grow easier. Marmee and father go early to bed these days, and I am left alone with nothing but the longing for my Beth that I think will never, ever cease. This evening, unable to sleep, I rose from my bed, lit the lamp, and went, as I often do, to the book that my dear German friend gave me when I was in New York. You remember he gave me such a fine copy of Shakespeare for a Christmas present, telling me I should find in it everything I need. Usually when I open it, I will find something comical or philosophical to make me smile or to do me good, but tonight the book fell open, as if of its own will, to poor King Lear lamenting his dead Cordelia — and when I read those saddest of all sad lines ever written — 'Thou'lt come no more/Never, never, never, never, never' — I laid my head down on the book's pages and wept and wept, very quietly so as not to wake Marmee, until even I could weep no more.

Is it very wicked to feel such sorrow, Meg? Father says that if I trust in God He will comfort me, but I will tell *you* this, Meg — although I'd never tell Marmee or father — that there are times in my wickedness when I am tempted to hate the God Who has been so cruel as to make us all suffer so. And — is this very wicked and selfish indeed? — it sometimes seems to me that He has made me to suffer the most, for Marmee and father have each other, and you have John and your two precious little ones, and Milady Amy in Europe has Teddy now for her very own knight in shining armor, while I had no one but Beth, and now that she's taken from me, I'm all wrong, Meg, all so very wrong.

Dear Meg, you do know — don't you? — that missing Beth so much don't mean that I love you any the less — if anything, you and Amy are the more dear to me than ever, now that we have lost her. I *had* three sisters but now have two, and am still a lucky woman for it, for some have none. One day, perhaps, I shall be able to be comforted by that.

That's all I will write for I think I have tired myself at last and might even sleep an hour before the dawn comes. Bless you for reading so far.

With love from,

Jo.

Lulu finished the letter, and sat staring for some time into the jumble of packing cases and broken furniture, turning the thin paper between her fingers. On the rare occasions when she had thought seriously of her Grandma Jo, it had been always as an old woman, rigid in her ways, and stern in her principles. But the woman who had written this letter was young — young and uncertain and torn with the pain of a loss Lulu now realized she could not begin to comprehend. Lulu had so far been happily unacquainted with too close a reality of death, although she had had friends from school and college who had lost one or another parent; and she remembered now that there had been a girl in the year above her at St Andrew's, a girl whom she had not known well, with thick brown hair and a broad friendly face, who had been killed in a skiing accident during a Christmas holiday. It occurred to her now to wonder whether that girl had had a sister, and, if so, how she could bear to live on.

'Lulu-belle! Looby-Lulu!'

Lulu jumped at the sound of Sophie's voice, rising from the landing below and wrenching her from the thoughts of a young woman who had lived to be old, mourning a sister who had not.

'What is it?' she called down the ladder, shocking herself by the sound of her own everyday voice, echoing from this room that held such ghosts from the past.

'Mom wants to know if you've been eaten by the spiders yet. You've been up there for over an hour.'

'I'm coming down now.'

Lulu replaced the letters and other objects into the case, set it back beside the bookshelf, and climbed down the ladder to join Sophie, child of the twenty-first century in worn jeans and a white blouse patterned with giant red daisies — Sophie had recently discovered the joys of vintage clothes markets.

'You were there for ages,' she said. 'You're covered with dust. What did you find?'

'Nothing much,' said Lulu. 'Lots and lots of bits of old paper and some photographs of Mom at the Women's Collective. But I forgot to bring them down, I'll go up again later and get them.'

'Mom's feeling guilty,' said Sophie. 'She thinks she's Hurt Your Feelings and you're sitting up there sobbing quietly into a little lace hankie.'

'No, I'm fine,' said Lulu. 'Just got a bit carried away looking at the photographs.'

'Well, don't tell her that! Let her go on feeling guilty and maybe she'll break out those posh chocolates she's got hidden in her bedroom.'

'What's it like?' said Lulu. 'To be without standards or shame? As a scientist, I'm curious.'

'Aha!' said Charlie as the two entered the room, arm in arm. 'It's the girl who never touches her sisters.'

'Doesn't count,' said Lulu. 'I was deliberately smearing dust on her. I didn't find the book, Mom, but the thrill of the hunt is on me now. I think I'll come back during the week and take another look.'

'You don't have to do that, honey,' said Fee. 'It was just a thought that Aunt Amy had.'

'No, I'm interested now to see what the recipes are like.' Lulu paused. 'Grandma Cissie was Grandma Jo's daughter, right?' she asked, then.

'Right.' Fee eyed her daughter warily, waiting for a sarcastic comment. To her surprise, it did not come.

'And Bethie-who-died-young was Jo's sister?'

'Yes,' said Fee. 'Why the interest in Grandma Jo all of a sudden?'

'Well, Charlie was asking about her. How old was she when she died anyway? Bethie.'

'Quite young, I think. I don't really know. It was a big family tragedy.'

'People were always dying young in those days,' said Emma. 'They always were in Dickens, anyway.'

'You didn't read that in this house,' said Fee, darkly: she had strong feelings about Dickens's treatment of his female characters. 'That man set the women's cause back by a hundred years.'

'Someone in the family once liked him,' said Lulu. 'There are lots of old copies of his books up in the attic, and they look pretty well read, too.'

In fact, the books looked as if they had been not so much read, as devoured, with cracked

37

spines and pages crumpled and spattered with stains by someone untidy a hundred years ago and more.

'They can stay in the attic,' said Fee, who did not share her ancestor's admiration for the writer.

'I'm Great-Great-Great-Aunt Beth! I'm *dyyyy-ing*!' Sophie cast herself dramatically on the worn green sofa in the corner of the room, one arm flung to the floor, and looked up for Lulu to join the charade.

Lulu looked coldly down on her younger sister.

'You have no heart, Sophie,' she said.

'What?' From her prone position, Sophie stared up at Lulu in surprise; making fun of Grandma Jo's family had been an entertainment the two of them had cherished since their childhood.

'Someone died,' said Lulu. 'Did you ever think how hard that must have been for the rest of them? What would you do if I died, just lie on the sofa imitating me and thinking it was funny?'

Astonished into silence, Sophie looked over at Emma, who only shrugged. Lulu crossed the room to the wall by the window to examine a photograph of all three sisters, laughing and windblown in their teens, on a family holiday in Scotland. 'When are you moving in to ruin my life, anyway?' she said.

'On Saturday.' Sophie sat up and pushed at her hair. 'It's all sorted. I phoned my friend Jamie while you were upstairs — he's got a van and he's going to help me. I haven't got much stuff, being a wandering gypsy player and all. But there are all those stairs at Charlie's and he's going to help me carry it all up.'

'Hm.' Lulu left the photograph, sat herself at the table, and pulled Toby onto her lap. 'And I suppose,' she said, 'you'll want me to cook a special supper for your friend Jamie to thank him for his help.'

'Oh, would you?' said Sophie. 'That would be amazing, Lulu, you're such an amazing cook. Would you do that beef thing with all the mushrooms? It's so fabulously yummy, and he'll have driven all that way, so I think he deserves it, don't you?'

'I think after carrying all *your* version of 'not much stuff' up the stairs, he'll deserve a starter and a dessert, too. Find out what his favourite pudding is and we'll surprise him.'

'And there you go again,' said Charlie.

'I'm not hugging her,' said Lulu. 'She's hugging me. And make no mistake, Sophie, if you don't behave yourself in the flat, you'll be down the stairs and back on the street before you can say Kate Winslet.'

'I think this calls for a little chocolate,' said Fee, making for the stairs to her bedroom.

2

Boddesley Brothers Publishing Company

Boston, October 1892.

Dear Mrs. Bhaer,

I hope that you will continue to consider my request for a selection of your private writings for my series of books, *Lives and Letters of Literary New Englanders*. I do understand that you 'don't care a pin for fame,' and thus can hardly claim surprise to learn that you 'abhor [your] sisters' sentimentality' in having retained so many of the letters that you have sent to them over the years; I, on the other hand, can only applaud their good taste for having preserved what is without doubt a lively and affecting correspondence. I thank you for your good efforts in having collected these letters from your sisters — and must also commend your honesty in acknowledging to me the doubtless vexing fact that they were there for the collection! — and hope that with a little more persuasion, I might yet incline you towards the idea of sharing them with your admiring public.

I intend to be in the neighborhood of Plumfield on Thursday next, and hope that I may call upon you there to discuss this further in person.

Your obedient servant,
Thomas Stauncey,
Editorial Director.

Lulu replaced the letter, its tidy masculine hand and crisply formal paper a contrast to the other letters in the pile, and sat carefully back into the tumbledown armchair she had dragged under the attic's window, frowning absent-mindedly into the weak stream of sunlight that fell through the glass to pool on the wood floor beneath. It was five days since she had first made the discovery of her great-great-grandmother's letters. She had not yet mentioned the find either to her mother or to her sisters, but it had remained in the background of her mind at all times since, and today, knowing that her mother was safely occupied at a seminar at the Institute of Psychiatry, she had taken her lunch break from Goncharoff's Antiques, the shop where she worked, to cycle over to the house for a further inspection.

Now, an hour later, she had learned a substantial amount about Josephine March. She had learned that she had grown up, with her parents and three sisters, in a little town just outside Boston in the latter part of the nineteenth century, in a household where money had been in short supply, but the family had taken pride in making do with what they had and had considered themselves fortunate. She had learned that Jo had loved to read, and to weave

41

dreams and to write stories — it seemed that the family story that she had had books published had been correct, and, indeed, she had apparently at one time achieved some recognition for them — that she had also loved to sleigh, and to skate, and had openly envied the freedom from convention that seemed taken for granted by the boys of the day. She had learned that Jo had admired Napoleon and George Washington, had hated pretension, had a habit of saying Christopher Columbus, which for some reason was considered shocking, and had sometimes made mistakes, for which she had always apologized afterwards. She had learned that the Marches had regarded their small family unit as the single most precious possession they owned. She had learned that Jo, like Lulu, had sometimes felt out of place in the world, had been odd and awkward and tactless, but that her family had loved her nevertheless.

Riffling through the pile, she picked up a letter at random, and reread, smiling, an account of an experiment that the youngest sister, Amy, had made with a piece of pokerwork and — according to Jo's enthusiastic recounting of the tale in a letter to Meg — had all but burned the house down. Amy had been artistic, it seemed, and Meg sounded efficient and organized: a little, thought Lulu, like Sophie and Emma. Sophie and Emma would enjoy the letters, but Lulu had decided that she would not reveal her discovery to either of them, not just yet. One day, of course, she would have to; but then everyone would know about them, not just her, and Lulu found she rather wanted to have Jo March all to herself for at least a little while.

The sudden harsh ring of her mobile phone pulled her back to the present day. She dragged it from the pocket of her jeans, inspected the name that flashed on the front and sighed: it was her employer.

'Hello, Mr Goncharoff.' Nikolai Goncharoff was Russian-born, firmly of the old world and formally inclined. He liked Lulu a great deal and she him, but he had never once suggested to her that she address him by his first name.

'Miss Atwater, I do not wish to disturb you, but I am wondering whether by any chance you intend to return to work this afternoon.'

'Oh, Mr Goncharoff, I'm sorry.' Lulu glanced at her watch and started — she had had no idea of how much time had passed since she had left the shop. 'Oh, no! Oh, Mr Goncharoff, I really am sorry, I hadn't noticed the time. Shall we just forget about this afternoon and call it my afternoon off?'

'Normally, I would be, if not pleased, then at least philosophically resigned to the dreary prospect of an afternoon unenlivened by your company. But you see, today is a very special day, and I must ask you to interrupt whatever delightful pursuit you are about and return. Today, we have sold a painting.'

'We have!' Goncharoff's Antiques had been struggling for business for some time. 'But that's amazing!'

'Truly it is, as you say, amazing, and the more so as it totals a full three such items we have sold this month. What a red letter day this is for the Goncharoff family. Irena is telephoning all the relations in Saratov to spread the good tidings, and Alexander is standing in the doorway of the shop, offering finest champagne to all who pass. If we can only sell another — oh, how many shall we say? — forty or so more before the month's end, we might just find we will be able to keep the shop open after all.'

Nikolai and Irena Goncharoff had been talking since Lulu had first started working for them of selling their dusty, ramshackle shop in a small side street off Haverstock Hill and retiring to a villa in the sun. Six months ago, Lulu had thought that they were mostly joking about this, but these days she was not so sure.

'Well, you never know, Mr Goncharoff,' she said now. 'This might just be the start of a trend.'

'It might, Miss Atwater. And, as the old people were fond of saying back in my country, the fish on the hill might whistle. But please come back to the shop as soon as you conveniently can, because we are in the unusual position of having paperwork to deal with.'

'I'll be there as soon as possible. I'll fly, I promise.'

'Your trusty bicycle will be of sufficient speed. But I will hope to see you later to join in all the rejoicing.'

Lulu gathered together all of the letters and replaced them in the leather case, allowing herself, here alone where no one could see her, a small frown of worry. It would make sense, she knew, for the Goncharoffs to sell their shop now:

business was slow, the land on which it stood was alone valuable enough to afford them a comfortable pension wherever they decided to live and their son Alexander had made it plain that when the time came he intended to take himself off to pursue a career at an auction house. But, for Lulu, leaving the Goncharoffs would mean having to find another job, and having to find another job would mean once again being required to confront the increasingly frightening fact that she truly did not know what she wanted to do for a career.

She cast one last, envious glance at the spidery writing of Jo March, who had known what she wanted to do, and had done it, and had even been successful at it, replaced the leather bag in its spot by the bookcase, crossed the attic and started to climb down the ladder. There was a trick to the second rung from the bottom; it had a weak spot which wobbled on the left side, and if you weren't careful you could miss your footing. Lulu generally made sure to take account of this, but now in her haste she forgot, and in order to maintain her balance was forced to jump back into the landing.

'Whoa, whoa, whoa. You might want to watch where you're going there.'

It was Tom the lodger, coming out of his room, a pile of books in his hand, stepping smartly back to avoid a collision.

'Sorry,' she said. 'I didn't see you there. Are you OK?'

'Small tip,' he said. 'Make things easier for the future. When planning to propel yourself backwards through the air, check first to make sure the surrounding area is clear of human obstacles, OK?'

'Sorry,' she said again. But he was smiling. He was not a handsome man, forty-ish, with sandy hair and mild brown eyes magnified by strong spectacles, but he had a surprisingly warm and open smile.

'Help you with the ladder?' he said.

'Thanks.' She watched him set the books down carefully on the floor, replace the ladder in the corner with one hand, and with the other reach for the pole to close the trapdoor: for a scholar, he had an unexpected fluidity of motion.

'I've been in the attic,' she noted, not especially necessarily, as they headed together down the stairs.

'I guessed so,' he said. 'I heard something up there, and figured it was either one of you guys or a troupe of ballerina squirrels rehearsing *Giselle*. You might want to brush your sweater down, it's dusty.'

'Thanks.' She swatted a hand across her front. 'It would only be me you heard anyway, because no one else goes there. My parents are too old, Emma's too clean and Sophie's afraid of spiders.'

'Did you find what you were looking for?' he asked. 'You sounded like you were hard at work.'

'I was.' Lulu hesitated. If she had not yet told her family about her great-great-grandmother's letters, she would certainly not tell a stranger. 'I'm looking for a recipe book my great-grandmother put together, in Massachusetts in

46

the 1920s. I haven't found it yet, so I might have to come back.'

'Well, I wouldn't get your hopes up for when you do,' he said. 'Early twentieth-century New England was not famous for its cuisine.'

'So they say.' It now occurred to her that she did not know which part of America he was from. 'Where are you from, anyway?'

'California.'

'Really? You don't seem like a Californian.'

'No? And what would a Californian seem like to you?'

She thought for a moment. 'Noisier,' she concluded.

He laughed. 'Well, I guess there are quiet ones there, too. If you wait till the shouting's died down and then listen real hard. You know, you really might want to look in at the bathroom before you leave the house. I don't want to be personal, but you are kind of dusty.'

*   *   *

There was a bare patch on the wall of Goncharoff's Antiques, which until that morning had held a gilt-framed nineteenth-century portrait of a handsome woman in a silk tartan dress, with rich jewels and an expression of profound sadness.

'It's the lady in tartan,' said Lulu. 'I shall miss her.'

'I, too,' said Mr Goncharoff. 'For many years I would look at her and think, *But the poor lady, what on earth in her life can be causing her such sorrow?* And then one day I discovered the answer, and ever since then I thought, *But the poor lady, how can her family have been so cruel as to have hidden from her her much-needed prune juice?* But she is on someone else's wall now, and it is for them to ask the question. Miss Atwater, the gentleman with the headgear has been into my shop again this afternoon.'

'Ziggy Lethbridge?' Ziggy Lethbridge was the proprietor of a coffee shop in Notting Hill, who was seeking to open another branch in Belsize Park. He was pudgily boyish and affected a turned-around baseball cap in order to disguise his receding hairline.

'You may call him that. I do not recognize the first name and cannot say the second. But I should warn you that the offer he is making me for this property is becoming more attractive. He has money, and you know what they say in this country — money talks.'

'*I* don't say that, Mr Goncharoff — I haven't got any.' Lulu laughed, and poured herself a cup of coffee from the pot in the corner of the office.

Mr Goncharoff looked at her, gravely, from behind his spectacles.

'What will you do, Miss Atwater?' he asked. 'If we sell the shop?'

'Oh, for heaven's sake, Mr Goncharoff.' Lulu was touched. 'You don't have to worry about me!'

'But I do worry, Miss Atwater. You have been with us for almost a year now, and we regard you as part of the family. Employment is not so easy

48

to come by these days as it once was. If we took your job away from you, what would you do? What do you think, Alexander?'

'Going to sell up the shop, old man?' Sasha Goncharoff, as everyone but his father knew him, loped in to throw an affectionate arm around the older man's shoulders. Sasha was twenty-eight years old, heavy-featured and lithely sinewy of build. He smoked Gauloises cigarettes, liked to go to nightclubs, and occasionally was visited at the shop by one or another leggily glamorous young woman with whom his exact relationship was never made altogether clear. He was a good-hearted young man who openly loved both of his parents, but there was that about him which made Lulu feel stiff and awkward in his company, as though she were wearing a dress that was supposed to fit her, but did not quite.

'And here is the answer to our question,' said Mr Goncharoff now, slapping his son's wrist, which looped his neck. 'You shall marry my reprobate son here, you shall exert your good influence to stop his wild ways and, at last, when Irena and I are gone, you shall inherit the untold-of wealth of the legendary Goncharoff fortune. What do you say, Miss Atwater, will you consider it?'

Lulu smiled, a little nervously. It was a joke of which Nikolai Goncharoff was fond, not least, she sometimes suspected, because it made both of its subjects uncomfortable.

'Hi, Sasha,' she said. 'Maybe we should just do it and get it over with, to get some peace?'

49

Sasha only smiled back, his eyes not quite meeting hers.

Lulu sipped at her coffee, trying not to feel foolish: she had never been able to banter with young men. With other girls, she knew, Sasha was able to laugh and be flirtatious, but when talking to her, for some reason, he became every bit as awkward as she was.

'Excuse me,' said a voice. 'Is Lulu Atwater around?'

At the door to the office stood Sophie, pretty as a spring day, in a short green and white flowered dress topped with a soft white cardigan.

'What are you doing here?' said Lulu.

'Come to see you,' said Sophie. 'I've just been to see the flat, and I thought I'd look in, if it's OK.' She perched herself on the edge of Lulu's desk and swept a smile at the two Goncharoff men. 'Hi, I'm Sophie. I'm Lulu's sister, is it OK to come to visit her?'

Sasha removed himself from his father and stood, slouching sensually, pinching his chin between thumb and forefinger.

'There's a sister who's an office administrator,' he said thoughtfully. 'And there's a sister who's an actress. And I'm guessing that you're the . . . office administrator, right?'

'Right!' Sophie beamed sunnily at him: charming the opposite sex had never posed a problem for her. 'I'm very bossy, I like to hand out memos, and I get really cross if people don't read them.'

'You sound terrifying. Would you like some coffee?'

'Love some, please. Ooh. Are those my sister's flapjacks? I'd know them anywhere, can I have one? They're amazing, does she often bring in stuff she's made? Aren't you lucky. She's always been a fabulous cook, we were heartbroken when she left home, reduced to eating plain digestives and those horrid cardboardy Bourbon things, it was terribly sad.'

'You could always have learned to cook yourself,' said Lulu.

'Well, but that was the problem, you see, you were always so good at it we all had the most desperate inferiority complexes, so we couldn't. Which reminds me. Super-important.' She swallowed a bite of flapjack, and leaned forward earnestly across Lulu's desk. 'Cheesecake,' she said.

'Excuse me?' said Lulu.

'Jamie's favourite pudding. You said we were going to surprise him with it, remember? Well, last night Esme and I got him into this whole complicated made-up game where we had to tell all sorts of secrets about ourselves, like first pets and childhood nicknames — his was Dinky-Ears, which I think is quite sweet, but you mustn't let on you know because I promised I wouldn't tell — and cunningly buried, right slap-bang in the very middle of all the other stuff, was, 'Hmm, OK, what's next on this list? Oh, yes. What's your favourite . . . ummm . . . *pudding*?' And it's cheesecake.' She stopped. 'Is that OK?' she asked. 'Can you make cheesecake?'

'Well, of course I can make cheesecake,' said

Lulu. 'Why wouldn't I be able to?'

'I don't know, a lot of normal ordinary people can't.' She turned to her by now enraptured audience to explain. 'My friend Jamie's helping me move into Lulu's flat this weekend, and because she's not only an amazing cook but the nicest and kindest sister in the entire universe, she's making just the most outstandingly yummy dinner for him, a runny sort of winey beef casserole that is just bliss, and she told me that if I could sneakily find out his favourite pudding we'd surprise him with it.' She smiled, proudly. 'So now I've done my part, and all Lulu needs to do is wave her magic cooking wand and it'll all be good in the 'hood.'

'You're moving in near here?' said Sasha.

'At the weekend. Want me to come and administrate the office? I sometimes pretend to be the actress sister and walk around quoting Shakespeare and posing, but that's just to lull you into a sense of false security. In my real identity, I'm super-stern and efficient, and very organized.'

'I think just the one Miss Atwater cracking the whip on us seems plenty for right now. But you're welcome to come in for coffee any time.'

'You know, I might just do that. If I find myself growing so weak with caffeine withdrawal that I can't make the five minutes' walk home. But you'd better enjoy those flapjacks while you can, because there might not be so many of them leaving the house after next Monday.'

'Now *that*,' said Sasha approvingly as the door

52

closed on Sophie's slim legs, 'is the sort of sister I like to meet.'

'That is kind of you, Miss Atwater,' said Nikolai. 'To cook dinner for her friend.'

'Oh.' Lulu laughed and shook her head, never comfortable with compliments. 'I feel sorry for Jamie. He lollops after her like a great big puppy dog, she orders him around most dreadfully and he takes it because he adores her.'

'Nice kind of boyfriend,' commented Sasha.

'Boyfriend! He wishes. He's just a friend, although if he could change things he would in a heartbeat.'

'Does she have a boyfriend?' he asked.

'I'm not sure right now. They tend to come and go.' Sophie was rarely without a boyfriend; but the regularity with which she changed them was such that both Lulu and Emma regarded their sister's love life with bemusement verging on awe. 'Would you like me to put in a word for you?'

She had thought she had spoken lightly, teasing as Sophie seemed so effortlessly able. But when she looked up, she saw that she had offended him.

'I don't think that will be necessary,' he said quietly.

'Sorry,' she said. 'I wasn't suggesting . . . People are always interested in Sophie, you see. Men, I mean. Guys.'

'She's very attractive,' he said. 'But I don't need help, thanks.'

'Sorry,' said Lulu again, but he had already gone through the door that led to the shop.

'Young men,' said Nikolai, shaking his head after his son. 'Do not marry him after all, Miss Atwater. You are far too good for him.'

★   ★   ★

'There's something I don't understand,' said Charlie, later that evening, sitting at the kitchen table and chopping mushrooms while Lulu expertly browned the meat in a large frying pan — Charlie was not a cook herself, but liked to watch her friend cooking. 'And that is why, when you're spending your own money on food for someone else, it's organic beef and wine and cheesecake fixings, but when it's my money on food for us, then I have to beg for anything posher than sausages and lentils. Can you explain that to me, please?'

Lulu smiled as she tossed another handful of steak into the sizzling oil of the cast iron pan, watching it splutter gratifyingly as it turned first golden, then crusty mahogany brown. The flat occupied the upper two floors of a pretty Victorian terraced house in a quiet street near Belsize Park Tube station; it belonged to Charlie's Aunt Maeve, who owned a cooking school just outside Cork and was particular about her kitchen. Having learned to cook on Fee's cheerfully dilapidated equipment, Lulu still pinched herself a little when she looked at the substantial pots on the six-burner kitchen range, the extensive collection of Le Creuset casseroles that lined the cupboard above, the bank of mixers, blenders and grinders that stood in the corner of the broad countertop, ready to spring to action at the touch of a switch.

'You don't get the good food,' she said. 'Mom said the other day that you're like another daughter to her, so you've been demoted to family status, I'm afraid. Have to wait for company for anything good. Anyway, don't you get enough fancy food at the hotel? Nice gourmet meals with *Javier*?'

Charlie was serving her apprenticeship at The Fitzcharles, her father's hotel in Covent Garden. The business manager was a young Spaniard, when mentioning whom she had lately taken to showing her Irish blood by blushing very slightly.

'I don't need the food to eat it,' she said, ignoring the jibe. 'I just want to have it on the table to look at and admire as a symbol of status. And — I thought that *you* might like to have steak for dinner occasionally. The budget does run to it, you know.'

'Not the way I run it,' said Lulu, firmly. 'I'm not wasting your money on over-priced filet mignon when there's perfectly good Bolognese sauce to be made. You never know when you might need a few pounds in the bank.'

'Um . . . ' Gently, Charlie looked around her at the spacious kitchen with its gleaming appliances. 'I think I'm OK for the time being.'

'And that's the danger of being rich.' Lulu turned from the stove to face her friend, her spatula raised in admonition. 'Rich people always think they're OK. And then sometimes it turns out that you're not, and then where are you?' The last of the meat was browned, and she turned back to tip glistening chopped onions into the rich, gelatinous fat. 'Mr Goncharoff is talking about selling up,' she said.

'Again? He's been saying that for months now.'

'Well, I think this time he might just mean it.'

'Hm.' Absent-mindedly, Charlie popped a piece of mushroom into her mouth. 'What will you do if he does?'

'I don't know. I'll think of something. Sophie says there are openings at her place.'

'Fulla Beanz?' Sophie worked at a coffee shop in Soho, where the clientele was young and the management understanding when the staff requested time off for auditions. 'Lulu, you'd hate it!'

'Would I?' Lulu turned from her pan to frown at her friend. 'Why?'

'Well, wouldn't you? All those trendy actress types?'

'As opposed to me? Thank you.'

'No, not as opposed to you! As opposed to . . . ' She stopped.

As opposed to old Mr Goncharoff, thought Lulu, with his grey beard and his world-weary jokes, or Irena, his smiling bottom-heavy wife whose skirts drooped unevenly over her stout calves. As opposed to Tom the quiet lodger, or frightening Aunt Amy in Boston, who lived alone with a housekeeper and snapped at sales assistants if she considered them insufficiently efficient, or old Mrs Scott-Ramsay, who lived in the lower part of the house, and pounded on the ceiling with her cane when they laughed too hard or played music too loud. And as opposed to me, she added to herself then, since that's the company I belong in; Sophie and Sasha and all the trendy, charming and attractive people opposed to me.

'Opposed to what?' she said. 'Little pink elephants in ballet skirts? Multicoloured ball-point pens? Out of season asparagus?'

'Actually,' said Charlie, thoughtfully, 'I was thinking more in terms of traffic lights.'

Charlie was one of the few people who could return Lulu from a borderline bad mood to a good.

'I think Sophie would make quite a good traffic light,' Lulu told her now. 'I can see her getting into it . . . picking a back story . . . deciding on her motivation . . . flashing . . . red . . . yellow . . . green . . . red . . . yellow . . . green.'

'You're a strange family,' said Charlie. 'Nice. But strange.'

'You invited us to live with you,' said Lulu.

★　★　★

Sophie arrived the next day, in a confusion of cartons of books and cases of clothes; boxes of jewellery and make-up; handbags and shoes; film posters; collages of photographs of herself and her friends; a prop sword; two wigs, one red and curly, one dark and straight; three hairdryers, one of them functional; a sewing machine; and several baskets overflowing with buttons, ribbons, squares of satin and pieces of lace, transforming the small, light-filled spare room into an exotic gypsy's tent.

'You're going to be a mad old lady one day,' said Lulu. 'Live in a house with cats and lace doilies and china figurines, and little children will be terrified to come and visit you.'

'They'll be dying to come and visit me,' said Sophie. 'I'll be a world-famous actress and young girls will sit at my feet, begging me for stories and kicking themselves because they never saw my Rosalind. Jamie, you are a superstar and a top banana and I love you to pieces forever.'

'I think this is the last of it.' Jamie staggered through the door carrying a box of theatre programmes topped with an elderly Paddington Bear. He was a tall, broad-shouldered young man with kind brown eyes under a mop of unruly hair; collapsing onto the small single bed under the window, his large form dwarfing its narrow frame, he stared in masculine befuddlement at the array of girlish accoutrements that littered the scrubbed pine floor. 'Where did you put all this at Esme's place, is what I'd like to know?'

'I have strange magical powers that make large items shrink to fit a tiny space.' Sophie surveyed the room, her nose wrinkled critically. 'Although I probably kept most of it in the basement,' she conceded after a moment. 'Very useful, that basement.'

'Well, there's no basement here, young Soph,' said Lulu. 'Just Charlie's room, my room, your room, and the communal bits downstairs. And your stuff stays up here, OK? All of it.'

'Yes, Mum.' Sophie dropped her shoulders to a servile hunch. 'Please, Mum, if I works ever so 'ard at polishing the grates, may Mr MacNichol take me out walking on my Sunday off? We 'as an understanding, Mum.'

'We has that, Mum,' Jamie assured her, soberly. 'And I'll see the girl right, I promise. There shall be no hanky-panky, you may rest assured of that.'

'God.' Lulu rolled her eyes in disgust. 'Never be in the same room with two actors together,' she reminded herself, sternly. 'I'm going downstairs to check on dinner, it should be ready in an hour or so.'

But when she reached the comforting confines of the kitchen, a pounding on the floor from below let her know in no uncertain terms that Mrs Scott-Ramsay wished to speak to her. Lulu sighed. Mrs Scott-Ramsay was a military widow who had lived in the bottom half of the house for many years. She did not approve of her high-spirited young upstairs neighbours, nor did she pretend to, and when in need of voicing her more pressing complaints was in the habit of pounding repeatedly on her ceiling with a long cane attached to one of her late husband's boots to attract their attention. Lulu now briefly considered ignoring the noise, but knew from experience that, if left unattended, Mrs Scott-Ramsay was capable of continuing almost indefinitely.

'What on earth is all that racket?' was her greeting when Lulu went to knock on her door.

She was a tall woman with waved white hair and a military bearing, and her faded blue eyes were now shot with indignation. 'It's simply deafening. I can hardly hear myself think.'

'I'm sorry, Mrs Scott-Ramsay, I thought I'd told you,' said Lulu. She knew she had, in fact, but Mrs Scott-Ramsay was not only bad-tempered but also increasingly forgetful. 'My sister's moving in to live with us. We've been carrying her stuff in all day, but we're more or less finished now.'

'Well, I should think so! You've been at it for hours.'

'I know, and I'm sorry, she's got a lot of stuff, it seems.' Unwisely, she tried a mild joke. 'She's a bit of a magpie, I'm afraid.'

'What?' Mrs Scott-Ramsay looked disapproving, and, too late to retract, Lulu regretted her attempt at levity.

'I said she's a bit of a magpie,' she said. 'She likes . . . things . . . you know.'

'A magpie, eh?' Mrs Scott-Ramsay's eyebrows raised. 'Well, I certainly hope she doesn't start liking *my* things, or there will be trouble, I assure you.'

'Oh, Mrs Scott-Ramsay!' Lulu was horrified. 'She's not *that* sort of a magpie, for heaven's sake! She's my sister!'

Mrs Scott-Ramsay said nothing.

'Of course I was only joking, Mrs Scott-Ramsay!' said Lulu. 'She's my sister, and she's really a lovely person. Shall I bring her down to introduce you, tomorrow morning? Then you'll know who she is, she's really lovely, I promise you.'

'Make sure you keep the noise down,' was all Mrs Scott-Ramsay replied, as she closed the door in Lulu's face.

★   ★   ★

'I'm going to wear a striped shirt,' said Sophie, mopping the very last of her meat sauce with a crust of bread and reluctantly pushing her plate aside. 'And a black mask. And I'm going to carry a sack marked SWAG which I'm going to put down by my chair and pat lovingly when she thinks I don't think she's looking.'

'You'll be lucky if you're asked to sit down,' said Lulu. 'She's really not what you'd call a cuddly bunny, is she, Charlie?'

'She's not our biggest fan,' agreed Charlie. 'I've tried everything, talking to her, taking a box of chocolates at Christmas but she told me she's diabetic, offering to pick up the Sunday paper for her but she says she doesn't read them because they're full of nonsense. She just won't come around. She told Maeve that if she'd known she was going to let 'Irish students' use the house, she'd have blocked the sale. Students! Can you believe it?'

'She doesn't sound very happy,' said Sophie. 'Maybe she's lonely.'

'I'm sure she's lonely.' Lulu rose to clear the plates. 'If I went around being like Mrs Scott-Ramsay, I'd be lonely, too. She called you a thief, Soph.'

'Well, for all she knows, I am. Great food, Lulu. Wasn't it amazing, Jamie?'

'Amazing.' Jamie's eyes, which rarely left Sophie for very long, found their way to Lulu with heartfelt appreciation. 'Truly amazing. You don't know how seldom I eat like this.'

'You should get a job in a restaurant,' Sophie told him.

'Or make your fortune on TV,' said Lulu.

'He can't make his fortune on TV till he's thirty,' said Sophie. 'The only roles for guys in their twenties are playing someone's son, and he's far too big to look like anyone's son.'

'Well, except for my dad's,' said Jamie.

'Your dad weighs sixteen stone, Jamie. Not big on on-screen charisma.'

'Mum likes him.'

'Oh, so do I, he's lovely! You'd love him, Lulu, Charlie, he's sweet. But he's a teddy bear type, like Jamie, and everyone knows that teddy bear types never work in their twenties. You mark my words, James, you'll wake up on your thirtieth birthday and the phone will be ringing off the hook with offers. So only five and a half years to go . . .'

'Six and a quarter, actually.'

' . . . and we'll all be boasting that we know you. Are you ready for some pudding?'

'Um . . . ' Jamie, who had taken three helpings of the casserole, hesitated.

'Oh, go on, say you're ready for pudding, please.'

'Oh, OK.' Laughing, Jamie shook his head and surrendered. 'I'm ready for pudding.'

62

'Are you indeed, sir?' Sophie tapped her chin with a thoughtful finger. 'Lulu, do we have anything for this young man's pudding?'

'Pudding?' said Lulu. 'You didn't mention anything about pudding to me.'

'Didn't I? What a regrettable oversight. Well, I suppose we'd better see if we have anything suitable that might just happen to be in the fridge.' Sophie rose, and gravely crossed the room to the capacious stainless steel refrigerator in the corner.

'Mr James MacNichol, sir, we are forced to serve you . . . ' With a flourish, she opened the refrigerator door.

' . . . *cheesecake!*' Triumphantly she bore to the table a creamy round, its surface lightly marbled with blackcurrant juice.

'Cheesecake!' said Jamie. 'Wow, that's my favourite. How did you guess?'

'Guess!' said Sophie. 'The whole of that game we played last Wednesday evening was a fiendishly clever masterplot made up by Esme, Jack and me specifically to worm the information out of you. Lulu whipped it up with her little wooden spoon this morning, and here we are, so enjoy.'

'You made this, too, Lulu?' said Jamie. 'Wow. You're amazing.'

'I've always cooked,' said Lulu. 'I don't know where it came from. Mom's very good, but she does it because she has to. I've always really enjoyed it.'

'It must be your way of being nice to people,' said Jamie.

Lulu paused, her spoon halfway to her mouth. 'What do you mean?' she asked.

'Oh, one of your many ways,' said Jamie, hastily. 'Obviously. That came out wrong, I'm sorry. All this good food has gone to my brain.'

But Lulu had seen the split-second glance that he had exchanged with Sophie before he spoke.

'I think,' said Charlie, speaking slowly and thoughtfully, 'that the problem with Lulu . . . is that she's probably one of the most hateful human beings I have ever met.'

'You'd noticed?' Sophie leaned across the table, eagerly joining the joke. 'She's completely ungenerous and never does anything for anyone, does she?'

'It's not just that,' said Charlie. 'I could probably live with that. But the roast babies for breakfast every morning are getting a little bit much.'

'Is she still doing that? We tried to stop her, but . . . '

'Very funny,' said Lulu. 'Most amusing. If it's going to be like this with you two from now on, I'm going to move home to my old room, dodgy ceiling and all.'

★ ★ ★

'Lulu!' said Fee the next afternoon, looking up smiling from the kitchen table where she was contentedly doing a crossword puzzle while the dishwasher hummed happily in the background. 'What a nice surprise.'

'Mom.' Lulu threw down her bag in the hall,

64

turned into the kitchen and blinked confusedly at her mother; she had understood her parents were taking themselves to the cinema this afternoon. 'You're home.'

'Well, yes, honey, I often am. I live here, remember.'

'Oh, what witty parents I have.' She bent to kiss Fee's upturned cheek, and perched herself on the edge of a chair. 'What happened to the film?'

'I opted out at the last minute. I decided I couldn't bear to sit through another two hours of Woody Allen's id-ridden avatar being fallen in love with by a girl younger than my daughters. For some inexplicable reason, your father is more broad-minded than I am about sexist fantasies involving gorgeous young women, so he's taken his friend Phil instead of me, and they can both leer at the jail bait to their hearts' content. How are you, Lulu? Did Sophie move in OK? Shall I make some tea?'

'Yes, she's fine, and no tea for me, thanks. I just came by quickly to have another look in the attic for that recipe book.'

'Oh, sweetie, you really don't have to do that. It was just a very passing thought of Aunt Amy's — she's probably organized half of Boston to raid their attics by now. It truly couldn't matter less.'

'Well, but I'm curious now. I want to see what sort of stuff she was cooking back in New England in those days. Lots of molasses and squash and boiled beef, I bet.'

'Well, *that* sounds appetizing.'

'It sounds really interesting, actually.' Lulu frowned reprovingly at her mother. 'And there are piles of old photographs up there, too.' She paused, leaned forward over the table, and gently caressed the egg-yolk-yellow trumpets of a bunch of daffodils, bright as sunshine in a blue and white Mediterranean ceramic jug: Fee was a gardener. 'These are pretty. They're the first, aren't they? I was wondering which of them might be of Grandma Jo — the photographs, I mean. What did she look like, do you know?'

'Not really.' Fee pursed her lips, trying to recall. 'One of the sisters was supposed to be a beauty, but I'm pretty sure it wasn't her. I think she was quite tall. And I do know she had all her teeth to the end, which she was quite proud of.'

'Oh, big help there. Thanks, Mom, I'll go and look for the old lady with lots and lots of really real-looking teeth. Hi, Toby, I didn't see you there.' She lifted the cat onto her lap, and tickled his substantial stomach. 'Did people like her?' she asked, then.

'Grandma Jo? Of course they did. The family adored her.'

'Well, the family would, wouldn't they? But what about other people? Proper people-type people out there in the world who didn't have to like her at all if they didn't want to.'

'Hmm.' Glancing surreptitiously at her daughter, Fee decided that this was not the occasion to point out to her that all families were not as unquestioningly loving and loyal as the Atwaters. Instead, she rose and filled

66

the kettle at the sink, her back turned to the kitchen table. 'She was a strong taste,' she said, after a moment. 'That was fine when she was older because people admired her and said she was a character. But I imagine she found it a little more difficult when she was young. Well, you and I both know that one, don't we, Lulu? We're both strong tastes, and I know I found my twenties quite hard sometimes. Sometimes other people do have problems dealing with a strong personality, especially if it comes in a girl, which seems unfair, but I'm afraid it's true. But a nice thing about getting older is that older people have lived a little more — some of us have maybe gotten a little less judgemental over the years, and others have maybe proved their worth a little more specifically in certain circumstances — so we're most of us able to see more clearly into the hearts of the people we know. And if you have a good heart — as I think we tend to, in our family — then the rest of the world will start to be aware of that, and it'll become more important to them. And the people who are worth having around will like you accordingly. And as for the others, quite frankly, screw 'em.'

'Mm.' Seen from the corner of her mother's eye as she plugged the kettle into the socket in the wall, Lulu looked for a moment as if she might ask more, but instead she rose, ejecting Toby from her lap, and pushed her chair into the table. 'I think I'll go and look for those recipes now,' she said.

'There's tea here if you want it,' said Fee.

When Lulu reached the attic, she knew exactly which letter she was looking for. It was towards the top of the pile, longer than some of the others, and adorned even more heavily than most with crossings-out, ink-blots and, towards the end, what looked suspiciously like tear-stains. She drew it out, took it to the armchair, and read.

Concord, September 1866.

Dearest Marmee,

Thank you for your letter, and what a comfort it is to know that Beth seems to improve there in the fresh air of the seashore. I delight to hear how she enjoys the sea breezes, and if she ain't much fatter yet, then surely she must soon be. We *shall* make her well between us and have our rosy-cheeked Bethie back again — I am determined on it.

Oh, Marmee, I've done a dreadful thing! Now, don't be alarmed, Marmee, it's not such a very bad scrape I've got into — indeed, Laurie seems to find it comical, which makes me want to shake him — but I'm covered in mortification and must 'fess all to you or I'll explode.

It concerns the dance at the Tudors' last night. You recall that Laurie was so looking forward to it as a diversion from digging so hard at his books all summer long, and that he was to escort Amy, who was to look lovely as an angel in her white silk with the blue ribbons, and make herself entrancingly agreeable to every single person there in order to delight the young men and heap coals of fire on the head of the wicked Miss Randal who scorned our boy so. Well, we've been preparing all week, and such activity we've had flying about making everything ready. The silk has been tried on, pronounced a perfect fit, and a small tear in a ruffle observed and skillfully repaired by Mantua-Maker-In-Chief Jo; the new sapphire bracelet (as we *will* insist on calling it although we know it's only colored glass, but it looks so jewel-like we all agree it might as well be 'waluable') considered on this arm and on that, and high upon the arm and low upon the wrist, until at last I suggested it be affixed to a pole and carried aloft in triumph for all to see and admire, which notion Milady did *not* find entertaining but which caused Hannah to clap her handkerchief to her nose and suddenly recall that she must attend to the potatoes in the kitchen. The scuff in the boots has been disguised by the very last remnants of the blue paint; *coiffures* have been paraded, discussed with Meg (not with me — hopeless on such matters, as you know), disassembled and reassembled into what looks to me exactly the same fashion but the others promise me is a different arrangement altogether; a small garden of flowers tried and discarded before the perfect nosegay was agreed upon. At last, late on the night before last, all was pronounced to satisfaction and Amy retired to her bed a happy and a hopeful woman.

Alas for human plans, she woke in the morning with a bad cold in her head — eyes sore and streaming, a painful cough, and a nose whose color rivaled that of Hannah's cranberry sauce at Thanksgiving. We tried every remedy we could (a plaster *and* a poultice, if you please, and sufficient Jesuits' drops to convert a Hottentot to Rome) but nothing availed, and as the day wore to evening, poor Cinderella was forced to acknowledge that — failing a fairy godmother with powers to heal the sick on top of all others — she would not be able to attend the ball after all.

Well, as Mr. Longfellow reminds us, 'Into each life some rain must fall,' and I was tucking the patient under her blankets and placing the invalid bell and a tall stack of handkerchiefs by her side preparatory to going downstairs for a quiet evening of apples and *Quentin Durward*, when she looked at me with those blue eyes streaming rivers of disappointment and rheum, and said, 'I suppose you will wear your tarlaton, Jo.'

'Why, what on earth do you mean?' I replied, thinking her delirious, for I was most comfortably clad in my old gray house-dress and had no more notion of changing into finer attire than of flying.

'To go to the dance,' she said. 'Of course you shall go in my place.'

'Of course I shall do no such thing,' I

retorted, for you know my love for both dances in general and the Tudors in particular.

'Oh, Jo, you must!' she cried, although in her poor croaky voice it sounded closer to, *Oh, Do, you bust.* 'We can't leave poor Laurie to go all alone, hard as he has worked and horrid as Miss Randal has been to him.'

'Fiddlesticks,' I said. 'He has all his college friends there to keep him company, and if you don't go then Mr. Laurence needn't chaperone, which I imagine will come as great relief to him, for he don't care for the Tudors any more than I do.'

'It would look rude and queer to cry off now,' she said. 'And besides, Mr. Laurence has given Bridget the night off, so has nothing for supper. Oh, Jo, please do this, and I'll never ask you for anything, ever again.'

Well, you know what a wheedling little puss Amy can be when she sets her mind to it, so at the last, there I was, best-bib-and-tuckered in my tarlaton and carrying Meg's stiffest embroidered handkerchief, uncomfortable as could be, entering the Tudors' house on Laurie's arm.

And, oh, Marmee, I wish you could have seen the dismay on the faces of Laurie's friends when they discovered that the 'Miss March' who was to accompany him for the evening was to be, not the youngest, but the eldest! Little Mr. Parker looked set to cry, and nor could I fault him for the sentiment, for if *I* had been promised an evening of gazing upon the beauteous Amy and been served instead with cross old Jo, I should have felt exactly the same way.

In we marched, and I did do my best to seem agreeable and not say anything odd, for I wanted not to make Laurie ashamed of me in all that elegant society. We fared well enough through supper, and then it seemed that Fortune had smiled upon me for a brief while, for old Mr. Tudor introduced me to his uncle who was visiting from Scotland, and a capital old fellow he was, with bonnie blue eyes and a shock of white hair that stood at all angles above his ruddy face. He had been a major in the British Army in India, and such stories he was telling me of 'In-ja,' as he called it, of men who walked on coals and made snakes dance by playing on a pipe, of ladies in bright-colored silks who rode in carriages upon the backs of elephants, that I do believe I could have listened to him all night long.

Unfortunately, our pleasant interlude was not to last, for, just at the moment when the major was arriving at the most thrilling portion of a confrontation he had had deep in the jungle with a prowling panther, his great-nephew, young Mr. Tudor, appeared as from nowhere, bowed coolly to his uncle, and said, 'My apologies, sir, for the interruption, but I fear I must request Miss March's presence in the drawing room. She has a message from home of some urgency.'

I flew behind him from the conservatory to the drawing room, my heart in my mouth, imagining who knows what having happened in my absence, to Amy, or to one of the twins, or even (oh, Marmee) the worst news of all having come from the seashore. But when we reached the drawing room, messenger was there none, only young Mr. Tudor, looking immensely pleased with himself among his group of friends.

'Wasn't that capital play, Miss March?' he demanded. 'I saw you all alone and enslaved by the old fellow's dronings, and knew that if I did not move to rescue you, you should be there hearing his endless tedious stories for the rest of the night. Now, ain't you pleased that I did so, and mightily grateful to me?'

Oh, Marmee, I was mad. I *tried* to do as you have taught me, to conquer my temper and to be still, and perhaps if Meg had been there to raise her eyebrows at me, or Amy to say something charming to make us all laugh and let the moment pass, I might yet have succeeded. But there was only me, Marmee, and my dreadful, wicked anger.

'You are the rudest and most disagreeable young man I have ever met!' I said, clenching my fists, for with very little further provocation I do believe I would have struck him.

I suppose he is not accustomed to hearing such frank tones, for he stood back, his hand upon his breast in outrage. He has horrid hands, Marmee, as white and as plump as a girl's, and — being the most dreadful dandy — he loves to load them down with heavy rings set with diamonds and rubies. As I looked at them, oh, dear, the devil came into me, and before I could stop myself, I had added,

'And you wear more jewels than my sister!'

The next few moments, I fear, remain something of a muddle to me. I know that Laurie ran 'haste-post-haste' to drop a quiet word to Mr. Laurence, who most suddenly and conveniently was stricken by his old affliction of the gout, that hasty adieus were made, and that within very short notice I was bundled into the carriage and taken home. Mr. Laurence, to whom the particulars of the incident remained happily unclear, clung gallantly to the pretense of his indisposition, while Laurie tried manfully to maintain a sober countenance, and for most of the journey succeeded. But just when we were turning the last corner onto the road home, Mr. Laurence, thinking to cheer me a little, most innocently asked me, 'Did you not think, my dear, that Miss Tudor's jewels were looking particularly fine tonight?' At which Laurie laid his head down upon his knees in a perfect fit of merriment, and did not raise it again until we had reached the house.

This morning, the story was all over town, and almost with the cock's crow, along came Meg, as regal as Empress Eugénie of France, to scold me on my deplorable want of breeding and lack of good manners. It *has* been a dismal day, mother. Meg has lectured, Amy has looked grieved, Hannah has whisked from parlor to kitchen with not a word, and even Miss Tabby has turned her striped tail up in disdain and refuses to talk to me. Matters were made worse when, halfway through the morning, came a ring at the door, and there stood a messenger with a box of flowers, such lovely roses and ferns and heliotrope, as fine as any from Mr. Laurence's conservatory, with a note addressed to Miss Josephine March, that read, 'To the only young lady last night who made me wish I were forty years younger. Respectfully, James Patterson (Major).'

For a moment, I thought that this might dampen at least a little of Meg's fury, but, on the contrary, it had the effect of stoking the fire. It is not sufficient, she tells me, to be pleasant only to the people I find charming or attractive; it is the duty of any person of good breeding to be amiable to every person they meet, and most particularly when they are a young woman and a guest in another person's house. I brought shame on the family last night, and if I cannot learn to hold my tongue now, while I am still young enough to learn new ways, I will grow into a cranky and eccentric old lady and the family will be most mortally ashamed of me forever. All these dreadful things she said to me and more, and, oh, Marmee, I know that she's right and I'm wrong, but I *can't* stand by and watch a young man make a mockery of an old, especially so shallow a youth as young Tudor and so splendid an old man as the major, so what on earth will become of me, and what on earth am I to do?

I long for you tonight, Marmee. Meg is so

cross with me, and only you understand how I struggle to be good and pleasant and womanly when it *ain't* easy and it *don't* come natural. Letters are very well, but if you were here at home we could sit as we do on our quiet restful nights together by the fire, with you in the easy-chair and me lying on the dear old shabby sofa with my head on Beth's little red pillow, and I could talk as I only can to you, and tell you all my troubles and see your dear smile of encouragement. I read your letters to console me but I'd far sooner have your smile to lift my spirits and your hand to stroke my brow. Ah, well, if I am down tonight it is only of my own doing, as Meg would no doubt remind me.

Write soon, Marmee dear, for it is so comforting to get your letters, and just now I'm in sorest need of my Marmee's comfort.

With love and a heavy heart from your black sheep daughter,

Jo.

Lulu sat with the letter for a long time, wondering what had happened afterwards in the little house in the town outside Boston all those years ago. Had Marmee laughed at the incident, like the young man called Laurie had, or had she lectured like Meg? Had the dandified Mr Tudor ever forgiven Jo, and what had the other people at the dance thought of it all? And Jo herself — had she really found it so amusing that the young men of the town had so plainly preferred her sister, or were her jokes a cover for an aching heart? But Jo had found love in the end, Lulu reminded herself quickly. Awkward as she had been as a girl, she had met a German professor, somehow or somewhere, and she had fallen in love and married him, and Mom had always said how happily married they were. Mom had also said, quite specifically this very afternoon, that the family had adored her. That was the word she had used. They had adored her.

★ ★ ★

The afternoon was almost over and Fee long finished with her puzzle when Lulu appeared again at the kitchen door.

'Is there any tea left?' she asked.

'I'll just check,' said Fee, who had brewed a second pot in anticipation.

3

Concord, September 1866.

Beth, dearie,

How you would have delighted in the theatricals that we held last night. *The Grandee's Revenge* played to tumultuous applause, with Mr. Theodore Laurence most ably taking the part of Don Pedro the Grandee; Miss Amy March, happily restored to health after a fierce battle with the rheum, appearing as Rosarita, his beloved Lady In Blue; Miss Josephine March, resplendent in the russet boots, as the wicked Don Felipe; and featuring, as a particular cause of excitation from one and all, no less a luminary than that most celebrated of all actresses, Mrs. John Brooke herself, tempted from her retirement into domestic bliss for one final appearance upon the theatrical boards in honor of Cousin Flo's birthday, to play the part of the Gypsy Queen.

I shall not pretend to you that the days preceding the performance were easy ones. Both the twins have had colic, requiring Meg to miss all of the final week's rehearsals; I discovered at the very last moment a broken heel on the boots, and had not kind Mr. Luft in town taken mercy upon me to keep open his shop until late, Don Felipe would have been reduced to playing his part while listing to the windward like a sailor; Teddy *wouldn't* learn his lines, driving us all to distraction and causing Amy to threaten the direst of consequences, until, on the very last rehearsal on the very day before the play, he turned up word perfect and smiling like a lamb, with an airy, 'You see — you fuss-pots needn't have worked yourselves into such a pother after all,' thus giving us at the last some compassion for the trials endured by his benighted tutors at college.

The day of the performance dawned bright and crisp. Amy was in her glory in her blue gown which she would insist on wearing all day long, claiming that it would 'take too much trouble to change later,' and that the parading abroad of this particularly becoming garment had nothing at all to do with the visit promised by a certain young Mr. Peebles, who had announced his intention of calling for coffee in the late morning.

Just after eleven, sure as his word, Mr. Peebles came calling, and particularly fetching Amy did look to greet him in her pretty blue dress with the pink ribbons and a pretty pink rose placed at a bewitching angle in her curls. Mr. Peebles clearly enjoyed the effect, and the two settled themselves in the parlor to enjoy a delightful visit over Hannah's finest coffee set upon the best tea tray. Unfortunately, just as Amy and Mr. Peebles were sitting in the parlor as properly as you please, young Tommy

Fletch was calling at the kitchen with the mutton chops for dinner, accompanied by his large dog, Caesar, who loves to play and whose eye fell straight away on what seemed to him a most likely playmate in Miss Tabby. And the next thing our elegant Miss March and Mr. Peebles knew, there careened through the parlor a harum-scarum procession of Miss Tabby with tail fluffed out like a fir tree in fright, pursued by Caesar who thought it all a huge joke, pursued by Miss March's sister with her hair in a duster and wielding a broom, which last she accidentally knocked into the coffee pot, sending a stream of brown liquid clear across the skirt of Amy's best blue gown.

Mr. Peebles behaved with most admirable gallantry throughout this unfortunate incident, inquiring tenderly as to the wellbeing of the victim, declaring stoutly (although we suspect with less than perfect dependability) that such accidents happen frequently in all the best of houses, and finally making his *adieus* with a true gentleman's courtesy and adding assurances that it would be his pleasure to return on a more opportune occasion.

The gown, though, was another matter. Hannah has soaked it in vinegar and believes that it can be rescued with sufficient scrubbing on Monday, but it was quite ruined for the evening, and for a while it seemed perilously probable that it would take the entertainment with it, for with no gown there could be no Rosarita, and with no Rosarita, no play at all.

'You could wear another gown,' I suggested a little doubtfully, for you know that when Amy has set her fancy upon an outfit no other will serve, were it stitched by angels themselves.

'I *could*,' she retorted, 'if you would like me to wear either of the only two other gowns I have fit to wear so close to wash-day and now that the silk has been put away. Which would you rather me be, Jo, The Lady In Turned Faded Drab, or The Lady In Gingham?'

Happily, Don Pedro himself, happening to call at the very height of this commotion, turned up trumps with a solution. It seems that old Mr. Laurence still retains in his possession several fine items that had once belonged to Laurie's mother that he could not bring himself to give away, for the old gentleman is often more sentimental than he likes to seem. Of course, he is not in the custom of lending them out, but Laurie can wheedle him so, and you know that the old man has a soft spot in his heart for Amy, so in the end she appeared that evening resplendent in a gown that was of a far deeper blue, and a far finer cut and cloth, than any poor garment our own humble wardrobes could dream of supplying.

And such a lark as followed, dear Bethie, would have had a Quaker stage-struck. Don Pedro by turns raged, lamented, shook his irons, and at the very last emerged so very gallantly triumphant with Rosarita at his side that the audience barely noticed that the spirit

81

gum had worn quite off his left cheek, requiring him to declaim his lines with jaw clenched like one with severe toothache, or half the beard would have slid into his romantically ruffed collar. Rosarita herself is happily evincing dramatic powers that have much improved since we were children — not that the gentlemen in the audience would have cared a fig if she had stood like a stone statue, lovely as she looked in both joy and distress, and fetchingly as her yellow curls fell down her white neck to the borrowed blue dress. Don Felipe schemed and cursed and smote his breast and was most gratified to hear an audible hiss of hatred arise from the dress circle each time he appeared upon the stage. But the star of them all was the Gypsy Queen, for Meg's voice grows richer with maturity even as her face and bearing grow more tenderly beautiful with all the sweet and womanly experiences that have come her way of late. Her performance was truly affecting, and when she told the story of her poor little daughter, carried away in infancy by the bandits and never seen since, I do believe that there was not a handkerchief left un-dampened in the entire house — in front of the stage or behind.

It was a *very* splendid occasion, Beth, possibly the most successful play that our little dining room has ever yet seen. Cousin Flo declares she never had a finer birthday celebration. And if *one* of our children or great-great-grandchildren don't *one day* become a famous actor or actress, then I will eat Don Felipe's wicked slouched hat, liniment stain upon the brim and all.

Ever your loving,

Jo.

For the first couple of weeks after Sophie had moved into Charlie's flat, everyone was on her best behaviour. Sophie was careful to tidy up after herself, refrained from slamming the door when coming home in the early hours of the morning, turned down her radio whenever Mrs Scott-Ramsay rapped on the ceiling and procured from a former acting teacher tickets to a first night at the Royal Court and an invitation to the party afterwards, which impressed both Lulu and Charlie considerably more than either of them admitted. In return Lulu, more heedful of harmony in her friend's home than she had ever been in her family's, bit her tongue on a variety of sarcastic comments that she would otherwise have voiced aloud and was pleasantly surprised to find how much easier her younger sister had suddenly become to deal with. But best behaviour, admirable as its intentions may be, was never meant to last.

'Has anyone seen my hair conditioner?' asked Charlie one soft Saturday morning when the sunlight streamed through the apple blossom, coming sleepily into the kitchen in her white cotton dressing gown. Charlie had inherited from her mother not only her metabolism, but also a head of dark glossy hair of which she was, quietly, extremely proud, and on which she lavished a variety of expensive products, causing Lulu to shake her head and mutter ominously about bailiffs knocking on doors and former heiresses reduced to living in cardboard boxes under the railway bridge.

'You mean the hundred-pounds-a-squirt American stuff made from albino skunk droppings and ground South Australian ants?' she said now. 'I don't even dare to look at it — I'm afraid the sight alone would bankrupt me.'

'You're welcome to use it if you want,' said Charlie. Passing behind Lulu, she pulled gently at her wild brown curls, roughly combed and pulled back, as usual, with a plain covered band. 'You have lovely hair, Lulu, if only you'd take care of it.'

'Lovely hair if only you'd take care of it,' mimicked Lulu mincingly. 'Stick you in a baggy skirt and an ethnic necklace and you could actually *be* Mom, it's really quite impressive. What's the occasion for the posh glop, anyway? Are you seeing Javier later on?'

'Possibly,' admitted Charlie, pinkening despite herself in the spring sunlight. 'There's a lunch at The Wolseley and he's going to try to be there if he can get away in time. But I want to use it anyway, and I just can't find it although I'm sure I put it out last night. It's quite strange.'

'Are you talking about hair conditioner?' Sophie, who had been engrossed in *Stage and Screen*, looked up. 'They're doing *Midsummer Night's Dream* at the Vagabond in Covent Garden — can you imagine the bliss? It's my favourite theatre in the universe. Did the conditioner come in a funny little kind of squishy white bottle with a blue top? Smells sort of coconutty?'

'Coconut and vanilla,' agreed Charlie. 'That's it. Have you seen it?'

'Well, there's a funny story about that,' said Sophie.

'Oh, God,' said Lulu.

'No, it's really funny,' said Sophie. 'You'll like it, I promise, OK?' She crunched the last of her toast and honey, sat back in her chair, and settled herself to entertain. 'OK, so it was last night, OK? And yesterday morning I went to the dentist — which, thanks for asking, Lulu, went mostly OK, all things considered — and then in the afternoon I had my voice class, and then I went straight off to the late shift at the Beanz, and when I was on my way there Maggie called to say I hadn't got the part in the *Sawbones* episode, which was soooo irritating because it was the third time I'd read for them, and they keep on telling me they're dying to use me because I'm — '

'Perfect for the demographic,' noted Lulu.

' — perfect for the demographic, right, but they're just waiting to find the right role to use me in, and they can't find it and it's just driving me mad, and then I got to Beanz and Julian was off ill and Beanz had even more than its usual weirdo quotient, which believe me is saying something for a Friday night.'

'What's your point, Sophie?' said Lulu. 'I'm supposing there is one.'

'I'm getting there, OK?' Sophie shook her

85

head at her sister. 'So I got to the end of the day, and by then I really, really needed a bit of a wind-down session, so obviously I called Jamie and he was down in Tooting so we agreed to meet at that place in Notting Hill, and what with one thing and another I didn't get home till after three and I know neither of you woke up when I came in, because I listened and you didn't.'

She paused and smiled proudly.

'Point, Soph?' said Lulu.

'So up the stairs I creep, quiet as a little mouse, creep, creep, creep, on my tippy-tippy-toes, past both of your bedrooms to the bathroom, floss my teeth, just like Mr Yugawa told me I should, then I remembered he'd told me a new way of brushing, too — you don't just go up and down like most people do, you go round in little individual circles on each tooth, and not too hard either, which is the mistake most people make because that weakens the enamel, you just — '

'Sophie!'

'OK, I'm getting there! God. So it's very late at night, I've had an incredibly long day, I'm very tired, and I don't have my lenses in. And . . . you know how when you move to a new place and you're really tired and you're reaching for something, then sometimes you reach to the place where you used to keep it in the old place?'

'Oh, God,' said Lulu.

'And you know how in this place we keep the toothpaste on the right side of the sink, but in

Esme's place we always used to keep it on the left?'

'Oh, God,' said Lulu.

'Well, it was just this little tubey bottle on the side of the sink, and I picked it up like this with my eyes all closed and everything, and I did think to myself, Well, that's funny, I didn't know toothpaste came in bottles, but I knew it had to *be* toothpaste because that's where we always kept it, you see. So I gave it a really good strong squeeze over my brush, and of course it all rushed out and down the sink, and I thought, And that's funny, too, this toothpaste is a bit gloopy, but I still had it in my head that it was toothpaste, OK? So the next thing was, I went to brush my teeth with it! And let me tell you something, hair-conditioner-flavoured toothpaste tastes really, really . . . '

Finally taking account of the expression on the faces of her audience, she stopped.

'Oh,' she said.

'I will kill you,' said Lulu.

'It's OK,' said Charlie. 'It's only hair conditioner.'

'I'm so sorry,' said Sophie. 'I had no idea it was so special, Charlie. I'll buy you another one, Charlie, I promise.'

'It cost more than a week of your wages,' said Lulu. 'I will kill you. I will.'

'It's no big deal,' said Charlie. 'It's only hair conditioner and you were always telling me I shouldn't spend money on it anyway, Lulu. Maybe this is a message from the universe to me that I don't need to have it and really shouldn't have it.'

'Well, you *don't* need it!' said Sophie. Brightening a little, she cast her eye over Charlie's abundant mane. 'You have such gorgeous hair you don't need to do anything with it, really.'

'Not the point, Soph,' said Lulu. 'Going to kill you.'

'But she doesn't need it! Look at her! Now, if she had really bad, difficult, frizzy hair like — '

'If you say one more word . . . ' began Lulu.

'I wasn't even thinking about you, actually! You're not the only person in the world with hair, you know. God. Actually, Charlie, I was thinking about my friend Esme, who's like my best friend in the world and I love her to pieces, but she has — and she'd tell you this herself — really terrible hair, all dry and horrible, and if *she* doesn't use conditioner, she looks just awful, like a clinically depressed haystack in a cyclone. But you look gorgeous without it, Charlie. OK, you look super-mega-gorgeous with it. But even without it you still look amazing.'

'Still not the point, Soph,' said Lulu. 'Still going to kill you.'

'Sorry,' said Sophie.

There was a silence around the table, while Lulu stared coldly into her empty coffee mug and Sophie collected sticky toast crumbs on her finger and licked them sadly.

'Shall I make some more coffee?' she said, after a moment.

'I'll do it.' Lulu began to rise from the table.

88

'No, I can!' Eager to redeem herself, Sophie shot to her feet. 'Just because you make the most super-gourmet coffee in the history of the world doesn't mean you have to do it all the time. Sit down and let me do it for once.'

'OK. Thanks, that would be nice.' Lulu sat down again, exchanging a shrug with Charlie.

Gawkily graceful in a faded blue T-shirt and tracksuit bottoms, Sophie loped to the cupboard and extracted the tightly sealed bag of meticulously blended coffee beans that Lulu travelled to Covent Garden once a week to mix for herself from the Monmouth Coffee Company. She took the bag across the room to the coffee grinder, her head bent, her hair shining gold as a halo against the snowy apple blossom in the window. She filled the grinder to the brim, closed the lid and pressed a button.

There was a whirring sound, followed by a click, followed by silence.

Charlie closed her eyes.

'Sorry,' said Sophie. 'I didn't know it was going to do that. Sorry.'

Lulu got up, went to the coffee grinder and inspected it.

'I can probably fix it,' she said at last. 'It'll probably take me all morning and it might not look as pretty afterwards. But I can probably fix it.'

'Sorry,' said Sophie.

'I don't mind how it looks,' said Charlie. 'But promise me I'll have coffee tomorrow morning.'

'You'll have coffee tomorrow morning,' said Lulu. 'I promise.'

'I really like coffee in the morning,' said Charlie. 'I feel I can face anything after I've had coffee in the morning. It's very important to me to have coffee in the morning. I don't mind how the grinder looks after you've fixed it or if you have to do something strange with it from now on to make it grind the beans. I don't mind if you go out and buy a cheaper grinder, or even if you go out and buy some coffee already ground — '

'Shhhhh!' Sophie leaped to cover her sister's ears. 'Don't talk like that to her, she's very sensitive about coffee. It's all right, Lulu, she didn't mean it.'

'You don't get to make jokes right now,' said Lulu.

'Sorry,' said Sophie.

'You'll have coffee tomorrow, Charlie,' said Lulu. 'I guarantee it. And as for you, Sophie, I don't know how you can make this up to Charlie, that's between you and her, but as far as how you can make it up to me, you can do all the supermarket shopping from now on. I'll buy the interesting things, like cheese and vegetables, but you can make sure we're stocked up with the dull stuff like tea bags and dishwashing detergent, OK?'

'OK,' said Sophie.

'And you don't just buy it and leave it in bags on the table either,' said Lulu. 'After you've brought it home, you unpack it and put it away, OK?'

'OK,' said Sophie.

'And this morning, while I'm hard at work

90

fixing the grinder, you can make yourself useful by doing the laundry. You can wash everything, whites and coloureds, two separate loads, remember, and then you can put it all into the dryer, and then you can take it all out and fold it and put it all away, too.'

'OK,' said Sophie.

'And no helping yourself to any of my clothes while you're at it, either.'

'I wouldn't help myself to your clothes,' said Sophie, 'if — '

'No jokes, Sophie.'

'Sorry,' said Sophie.

★ ★ ★

'It's just so embarrassing,' said Lulu a few days later, sprawling at the scrubbed hardwood table in Emma and Matthew's small, immaculate kitchen: Emma took pride in keeping her surroundings tidy. It was Tuesday evening, when Matthew played squash with his friend Cheng, and Lulu had acquired the habit of dropping into the flat for a sisterly visit. 'Charlie *says* she doesn't mind, but I'm sure she does really, and even if she doesn't mind now I know she will one day, because in the end you do, don't you? I've minded about Sophie ever since she was two.'

'Charlie was the one who invited her, though, wasn't she?' Standing at the stove, Emma poked gently at the vegetables in the pan and turned her head to peer at the pasta bubbling in the pot beside it. 'I was there, remember, I heard her.'

'Yes, but she didn't know what she was taking

on! We know what it's like to live with Sophie, but she doesn't. Didn't, anyway — I've a horrible feeling she's starting to find out.'

'And you tried to warn her about that, too, and she went ahead anyway. I wouldn't worry about it too much, Lulu. Charlie can take care of herself, and you know Sophie — everyone ends up loving her anyway. And it's not as if she's going to attack you in your sleep with a machete.'

Despite herself, Lulu produced a smile.

'Not on purpose, anyway,' she commented.

'Sorry!' Emma widened her eyes, slipping with ease born of long practice into their Sophie imitation. 'Oh, Lulu, was that your leg? I'm soooo sorry, I didn't mean to, but never mind, you've still got the other, whoops, no, you haven't, oh, and there goes your head, too, I've killed you! Mom! Charlie! Emma, you'll never guess what's happened!'

'Well, if she ever does, feel free to kill her back on my behalf.' Lulu reached across the table to pull towards herself a large book with a picture of a young woman in white on the cover.

'What's this?' she asked.

'It's a book,' Emma told her.

'I can see that. *How to Plan the Perfect Wedding*.' She looked at it, frowning. Like many people who are academically gifted, Lulu had a tendency to overlook the more mundane details of the practical world around her; although she knew quite well that Emma and Matthew were planning to get married, it had not seriously occurred to her until now that this would involve having a wedding. 'Do they have books about that?' she asked.

'Apparently,' said Emma.

'Hmm.' Lulu opened the book and flicked through its pages, staring at pictures of roses, and shining gold rings, and tables set with crisp white linen. 'Are you really going to do it?' she asked then.

'No, Lulu.' Well used by now to her sister's scattershot grasp of social customs, Emma shook her head sadly as she hooked out a piece of pasta to taste for texture. 'We're not really going to get married, Matthew and me. That announcement we made to the family a few weeks ago, and this ring I've been wearing ever since, were all part of a cunningly devised master plan to get Dad to open the good champagne. Of course I'm going to do it — what a weird question. Truly, even for you, that is seriously a weird thing to ask.'

'Sorry.' Still leafing through the pages Lulu paused at a picture of a canapé. 'I wouldn't put caviar on top of smoked salmon, it's too much fish. It just seems so sort of grown-up, somehow. Having a wedding.'

Looking down at her seated sister, Emma sighed and once again shook her head.

'But we are grown-ups, Lulu,' she said, 'and that's what grown-ups do. They fall in love, and they get married. Didn't anyone tell you?'

'I suppose they didn't,' said Lulu. Lulu had never yet been seriously in love. She had had boyfriends, of course she had, but they had never been very serious, and the idea of finding, as Emma had, the person with whom she could consider sharing the whole of the rest of her life — let alone one who would consider spending the rest of his life with her — seemed as unreachable to her as the dreams of flying she had sometimes had as a small girl.

'Someone will come along,' said Emma. 'You'll see. He'll turn up and it'll all fall into place.'

Which was all very easy, thought Lulu, with a private little shiver, for Emma to say, she who had fallen in love so happily and with so little effort. Emma liked people and people liked Emma: of course she would fall in love with someone who would fall in love with her, just as someone would fall in love with Sophie one day — Emma was right: everyone loved Sophie. But Lulu was so different from Emma and Sophie, she was spiky and strange, and could not even make Sasha Goncharoff laugh. Who would she ever find whom she could fall in love with — and who in all the whole wide world would ever fall in love with Lulu?

'When he does,' she said, 'I'll tell him to bring extra shaving cream — Sophie's running short on shampoo.'

Emma smiled. 'Food's coming,' she said. 'It's sauce-y, so watch out for the book, please.'

Nudging Lulu aside, she removed the wedding book from the table to a safer spot on a shelf, and set down two plates of pillowy pasta studded with jewel-coloured vegetables: red cherry tomatoes, yellow squash, and purple aubergine.

Lulu tasted, and nodded approvingly. 'Nice,' she said. 'Next time, you might want to use just a little less crème fraiche and possibly cook the pasta just a minute more.'

'And maybe add a generous helping of shut up and eat or cook your own,' Emma returned, amiably. 'Mom seems quite pleased about the wedding, actually. I thought I'd get a lecture on patriarchal tyranny and young women as goods for barter, but she actually asked me what I wanted her to wear.'

'Did you tell her no hippie skirts?' Fee was an attractive woman for her age, but in the eyes of her daughters, still a little too fond of the fashions of her youth.

'I'm doing better,' said Emma. 'I'm going shopping with her. Will you be my chief bridesmaid?'

'Me?' Lulu narrowed her eyes suspiciously. 'What would I need to do?'

'Not very much, just organize the hen party, sign the register and hold me down when I panic on the day. It's not going to be a fancy wedding.'

Not fancy, thought Lulu, but beautifully orchestrated: Emma did everything beautifully. And the chances of Emma's panicking, on that day or any other, were about on a par with those of Fee's applying for Botox.

'I can do that,' she said. Then frowned. 'It doesn't mean being nice to people, does it?'

Emma laughed. 'No, it doesn't mean being nice to people, we'll leave that to Mom and Dad.' She stopped herself: Emma had always had excellent self-control. 'And I'm trying not to talk about it too much because I don't want to turn into one of those brides who bangs on until everyone's bored rigid. So.' She reached for the water jug and poured herself a glass. 'What's going on with you, apart from wanting to kill Sophie? How's work? How's Mr Goncharoff? Is he really going to sell the shop?'

Lulu sighed, irritably: it occurred to her that she knew precisely which question would follow this. 'Probably,' she admitted after a moment.

And, sure enough, the question came.

'And what will you do when he does?' said Emma.

'I don't know, Emma,' said Lulu. She laid down her fork and stared mock-intensely into her sister's eyes. 'Now I want you to watch me very carefully, and listen to me very hard, and you can feel free to read my lips as I go if it helps you to understand. OK, here goes. I. Don't. Know. It's the answer I've been giving you for ages now when you ask me that question. And any time you decide to ask me again, and any way you decide to ask it, the answer will still be the same. I don't know. And I won't know until I do know, and when I do, I'll tell you, OK?'

'Sorry,' said Emma, mildly. 'I just care about you, that's all. Sisters do tend to care about each other, if you'd noticed.'

'Hmm.' Lulu reached for the pepper mill and ground flakes over her pasta. 'What do you know about Grandma Jo?' she asked suddenly.

'What?' Emma blinked at the abrupt change of subject.

'Grandma Jo,' said Lulu. 'I've been thinking about her lately for some reason, wondering what she was really like. Mom goes on about her, but you know how she exaggerates. What do you really know about her?'

'Well, only what Mom's told us, for what that's worth.' Emma paused, searching her memory. 'She ran the school. She wrote a couple of books. And Grandma Jojo once told me she broke her arm falling out of a tree when she was small.'

'You remember Grandma Jojo?' Lulu had been only five when Fee's mother had died, suddenly, of a virus caught on a trip to Africa.

'Sort of. She came to visit us a couple of times. She was rather glamorous. She smelled of lily of the valley, and she was always on at Mom to comb her hair.'

'Was she, now?' Lulu filed for future reference this useful piece of information.

'And she was very pleased when *you* came along,' said Emma. 'I think she'd wanted to have more children than Mom but she couldn't, I don't know why. So she was pleased about you, and she was just delighted about Sophie.'

'Little did she know,' said Lulu.

★   ★   ★

'I have an announcement,' said Sophie one lazy Sunday as the flatmates lounged in the living room in the lengthening spring evening, happily sated with weekend leisure.

'Oh, God,' said Lulu from the depths of a capacious armchair, where she was entertaining herself with a Sudoku. 'What have you done now?'

97

'I haven't *done* anything,' said Sophie. 'Do you think there's any way you might just manage to stop being so revoltingly suspicious of me for just one minor fraction of a micro-second, please? Actually, I've got something to say that you'll both really like.'

'You're moving out?' Lulu sat up hopefully. 'Can I help you pack?'

'What I have to say,' said Sophie, addressing herself with dignity to Charlie, 'is that I'm inviting you both to dinner here at the flat on Saturday night. I've spoken to Mom and Dad and Emma and Matthew, and they've accepted with pleasure. And I'd be delighted if you — if both of you — would do me the honour of joining us, too.'

'Interesting,' said Lulu. 'Interesting and hospitable. And, just to satisfy my curiosity here, exactly who is supposed to be cooking this sumptuous feast?'

'Me,' said Sophie.

'Oh, God.' Lulu lay back in her chair and covered her face with a cushion.

'This is so not fair!' said Sophie. 'That is exactly — exactly, precisely and word for word — what Emma said. You neither of you believe me that I can cook, but I really can. I learned while I was at drama school, and I did lots of cooking at Esme's place, and she really liked it, so there.' She looked down at her jeans-clad legs, and became busy rubbing at a rip in the knee. 'And you two have been so nice to me,' she added, quietly, addressing the faded denim, 'letting me live here which has really saved my

98

life, and Charlie's been so wonderful when I've messed things up, and even Lulu hasn't been too horrible considering, that I'd really like to do something nice for you in return. So I'd like to ask you to dinner, please. I'd really like to cook dinner for you.'

There was a pause while Lulu and Charlie exchanged glances.

'Well, that would be very kind of you, Sophie,' said Charlie then. 'Thank you very much, I'm looking forward to it. Aren't you, Lulu?'

Lulu looked at Sophie, and sighed.

'Really looking forward,' she agreed. 'That'll be nice, Soph. Want me to help you with the cooking?'

'No!' Abandoning the tear, Sophie threw up her hands in frustration. 'You always do this, Lulu, you always try to take over, and it's really irritating. I *don't* want you to help, that's just the point. It's something *I* want to do for *you*, OK? I want to do it and I can do it, so could you just for this one occasion, please, just find a way to believe it and accept it and say thank you for the invitation?'

'OK,' said Lulu, surprised by this into civility. 'Sorry.'

'You haven't thanked me for the invitation yet,' said Sophie.

'Sorry,' said Lulu again. 'Thank you for the invitation, Sophie. It's very kind of you.'

'You're welcome,' said Sophie.

★　★　★

For all of the following week, Sophie flung herself into preparations. She spent hours in her bedroom, doing what she referred to as 'research', emerging with a satisfied face and a barely suppressed smile of excitement whenever she looked at Lulu or Charlie. On Friday she enlisted the help of Jamie and his van for a shopping trip, returning laden with bags full of chicken and vegetables, fruit, curry powder and wine, which they carried up the stairs with much clatter, oblivious to the disapproving face of Mrs Scott-Ramsay, being helped out of a taxi by her housekeeper at the height of their activity.

'I hope you bring a doggie bag tomorrow,' said Lulu to Jamie, watching Sophie cram tomatoes into the fridge and heroically refraining from commenting that the cold would diminish their flavour. 'There's enough food here to feed a starving army.'

'Oh, that's a thought,' said Sophie. 'D'you want to come to dinner tomorrow, Jamie? There's loads of food.'

'Hadn't you asked him already?' said Lulu. 'After all the work he's been doing?'

'I'd have got around to it,' said Sophie. 'Wouldn't I, James? Anyway, I'm asking you now. Would you like to come to dinner?'

'Uhm.' Jamie tried to seem to think it over: if this were a sample of his acting skill, thought Lulu, it did not bode well for his professional future. 'OK,' he said then. 'It'd be nice.'

'You see? Sorted.' Sophie beamed happily at her sister. 'You like my cooking, don't you, Jamie?'

100

'Oh, yeah,' said Jamie. 'It's really good. She's a beautiful cook, Lulu, really she is.'

Sophie nodded triumphantly. 'And just you wait till tomorrow,' she told them both. 'You're in for a real treat.'

★　★　★

On Saturday, both Lulu and Charlie were forbidden entrance to the kitchen. Sophie barricaded herself in amid a furore of savoury smells, clanging pots, exclamations of satisfaction and distress, and occasional celebratory bursts of 'Food, Glorious Food', emerging only at lunchtime in response to Lulu's howls of hunger to pass them both a ham and cheese sandwich from a tomato-smeared hand.

'It's a good sandwich,' said Charlie, hopefully, as they munched in the living room.

'It's a sandwich,' said Lulu.

'Even so,' said Charlie, 'it's a good one.'

'You've been talking to Jamie,' said Lulu.

★　★　★

'I must say, honey,' said Fee when they all at last were gathered at the dinner table in the long, light kitchen, 'that this food is truly excellent. Isn't it excellent, Lulu?'

'Wonderful,' said Lulu. She inspected a slice of French bread covered with roughly chopped tomato. 'Really wonderful, Soph. Congratulations.'

'It's terrific, isn't it?' Jamie smiled proudly at

101

Sophie. 'Amazing, Sophie. I think it's your best yet.'

'The secret to bruschetta,' said Sophie, 'is not to put the tomatoes on the bread too early. I used to do that for ages, didn't I, Jamie, and I used to wonder why the bread was always all soggy, and it was horrible Ruby, oddly enough, who told me that trick. Now, for this, I put the tomatoes on just before I brought it all to the table, and isn't the bread nice and firm?'

'Firm,' said Lulu. 'Nice.'

Sophie frowned critically at her plate. 'I suppose the tomatoes could be a little riper,' she admitted. 'And some recipes say you should do fiddly stuff like skinning them and toasting the bread, but I don't think that's necessary, do you? Have some salad.'

'Salad, too!' said Fee. 'Goodness, Sophie, you're spoiling us. Isn't it all wonderful, David?'

'It's a feast,' said David. He was a tall man, lean and gently balding, with the look of someone quietly and always enjoying a private joke. He smiled now at his youngest daughter. 'Well, well, Sophie! First you teach yourself to sew, and now you learn to cook. Next thing, you'll be putting all this career nonsense out of your head and settling down to marry like a young woman should.'

Sophie simpered prettily back at him.

'Only if I can find someone as big and strong and clever as you, Daddy,' she lisped.

'That's my girl.' David nodded approvingly. 'True femininity,' he noted to no one in

102

particular. 'She gets it from my side of the family.'

'Ignore them, Charlie,' said Fee. 'They do it to get a rise out of me. It's never yet worked, but I guess hope will spring eternal. Have some of Daddy's little girl's salad.'

'Thank you, it looks delicious.' Charlie helped herself to a portion, tasted and was silent.

'I made the dressing myself,' said Sophie. 'I used less oil than usual because Emma's always worrying about weight, so it might be a bit vinegary. But it is homemade.'

'Maybe,' suggested Lulu gently, 'just as a thought, really, just as a sort of idea, we could perhaps bring out a little more olive oil and have it on the side. Just for any people to add who don't like it quite so, um, sharp.'

'Sharp flavours refresh the palate,' Sophie told her. 'Oh! Oh! I've got an announcement!' She rapped on her glass with a spoon, and stood up. 'Listen up, everyone, I've got something to say.'

'I do not like the sound of this,' Lulu murmured to Emma.

'You never know,' said Emma, trying to seem more confident than she felt.

'Listen to me!' Sophie at last achieved silence. 'OK, everyone, Mom, Dad, everyone. I want to say thank you both to Lulu and to Charlie for taking me in when I had nowhere to go. It was kind of both of them, and it was kind of Lulu, but it was even kinder of Charlie because Lulu's my sister and she's sort of stuck with me, but Charlie didn't have to be this kind, and I really appreciate it.'

'Hear, hear,' said Jamie, rapping on his own glass in approval.

'That's very nice of you, Sophie,' said Charlie. 'But honestly . . . '

'And I've been thinking,' continued Sophie, 'about a way of thanking Charlie particularly. Tonight is all very well, but it's for everyone, not just you, Charlie, and I wanted to do something specially for you.'

'Oh, God,' said Lulu.

'You never know,' Emma reminded her, less certainly still.

'You might not know this, Charlie,' said Sophie, 'because I don't go on about it because it's the sort of thing that if you let everyone know about, they're always on at you to do it. But I just happen to be just a little bit of a whizz at the sewing machine, aren't I, Mom?'

'*Not* taught by me,' noted Fee. 'Learned over my objections, in fact. But then, I did bring you all up to question authority.'

'And you know those black jumpers you like to wear, Charlie?' continued Sophie.

'Oh, God,' said Lulu.

Emma said nothing.

'The ones you always look so super-sophisticated and elegant and grown-up in,' Sophie added hastily. 'But let's face it, they do all look more or less the same, and I had the idea you might like to wear one that looked just a little bit different occasionally. And last week I happened to spot one of them lying around in the clean laundry basket. And . . . '

She reached behind herself to rummage in a

drawer and produced a package wrapped in tissue paper.

'Here you are,' she said. 'I hope you like it.'

Emma became interested in her salad. Lulu slid down in her seat, covering her face with a hand.

Smiling just a little nervously, Charlie unwrapped the package.

'Oh!' she said then, softly. Around the neck of her plain black jumper was sewn a delicate tracery of Victorian beads and buttons in carved bone, ivory and mother of pearl.

'Do you like it?' said Sophie, watching her and biting her lower lip.

'It's beautiful,' said Charlie, running a caressing hand over the newly adorned garment. 'Sophie, it's just . . . beautiful.'

'I hope it's OK,' said Sophie. 'It's what I've been doing all week up in my bedroom. I got the buttons and things in Camden Market, I thought they'd show up nicely against the black.'

'It's amazing,' said Charlie. She handed the jumper to Fee. 'Look at it, Fee. Did you really do this yourself, Sophie?'

'Designed it and everything,' put in Jamie. 'Isn't she amazingly talented?'

'Yes, she is,' said Fee. 'I have no idea where she gets it from but, honey, that is truly gorgeous.'

'Sophie, thank you so much,' said Charlie. 'It's so original and just lovely. Look, Lulu, isn't it pretty?'

'Yes, do look, Lulu.' Sophie rounded on her sisters. 'Look, Lulu, look, Emma, sniggering and whispering together there, I did something right for once. Had the idea, did it, and didn't mess it up, how about that? Your sister did something right. Remember that the next time you're so sure I'm going to get it all wrong, OK?'

'You know something?' said Emma, after a moment. 'You've got a point, Sophie. We probably do tend to put you down a little bit, because you're the youngest, and it's really not fair. I'm sorry, and I'll try not to do it in the future.'

'Thank you,' said Sophie. She looked at Lulu. 'Lulu, do you have anything to say?'

Lulu sighed. 'She's probably right,' she said. 'It is a beautiful jumper. Sorry, Soph.'

'OK,' said Sophie. 'All right. I'm glad you like your present, Charlie. And now I'm going to serve the chicken curry because believe it or not, I'm capable of cooking that, too. Just look at this.'

She walked proudly to the stove, removed the casserole from the top, set it on the table, and with a flourish removed the lid.

A cloud of acrid smoke arose, smelling of burnt onions and charred spices.

Firmly, Lulu replaced the lid, and rose from the table.

'I'll cook some pasta,' she said, beginning to fill a pot with water.

★   ★   ★

'What on earth is that noise?' said Fee some half hour later as they were consuming Lulu's hastily prepared meal.

106

'Mrs Scott-Ramsay.' Charlie sighed as the now familiar pounding on the floor began.

'She's getting worse,' said Lulu. 'We try to be nice to her but she won't have any of it. She doesn't approve of Charlie because she opened the flat to undesirables like me, and she doesn't approve of me because . . . well, I don't know why, actually, but she doesn't.'

'I hope you've been polite to her,' said Fee.

'Mom!' Lulu glared at her mother. 'Of course I've been polite to her, I'm not twelve years old any more! I'm very polite indeed. Sophie's seen me, haven't you, Soph?'

'She's spookily polite,' agreed Sophie. 'Unrecognizably polite. It's actually a little freaky, almost like she's channelling Emma.'

'You poor man.' Emma addressed herself compassionately to Matthew, who sat smiling quietly, as he usually did at these gatherings: Matthew's presence was genial, but in company he was not a talker. 'Marrying someone who likes to be polite and pleasant and considerate of other people's feelings. How on earth will you stand it?'

'You're a brave man, Matthew,' said David. 'Marrying into this bunch. I was telling Claire only this morning that if I didn't have her I don't know what I'd do.'

'Oh, God.' Lulu groaned and shook her head. 'Not Claire again, Dad, please, not in public.'

'Claire's David's fantasy wife,' Fee told Charlie and Jamie. 'She's his ideal woman. She lives to serve him, only speaks when she's spoken to and has no opinions at all about anything whatsoever. I'm quite fond of Claire in fact — she has a good heart, in spite of her unfortunate breath.'

'I don't know, Mom,' said Sophie. 'Sometimes she gets this sort of gleam in her eye that makes me wonder if she's plotting something.'

'Don't encourage them, Sophie,' said Lulu. 'We've discussed this, it only makes them worse.'

'My Claire wouldn't know how to plot,' said David, proudly. 'She doesn't have two brain cells to rub together, bless her. And I've explained about the breath, Fee. She hasn't had time for the dentist because she's still too busy monogramming my summer handkerchiefs — she had to throw the last lot out because she'd thought David began with Q. She's the woman of my dreams,' he added to Matthew.

'Atwater family humour,' Lulu told Charlie. 'So now you know where we get our strangeness from. Oh, God!' she added as the pounding on the floor picked up its pace. 'Please, Mrs Scott-Ramsay, it's not like we're dancing the Highland Fling up here. We're entertaining our parents, for heaven's sake!'

'I feel bad, though, for disturbing her,' said Fee. 'It is annoying to have people making a noise upstairs, although I don't see how we can help having fun. Here's a thought — the lilac's quite lovely at the moment, so why doesn't one of you come over to the house tomorrow and pick some from the bush to take to her with my apologies? Sometimes it can help to hear from people's parents.'

'I'll do it,' said Sophie. 'She doesn't know me

well enough to disapprove of me yet.'

'That's very generous of you, Sophie,' said Lulu. 'Are you planning to go before or after you clear up all the dishes from tonight?'

'In between,' said Sophie, injured.

★　★　★

Halfway through the following afternoon, Sophie presented herself at Mrs Scott-Ramsay's door, her hair neatly combed and wearing an inoffensive white blouse, with her arms full of lilacs.

'What do you want?' was her neighbour's not auspicious greeting. 'I don't sign petitions and I already give to the charities I choose to give to.'

'I'm Sophie from upstairs,' said Sophie. 'My mother sent you these lilacs to say sorry for the noise we made last night. She and my father and my other sister came to dinner, and I'm afraid we got a bit what my father would call rackety. So she wanted you to have these as an apology — they're from our garden.'

'Lilacs.' The old woman sniffed and reached to the purple flowers a surprisingly caressing hand. 'That's very civil of her,' she admitted. 'I'm going to have to ask you to come in and put them in water. It's my housekeeper's day off.'

Sophie followed Mrs Scott-Ramsay down the hallway and through the living room to the kitchen, where a large window over the sink showed sparse appointments and a blue and white plate still on the table holding crumbs from a sandwich lunch. Mrs Scott-Ramsay sank into the chair beside it and brandished her stick towards a cupboard above the counter.

'Up there,' she said. 'And don't break anything.'

Standing on tiptoe, Sophie opened it and withdrew a large white china vase decorated with dark red chrysanthemums and yellow butterflies.

'I think they'll look pretty in this, don't you?' she said. 'The flowers are sort of purplish so they'll pick up the colour.'

'Hmm,' was her hostess's only response. 'Do you know what to do with lilacs?'

'Absolutely!' Sophie smiled. 'My mom's a lilac freak, and it was just about the first thing she ever taught us. Cut them diagonally like this ... lukewarm water, not too hot, not too cold ... and then you add sugar, which I see here beside the teapot, and ... do you have any lemons?'

'Refrigerator.'

Sophie opened the fridge to see a small covered casserole dish, a box of eggs, three and a half lemons, and several individual bottles of tonic water.

'Here it is,' she said. 'And there they are, sorted. Now! Don't they look lovely!'

'Hmm,' said Mrs Scott-Ramsay again. 'Your mother grows these, does she?'

'My mother grows everything. We only have a small garden, but she grows the most amazing flowers, freesias and lilac in the spring, roses and peonies in the summer, herbs all the year around, we even have a little vegetable patch. She says she was born with a green thumb.

110

That's what they call it back in Boston, apparently.'

'American?' Mrs Scott-Ramsay raised her eyebrows in disapproval.

'Absolutely.'

Mrs Scott-Ramsay snorted. 'Still, it was very civil of her to send flowers,' she allowed. 'I've always been fond of lilacs.'

'Me, too!' Sophie drew up a chair at the table and perched herself on it. 'They're so pretty, aren't they! Look at that beautiful, amazing colour! They're just like . . . '

She stopped herself, becoming suddenly aware that since she had arrived Mrs Scott-Ramsay had looked neither at the flowers nor directly at Sophie herself, but instead was staring, fixedly, at a spot somewhere between the two.

'And the smell!' she added quickly. 'Isn't it just the most heavenly springlike smell you've ever imagined, like wrapping your whole nose in a silken sheet of gorgeousness?'

'It is a pretty smell,' conceded Mrs Scott-Ramsay. 'We used to have a bush when I was a girl in Lincolnshire, and it always takes me back. Well, we can't just leave them on the kitchen table. Bring them in here.'

She struggled to her feet, and made her way stiffly into the living room. It, too, was a well-lit room, the afternoon sunshine casting oblongs of light onto the deep carpet and the substantial upholstered furniture. There was a portrait on one wall of a stern-looking man in military uniform, and on the mantelpiece beside the clock a silver-framed photograph of two young women with hard faces wearing the fashions of thirty years ago. Sophie looked around at the rest of the room and felt in her heart a sudden sharp pang of sadness.

Most of the available wall space was taken up with books.

★　★　★

'If she thinks,' said Lulu a couple of hours later, gazing resentfully at the sinkful of remaining dishes and the soaking pan that had held the curry, 'that if she stays out long enough we'll get fed up with waiting and do the rest of it ourselves, then she's got another think coming. Charlie, what are you doing at the dishwasher?'

'Inhabiting my own kitchen,' said Charlie, beginning to unload plates. 'If that's OK with you, please. She did do two loads, and it won't take me two minutes to unpack these and start another.'

'Well, if you want to indulge the brat, on your own head be it. But you are not — do you hear me, *not* — to touch or even so much as look at the curry pot, OK? That's all hers.' Carefully, she held the kettle over the dishes in the sink to fill it from the tap. 'Do you want a cup of tea?' she said. 'I was going to do the vegetable thing for supper, but we used them all last night, so I suppose it's sausages and beans instead.'

'She offered to go out and buy some more vegetables,' said Charlie.

Lulu shuddered.

'I wonder where she is,' she said after a

moment. 'I know she came back because her bag's here, and I'm supposing she took the flowers down to Mrs Scott-Ramsay because I don't see them anywhere. But what she did after that is anybody's guess.'

'Well, if her bag's here she can't have gone far,' said Charlie.

'You don't know Sophie,' said Lulu. 'Oooh, look, there's a pretty beam of sunshine coming through the front door, I think I'll go out and follow it, oh, tra-la-la, isn't it pretty out here, whoops, you'll never guess what's happened, I've been abducted and sold into white slavery, and because I didn't bother to take any identification with me when I went out, no one will ever know what became of me, and just try explaining *that* to Mom and Dad.'

'What about Mom and Dad?' Sophie wandered into the kitchen, a thick leather-bound book in her hand, and sat herself down at the table.

Lulu directed a stern arm at the kitchen sink.

'Curry pot,' she said.

'I'm going to get to it,' said Sophie. 'Give me a chance. God. By the way, it's lovely to see you, dear sister, have you had a nice afternoon? I have, actually. I've been downstairs talking to Mrs Scott-Ramsay.'

'Yeah.' Lulu added an extra tea bag to the warmed pot and poured steaming water on top. 'Right. Curry pot, Soph.'

'I *have*,' said Sophie. 'Really.'

Sitting across the kitchen table from Sophie, Charlie looked at her and frowned.

113

'I think she means it,' she told Lulu.

'Right,' said Lulu. 'Welcome to Sophie. The guided tours leave on the hour, and there's an excellent brochure available at the kiosk.'

'I do mean it!' said Sophie. 'Lulu, for God's sake.'

'Really?' At last registering her sister's tone, Lulu left the tea to steep and joined the others at the table. 'You've been with Mrs Scott-Ramsay?'

'That's what I've been trying to tell you! Actually, we got along really well. Once you get talking to her, she's really quite sweet.'

Lulu reached across the table to feel her sister's forehead.

'No temperature,' she announced. 'She must just be going insane. Sad in one so young.'

'And that's the problem!' said Sophie. 'You two think she's going to be awful, so she is. I didn't think she was going to be awful, and she wasn't. And she's actually had quite a hard time. She's been widowed for twenty years and she still misses her husband who she says was the handsomest man she ever knew, and she didn't say so but her daughters sound horrible, really selfish old bags. Her health's bad, her best friend's moved to Newcastle to be near her son's family, and the worst thing of all is, she's got diabetic retino-something which means she's going blind, and there's nothing they can do.'

'She's going blind?' said Charlie, sobered. 'I didn't know that. Poor old thing.'

'Well, she doesn't like to talk about it because she's embarrassed by it. She only really told me when I started to read for her, although I'd

114

already guessed because when I brought the lilacs in . . . '

'Wait, wait.' Lulu waved a slowing hand. 'You've been *reading* to Mrs Scott-Ramsay.'

'It's so sad,' said Sophie. 'She loves books, really *loves* them, she's been reading all her life, and now she can't read any more, and she hates Books On Tape because she always wants to stop them and go slower but she can't work out how, so we've worked out a deal, she and I. I'm going to go down there every day and read *David Copperfield* to her, which is, like, her favourite book in the whole world, it'll be good for both of us, because it'll give her a reading fix, and it'll be good practice for me at the same time, and if you want to know, I think it'll be good for all of us up here, too, because I bet you anything you like that once she gets into a bit of a better mood with life, she'll stop pounding on the floor.'

There was a silence while Lulu and Charlie exchanged glances.

'Sophie,' said Charlie. 'If you can manage that, I will bless you forever and a day.'

'Then get exercising that blessing hand, Charles,' said Sophie, 'because she's really excited about this.' She picked up the leather-bound book from the table and brandished it. 'Look, she's given it to me so I can read ahead and know what's going on. It's long, isn't it? Seven hundred and twelve pages in teeny tiny print. But so much the better, she says, because there's that much more of it to enjoy.'

'Huh.' Lulu picked up the book and flicked through it. 'Can I ask you a major favour?' she

115

said, after a moment.

'What?' said Sophie.

'Please,' said Lulu. 'Please, please, *please* can I be there when you tell Mom you're going to spend the summer reading Dickens?'

Sophie grinned.

'It'll be good, won't it?' she agreed.

Concord, January 1868.

Dearest Amy,

What a relish it was to receive your fine fat letter, so full of romantic castles and lofty mountains and glassy-surfaced lakes that I shouldn't think you'd ever in your life be sad about anything again for very long, for every time you felt blue you could go to the little secret place in your mind that remembered such wonders and see them all over again and marvel anew. Dearie, I don't suppose for one moment that aunt and uncle would be 'offended' if you were to present them with a collection of your sketches at the end of the trip. I would think it altogether proper and graceful on your part to give them such a handsome thanks for their generosity, and one which is particular to them, besides, which must surely make it more precious still. They can always purchase pictures to hang in their home, but they *can't* buy your skill and they *can't* buy sweet memories, and both of these your sketches will have aplenty.

In the meanwhile, I must tell you, dear, of a clever way that Meg has devised to thank

Sallie Moffat for all of her generosity. You know how she is always giving Meg little gifts of clothes and pretty trifles, and last week she took her into Boston to hear Mr. Verdi's *Ballo in Maschera* — no performance near so fine, you may be sure, as you will hear when you at last descend from your mountains to reach Milan, but Meg was in her delight, and has been singing like a lark ever since of witches, doomed lovers, and assignations in gallows places. Marmee frowns at the unsuitability of this for the children's ears; but she need not trouble herself, for, happily, the twins' understanding of Italian is so far even more limited than that of their English, so they both lie contentedly cooing in their cradles as their mama warbles away, enjoying the sound of her sweet voice, and blissfully unaware of the import of the words attached to the music.

Meg's despair was in finding a way to thank Sallie. You know how proud she is, and how she abhors to receive charity with no way to return it, but the truth is that she *don't* have much money and Sallie *does*, and prettily homemade gifts are all very fine, but what is the purpose of taking a nicely made blancmange to a house whose cook has served in the finest houses in Boston, or working a pair of slippers for someone who orders her shoes from Paris?

The answer came when Meg and I paid a call upon Sallie last Tuesday. She welcomed us into that great splendid house as heartily as she always does, for she is a kindly person and quite without airs, and I've always thought well of her for all that you think her so vulgar. Ned has bought her a new writing bureau for the drawing room which is her particular pride, and nothing would serve Sallie when we arrived but that we must go directly into the drawing room to see and admire. In we marched, and, Amy, such a monstrous thing I never saw, with drawers and carvings and cupids and garlands and I know not what else besides, but Sallie had ordered that it be set in pride of place against the great wall, where it jumbled between a velvet sofa to one side and a great Indian teak cabinet to the other, all of them set higgledy-piggledy against each other so the sunshine hadn't a chance of entering and all looked gloomy as a robbers' den. At first, I couldn't understand why the room was so dark, and looking around said before I could stop myself, 'But such a great room as this is, why does it seem as poky and dismal as my little garret at home?'

Meg's eyebrows shot up so far they near vanished into her hair. But Sallie, good-natured soul that she is, only laughed and said, 'Why, because I lack your sister's good taste, of course. If I could arrange my rooms to look as pretty and peaceful as the rooms at Meg's little house, I'd do so with a relish; but since *she* has heaps of taste and *I* have little to none, I am condemned to live my life in a fine big house but one that will never please the eye, no matter what I do to it.'

Well, it didn't take but a minute for Meg to

say, 'Would you like me to help you make your house more pleasing, Sallie?'

And that's when I became *de trop*, for they both spent the next hour and more walking from room to room through the whole house, with Meg 'marming' it most splendidly, ordering this piano to be moved to that wall, and that curtain to be draped in the other becoming fashion, as if she were accustomed to pass her days as chatelaine of a splendid castle, instead of mistress of the little Dovecote, while Sallie scurried after, taking notes upon a tablet, with her tongue protruding from her mouth, and looking for all the world like poor Bob Cratchit being ordered about by Mr. Scrooge. I didn't care — made friends with the cat and had a splendid time playing 'mouse' with my second-best gloves. And now Sallie is happy as a clam with her 'spandy-new' house — which does indeed look immeasurably improved, for Meg *does* have 'heaps of taste,' which Sallie will always want and even Ned can't buy for her, and, oh, what good it does our sister to have at last discovered something of value that she can give to a friend who has given so much to her.

And so it seems that both you and she are putting into effective action that most stirring of all of Marmee's pet speeches, delivered (you will recall) with that toss of the head and her very highest and mightiest Empress Maria Theresa of Austria air: 'Although our circumstances might not permit grand gestures, that is no reason for us not to return kindness to

119

those who have been kind to us. There are many gifts to be given, girls, that are more valuable by far than those that have been purchased with mere money.'

Ever your loving sister,
Jo.

4

Concord, November 1865.

Dearest Meg,

Marmee has told me that you 'sold' the violet silk back to Sallie Moffat, and, oh, Meg, I am so sorry that you had to make that sacrifice, for I know how you delighted in it. It *was* a particularly lovely shade of silk, and it would have looked so elegant on you, especially for your first winter as a married woman. I know Marmee says that fine feathers don't make fine birds, and that is well enough for me, plain-faced and awkward as I am, but you are *so* pretty, Meg, and it don't seem right that you can't rig up to show yourself off from time to time.

Well, as Pa says, 'What can't be cured must be endured,' and when my cold is better I'll come over to the Dovecote to see what we can do with the clothes you already have for the season. The blue house dress will look almost as good as new when it is turned, we'll take the ruffles off the green skirt and add a frill to the maroon, and once the jacket is altered, the brown street suit will be mostly *à la mode*, or as near as we can hope for, and we must comfort ourselves with the thought that there's not a faded hue or a worn fabric in the

121

world that can make your face less pretty than it is or your skin less fair.

Oh, Meg, *one day* I shall get rich from my writing and shower you with silks and fine jewels that will put Sallie's entire wardrobe to shame. But until the day comes, my dear, we must once again pick up our burden of poverty and continue to carry it as far as the road goes, however sore our shoulders or heavy our hearts. I know that Marmee and father are proud of you for your good sense and good judgment, and if I were a better person, I would doubtless be so, too. But I ain't a better person, and I think it's too bad that you must forego something so pretty that you wanted so, and so I will finish this letter by sending you love from your own,

Jo.

Although Emma was careful not to burden those close to her with the minutiae of her wedding preparations, she was nevertheless quietly pleased with their progress. Hers and Matthew's would not be a splashy wedding, they had decided: they were neither of them splashy people, and Emma in particular, the prudence of New Englanders in her blood, took pride in planning an occasion that, while celebratory, at the same time avoided unnecessary show or expense. She had always been sensible with money, had never overdrawn her bank account, and derived secret, but nevertheless substantial, satisfaction in never having so much as used the one credit card which she carried with her in case of emergencies. Their

122

wedding, she had declared to Matthew, would reflect that.

The venue was to be a simple one, a former pumping station now rented out for parties, set beside a reservoir in a small park hidden surprisingly behind a busy North London street, an angular building from the 1930s with high ceilings and long windows to capture to its fullest the dark and silver February light that both Emma and Matthew found more beautiful than summer's blaze. Favours from friends were being called in as wedding gifts: the photographer would be a friend of Matthew's, the musicians friends of Sophie's, Sophie had offered to sew the bridesmaid dresses for herself and Lulu, and Lulu to provide the wedding cake. The registrar had been booked, the caterers commissioned, and Emma had even bought her wedding dress, a sensibly glamorous outfit that she could wear again if she wanted to, a silk skirt and pearl-buttoned top in a soft romantic shade somewhere between champagne, oyster and palest almond pink, which hung now in a corner of her cupboard in which Matthew was forbidden for the duration to look, with a pair of simple satin court shoes, pretty but comfortable enough to dance in, dyed in the same colour as the dress, sitting patiently beneath the hanger awaiting their day of splendour.

'It's actually coming together quite well,' she said to Matthew one sunny Sunday morning in June, leafing through her wedding books as they sat lazily in the kitchen, finishing a pot of coffee and revelling in the luxury of little to do. She smiled. 'Although it's still not exactly the sort of day Sophie's hoping for.' Sophie had lately taken to producing a string of suggestions for the wedding, each more outrageously extravagant than the last. 'Her latest idea is for me to arrive in a glass carriage pulled by six white horses with Jamie on top playing Gershwin on the clarinet, but I think I can talk her down.'

Matthew smiled, too, then frowned a little anxiously. 'She is joking, right?' he clarified — with Emma's family, he was not always entirely sure.

'I'm pretty sure she is.' Nor, now that she thought of it, was Emma. Emma occasionally wondered just how it had come about that such a practical and sensible person as she had emerged from the Atwater household. 'It's hard to tell, sometimes,' she admitted. 'But it doesn't matter because she's not the one in charge, is she? I am, and I think I'm doing a pretty good job of it.'

'Of course you are,' said Matthew, smiling at her with quiet pride: a practical man himself, he took considerable pleasure in his fiancée's administrational skill. 'You were always going to. If anyone in your family can organize a wedding, it's you. I worry about Sophie's husband, though, whoever he is. If that's her idea of a wedding, I hope he's a rich man.'

'If he isn't, she'll decide it's the height of romance to trip down the aisle wearing something from the Oxfam shop,' said Emma. 'Sophie'll be OK, she always is.' She frowned a little. 'I wish Lulu would find someone nice, though,' she added. 'We're not allowed to talk about it, but I know she'd like to.'

Unwisely, Matthew allowed himself a snort.

'Now, I'd *really* worry about him,' he commented.

'Hey.' Emma had made it plain early on that, while she and Sophie were allowed to criticize Lulu on occasion, no one else was, and most particularly no one male.

'Sorry. Can I help it if you're my favourite?'

'What, not Mom?' Matthew and Fee were particularly good friends. Emma smiled at her boyfriend, forgiving him, splashed milk into the last of her coffee and rose, stretching luxuriously in the sunshine and savouring the brush of her cotton skirt against her summer-bare legs, to replace the bottle in the fridge.

'It's louder,' she said.

'Saturday,' said Matthew.

'Can't wait.'

Closing the fridge door, Emma smiled again secretly to herself, overhearing their own conversation as a stranger might, impenetrable to the rest of the world, but to them and only them a crystal clear update on the hum in their elderly fridge, which they were planning to replace, with a sensibly priced model they had already selected at John Lewis, their favourite shop for such purposes, at the end of the following week, when Matthew's next pay cheque would have brought up to budget the account they had established for such expenditures. It was the sort of conversation she loved to have with Matthew, the sort of conversation that grown-up couples had with each other, expressing quietly but unmistakably their domestic stability, their shared priorities, their good sense with practical matters like money.

'Mom's funny about the wedding,' she said, sitting down again. 'She keeps peering at me like a professor studying some little-known Aboriginal tribe and asking things like would it be better luck or worse if your borrowed thing was also blue, and what would happen if you forgot to give it back afterwards.' Fee and David had been married by a Native American shaman on a beach in Rhode Island, with readings from *The Prophet* and plaited twine for rings; the ceremony had not been considered legal by the British immigration authorities and they had later been required to perform another in a registry office in order to qualify Fee for citizenship. 'She seems to be happy for me, though. Even though weddings aren't necessarily her sort of thing.'

'That's the nice thing about Fee,' said Matthew. 'She lets us get on with our life instead of trying to impose her own ideas.' He grimaced apologetically. 'I think I'm going to be luckier in my mother-in-law than you are in yours.'

Matthew's mother was a difficult woman, bitterly divorced from Matthew's father, and demanding of Matthew, her only child.

'Caroline's all right,' said Emma. 'She's quite nice to me, actually.'

'Well, of course she's nice to you!' Not a man given to poetic flights of fancy, Matthew nevertheless had yet to identify a serious flaw in

Emma. 'She'd be mad not to be, you're the daughter-in-law of anyone's dreams.'

'That's no guarantee,' said Emma. 'I have friends who are as nice as me who have terrible mothers-in-law. Rosie at work's mother-in-law is awful to her. Caroline could be a lot worse. And, anyway, I'm not marrying her, I'm marrying you. And very much looking forward to it, by the way.'

★　★　★

It would be a good marriage, she thought an hour or so later, still smiling to herself as she strolled up Upper Street to her parents' house for brunch, while Matthew stayed at home to catch up with his month's paperwork. They were a good fit, they two, sensible and intelligent, neither of them dramatic, but both, in their own way, romantic; they both shared a good heart as well as good sense, qualities which they had both seen and loved in each other immediately, and were such as would hold them strong against all the tempests that life might throw their way. A good marriage, its tone set from the start by a wedding which would be not a spectacle of excess, but a quiet celebration of two people who did not need extravagance to prove their own worth. Sophie might bemoan the lack of horse-drawn carriages, but there were other things, Emma thought, still smiling, that were almost as lovely as a wedding and certainly more lasting, to spend their money on, too. First, there was a fridge to buy . . . then there would be holidays to be taken, and possibly the car to trade in for a newer model . . . One day there would be a house to move into with a garden for children to play in.

People smiled at Emma as she walked along in the sunshine, and she smiled back at them, loving her life, and the kind warmth of the summer morning, and the swish of the skirt about her legs.

Halfway along Upper Street she passed a small flower shop, and stopped to enjoy the display — windows bursting with delphiniums as blue as the June sky, and early hydrangea as white as the small fluffy clouds that scudded cheerfully across it. She had not yet hired a florist for the wedding: maybe during the week she would go into the shop and check out their prices, although she thought they would probably be out of her range. Upper Street had changed since Emma was a child: the small family-run shops and workmen's cafes where Emma remembered her mother taking her to buy ballpoint pens and notebooks for school, vests and thick pyjamas for the winter, and sweets and giant cream buns for a treat, had mostly gone, edged out by fashionable restaurants and upmarket stores selling expensive designer clothes and housewares. Shops that thrifty Emma could not aspire to shop in, but nor, she thought now, did she especially care to. Saving up for a fridge at John Lewis was far more her speed, thank you.

'Nice legs,' said a friendly London accent. Emma started, and turned to see a young man with a wide, good-natured Saxon face, lounging contentedly in the entrance to the shop next door.

'I said, you've got nice legs,' he repeated, indicating. 'Very nice, in fact.'

'Thank you,' said Emma, smiling back — he clearly meant no harm, and she did, in fact, have nice legs. 'My boyfriend likes them, too.'

'So would mine,' said the young man. 'But I just wanted to say.'

'Well, thank you,' said Emma. 'That's a nice compliment. You've cheered me up.'

'You looked pretty chipper already,' said the young man. 'Been inside my shop?'

She looked past the doorway to the shop behind. Shoes By Manolete, one of the new breed of Islington shops, and highly priced even for that section of the road. A shop into whose window. Emma — who did know that her legs were nice and who liked to flatter them, within reason, with pretty shoes — had occasionally peered and wondered who on earth could justify paying such prices for shoes while people were homeless.

'Ah,' she said. 'Nice try.'

'I'm not looking for custom,' he said. 'I'm filthy rich, actually. I'm Manolete. I'm the next big thing — you might have read about me in *Grazia*.'

'Sorry,' she said. 'I didn't mean to offend you. I'm sure you're very popular.'

'That's OK,' he said. 'Actually I'm really called Nigel, but you know how it is. I just thought you'd look nice in my shoes.'

129

'They're lovely shoes,' she said. 'I look at them when I go past. I'm sure anyone would look good in them.'

'You'd be surprised,' he said. 'I just sold a couple of pairs this morning.' He stopped and sighed, his face clouding. 'Tragic ankles,' he said. 'Just plain tragic. Lovely girl, mind you, and it's not her fault or anything, but there's nothing you can do about an ankle, is there? It broke my heart to see my shoes go off with her.'

'I'm sorry,' said Emma 'That must have been, um, difficult.'

'It was tragic,' he said. 'Heartbreaking. Criminal. That's why it's nice to see a nice pair of legs like yours. Gives me back a bit of hope.'

'Well, that's good,' said Emma. 'Your shoes are lovely, really. But they're way beyond my budget, I'm afraid.'

'Oh, my love.' Nigel known as Manolete clicked his tongue disapprovingly. 'Lovely shoes are in everyone's budget. A private yacht, now that's going too far, but shoes?' He brightened. 'Tell you what. Why don't you give him a treat on his wedding day?'

'Excuse me?' Emma blinked, unsure whether to be amused or offended.

'Well, you are getting married, aren't you? I see them all the time, girls like you, stopping outside next door with the ring, the little smile, the looking at the flowers . . . I think it's lovely. You said he likes your legs, so give him a treat on his wedding day — wear some really gorgeous shoes.' He narrowed his eyes and squinted appraisingly downwards. 'Tell you what you'd look good in,' he said after a moment. 'The Empress line. Now, I don't say that to just anyone 'cause the Empress line's a bit of a challenge. You need nice feet, as well as nice legs, for Her Imperialship, but if you are up for it they knock your socks off, and I think, yes, I really do, that you just might qualify. The Catherine, maybe. Or . . . no, wait. I've got it. The Josephine. Josephine's the girl for you.'

'Josephine.' Emma smiled. 'That's my name.'

'Well, there you are, my love. It was meant to be. And there she is in the window, look, waiting for you.'

He pointed to a stand in the window that held a concoction of dark pink straps and rosettes set high on a slender heel. It was an absurd shoe, which would begin to pinch after an hour, would fall apart after half a dozen wearings, and which, by coincidence, cost precisely the sum that Emma and Matthew had in the fridge fund.

Emma looked at it, and wanted it as she could not remember having wanted any inanimate object in her entire life.

'Aha.' Nigel-Manolete identified her expression and winked. 'When she's the one for you, you know, don't you, Josephine? Size five, am I right? Come in and try her on.'

Whirling through rose petals and bird songs in a vortex of clouds the colour of the sunset, Emma caught herself, and returned herself, firmly, to earth.

'I can't afford new shoes,' she said. 'I have to buy a fridge.'

131

Nigel looked pained, as if he had caught her kicking a puppy.

'A fridge?' he said. 'A refrigerator, Josephine? We're talking about your wedding day, my love.'

'A fridge is very important,' she told him. 'You use a fridge much more often than you use shoes. Our old one hums when you open it, and the freezer drips. We really need a new one, and we've decided on the one we're going to buy. In John Lewis at the end of the week when Matthew's next pay cheque arrives.'

'A refrigerator,' he said again, shaking his head uncomprehendingly. 'In John Lewis. That's criminal, that is, Josephine.'

'And by the way,' she said. 'My name's not Josephine, it's Emma. Actually, it is Josephine, but it's Josephine Emma, and everyone calls me Emma. And I have to buy a fridge. Goodbye, Nigel.'

'A refrigerator,' he said sadly.

★   ★   ★

In a secret corner of her mind, Emma had always wondered whether she might not have turned out differently if she had continued to be known as Josephine. She had been very small when Lulu's inability to pronounce the name had caused the family to adopt her middle name instead, but even so, she had memories, faint but wonderfully warm, of the time when she was called by the name she had been given. It had been a good time when Emma was Josephine, a time when she was the only child in the house,

132

the smallest one, the sweetest one, and the world, it seemed, had revolved around her; and sometimes still, in idle or dreamy moments, Emma would entertain herself by fancying that out there somewhere, in an alternative world where younger sisters had not presented themselves with their needs and their fuss and their pulls on her parents' time and attention, there was another self who was still called Josephine.

Josephine was not like Emma. Josephine was self-indulgent and more than a little lazy. She lay on a Victorian reclining chair covered with brocade in a sunny upper room filled with out-of-season flowers in ornate vases, and ate exotically filled chocolates from a pink oval box, smiling placidly on the admirers who thronged at her feet and occasionally sweeping a dramatic gesture with a rounded, pampered arm. Josephine wore flowing, feminine clothes in sensual fabrics, silks and satins and lace, used just a little too much make-up and looked lovely in it, and let her hair grow long and loose and tousled. Josephine had a string of credit cards, which she ran up with abandon and never ever worried about how she would pay them off. Josephine adored — simply adored — beautiful shoes.

'What sort of shoes did you wear at your wedding?' she asked Fee over brunch, nibbling carefully — because now of all times was not the time to start gaining weight — at a medium-sized portion of asparagus frittata.

'I didn't wear shoes,' said Fee. 'I went

barefoot, which seemed like a romantic idea at the time, but turned out not to be so smart, because the sand was cold and you'd be surprised how many sharp stones and broken shells there are around.' She peered, mock-sternly, at her daughter over her coffee mug. 'Take your mother's advice, honey. On your wedding day . . . wear shoes.'

'Seriously, Mom,' said Emma.

'I am serious,' said Fee. 'I ended up filching a Band-Aid from the shaman — he had a whole store of them, which I thought was interesting — and begging for your father's socks to stave off frostbite. It was not pretty.'

'OK.' Emma tried again. 'Then what shoes did you wear to the registry office?'

'I don't know. Probably a pair of patriarchy-friendly high heels because I wanted to please your Granny Atwater by trying to look respectable for the occasion, and high heels were the only way you could in those benighted days. No, wait.' She thought for a moment. 'It's coming back to me now. It was just around the time Lady Diana was getting together with Prince Charles, and she was always trying to pretend she wasn't taller than him, so she'd made flat shoes socially acceptable for the first time. I was actually able to be comfortable on my wedding day at the same time as making Granny Atwater happy, and I remember thinking, God bless you, Lady Di, and God help you, too, marrying into that crowd. And I was right on both counts, sadly.'

'You should wear high heels sometimes,

Mom,' said Emma. 'You have nice legs, you should show them off. Wouldn't Dad like you to?'

'I don't know,' said Fee. 'I've never asked him.' She looked thoughtful for a moment. 'We're not into playing dress-up, if that's what you're asking,' she added helpfully.

'Mom!' There were times, Emma felt, when having an American-born family therapist for a mother was overrated. 'Of course I'm not.'

'Well, you *can* ask, honey, if you want,' said Fee. 'You do know that, don't you? You can ask me anything about anything.'

Anything but shoes, Emma thought, a little sadly; but to have voiced the thought would only have hurt her mother's feelings.

'OK!' A whirl of intensity, Lulu burst in, a smudge on her cheek and her hair wilder than ever, hugging to herself a selection of photographs printed on old-fashioned card. 'I've narrowed it down to these, so one of them must be of her. Let's take a look.'

'Not necessarily, sweetie,' said Fee. 'There were a lot of them in the family at one time, remember. But hand me my glasses and we'll look anyway. We're looking for Grandma Jo,' she explained to Emma. 'Lulu's been back up in the attic and it seems she thinks she's found her.'

'Grandma Jo again?' said Emma. 'You're awfully interested in her these days, aren't you?'

'That's odd.' Lulu frowned at her sister in feigned puzzlement. 'I don't recall having asked your opinion. Remind me again exactly when I did.'

'No need to jump on me, Lu,' said Emma. 'I'm the one who's always been interested in her, remember?'

Not for the first time lately, Emma reminded herself to go gently with Lulu. Mr Goncharoff had not yet sold his shop, but it was becoming increasingly apparent that one day soon he would, and when that happened no one, least of all Lulu herself, seemed to have any idea of just what would become of Lulu. Lulu had never been good at showing vulnerability, but Emma knew nevertheless that beneath her younger sister's carapace of jokes and sarcasm lay insecurities that she herself could not begin to imagine. Emma sighed a little, quietly, to herself. She did not feel she had even nearly finished with her own conversation with their mother; but if hunting for Grandma Jo would help to divert Lulu from the uncertainties facing her, well, Emma was accustomed by now to having her own immediate needs upstaged.

'OK.' Lulu sat down and arranged the photographs in front of her, like a giant pack of playing cards. 'It's hard to tell because not many people in the family seem to have made notes of who was who. Not organized, Mom.' She glanced reprovingly at her mother. 'But this one here seems to be the most likely. It's obviously of this person's birthday party, and I'm wondering if it's Grandma Jo's.'

'Let's see.' Fee took the photograph and inspected it: a group of people wearing the fashions of sixty years before, a few of the younger ones in Service uniform, grouped

136

affectionately around a bent old woman sitting behind a cake, her face criss-crossed with wrinkles, her long New England chin still defiantly firm, her eyes alight with intelligence across the years.

'I know that Grandma Jo was born in November 1845,' said Fee, 'and that she lived to be a hundred, which would call for a big party, wouldn't it? This is definitely our family — there's my mom, and there's my Uncle Alan in his naval uniform — isn't he young! Those two are Aunt Amy's parents, Aunt Margaret and Uncle Ted, and I guess that little girl with them must be Aunt Amy . . . yes, she'd be about eight — it's funny that there are some people you never quite imagine as having been children.' She frowned, thoughtfully, over the image. 'I wonder if we can pinpoint the exact date,' she said. 'It's obviously around the time of the Second World War, because of the uniforms . . . oh, but, look, Mom's in civilian clothes, which makes it certainly later than 1944 because the women pilots were disbanded just a few months before the war was over — they were told because they were 'too expensive'. Mom was mad about that till the day she died. So it's probably 1945, and it's not summer, because look at those thick sweaters, and . . . aha! You see that?' She pointed to a cone-shaped basket set beside the cake holding an arrangement of pears and grapes. 'That's a horn of plenty — it's a Thanksgiving decoration, so it must be November. November 1945.' She brought the photograph closer to study it. 'Do you know, Lulu,' she said

137

after a moment, 'you're a genius, I think this must be her. How very interesting, I don't think I've ever seen this before.'

'I thought so.' Lulu nodded as they bent to inspect the group. 'It seemed about the right time for it. And whoever this woman is, you can tell the others all loved her — look how they're clustering around. And you said the other day that they adored her, didn't you, Mom? That's what you said. They adored her.'

'They did.' Fee smiled at her middle daughter, whose voice only she had heard shake slightly, and reached a hand to replace a curl behind Lulu's ear. 'They did all adore her, and you can tell that these people all adore this woman. I think this must really be her, Lulu. Aren't you clever? This is a real find.' She picked up the photograph again. 'An interesting face,' she said. 'Not pretty, they always said, but interesting. She was fifteen when the Civil War began, and seventy-five when women got the right to vote. What stories she'd have had to tell. But I guess we'll never know them now. David has to see this. David!' She leaned back from the table to call down the hallway to where her husband was working in his office.

After a moment, David appeared, Sunday rumpled and unshaven, his coffee mug in hand.

'You screeched,' he observed, mildly.

'I raised my voice in order to attract your attention,' Fee told him. 'It's a common form of human communication. I'll bet even Claire does it from time to time.'

'Claire never wants attention,' he said. 'She

138

has no needs or desires. She sits quietly in the corner and waits for me to speak and then she waits for me to finish speaking and then she says, 'How wise you are, dear, do tell me more.' She's the most interesting woman I know. What've you got?' He sat, resting his arm on his wife's shoulder with the ease of long companionship, and picked up the photograph.

'That's Grandma Jo,' said Fee. 'Lulu's been up in the attic, and she quite brilliantly found her.'

'Did she now?' David inspected the face. 'Blimey, I wouldn't mess with her,' he commented.

'The family adored her,' Lulu told him.

'From the look of her they wouldn't have dared not to,' he said. He looked closer. 'Intelligent face,' he added. 'Was she the one who was a writer?'

'So my mom used to say,' said Fee. 'There was a story she was once quite successful but you know how family stories get blown up, and I've never seen any of her books anywhere.'

'It's still possible,' said David. 'Literary fashions come and go like any others.' He looked up at Lulu. 'Here's a thought, Lu — if you ever want to try your hand at writing, there are any number of people I could put you in touch with to help you.'

'Here's another thought, Dad,' said Lulu. 'If you ever want to try your hand at not making helpful suggestions about *my* life not yours, I'd really, really encourage it.'

'Grandma Jo.' Emma took the photograph from her father: she could have enough, she felt,

139

of bickering between Lulu and her parents about Lulu's career path. 'Grandma Josephine, actually. I wonder if she minded having her name shortened like that?'

'No, she preferred it that way.' Lulu checked herself. 'I would have anyway,' she added, quickly. 'It'd be such a fuss to go through life as Jojo-Shusha-Feffa, I'm sure she'd have preferred plain old Jo.'

'I think Josephine's a pretty name,' said Fee. 'You were going to be the first to be called it in full, Emma, but poor old Lu here just couldn't get her tongue around it, so it had to be Emma instead.'

'I don't remember anybody consulting me about the change,' noted Emma. 'Perhaps I'd have liked to carry on being called Josephine, but did anyone ask? Noooo.'

'Josephine wouldn't have suited you,' said Lulu. 'Emma's such a bossy name, and you were born to boss.'

'No I wasn't. And wipe your face, it's all dusty.'

'Oh, har-di-har, my sister's so amusing.' But Lulu laughed anyway, and stuck out a cheerful tongue; finding Grandma Jo had clearly pleased her.

'We did feel bad taking your name away from you, Emma,' said Fee. 'But Lulu just couldn't do it. Remember how hard she tried, David? She'd sit there going 'Joo-Joo, Joo-Joo', you used to say she sounded like a rare African primate calling across the jungle to its young.'

'Happy days,' noted David. 'When I was

140

allowed to get a word in edgewise. Long gone now, of course.'

'And then it turned into Choo-Choo, and oh, Emma honey, it was so sweet because she just loved her Choo-Choo to pieces, and I'd take her to pick you up from school and she'd just roar at the top of her lungs, 'Where's my Choo-Choo? Come to meet my Choo-Choo!' It was the cutest little thing I'd ever heard in my life.'

'I called her Choo-Choo?' said Lulu. 'That was clever of me.'

'And one day Emma turned to me — she was a very grown-up little five-year-old, wasn't she, David? — and said, 'Mom? Would you please *explain* to my sister that I'm a *girl*, not a train?' So we had a conference, didn't we, David, and decided to call you Emma instead.'

So even at five, thought Emma a little sadly, she had been perceived as too grown-up for her pretty, romantic name.

'You see?' said Lulu. 'Born to boss. You were never going to be Josephine.'

★   ★   ★

'My mother has just told me what my sister Lulu used to call me when we were small,' said Emma the next day to Rosie, her workmate, in the small, sunny office they shared in a building just behind King's Cross. 'She couldn't pronounce my name so called me Choo-Choo. Mom just told us yesterday. What a weird little girl.'

'Choo-Choo?' Rosie frowned at her, puzzled. She was a rather stern young woman with blonde, bobbed hair and horn-rimmed glasses, who tended to look at the world from a literal point of view. 'How did she get Choo-Choo from Emma?'

'Emma's my middle name, actually. My first name is Josephine.' Emma snorted. 'Or, according to my sister the train-spotter, Choo-Choo.'

'Well, if she was small, that was probably the best she could do,' said Rosie. Rosie had a good heart, but did not always recognize the subtler shades of humour.

'Probably.' Emma decided to abandon her mild attempt at levity. 'Haven't I ever told you my real name's Josephine? It's pretty, isn't it? I sometimes think about taking it back again, but it's probably too late now. Have you ever wished you had a different name?'

'No.' Rosie stared at her in surprise. 'Why would I want that?'

'I don't know. Some people do.'

'Well, I don't see the point. Why are you talking about names, anyway?' Her eyes widened. 'You're not . . . '

'God, no. What sort of idiot do you think I am?' Neither Emma nor Rosie was the sort of young woman who would find herself unexpectedly pregnant.

'Good. We've got a busy summer coming up. How are the wedding plans, anyway?'

'Fine, thanks.' She smiled. After brunch, she had gone back with Lulu to Belsize Park for tea. 'My sister Sophie's latest plot has me descending from the sky by hot-air balloon accompanied by a harpist in medieval dress while the bridesmaids release a flock of doves to meet me coming down.'

'Doing *what?*'

'She's just joking. Sophie's an actress; she likes to weave fantasies.'

'Well, just so long as they stay that way. Weddings can get out of hand, remember, and even sensible people can get carried away.' She smiled, reassuringly. She was fond of Emma. 'Can't see it happening to you, though,' she added.

'Probably not.' Emma sighed a little. 'I saw some beautiful shoes in Manolete's,' she said after a moment.

'Manolete's?'

'The shoe shop on Upper Street? Sort of halfway down, next to Lily's Flowers?'

'Don't know it.' Rosie was not a person who sighed over shoes.

'Manolete's?' Poppy, the office junior, had wandered in. 'Is that the place that had the write-up in *Grazia*? Manolete the Michelangelo of the foot? My sister went there. She bought some amazing shoes, but they cost an arm and a leg. Her boyfriend said she'd spent more than he'd spent on his car. It's a terrible old banger, mind. And they are seriously gorgeous shoes.'

'I couldn't justify that money,' said Rosie. 'Not for shoes. People are homeless.'

'Her boyfriend said *they'd* be homeless if she ever went there again. He was quite cross, actually. They're seriously truly gorgeous shoes, and she and I thought they were worth every penny, but he said he'd like to take this Manolete and Michel his Angelo all the way to the bank.'

'I don't understand people like that,' said Rosie. 'Persuading people to spend more money than they can afford. It's just wrong.'

'It depends on how you look at it,' said Emma. 'Some people think that for really special shoes, it's worth the money. And I met Manolete actually, yesterday. He seemed very nice.'

'*You?*' said Poppy. 'Met Manolete? How?'

'We just met,' said Emma. She frowned at the younger girl. 'Why? What's odd about that?'

'I don't know,' said Poppy. 'I'd never have put you and him in the same room somehow. He's all sort of fashionable and cutting edge.'

'Cutting into other people's money from the sound of it,' said Rosie. 'Where did you meet him anyway? Bet it wasn't giving out soup at a homeless shelter.'

'We met on Upper Street,' said Emma. 'He was standing in his shop and I was walking past. We had quite a nice chat, he seemed nice.'

'Anyone can seem nice,' said Rosie. 'If they're trying to sell you overpriced shoes.'

'If you want to know,' said Emma, 'he told me I had nice legs.'

'Course he did,' said Rosie, patiently. 'He was trying to sell you shoes. I bet his real name's something like Kenneth, or Trevor.'

Emma, deciding not to reply to that, exercised some material self-restraint in abstaining from wondering what comments Nigel-Manolete might have passed on Rosie's own legs. She wanted to ask Poppy whether her sister's

144

boyfriend had ever recovered sufficiently from the financial blow to enjoy the effects of the shoes on Poppy's sister's legs, but by the time she had emerged victorious from her battle with her lesser self, Poppy was gone.

★ ★ ★

That evening, Emma took off a little early from work and, instead of cycling straight home, went first to Upper Street to check out Lily's Flowers for the wedding. They would probably be too expensive, she thought, weaving her way through the traffic around the Tube station, but as they were in the neighbourhood they were worth a look anyway. They would doubtless be too expensive, in fact, in this new shop in so fashionable a section of Upper Street, and Emma, having been so careful so far, was not about to blow the wedding budget at this point. But it cost nothing to look, she thought, and with a shop with such pretty flowers so close to where she lived, it would be plain silly not to check them out.

She reached the row where Lily's was, and chained her bicycle to the lamp post that was most convenient to the shop. That it meant walking past Manolete's to get from it to Lily's was hardly her responsibility: the lamp post on the other side of Lily's was considerably further down the street, and besides, she had noticed as she passed that it had two bicycles chained to it already. She walked towards the flower shop, and, since she always did turn her head to look

145

in Manolete's window when she walked by, it would have been unnatural for her not to do so now. But when she did, her heart gave just the one dull thud and sank like a stone. The stand where the Josephine had been was now empty.

It was just as well, she told herself then, quickly, firmly and sensibly. She was not in a position to afford the Josephine, and knew perfectly well that she never would be. The shoe had been nice to look at, nice, even, admittedly, to covet for oh so brief and unrealistic a moment. But there was the budget to consider, the fridge to buy, the house with the garden in a couple of years to save for, not to mention the children's education further down the line. Besides, she already had the shoes for her wedding, the perfectly nice and perfectly pretty low-heeled satin court shoes, that had been specially dyed to match the dress and that would, unquestionably, be far more comfortable to wear. The sight of the Josephine with its slender straps and little silk flowers would have served no purpose but to torment her. So, all things considered, it was just as well that it had gone.

'Josephine!' Nigel-Manolete, reaching into the window for a pair of delicate satin boots in light baby blue, hailed her with the comfort of old familiarity. 'What a sight for these sore old eyes you are. I was hoping you'd come by today, come in, I've got something to show you. Excuse me,' he added to the customer sitting patiently on a chair. 'This here is a very important professional-type contact of mine, on account of which I just have to reach out and grab her whenever she does me the honour of passing by my shop.'

'How wonderful to be so important,' smiled the customer. 'Are you someone amazingly high up in shoes?'

'Hardly.' Surprised by the ambush, Emma perched herself on the edge of a chair. 'He's just kidding you, I'm nothing to do with fashion at all.'

'Well, you're obviously very special anyway,' said the customer. She had a vibrant contralto voice, a great deal of blonde hair and a pretty, slightly old-fashioned face, which looked to Emma somehow familiar. As, of course, it would, Emma told herself then. This was Alice Weathers, Oscar winner and darling of the BAFTA crowd. Alice Weathers, who commanded more money per movie than Emma would probably earn in her entire lifetime, who famously lived with her film director husband in one of the most splendid of all the Georgian houses in Canonbury Square. Alice Weathers, who was about to buy the Josephine shoe which Emma now saw winking saucily at her from the counter, as it was only right and fitting that she should because Alice Weathers was the sort of person who could afford it.

'I am absolutely heartbroken,' Alice announced to Emma. 'I have the most fabulous party coming up and I've just fallen head over heels in love with these perfectly exquisite shoes here, but Manolete says he doesn't have them in my size. Don't you just want to go into a corner and *sob* when that happens?'

'The problem with size five,' said Manolete, 'is it's a popular size in a shoe 'cause it's the pretty size. Now, we do have a five in this lovely little boot here, which is a really very lovely little boot, and listen up, ladies, because you're hearing it here first, it'll be all over the place for the summer. How about you give it a whirl?'

'Mm.' Alice pursed her lips for a moment, thinking, then shook her head. 'I don't think so. It's my birthday party, and a girl wants to show off her legs, doesn't she? Oh, what a shame. Well, I'll leave you two to your important business and go off and sulk somewhere. Bye, Manolete, Josephine. *Abrazos.*'

She gathered her bag, and tripped out into Upper Street. As soon as she had gone, Nigel-Manolete's body sagged, and he gripped Emma's arm, his mouth agape with emotion.

'Did you see that?' he demanded. 'Oh, my Little Red Riding Hood's Great-Aunty May, did you bleeding *see* that?'

Emma smiled: write-up in *Grazia* or not, Nigel-Manolete was apparently not above being impressed by a little celebrity glamour.

'Quite something,' she commented sympathetically. 'You handled yourself pretty well, though.'

'You think so?' he asked hopefully. 'I couldn't believe it when she walked in. I didn't know where to look. As God is my witness, I did not know where to look.'

'Well, you never know,' said Emma. 'If things go the way they seem to be, you might be seeing more like her in future.'

He shuddered, turning faintly pale.

'I hope not,' he said. 'Did you *see* the legs on her?'

'Um . . . ' Curiosity now aroused, Emma turned to peer from the window. He sprang ahead of her, blocking her view.

'Don't look,' he advised. 'It'll haunt your dreams. No wonder her agent keeps sending her for period parts. And she wanted to buy the Josephine! I do not know what we are coming to.'

He bustled to the back of the shop, and rummaged in a drawer.

'I don't hold it against them,' he said. 'Having tragic legs. It's not their fault, after all. My mum's got terrible legs, lovely woman, heart of gold, but great thick legs like an antique Steinway grand, my dad always says the first time they met he wanted to sit down and tinkle out 'Chopsticks', and I say to her, 'Mum, that's why they have nice knee-length boots, to hide your terrible old piano legs.' Lovely boots I made her for Christmas, she looks just lovely in them, and no one's the wiser. But when it gets criminal, Josephine, is when they don't hide them away in nice boots — they go out and wear shoes that'll draw attention. It doesn't make the legs any better. It just makes people look at them, and who wants to do that? Show them off, indeed. Anyway, here she is, waiting for you.'

From the drawer, he withdrew a box, and from the box withdrew another Josephine shoe, which he held out to her expectantly.

Emma looked at it and thought her heart would shatter into pieces.

'But I'm size five, too,' she said.

He looked up, puzzled.

'Sorry?' he said.

'I'm size five,' she said. 'Like she is. And you told her you're out of size five.'

'Oh, Josephine!' He shook his head, reprovingly. 'You didn't believe that load of tosh, did you? Size five's the pretty size my Uncle Arthur, you need to sharpen up, my girl, or someone's going to take you for a ride. I wouldn't let my Josephine go prancing out at the end of those great tree trunks, I don't care how famous they are, she'd never forgive me. I was saving her for you. I knew you'd come back for her and now here you are. Try her on, not that you need to — I can tell.'

The shoe was size five. Looking at it, Emma had once again that curious sensation of being borne on soft winds through a cloud of pink-coloured petals. And once again, she caught herself and brought herself down.

'I'm not trying her — them — on,' she said. 'There's no point because I can't afford these prices. I'm not very rich like you and Alice Weathers and all the other people who come in here. I'm not a fashion designer, or a film star, or a rich man's wife. I work for a medical company, my boyfriend and I have a budget for our wedding, we have the fridge to buy at the weekend, we want to buy a house in two years, if we can afford one, and then we want to start a family, which will cost money. And

I'm not called Josephine either, I'm called Emma.'

'No you're not,' he said. 'Emma's an orthopaedic nurse's shoe. You're Josephine. And Josephine size five is you. Come on, try her on, I haven't got all day.'

Before Emma knew it, she was sitting on a chair, her leg extended.

'You're an eldest, aren't you?' he said. 'I can always spot 'em 'cause I was one myself. Bleeding pain in the neck, wasn't it? Be a big boy, share your toys, set an example, lucky I had sisters, can you imagine me setting an example to boys? I said to my mum once, I said 'Mum, I'm only six,' she said, 'So what, your sister's only three and there'll be another one soon who's younger still.' I thought, Oh, great, just what I need. But the thing about being an eldest is, oh, Josephine. Oh, Josephine. Oh, *Josephine*.'

The shoe was on Emma's foot. It was, quite simply, spectacular.

'You can't have her yet,' he said. 'I've got to savour the moment. I deserve this after what I've been through this afternoon. Oh, Josephine.'

'I'm not going to have her at all,' said Emma. 'I keep telling you, I can't afford it.'

'I can't savour for too long,' he said. 'I've got to get home for *Come Dine with Me*. But just give me a moment, OK? Me and Josephine.'

'I'm taking them off now,' said Emma. 'Then I'm going home. It's been nice talking to you, but this is just not in my budget.'

He looked up at her, sharply. 'Don't toy with me, Josephine,' he said. 'Size five was made for you. If you can afford a refrigerator, you can afford a shoe.'

'That's just the point,' she said. 'I can't afford both. You might not understand that, but your mum would.'

'That's why my mum has a credit card,' he said.

Emma looked down at the shoes on her feet. The straps wound delicately around her toes, and she noticed for the first time that at the centre of each rosette was sewn a tiny seed pearl.

Moving briskly, Nigel-Manolete removed the Josephine, strode to the counter, and held out his hand. 'Come along,' he said. 'Give it over. Like I said, I haven't got all day.'

As if she were watching from a great height, Emma saw herself remove from the fold of her wallet the never-yet-used credit card, and surrender it to him.

'Good girl.' Nigel-Manolete nodded approvingly. 'Now just put your PIN in while I wrap her up. Goodbye, Josephine Size Five, you lucky little darling, aren't you happy I rescued you from tree trunks back then? I do love a happy ending, don't you, Josephine? There you go, take her home with you, and I don't want you coming back with second thoughts because I'd laugh in your face, OK? In your face.'

'How do you know I won't sell them on?' Emma attempted weakly. 'To someone who can afford them?'

'You, sell the Josephine? Oh, Josephine Size Five, she's a laugh a minute, isn't she?' He gave the stiff paper bag a last, affectionate pat, and handed it over. 'Now, I don't want to see you coming into the shop again, Josephine,' he said, 'because you're right, you can't afford to shop here regular, and I might not be able to control myself and it might all lead to ruination like in *West Side Story*. But I want you walking past as often as you can in your nice little short skirts with your lovely legs, and we'll wave as you go by. And I want you to treat the Josephine right, which I know you will, and to have a wonderful wedding day, which I know you will, too, and to have fun buying the fridge, too, if that's something that rings your jingle bells, 'cause we all need them rung whatever way we can. Bye, Josephine.'

★　★　★

What have I done? thought Emma as she loaded the bag with the shoes into her bicycle's basket and cycled through the light early evening back to the flat. Spending in just ten minutes as much money on a pair of shoes as it had taken her and Matthew months to save for a fridge. Spending on herself money that could have been spent on both of them, and, worse, not even spending it outright and honestly, but committing to spend, on the credit card she had never yet used before, the card that would rack up interest and lead to financial ruin, the card she had so proudly held back for emergencies, only to squander on a pair of shoes.

What have I done? she thought, chaining her battered but serviceable bicycle against the railings outside the flat, and taking into the narrow hallway of the converted Victorian labourer's cottage the package in the stiff white bag that should have been brought home by someone else, someone travelling by taxi to a house with a heavy double door leading to a marble hall and an important staircase, the package that now as she climbed the flimsy stairs to the flat felt barely heavier than the air around it, as what should it have to weight it, its content being nothing but straps and rosettes, straps and rosettes that had cost her as much as a fridge.

What have I done? she thought, unwrapping the shoes in all their gaudy frivolous glory and setting them shamefacedly beside the perfectly pretty, perfectly serviceable, perfectly affordable shoes that she already had, that now seemed to shrink in rejected humiliation beside their wantonly glamorous rivals, her heart suddenly and absurdly breaking with pity for them and remorse for the pain she had caused them, what have I done? what have I done? what have I done?

The telephone rang, startling her disproportionately. It was Matthew.

'I'm still at work,' he said. 'Just leaving now.'

'No rush,' she said. Why did she feel suddenly guilty? Then, oh, she thought, that was why. 'I've only just got in myself.'

'Are you OK?' he said. 'You sound sort of out of breath.'

'No, I'm fine,' she said. Although she was far from fine, very far, very far from fine. 'Actually, I did have quite a long day.'

'Me, too,' he said. 'Let's go out to dinner tonight.'

Go out, she thought. To a restaurant, with restaurant prices for food she could cook herself, probably with wine, and a tip for the waiter on top. Emma could never go out to a restaurant again.

'I'll cook,' she said. 'We've got the chicken, I'll just throw it into the oven.'

'Let's go out,' he said. 'There's that Italian place I want to try. We haven't been out for a while. Let's celebrate having nearly bought the fridge.'

And because Matthew was not the one who had spent the cost of the fridge on shoes, if Matthew wanted to go out to dinner tonight, then surely he deserved to go.

'OK,' she said. 'Why don't you make a reservation?'

She hadn't not told him, she thought after he had hung up. It just wasn't the sort of thing she would tell him over the telephone. She would tell him when he came home tonight. Or, at worst, she would tell him when they were at the restaurant.

Except that she didn't tell him when he came home for the simple reason that he didn't come home. He had been about to leave when a manager on one of the projects he was working on had called him with a minor detail in a text he needed to review, which led to a further minor detail, which led to yet another minor detail, adding up in the end to an extra two hours at the office, with the result that he met her not at home but at the restaurant, tired, tense, and in need of a little indulgence. She did not tell him over the vitello tonnato, which he had ordered for her in advance, knowing that it was her favourite entrée, because his face was beginning to relax and she wanted to see it more so; she did not tell him over the evening's special of wood pigeon with house-made wild-boar sausage and fresh porcini mushrooms (for him) and spaghetti alla puttanesca (for her), because she did not want to spoil his enjoyment of the pigeon; she did not tell him over the tiramisu which he liked her to order so that he could steal half, and the zuppa inglese which he added for himself on an impulse, because he was too deeply involved in explaining to her an elaborate practical joke involving telephones and Sellotape that he and his cubicle mate had played on their arch enemies in the next cubicle; she did not tell him over the coffee (for both of them) and grappa (for him), because by that stage she could not bear to. She would tell him, she thought, the next night.

Except that the next night was Tuesday night, which was his squash night with his friend Cheng, who was breaking up with his girlfriend and wanted to go to the pub afterwards, where he uncharacteristically drank so very much too much that Matthew ended up escorting him home to Wandsworth in a taxi (a taxi fare to Wandsworth!). And on Wednesday, they had opera tickets (opera tickets!) with a college friend of Matthew's and his wife, and on Thursday Emma had her book group, who were discussing a new biography of Marie Antoinette and remarked that Emma seemed unusually quiet on the subject, which she attributed to stress at work and a headache; and, before she knew it, it was the rain-soaked, thunderous evening before the day when she and Matthew were to go fridge shopping, and she had not yet once mentioned to him that at the beginning of the week, she had spent an outrageous sum of money on a pair of completely ridiculous shoes.

'Do you like my name?' she asked him as they sat down to their traditional Friday supper of pork chops and butter beans.

'Atwater?' he said. 'Yes, it has a good solid ring to it. Are you thinking of keeping it? The only thing is, it'd get complicated when the children start going to school.'

'Not Atwater,' she said. 'Emma. Do you like Emma?'

'Emma.' He thought. 'Yes, I suppose I do. I mean, it's you, isn't it, and I like *you*. Is that your pork chop? It's a midget. Why didn't you get a bigger one?'

'I'm trying not to gain weight,' she said. 'I sometimes wonder if Emma's a bit . . . I don't know . . . dull as a name. Don't you sometimes wish I was called Josephine instead?'

He smiled. 'Or Choo-Choo,' he said. Last Sunday evening, back in that now barely imaginable time of innocence, they had been able to laugh about Choo-Choo. 'You'll starve to death on that, it's the smallest chop I've ever seen. Do you want some of mine?'

'No I don't,' she said now, irritated. 'And I'm

not talking about Choo-Choo.' Choo-Choo, the untainted little girl who wore sturdy sandals fastened by a buckle to school and who afterwards went home to a clean conscience and a younger sister who loved her to pieces. 'I'm talking about Josephine. It's such a pretty name. The other day I saw a pair of shoes on Upper Street called Josephine.'

'What do you mean?' he said.

'What do you mean, what do I mean?' she said.

'What do you think I mean? You were walking down Upper Street and a pair of shoes came up to you and said, 'Good afternoon, our name's Josephine, could you please tell us where we catch the Number 19 into town?' Were they tourists? Did they have an American accent? Did you call them Choo-Choo and did they kick you?'

'They were in a shop window, Matthew. Designer shoes. They have names, you know.'

'Do they? I didn't know that.'

'Well, they do. And these were called Josephine. And they were . . . ' She paused, and, despite herself, her voice caught a little. 'They were the most beautiful shoes I've ever seen,' she finished.

Matthew laid down his knife and fork. Emma did not generally fish for compliments, but it was clear that something gallant was expected of him here.

'You don't need beautiful shoes, Emma,' he said. 'Your legs are good enough without them.'

Emma rose. 'If you had wracked your brains

all day,' she said, 'you could not have come up with a less sensitive or more hurtful thing to say to me. Enjoy your dinner. I'm going to visit Mom.'

She made for the door to the kitchen, where she turned.

'And I'm taking a taxi,' she added defiantly, before closing the door in his bewildered face.

★ ★ ★

On the other side of Islington, Fee was standing in her own kitchen fixing her favourite solitary supper of vegetable barley soup and a chicken sandwich when she heard a car draw up in front of the house, followed by light footsteps and the impatient scrabbling of a key at the front door.

'That'll be Lulu,' she told Toby, Lulu infuriated again by Sophie. No, not Lulu, who never took taxis, it must be Sophie, who often took them although she could not afford them, and even more often, in a way that Fee had never entirely understood, just happened to find someone with a car who just happened to be going in the exact direction in which Sophie wished to go. It would be Sophie, bursting in with rain-drenched hair and a highly wrought story of love or friendship, work or betrayal. Well, there was plenty of food for two — Fee had learned over the years to be generous when calculating supper portions. She looked up to see Emma, her controlled, confident Emma, standing in the doorway clutching a wad of damp tissue, tears running down her face like the rain outside the window. Fee's heart froze with fear.

'Honey, whatever has happened?' she said.

'He said my legs were good enough!' choked Emma, collapsing into her mother's arms.

★ ★ ★

'And I know it was wrong,' she said some time later, when the supper had been consumed and the whole tale told. 'It was greedy and mad and I don't know what came over me. And now I have a pair of stupid shoes that I'm too ashamed to look at, never mind wear, and a credit-card bill that's going to come in for the first time in my life, and I feel like I've taken something completely precious and pure and beautiful, which was our life together, Matthew's and mine, and thrown something dirty at it that's ruined it forever.'

Fee looked at her daughter, and sighed. Then she rose, and went to the kitchen counter, returning with a bowl of cherries and a box of Bendicks mints.

'Dessert,' she said. 'I've retired from making them so if you want something fancy, go visit your sister . . . Emma, I want you to listen to me because I'm going to tell you a secret about marriage.'

Unwrapping from its cool green foil the one chocolate mint she decided she would allow herself, Emma glanced up at her mother warily.

'It's not going to be one of the fish and bicycle secrets from the Collective, is it?' she asked.

'No, it's not.' Fee smiled. 'But it is a piece of

advice from someone who's been married since before you were born, and if you're smart you might want to hear it.'

'OK.' Emma sighed, crumpled the foil, and settled herself for a lecture.

Fee sat for a moment, pursing her lips with the look that Emma knew meant she was composing her thoughts.

'Times have changed in the last hundred years,' she said then, slowly. 'Good lord, they've changed since I was a girl, and if Grandma Jo, for instance, could see the world today, heaven knows what she'd make of it. She was unusual, I think, because she was a writer and helped her husband run a school, but most women of her time sat at home and tended the house while the men went out to work. These days, thank God, we're far closer to being partners with our men than we've ever been, but the truth is, we're not quite there yet, and maybe we never will be. Matthew's a good man, Emma, as your father is, and I think you'll be very happily married. But . . . I've noticed that already you do more than he does. You cook far more often than he does, you're the one who notices when you run out of milk, you're the one who does the laundry, you were the one who chose his mother's birthday card. It always happens. The woman works far harder around the home than the man does, and, good God, just wait till the kids come along and see what it's like. Don't get me wrong: a happy marriage is wonderful — it's one of the greatest blessings that life can bring. But it's also true that a very great deal of it is tedious and

161

repetitive, and if we women aren't very careful, the best of us can find ourselves turning into a drudge. So — do you know what the answer is?'

Emma thought. 'Communication?' she hazarded. Maybe if she had asked Matthew to cook dinner more often, she would not have fallen prey to Monday's madness. 'Drawing boundaries and sticking to them? Educating him to take his share of the work?'

Fee shook her head, leaned forward across the table and laid a hand on her daughter's.

'Treats,' she said, firmly.

There was a pause while Emma blinked in surprise, and unwrapped another mint.

'Treats,' she repeated.

'Correct.' Her mother nodded. 'I love my husband dearly, and you know how much I love Matthew, too. But over many too many years and much too much beating of my head against a brick wall, I've come to accept that there are things about men that we're just plain old not going to change. And here's where we get to one of the good things about being a woman, which is that, once we've accepted a situation, we're quite good at adapting ourselves to it, and one of the most effective ways of adapting is to take on the protective colouration of the environment. I've noticed over the years that men have very little hesitation in buying themselves treats when they feel they deserve one — you did say, didn't you, Emma, that Matthew ordered the wood pigeon on Monday? And my philosophy is that, if they're allowed to reward themselves on occasion, then I don't see why we shouldn't be,

162

too. And now that we are — thank God — no longer dependent on them for every penny we spend, it's very important indeed that we allow ourselves to splurge occasionally on things that will make us feel good about ourselves. It's very healthy, in fact.'

Emma took another mint. Counting the wrappers on her plate, it seemed to be her fifth.

'But, Mom,' she said, 'those shoes cost as much as a fridge. I can't believe I spent that much.'

'Are they the most beautiful shoes you've ever seen in your life?' asked Fee.

'Yes, Mom,' said Emma after a moment. 'Yes, they are.'

'And will they make your legs look perfectly lovely on your wedding day?'

'Oh, Mom,' said Emma. 'They'll make them look just amazing.'

'Well, then.' Fee smiled at her daughter. 'I don't suggest buying designer shoes every day of the week. And I certainly don't suggest spending that sort of sum in the future without discussing it with Matthew first. But I do most strongly believe that if you find something makes you feel truly, wonderfully, fabulous, then in the long run it's the best and the healthiest thing, both for you individually, and for the marriage you'll create with Matthew, if you allow yourself to have it.'

'I don't get it,' said Emma. 'You don't even like shoes.'

'I have other treats,' said Fee. 'I know you girls think I look like some crazy old hippie because I don't always follow the latest fashion. But I happen to feel extremely good about my body because it's the way I like it to be — it's clean and it's healthy and it's in reasonably good shape for my age, and if you want to know more, your father and I — '

'Enough information, Mom,' Emma interrupted.

Fee smiled again. 'All I'm saying,' she said, 'is that we all have different styles of making ourselves feel good about ourselves. And it happens that shoes don't mean so very much to me, so if I were to spend a deal of money on them that would just be money wasted. But if they happen to make *you* feel like a million dollars, then you should by all means go ahead and treat yourself from time to time, and what better occasion to do so than your wedding day?'

'That's all very well,' said Emma. 'But there's still a credit-card bill coming in that I have no idea how I'm going to pay.'

'How much did you say it was for?' said Fee.

Emma groaned. 'The same as the fridge,' she said.

Fee rose, went into the hallway and returned with her handbag. She opened it, rummaged and produced her chequebook.

'This,' she told Emma, reaching for her glasses as she flicked open the cover, 'is one of *my* treats.'

5

'Miss Atwater, will you come into my office, please. There is that which I wish to discuss with you.'

So it was happening, thought Lulu dully, following her employer into the narrow cubbyhole which he referred to as his office. It was a windowless space, with room only for a small desk and a chair on either side, and Mr Goncharoff rarely used it but for matters of solemnity or importance. Matters, thought Lulu, such as the announcement that he was about to sell the shop.

'This morning,' said Mr Goncharoff, 'I go to meet with the gentleman with the headgear. We will exchange contracts. At the end of the month, Goncharoff's Antiques will become another coffee shop for the people of Haverstock Hill, Irena and I will move to Spain. Irena is pleased about this, and says she hopes to be swimming in the sea on Christmas Day. Alexander has been accepted into a training course at Sotheby's. He is pleased with this, too, as it is something he has wanted.'

He stopped, and peered at her over the top of his spectacles. 'So much for the Goncharoffs,' he said. 'But it leaves us with the question of you, Miss Atwater. I know that none of what is about to happen will come as a surprise to you. Have you thought yet what you will do with yourself?'

Lulu sighed to herself. There had once been a time, she remembered, when people had not been asking her that question, and she supposed there would come another time in the future when they would not be again. She hoped that, whenever that time did come, she would remind herself to enjoy it to its fullest.

'Well, I don't know, Mr Goncharoff,' she said now. 'I suppose it's time to start deciding, isn't it?'

'It seems that it is.' He sat back in his chair, and looked at her, thoughtfully twirling his thumbs. 'You could not spend all of your life bringing biscuits and keeping the files for the Goncharoffs. Work is not so easy to find these days, but — although you do not talk about it much — I remember from your letters of reference that you were a gifted student at the university. The world needs scholars always, and in particular now in these troubled and exciting times. Perhaps you should take the rest of the day off to put your thinking cap on about what it is you really want to do.' He stopped, and frowned. 'What is a thinking cap, by the way, Miss Atwater? I have often wondered.'

'It's sort of tall and pointed,' said Lulu, 'and quite sort of scholarly and stern. You want to watch your grammar when you're around a thinking cap.'

'I had thought so.' Mr Goncharoff nodded. 'I shall miss you, Miss Atwater. Take today off. There will not be so much for you to do before the end of the month, so I hope you are able to use your thinking cap to good effect.'

166

Lulu left the shop and walked up the hill and around the corner to her house. It was all very well, she thought, for Mr Goncharoff to make jokes about thinking caps and decisions; Mr Goncharoff had already made most of the big decisions of his life, and made them, on the whole, successfully. He had decided to move away from his city on the Volga in the south-west of Russia, and go first to Paris, and then to the north-west of London; he had decided to mix his knowledge of art and history, which was extensive, with his business acumen, which was adequate, to pursue a career in antiques which had kept him interested and supported his family for the last three decades; today he had decided to sell his shop in the side street off Haverstock Hill, and retire to a place where his only decisions from now on would be whether to sit in the sun or the shade for his morning coffee or whether to dine at home on the calamares that Irena would buy from the market or to walk to the restaurant in town for paella.

For Lulu, it was more complicated. She was sure that she did not — as Mr Goncharoff had hinted and as her parents would doubtless begin once again to suggest — want to go back to university. But if not university, what then? Lulu's big decisions in life lay ahead of her; and the harder she tried to make them, the more, it seemed, her brain froze in confusion.

It was not until she had reached her house and was standing outside the front door that she realized she did not want to go in. Sophie was there, awaiting a call from her agent — or, worse, having already received a call from her agent and being either ecstatic or heartbroken at the result — and Lulu had not the energy for Sophie right now. She sat herself down on the low stone wall outside the house, and squinted into the summer sun, trying to decide just where it was she did want to go on this disconcerting morning of sudden and unfestive freedom. A park or coffee shop, she thought, would be too public; a library too redolent of the academic world into which she knew her parents would now try to urge her. Borough Market, on the other side of London, its stalls heaped with vegetables and spices, a luxury for days of leisure, was only worth going to during the weekend. After a while, she realized that in this instance if in no other she knew exactly where it was that she wanted to go and what she wanted to do, and a moment's calculation told her that the coast was clear: her mother, she knew, would be safely ensconced in Sophie's old room seeing clients for most of the day, and her father was at his office in Russell Square. She stood up, stretched in the sun and began to unchain her bicycle from the railing.

*   *   *

In the weeks since she had first discovered Grandma Jo's letters, Lulu had gradually cleared for herself a little corner among the dust and the spiders of her parents' attic, in which she had formed a neat, if not elegant, little nook, consisting of the broken armchair, which proved

168

perfectly serviceable once she had replaced its missing leg with a stack of chemistry textbooks; a paint-spattered side table, victim of a brief artistic fling of Emma's; and a discarded desk lamp, which she had doctored with duct tape and fitted with a new bulb. She still had not mentioned the letters to anyone else in the family, although she knew that she could not keep them a secret forever; one day, she knew, she would have to bring them down from the attic and show them around. This would not be something she would do casually, she had decided: she would find a pretty box to place them in, and pick a time to present them, properly and with the ceremony they deserved, possibly to her mother at Christmas, or to Emma just before her wedding day. To tell the truth, she was in no particular hurry to do this. Once the letters were out in the open, they would become not Lulu's letters, but the family's, to be examined and exclaimed on, pored over by Fee and Emma, read dramatically aloud by Sophie, photocopied, no doubt, and sent in a package to Aunt Amy in Boston to do with who knew what and show to who knew whom. But for this time when no one but Lulu knew about them, Grandma Jo, fierce, funny and awkward, who had struggled against the world and found love at last, was hers alone; and at the moment she felt she rather needed something that was only hers.

Meanwhile, she had set herself the task — under the guise, should anyone ask, of searching for Grandma Cissie's now long-vanished recipe book — of sorting through the large trunk of family papers, searching for further items of interest. The undertaking was a substantial one, as the papers seemed endless and were stuffed into the trunk in no particular order, letters jostling laundry lists, newspaper clippings tattering between electricity bills, half-used ration books from the war tossed carelessly between sheafs of outdated tax returns. Occasionally she would come across a treasure — a pile of half-century-old theatre programmes, which would delight Sophie; Grandma Jojo's old passport, much battered and crammed with stamps, the photograph showing the same young woman with the cigarette in the photograph on the bookshelf — but most of it was the pedestrian stuff of day-to-day living, domestic accounts from households unnamed, announcements of lectures and concerts given and many years forgotten, receipts for clothing long worn out and food long consumed, bought by who knew whom for who knew what occasion, with what satisfaction they had provided, or failed to provide, unrecorded.

Nevertheless, Lulu was enjoying herself. She was beginning to piece together a family history: Jo March had indeed married a German professor, Professor Bhaer, so that part of the story was true at least; Cissie Bhaer had married a businessman called Bill Fraser; Jojo Fraser had married a rather dashing young pilot called Robert Chamberlain, whom Lulu remembered faintly from a childhood visit to Boston as a stooped and kindly old man called Grandpa Bob. The family had moved to the city when Grandma Jo's school had failed during the Depression, and had stayed there ever since, witnessing — since someone in the family had been in the habit of collecting newspaper clippings — school reforms and society weddings, baseball matches, natural disasters and the end of Prohibition, a new bus line through town, a variety of fights for women's reproductive rights, the Second World War, the death of President Kennedy in Dallas, and a Beatles concert at Boston Garden. They had shared long faces — which Fee and Sophie had inherited, but not Emma or Lulu — political awareness, and an interest in the arts. Lulu thought that on the whole, they were a rather nice family.

A high-school yearbook from the 1930s now caught her eye, and she flicked through it, smiling at the pictures of youngsters, boys with jug ears, girls with bobbed hair or skinny pigtails, bundled up to ski in the winter, rowing on the river in the summer, their crowds of happily unformed faces squinting merrily into the camera, possibly, or possibly not, including that of a family member. Beneath the yearbook was a large envelope, addressed to Mrs Josephine Bhaer in a tidy hand that Lulu by now recognized to be that of Grandma Jo's sister Meg. Lulu screwed her nose a little — Meg's letters, she had discovered, tended to the domestic and paid particular attention to the topic of children's diets — but decided to open it anyway. Maybe Emma would be interested when she started to have children of her own.

Inside the envelope were five smaller envelopes, all addressed in the now familiar scribbling hand of Grandma Jo. The accompanying note from Meg was simple and short.

Plumfield, September 1892.

Dear Jo,

I've sent you a package with your letters as you requested for Mr. Chauncey. I know Amy hopes very much that you'll look favorably on his request for publication. But I know, too, how very little *you* care for being lionized, so I fear her hopes will be dashed. Nevertheless, I am sending you these letters separately, for, whatever you decide about the book, I cannot think you will want them made public. What a very long time ago all of that was, to be sure.

Ever your loving sister,

Meg.

The five envelopes were smaller than those Grandma Jo generally used, and made of thinner paper: they were addressed to Meg and bore, not the usual Concord postmark, but that of New York. Her curiosity now piqued, Lulu opened the first one and read.

New York, December 1867.

Dearest Meg,

Thank you most heartily for the poems. They are perfectly beautiful and you were an angel to translate them for me — *one day*, I shall be able to read Schiller in the original, as my accomplished sister can. I'm still grubbing away at my German lessons, although the tongue don't come easy to me, and even though my kindly old professor friend who is teaching me *says* that I'm making progress, I fear he is letting his good nature, which is considerable, cloud his better judgment. I am a sore trial to him, I know; he has a trick of pulling upon his beard when he is distracted and by the time our lessons are concluded, it stands out in strands like a great towzled brown bush. But I *will* master the tongue; I am determined upon it. It is the native tongue of the divine Herr B., and as such the tongue of seraphim, not men — however badly I mangle it!

Oh, Meg, Herr B. is *such* a handsome man! His hair is as thick as a haystack and as yellow as a field of corn in the highest day of summer, his eyes are as blue as the heavens, and when we pass each other in the hallway and he gives me that queer little bow that Germans give, then my heart goes all into a flurry and I know not where to look, just like the foolish girls in the novels. He comes from Cologne, he's in New York to study philosophy at the university, and I know (for I couldn't help it, I peeped at his mail on the hall table) that his first name is Friedrich. Isn't that a heavenly name? Is this love, Meg? I can't think what else it can be, so fancy it must. Here's a merry how-d'ye-do — your thorny old sister takes work as a governess, and goes and falls in love like a sentimental damsel in a story!

I think he has noticed me, too, although it is hard to say for I am so shy with him. He is gallant — oh, Meg, he is so very gallant, so very charming — to everyone, with a smile and a cheery word for all, and everyone in the house is enthralled by him, from little Kitty and Minnie, who giggle and toss their heads when they see him and *won't* pay me heed afterwards, to clever Miss Norton, who has praised his head to me as 'perfectly classical in proportion,' to poor little Annie the under parlormaid, who turns red as a beet in his presence and clatters the coal against the hod like so many castanets in confusion. But I fancy I notice an extra attentiveness in his bow to *me* of late, a tenderness in those rich cerulean eyes as he says, in that melodious voice of his, 'Gut morning, Mees Marsch.' I *can't* feel as strongly as this and not have it returned at least a little bit. It isn't possible.

Don't say a word to Marmee or Beth of any of this. But I am fancying a day when we sit together, he and I alone with each other, before a fire — in a garret somewhere; we shouldn't want much — and I lay my head upon his shoulder, and he touches my face with his long slender hand, and I call him Friedrich and he calls me Jo . . .

Meanwhile, the dear old Professor awaits me in the parlour, to *try* to assist me in making some sense of Hans Andersen's tale of the Little Mermaid. Poor man, I pity him sorely

. . . when I am not weaving dreams about Herr B.

Ever your loving (and, these days, dreaming and sighing),

Jo.

Lulu dropped the letter and looked up into the blue sky above the attic window, smiling at what must surely be her great-great-grandmother's first sight of her great-great-grandfather. Until now, Lulu had always pictured her great-great-grandfather, Professor Bhaer, as a staid and middle-aged man; but before he became Professor Bhaer, he must of course have been plain young Herr Bhaer, and how curiously gratifying it was to know that he had been handsome, too. Lulu's boyfriends had so far tended to the scientific and eccentric: she had never attracted the attention of a handsome man. Handsome men fell for Sophie with her blonde hair and easy charm, while Emma had always drawn the solid and dependable types, beginning with a brown-haired and rather solemn little boy whom she had known in kindergarten, who had spent endless evenings at their house doing jigsaws and who had gone on, Lulu thought, to become an architect, and ending with Matthew, who was about as solid and as dependable as it was humanly possible for a person to be.

If Lulu were asked to identify the sort of man who was attracted to her, she could not precisely say, and the truth was that no one much seemed to have been attracted at all lately; in fact, now that she thought of it, she had not had a serious boyfriend since university. It was probably as well, she reminded herself sternly: she had never seen the point of having a boyfriend just for the sake of having one, and there were, besides, so very many other questions currently surrounding her life that the idea of romance was probably too distracting to take on. Nevertheless, she thought now, it would be nice to be fallen in love with; and to be fallen in love with by a handsome man would be positively luxurious.

Just for the pleasure of it, she picked up the letter and read it again, piecing together the story behind it. It seemed that at one point, Grandma Jo had taken a position as a governess in New York, staying in what appeared to be a boarding house, and teaching, from the sound of them, two rather spoilt and precocious children. The other boarders, it seemed, included an educated single woman (for a moment, Lulu wondered just what her life had been like, and what circumstances might have led her to live in a New York boarding house), an older professor and . . . yes, there he was, Friedrich Bhaer, her great-great-grandfather, with 'hair as thick as a haystack and yellow as a field of corn . . . eyes as blue as the heavens'. He had been fair-haired, attractive and charming, and, yes, of course, thought Lulu a little wistfully, now it fell into place, had provided the almost too perfect genetic blueprint for his great-great-granddaughter Sophie Atwater. But there was a twist to the story, she reminded herself, then. It turned out that yellow-haired and charming young Friedrich Bhaer had fallen in love, not with another charming beauty, but with gawky and outspoken Grandma Jo. He had not been embarrassed by her, as Sasha Goncharoff had by Lulu, or looked at her sister in alarm when she spoke, as Lulu knew that Matthew sometimes looked secretly at Emma; on the contrary, he had fallen in love with her, he had married her, and he and their children and their grandchildren had all adored her. That was Mom's word. They had adored her.

From the pocket of her jeans, her mobile phone rang. It was her mother.

'Hi, honey,' said Fee. 'Are you OK? I looked into the store to see you, but Sasha said he thought you'd gone home.'

'Yes, I'm fine,' said Lulu. 'Why were you at the store? I thought you had clients today.'

'A couple cancelled this morning, so I made a run to that nice bookshop. Are you all right? You're not sick or anything?'

'I'm fine, Mom.' Lulu paused. This was not how she had planned to deliver the news to her mother, but there appeared now to be little alternative. 'Mr Goncharoff's sold the shop,' she said.

'Oh.'

In spite of everything, Lulu smiled to herself as she pictured her mother weighing the most appropriate blend of supportiveness, encouragement, discretion, and concern.

'How are you doing?' she asked after a moment.

'OK,' said Lulu. 'I'd known it was coming, after all.'

'That's good,' said Fee. 'You sound OK, anyway, so that's something. Where are you?'

'At home, actually. In the attic. Mr Goncharoff gave me the day off, so I thought I'd have another look for the recipe book.'

'Oh.'

There was a pause while Fee struggled with herself, and lost.

'You know, sweetie,' she said slowly, then. 'We still have eight weeks left before September.'

At which, Lulu lost all inclination to smile.

'Mom,' she said. 'If you so much as mention the word university to me, I am terminating this conversation.'

'My darling child,' said Fee, 'I'd be delighted never to mention the word again, if you were able to suggest some sort of alternative.'

'Well, I'm sorry I can't,' said Lulu. Alone in the attic, she scowled at the phone: the pleasure she had been feeling from the new letter had now dissipated into irritation with her mother. 'I'm sorry I'm not Emma or Sophie, sorry I can't come to you with nice little plans for my future all neatly wrapped up with a shiny ribbon on top, nice steady job and respectable marriage for Emma, nice exciting acting career for Sophie. Sorry I'm only messy old mixed-up me.'

If she had hoped to induce guilt in her mother by this speech, she was disappointed.

'Oh, honey!' said Fee. 'That is just plain unfair. Of course I'm happy you're you. But that includes wanting you to be happy, too, and I don't see how you couldn't be happier than being unemployed by at least giving that place

I'm not allowed to name a try.'

'Well, I see how,' said Lulu. 'I'll talk to you later, Mom, I'm going back to the flat now.'

She would not, she decided, read the remaining letters from Grandma Jo just now: her mother's call had put her out of sorts, and she wanted to be in the frame of mind to appreciate them. She replaced them instead in the larger envelope, and laid it, carefully, at the left end of the top bookshelf, promising herself that she would come back to discover the rest of the romance at some time when she needed to be cheered up. She had a feeling the need would be felt more than once over the forthcoming weeks.

She closed the trunk, crossed the attic and climbed down the ladder to the landing, remembering this time to go gently down the last two rungs. What she had not reckoned with was a splinter on the side that caught her hand as she put the ladder away, scratching her.

'Ow.' She jumped back and shook her stinging hand. 'Damn. Ow.' She kicked the ladder's side crossly. 'Bloody object.'

'Are you OK?' Tom the lodger was once again coming out of his room, the now familiar pile of books under his arm.

'Yes, I'm fine.' Lulu inspected her hand: beyond the shock, the damage was negligible. 'The ladder doesn't seem to like me, though.'

'You do seem to have a couple of issues there.' Gently, he took it from her, and completed the task of stowing it in the corner. 'Have you maybe done something to offend it?'

'Possibly.' Lulu looked at it thoughtfully. 'We

were neighbours for several years, although I don't remember any bad blood. But that's the problem with causing offence, isn't it? You don't always know when you do.'

'Maybe you should book a joint session with your mom, get matters out into the open and let the healing begin.' He looked at her more closely. 'Are you sure you're OK? You look kind of jumpy.'

'Oh.' And now that she started to descend the stairs, she realized that she did feel a little on the shaky side. 'It's one of those days, you know. I lost my job this morning, and I suppose it's just sort of sinking in.'

'Too bad,' he said. 'Remind me again what you do.'

'Well, that's the problem, I don't really do anything properly.' They had reached the hallway of the house, and she stopped and looked at him. 'You're an academic, aren't you?'

'Lecturer at Birkbeck,' he nodded. 'The eighteenth-century novel.'

Hardly her field, she thought, but it was the right area, anyway.

'Can I ask you what it's like?' she asked. 'The academic world.'

'Sure. Want a cup of coffee?'

'Um . . . '

Fee drove fast through the streets of London and would be home very soon; a cup of coffee would keep Lulu in the house, and she really did not feel like confronting her mother right now.

'I'm going to Carroll's for breakfast,' he said. 'Care to join me?'

Carroll's was a different matter. It was a remnant of old Islington, the shabby borough Lulu had grown up in before the fashionable people had moved in, a workman's cafe tucked in a side street off the Caledonian Road, with Formica-topped tables and windows that misted in the winter.

Lulu did not often go out to eat, but she had always had a fondness for Carroll's.

★   ★   ★

Tom appeared to be well liked, she noticed, approvingly, when they reached the cafe. He was greeted with affectionate warmth by Maureen, the owner, and speedily served with a full English breakfast, the plate heaped high with food: Maureen, who was a maternal soul, liked to fatten her favourites.

'Do you always do that?' she asked, watching with interest as he doused his scrambled eggs with the Tabasco sauce Maureen had brought to accompany them.

'Yeah.' He looked up, surprised. 'Don't you?'

'No! No one does here. Hadn't you noticed?'

'Not very good at noticing things, I'm afraid. It drove my ex crazy.' He stopped, frowning a little, and shook his head, as if to dislodge some memories. Then smiled that kind smile at her. 'So what's up with you?' he asked. 'You look like you could use a friendly ear.'

'Oh.' Lulu sighed, and swallowed a mouthful of her bacon sandwich. 'Probably something terribly tedious and young person-y, that everyone's heard a million times over and is bored halfway into a coma by.'

'I'm not quite your grandfather's age, you know. Try me.' He forked a healthy mouthful of baked beans and nodded encouragingly.

'OK.' It was surprisingly difficult, though, to know where to begin. 'Have you been an academic all your life?'

'I guess I have. Wow.' He raised his eyebrows behind his glasses. 'That sounds kind of disturbing, doesn't it? To have never done anything but what I do.'

'I suppose not, if you enjoy it. *Do* you enjoy it?'

'Absolutely.' He nodded. 'I'm very fortunate because my work is my joy. A lot of people wake up in the morning thinking, Oh, God, I have to go to work today. Me, I wake up thinking, Oh, boy, I get to go to work today!' He nodded again, firmly, and a little sternly. 'I'm a very fortunate man,' he repeated.

Yes, thought Lulu, but his work meant reading eighteenth-century novels. Sophie had appeared in an adaptation of *Tom Jones* at drama school, and had come home bursting with tales of unruly love, bold wenches and erotic meals leading to tumbles in rumpled sheets in coaching inns. There were not many coaching inns, thought Lulu sadly, in the biochemistry department.

'What's up?' he said. 'Are you thinking of going back to college? Your mom tells me you're some kind of genius at science.'

'And that's another problem,' she said. 'I do

seem to be quite good at that stuff. And people keep telling me I should pursue it, but I just don't want to, although I don't know what else I do want to do. I do know I don't want to do that, though.'

'Then don't do it,' he said, immediately.

'No?' She looked at him in surprise. It was the first time an older person had ever not tried to persuade her in the academic direction.

'Uh-uh.' He shook his head, firmly. 'It's really one-dimensional, the academic life. If you go into it, it takes over your world and can become all that you do and think about. It suits me because I happen to be in love with my subject. But if you don't really love it to the point that you're almost obsessed with it, then it's not for you.'

'Ha.' She was silent for a moment, digesting this new perspective. 'But I do have to do something,' she said. 'I'll be twenty-five at the end of the year.'

He smiled. 'That's not so old,' he said. 'And you don't have to know yet what you're going to do forever. Back in California people take years to figure out what they want to do. Of course, some of them end up never figuring it out at all, and that's not so good. But there's not as much hurry as you seem to think there is. Why don't you just try doing something you like? What *do* you like?'

'I don't know.' She thought for a moment, watching Maureen's cat pick her way regally through the chairs to land and stretch in a puddle of sunshine. She liked cats, she thought.

Cats didn't feel the need to ingratiate themselves. 'I like animals,' she said. 'I don't want to be a vet, though. And I definitely don't want to work in a pet shop, because I don't approve of them. But I do get on with animals, I always have. Sometimes I think I get on with animals better than I do with people.' She sighed. 'I'm not very good with people, to tell you the truth.'

'In the eighteenth century,' he told her, 'landowners used to think it was picturesque to have a hermit living on their properties. They'd build a hermitage and actually go out and hire someone to live in it. Maybe that's a career path to consider.'

Lulu thought. 'It'd be a healthy life,' she said, then. 'All that fresh air. Would they feed me?'

'Not as such, I don't think. I think you'd have to go out into the grounds and forage for nuts and berries.'

'I can forage. And I love nuts and berries. Mom says I was a bear in a previous life.'

'Well, I guess we've solved the problem, then.' He laughed, then stopped, remembering that he was the older one, to whom she had come for advice. 'You know what I'd really do if I were you?' he said. 'I'd give my brain the afternoon off. It's a beautiful day — why don't you get on that bike and go for a good long ride, get some fresh air and exercise, maybe find some animals to look at?'

'You mean the zoo?' Lulu wrinkled her nose. She was not sure whether she approved of the zoo any more than of pet shops. Besides, it was

184

summer and would doubtless be full of more people.

'Or just go to the park and watch the ducks,' he said. 'Everything doesn't have to be as big a deal as you seem to want to make it. There are animals everywhere if you look. Just go and hang out for a while. And, uh . . . ' He paused, and sipped at his coffee. 'We might not tell your mom about the hermit thing, OK?'

'I don't think she'd see the funny side,' Lulu agreed.

★   ★   ★

When she arrived at home a few hours later, she found Sophie sitting bolt upright in the living room, her hands folded demurely on her lap, a spot of colour blazing in each cheek.

'Good afternoon, Lulu,' she said. 'Has anything of interest transpired for you today? I've had a fairly humdrum sort of a time myself. I got up . . . brushed my teeth . . . fixed some food . . . watered the busy Lizzie . . . ' Suddenly, she leaped to her feet with a shriek of joy. ' . . . heard that I've landed the part on *St Luke's*!'

'You haven't!' Her worries abruptly obliterated, Lulu caught her sister around the waist and led her in a triumphant waltz around the room. *St Luke's* was one of the most popular hospital shows on television, more popular by far than *Sawbones*. 'That's amazing, Soph, I am so proud of you!'

'Maggie's just phoned to tell me.' Sophie seized the back of a chair and beat a triumphant tattoo with her fists. 'Is she the best agent in the entire universe, or what? I knew it was good news straight away because she had her happy voice on. It's really good, Lulu, because Dr Brodie gets wrongly charged with sexual harassment and I play a nurse who stands up for him. Three good scenes with other nurses and — get this — a four-minute two-hander with Colin, just him and me in a room.'

'Just you and Dr Broody?' Lulu laughed and poked at her sister with a mischievous finger: Colin Hobbes, the dark-haired actor who played St Luke's maverick young registrar, was the material of many young women's dreams. 'Emma's going to be jealous.'

'He's a very good actor, actually.' Sophie frowned her disapproval of Lulu's tone. Then brightened. 'And four minutes is great because it pretty much guarantees a close-up. *And* I'm a nurse, not a sad old patient like they wanted on *Sawbones*, which means I don't die or get discharged so I might even be asked back if I do well enough. I report on set three weeks today. Oh, Lulu, this is so exciting!'

'I think it calls for a celebration,' said Lulu. 'It's Tuesday, isn't it, let's ask Emma to come here for dinner, and I'll cook something nice. Do you want to ask Jamie, too?'

'Oh.' Sophie, who had been doing plies in front of the window, stopped. 'That's so sweet of you, Lulu-belle, it would have been lovely. But I'm going out to celebrate with Rupert.'

'Rupert?'

'You met him on Saturday? Tall, sort of dark, a

186

bit pink shirty, but very nice? He's taking me to Baldini's, the place in *Time Out*, it's supposed to be amazing.'

'Oh, him.' The young man who had come to pick Sophie up for her date last Saturday. He was handsome, of course, and had not cared for Lulu, nor had he pretended to.

'Didn't you like him?' said Sophie. 'He's really interesting once you get to know him. He does an amazing trick with a beer bottle and a five-pound note.'

'Sounds electrifying. Where did you meet him?'

'Around.' Sophie shrugged: she was accustomed to meeting, and attracting, young men wherever she went. 'And speaking of him, I have to go and make myself beautiful for him. Let's celebrate later on, Lulu, you and me. Shall we go to the pub tomorrow? I'll buy you a drink. Play your cards right, and I'll throw in a Scotch egg.'

She would not have to work very hard to make herself beautiful, thought Lulu a little sadly after her sister had left the room. Blessed as Sophie was with prettiness as well as charm, it was no wonder that men sought her out. She wandered to the mirror above the fireplace, and inspected her own face — ordinary of feature, she had always thought, the eyes a little too intense for comfort beneath the curtain of wild hair — and wondered, as she sometimes did, how it would feel to be blonde and lighthearted and be taken to dinner in fashionable restaurants by young men who did amazing tricks with beer bottles. Of course Sophie would want to go out tonight instead of celebrating with the family, she reminded herself; she could enjoy Emma's company and Lulu's cooking any time she chose. If Lulu had been in Sophie's place — if she had known what she wanted to do professionally, and had just been given an extraordinarily exciting opportunity to do it, and if, besides, there were a young man in her life who was offering to take her to dinner at a fashionable restaurant to celebrate this — then Lulu would doubtless have gone out to celebrate, too. But there was no young man who was offering to take her to dinner currently, and no young man she particularly wanted to be invited by, either, and, Lord knew, there was little enough to celebrate on the professional front. She frowned at herself, realizing that she had not yet told Sophie her own professional news. Well, it could wait till tomorrow, she thought: there was no point in dampening Sophie's evening as well as her own.

★   ★   ★

Emma was already cooking when Lulu arrived at her flat, the pale evening light streaming through the window, a bunch of Fee's roses the colour of sunset splashing orange and red across the dining table.

'Matthew's been waxing romantic,' she said. 'He went into Mom and Dad's garden on Sunday and picked them for me himself. Useful sort of in-laws, aren't they? Nice to see you, Lu. How are you doing?'

Lulu sighed at her sister's carefully casual

188

tone, and dropped into a chair.

'Mom's told you, hasn't she?' she said.

Emma looked up from the vegetables she was stirfrying, and smiled.

'Did you think for one mad second that she wouldn't have?'

'Not really.' Lulu yawned, feeling suddenly more tired than if she had worked a full day for the Goncharoffs. 'What are you cooking?'

'Sea bass. I decided you need a treat. We all need treats from time to time; they're very important. Glass of wine?'

'Wine?' Lulu frowned suspiciously: they did not usually drink with their Tuesday supper. 'Are you going to ask me for a kidney later on?' But she took the glass anyway, and sipped at the liquid, pale yellow in the evening light. 'Nice,' she commented.

'Matthew and I have joined the Wine Society. We both agreed you deserved something good tonight. How's the rising new TV star? On an insufferability scale of one to ten?'

Relaxing just a little into the comfort of being cooked for, Lulu laughed.

'Hovering around thirteen and a half,' she said. 'But it's OK because it's only when she touches the earth, most of the time she's orbiting around Saturn and out of reach anyway. Have you heard she'll be sharing a scene with Dr Broody?'

'She did just get around to mentioning it. But only about fifty or sixty times, so not too bad.' Emma smiled into the vegetables. 'It's funny to think about, though, isn't it?' she said. 'Our grubby little sister and Dr Broody. It's quite exciting, really, I'm dying to hear what he's like.'

'Colin,' Lulu corrected her, 'is the consummate professional. And so is Sophie. So if you want vulgar gossip, you'll have to read the tabloids, I'm afraid.'

'I wonder how tall he is,' said Emma. 'I've been trying to measure him against the other actors, but I can't quite work it out. I do hope he's tall; I don't like short men. If he's short, I'll have to stop fancying him.' She gave the vegetables one last stir and turned off the heat under the wok. 'Sophie doesn't seem to know about your news yet,' she said.

'I haven't told her,' said Lulu. 'She's so excited — I decided it could keep till tomorrow.'

'That was nice of you,' said Emma.

'Right.' Lulu snorted. 'I'm very nice. That's why everyone finds me so easy to get along with. That Lulu, they say, she's so . . . nice.'

'I'm serious,' said Emma. 'It really was nice of you. You should do what Mom says and give yourself positive feedback when you've earned it. And while you're at it, you might just learn to take a compliment when it's offered.' She reached down to ruffle Lulu's hair before turning back to the stove. 'Watch out, food's coming.'

She set before them plates of moist fish, herb-flecked rice and the vegetables, and raised a forestalling hand.

'In answer to your question,' she said, 'it's parsley, black pepper and a little lemon rind. And in answer to your extremely helpful and considerate suggestion, the way you'd cook it might very well be the way *you'd* cook it if you happened to be cooking, but this is the way *I* cook it, because I am not you, but me, OK?' She passed extra quarters of lemon, and squeezed hers over her fish. 'Now, do you want to talk about stuff?'

'Not really.' Lulu sighed again and tasted her sea bass. 'This is very good, by the way, thank you. But I suppose we'd better get the conversation over with because I know you're itching to have it.'

'Well, it seems someone has to,' said Emma. 'Mom says you bit her head off this morning when she tried it.' She laid down her knife and fork and looked at Lulu for a moment. 'We're all quite worried about you, you know,' she said. 'And I know you don't want to talk about this, and I know I'm not allowed to ask you if you have any plans for what you're going to do next. But, just out of curiosity, *do* you have any plans?'

'Not for the long term,' said Lulu. 'But, since you're so eager to know, I was thinking that just for the time being I might look for something to do with animals.'

There was a pause.

'Animals,' said Emma.

'What's wrong with animals?' said Lulu. She looked up, sharply, from her plate. 'Do you not like them or something?'

'Of course I like them! It's just that . . . ' Emma paused, seeking diplomacy. 'Well, you've never really particularly talked about them before.'

191

'I'm very good with them,' said Lulu. 'Hadn't you noticed?'

'Ummm . . . ' Emma searched her memory, trying to trace an especial bond between Lulu and the animal world.

'I talk to Toby much more often than you do,' said Lulu. 'I like Toby a lot. And Mrs Goncharoff has a sweet little pug who always wags his tail when he sees me.'

'Animals,' said Emma. 'So you're thinking of going to veterinary school.'

'No!' Lulu reached for the pepper and ground it vigorously over her fish, shaking her head in frustration. 'I'm not thinking of going to any sort of school! Don't you listen to anything? I'm thinking that obviously I have to get some sort of a stopgap job until I decide what I really want to do, and, just as a stopgap job, just to fill in the time, just temporarily, I might start looking around for something to do with animals.'

'Well, what to do with animals? A lion tamer? A snake charmer? A cowgirl?'

'I don't know,' said Lulu. 'Maybe a vet's receptionist.'

'A vet's receptionist,' said Emma. 'Oh, Lulu, you've got a first-class degree in biochemistry. Wouldn't you be bored out of your mind?'

'Not half as bored as I'd be if I went back to university,' said Lulu. 'I know that's what you all want.'

Emma sighed, abandoning her attempt at discretion. 'Mom and Dad think you should at least give it a try,' she said.

'I know they do,' said Lulu. 'And I know you

do, too. And I'm sure Matthew agrees with you, and I'm pretty sure Mr Goncharoff thinks the same way, and probably so do Sophie and Mrs Scott-Ramsay and Dr Broody, too, if you asked them. But interestingly enough Tom the lodger, who is the only person in this entire line-up who is actually *at* a university, thinks I shouldn't. And I'd like you, please, to put on your thinking cap and think very, very long and very, very hard about this, and after you've had a good long hard think in your thinking cap, I'd like you to tell me if this might just conceivably suggest anything to you.'

'You talked to Tom the lodger?' said Emma.

'We had coffee together this morning,' said Lulu. 'We had quite a long talk about things, actually.'

'Did you, now?' said Emma, raising an interested eyebrow.

Which was, quite possibly, the sole thing that Emma could possibly have said that was more irritating that anything she had already said.

'Tom the lodger,' said Lulu, 'is a hundred years old.'

'He's thirty-nine,' said Emma. 'We share the same birthday, funnily. Mom gave him a card last year, and he and I compared dates.' She twirled her wine glass thoughtfully, diverted now from the question of Lulu's career. 'He seems like a very nice guy, actually,' she said.

'He's thirty-nine years old,' said Lulu. 'He's Mom and Dad's lodger.'

'Thirty-nine's not that old. And Dad's always said you were an old soul.' Emma nodded, examining the idea and liking it. 'He's obviously intelligent, and you need that.'

'I don't *need* anything,' said Lulu. 'I had a cup of coffee with my parents' middle-aged lodger to ask him, as someone who spends his life in the academic world, if he thought I should pursue an academic career. Which, by the way, he said he didn't recommend, which I thought was very interesting and quite sensible.'

But Grandma Jo had married a professor, she thought then, a little alarmedly.

But when she had fallen in love with him he had not been a professor, but a student at the university, with thick yellow hair and deep blue eyes.

'It was a bit like being back in a tutorial,' she said. Although with a particularly kind and understanding tutor, she carefully did not add. 'He's really absent-minded. He puts hot sauce on his scrambled eggs and hadn't even noticed that no one in England does that. He said he drove his ex-wife crazy.'

'Well, there you are,' said Emma. 'You're like two peas in a pod. You can both be absent-minded and drive each other crazy.'

But people were not required to fall in love with the next pea in the pod, thought Lulu. Grandma Jo had fallen in love with a charming young man with thick yellow hair, and he had fallen in love with her, and he had adored her.

'I wonder what he's doing,' said Emma, 'lodging in a room in someone else's house.'

'Don't know,' said Lulu. 'Don't care. His business, not mine.'

'I bet there's a story there,' Emma continued. 'You should ask Mom.'

'You must be mad,' said Lulu. 'I'm not going to ask Mom to pry into her lodger's secrets.'

'Aha!' Emma pointed her fork in triumph. 'You respect his privacy. That's a *very* good start.'

'You know something, Emma,' said Lulu. 'There are times when you can be really, really annoying.'

Concord, July 1867.

Dearest Amy,

It's late at night, but I can't go to bed without telling you of my vexation with Meg, for I fear if I don't tell *someone*, I shall fall prey to spontaneous combustion like wicked Mr. Krook in *Bleak House*. You recall how she plotted all last year to get me to marry John's work friend, the good-hearted but altogether uninteresting Jack Scott, bringing him to endless calls upon Pa when I 'happened' to be at home, issuing sudden invitations to walk into town at the precise time when he 'happened' to be there about his own errands, giving hints and sly looks in his presence, followed in his absence by rapturous sisterly lectures about the blessed companionship of the married state — although what precise manner of companionship she was recommending for *me* remains mysterious, since neither Jack Scott nor I have ever had two words to exchange with each other beyond

195

'Good day, Mr. Scott,' 'Good day, Miss March,' and on a particularly resplendent occasion, 'What agreeable weather we are enjoying, are we not?' You will recall how hopeful I was to hear he had begun to court Nan Green from out along the Lexington Road, you will recollect the jig of glee that I danced around the parlor to hear of their betrothal, you will remember my declaration on the day when the church bells rang out for their marriage, that that day was the happiest, not only of his life but of my own, too.

Well, it seems that our sister is not satisfied yet. This morning, Meg just 'happened' to pay a call while she was about her errands, and while she was here, just 'happened' to invite me to dinner tonight, adding that we would have the company of Jack and Nan Scott. Of course I said yes, for although I don't care to *marry* Jack Scott, I *like* him well enough, and Nan has vivacity enough for both of them, so the conversation would be assured to be amusing (why is it, Amy, that the jolliest of girls will sometimes marry the dullest of men?); and when Meg added that Demi had been particularly asking for Aunt Dodo, well, my presence was secured, for you know how those two little tyrants have me in their thrall, spoilt as they are.

Up I turned at the Dovecote at the appointed hour, bib and tucker on, bearing a large slice of Beth's gingerbread for the twins, a book from father for John, who is still Meg's

196

despair when he loses himself in his reading, and a couple of pots of Hannah's jelly and a posy of roses for Meg . . . only to find that Demi was not the only 'bacheldore' who was awaiting my arrival. There in the parlour were Jack and Nan Scott at one end of the sofa, and at the other, a stout gentleman with a high complexion and particularly well-polished boots, whom Meg presented with a flourish as 'Jack's brother George, newly arrived in town from Pennsylvania.'

To do Mr. George Scott credit, he appeared every bit as alarmed by my presence in the company as I was by his. For two pins, I'd have made my bolt for freedom right there and then, and spared both of our blushes; but before I could so much as move, Meg had steered me to the chair beside him, and begun.

Was I aware, Jo, that Mr. Scott was a voracious reader?

Well, hardly, since until five minutes before this, the fact of his very existence in this world had been a matter of blissful ignorance to me, let alone the question of how he was accustomed to spend his leisure hours.

Did he not observe, Mr. Scott, how tenderly Mrs. Brooke's sister played with the babies and how dearly they loved her?

Quite so, replied Mr. Scott, staring in appalled fascination as Demi smeared grass and molasses down one of Mrs. Brooke's sister's cheeks and onto her collar, while Daisy's latest caress effected total destruction on what few shreds remained of her hairstyle.

How were Papa's new slippers coming along, Jo, and was he aware, Mr. Scott, that Mrs. Brooke's sister was a particularly accomplished needlewoman? How was he settling into Concord, Mr. Scott? The town had a remarkable history and had played a prominent role in the Revolutionary War — perhaps Mrs. Brooke's sister might be prevailed upon to accompany him to visit some of the more interesting parts?

And so on and so on until by the end of dinner, Mr. Scott had pushed his chair back away from the table and halfway into the kitchen broom closet in terror, while I had retreated almost to the garden on mine in mortification.

'What on earth can have possessed you!' I said when they had left, which they did early, for Nan requires much rest these days and Mr. Scott had the appearance by this of one hunted by savages or bears. 'I don't know who was the more discomfited, him or me.'

'That you both were reluctant to push yourselves forward speaks well of your modesty and of his good sense,' she replied serenely, having picked up Demi's torn nightshirt and sewing away on it as if she had no other care in the world. 'I, for one, thought the occasion went particularly well, and look forward to many more until you become more at ease in each other's company.'

Is it marriage that has so addled our sister's wits, Amy? Why can she not understand that every woman in this world who still remains unmarried does not yearn to be coupled with any man who happens to be a bachelor? Meg used to be a good and sensible creature, but if this is the effect that domestic felicity has upon one, I might just choose to live out my days as a spinster instead.

Your loving — and determinedly heart-whole — sister,

Jo.

6

New York, Monday December 1867.

Dearest Meg,

Another encounter with my Herr B. upon the staircase, and, oh, how my heart soars. He spoke to me, Meg! He said, 'Gut efening, Mees Marsch,' and when I blushed and stammered like the foolish creature I become in his presence, he inclined that noble head — for *he* don't snub me, unlike some of the other young men, for being 'only a governess' — and added, 'I trust it goes vell viz you.' 'Very well, thank you,' I managed to reply, and then, visited by an inspiration, was emboldened to add, '*Zehr gut, danke.*' Those glorious blue eyes blazed as he looked at me with interest. 'You learn my language?' he asked. 'Trying to,' I told him, thinking of the poor old Professor who had all but plucked his beard from his chin in despair at me but an hour before. 'I am sure you vill do zehr vell,' he said. Zehr vell! Oh, Meg, I am in the very seventh heaven!

Your blissful sister,
Jo.

Wednesday.

Dear Meg,

A bleaker mood prevails today for I discover I have a rival. One of the Professor's other students of German, who is even more stupid at the language than I am, a pretty, lively young thing called Lucy, the daughter of a rich city merchant and stuffed to bursting with little airs and graces, whom I espied in the hallway from the second landing, standing with a confiding air and her hand upon *my* Herr B.'s arm, blushing and dimpling and tossing her curls, and begging him, oh, so coquettishly, to explain, 'Exactly where do your umlauts come from, Herr B., and why is there not one upon the word itself?' 'Out, you little hussy, and go to plague the homely stout old Professor with your foolish questions,' was my impulse to shout down the staircase at her. But I resisted, of course, and so must stand helpless and watch while Herr B., gallant as ever, smiled indulgently upon her and even seemed to enjoy her prattle just a little. But I was gratified to notice that he did not tell *her* that she 'vould do zehr vell' with the language, and, while it is true that all young men do like to be flirted with, I am sure that my Herr B. is far too sensible to fall too far for such silly girlish wiles. He is to be a professor of philosophy, for mercy's sake!

Yours, sobered but undaunted,
Jo.

Friday.

Dear Meg,

I have formed a plan. On New-Year's eve, there is to be a masquerade at the house, and quite the gala it is to be, I am told. I shall contrive a costume — don't know what, haven't any fine clothes, but I'll think of something, as we used in the theatricals at home — and disguise my voice, and when I have distracted myself by acting another character I know I'll be rid of this bashfulness which so hampers me when I'm in my Herr B.'s presence. I'll dance with him, and talk to him, and amuse him with nonsense, and fascinate him with conversation such as silly little Lucy never dreamed, and — once we are unmasked and he sees how jolly the stiff and awkward Mees Marsch can be when she unbends — he *will* fall in love with me! He must!

I kiss this letter as I send it to you, and let us hope the next one will bring the happiest tidings of all from your own,

Jo.

It was a glaring afternoon in the baked dusty heat of late summer, and for three weeks Lulu had been working in a pub. The people in the local veterinarians' offices she had applied to had been polite and friendly, and pleased to meet a fellow animal lover; they had taken her name and telephone number and promised to contact her should a post become available; however, they had all explained, the turnover of jobs in their pleasant and leisurely line of work was exceptionally slow unless someone were either pregnant or approaching retirement, which no one seemed to be. If Lulu needed work, they all recommended, she should not wait for a call from them, but find something else instead to fill in.

In fact, Lulu did not particularly need to find work immediately: Mr Goncharoff had left her with a severance pay which, while not lavish, would give her enough to live on for a few weeks at least, if she were careful, as Lulu was. But, partly through stubbornness, and partly in order to keep herself safely occupied until the academic year was underway without her, Lulu had decided to plunge straight into another job. Goncharoff's Antiques had closed on a Friday afternoon; on the following Monday morning, she had started to work the day shift as a summer relief barmaid at the Crown & Sceptre, in Islington.

Despite the regality of its name, the Crown & Sceptre was not a prepossessing pub. It did not offer a garden with shady trees and flowers hanging romantically from baskets, like the Albion, where Lulu's parents would sometimes stroll for a glass of wine on a light evening; it did not boast an attractive menu of organic foods simply but deliciously prepared, like the Barnesbury, where they would take themselves to dinner when neither could be bothered to cook. Summer positions in those pubs had long been taken by those luckier than Lulu, students and foreign visitors, who had applied early enough in the year to pick and choose their places of employment.

The Crown & Sceptre was a dank space at the unfashionable end of Upper Street, set between a dingy grocery and a chemist's shop smelling of cheap perfume; the beer it served was thin, and the Tasty English Fayre boasted on its menu consisted of watery shepherd's pie and questionable chicken curry, trundled into the kitchen daily already cooked in industrial-sized vats, and thrown into the microwave in individual portions, should any customer be unwary enough to order. The clients were few and depressed, sad men in fraying business suits who may, or may not, have been in employment, tight-curled elderly women exchanging medical histories between tuts of dismay and emphysemic coughs. It was the sort of place where a person would have to be desperate to accept employment; and Lulu, as Michelle the manager quickly made plain, the sort of person they would have to be desperate to employ.

Michelle was a thin-faced, thin-lipped young woman, with dyed jet black hair, and, at barely thirty, the beginnings of a frown line already discernible between her thinly plucked brows. She had disliked Lulu on sight, and her ill opinion had been confirmed when Lulu had mentioned that she had had previous experience serving behind the bar at her student union: Michelle did not approve of university graduates. Michelle, it quickly became plain, did not approve of anyone whom she perceived as coming from a more privileged background than her; and when she learned that Lulu lived in Belsize Park, and that her father travelled the world for his profession, then Lulu became irredeemably identified in her eyes as a spoilt rich girl who needed to be taught a lesson in life's realities. Behind the bar at St Andrew's, Lulu had been known as being rather efficient; at the Crown & Sceptre, try as she might, her counter top was never cleaned sufficiently for Michelle, her glasses never arranged neatly enough, her beer never drawn fast enough. But the Crown & Sceptre was desperate for a relief barmaid, and so had hired Lulu until the end of September, although Michelle doubted whether she would last until then: Lulu's sort, she knew, were not the type to honour their commitments.

'Don't worry about her,' the other daytime barmaid, Jasmine, would tell Lulu, reassuringly. 'She's just a miserable old cow.' Jasmine was plump and radiant, with coffee-coloured skin and a broad moonbeam of a smile. Jasmine's mum had been a school dinner lady and her gran a bus conductress; Jasmine liked pub work, she said, for the same reason her mum had liked the school and her gran had liked the buses, because it got them out into the world and around people. Jasmine liked people, and Lulu liked Jasmine, who was sunny and friendly, and hummed softly to herself as she worked. Unfortunately, it was not Jasmine who was in charge.

One of the few benefits of working at the Crown & Sceptre was that it was close enough to her parents' home for Lulu to visit the attic in her off hours. She was slowly eking out the unfolding of her great-great-grandmother's love story, allowing herself to open one envelope a week to savour the tale and picture the players: Grandma Jo hiding behind her hair as Lulu did when she felt insecure, wearing a sturdy skirt suit of brown or grey, with a tailored jacket over a plain white blouse; pretty little Lucy, all ruffles and ribbons in sickly sugary pink; and in between the two, handsome and dashing Herr B., who was as charming to poor girls as he was to rich, and in the end would choose Jo over Lucy to be his wife. Tracing back from the hundredth birthday party, Lulu had found photographs that she was almost sure were of Grandma Jo, going back to the turn of the last century. She had an intelligent face, as Lulu's father had remarked, but no one could ever have called her a beauty. Luckily, she had had other qualities, which had attracted the love of the yellow-haired and glamorous Herr B., of whom, for some reason, Lulu could not find a single likely image. Maybe he had not liked to have his photograph taken.

Sitting now in the dusty comfort of the cool attic, Lulu looked at her watch and sighed, wishing she could spend longer there, looking through photographs, half dreaming, half imagining the long ago love affair between the ugly duckling governess and the handsome young student. The last envelope from New York bore a January postmark, and Lulu had been saving for a special treat the occasion when she would open it and read the story of how love must finally have bloomed at the New Year's Eve party. She looked at it wistfully now, feeling she could happily use a treat at that moment; but Jason, the evening bartender, had developed stomach flu and Michelle had informed Lulu that afternoon that she had volunteered to take his shift on top of her own. 'Unless,' she had added, sarcastically, 'you've been invited to dinner at Buckingham Palace instead.'

'Don't let her bully you,' Jasmine had advised. 'Tell her you have been invited to Buckingham Palace, that'll shut her up.'

But that was all very well for Jasmine to say, whose family had even fewer advantages than Michelle's. Lulu was due back at the pub in less than an hour; and the letter where Grandma Jo finally found her love was one which deserved a certain ceremony. She replaced the small envelopes inside the large one, laid the package on the shelf, and left the attic.

★   ★   ★

'Hi, honey.' Fee was coming in from the garden, a bowl of freshly picked tomatoes in her hand. If she had noticed the volume of time that Lulu was spending in the attic lately, she gave no sign. 'Would you like a cup of tea? Your father's on his way home — he's off to Greece first thing tomorrow, so we're having an early supper.'

'Ummm . . . ' Lulu had been avoiding seeing her parents together lately. Neither of them approved of the Crown & Sceptre — her mother because she thought they worked her too hard, her father, he said, because its beer made him yearn for the rich, full flavour of yesterday's dishwater — and when together they tended to gang up on her about it.

'Do stay, sweetie,' said Fee. 'He asked me the other day if he'd been fantasizing having a middle daughter as well as an extra wife. I think he thinks you're mad at him.' She set the tomatoes on the table, and frowned at Lulu. 'You're not, are you?'

'No.' Although occasionally irritated by her father, Lulu did not on the whole get seriously angry with him. But it was true that she had seen less of him lately than she had of her mother; and, having been challenged, her instinct was to become defensive. 'Although he can talk about not being around — he's never here.'

'Would you have liked a dad who was around more?' Setting out plates of food, Fee looked up a little anxiously at her daughter. 'My dad wasn't there much, either, he was always off flying somewhere, but I never really thought about it — he was sort of there when he was there, and I always knew he loved me, which was the important thing. Would you have liked a dad who came home every evening like other dads?'

'No, Dad's fine.' Or rather, thought Lulu, but knowing better than to voice the thought aloud, he was fine when he was not trying to talk her into a career choice. 'Well, he's fine if you like that sort of thing.'

'Good, because it's kind of late to trade him in at this point.' Fee inspected the table — pink

208

ham, brown bread, scarlet radishes and tomatoes, green salad leaves and a jar of many-
coloured zinnias from the garden. 'I used to
cook,' she said a little doubtfully. 'But with
summer food you don't really need to. Anyway,
it's far too hot tonight to slave over a stove.'

'Claire cooks proper meals.' David Atwater,
tramping in on heavy feet, exuding masculine
bonhomie. 'Soup for a starter, home-made meat
pies with mashed potatoes and gravy, and suet
pudding and custard for dessert. Winter and
summer alike, she says it's what she was put on
this earth to do.'

'It's just as well I have Claire around, then,'
Fee told him. 'She'll keep me company when
you drop dead of a heart attack.'

'I'm not going to. Claire's already donated me
her heart as a spare. She keeps going on a little
kitchen timer — she asked for a battery but I
told her it was too expensive. Good evening, ball
and chain.' Perhaps in reaction to his wife's
liberal sprinkling of her conversation with honeys
and sweeties, David tended not to use
conventional endearments for those he loved
best. He kissed Fee, and reached into a cupboard
for a bottle of wine. 'Hello, Lu, what a nice
surprise. Glass of wine?'

'I'll just have a cup of tea,' said Lulu. 'I have to
get back to the pub.'

'Ah, yes, the pub-a-grub-dub.' He poured
himself a glass and sipped appreciatively. 'It
wouldn't do to go back smelling of real wine
— you'd only confuse them. How's it going
there, anyway?'

'It's going.' Lulu tipped milk into her tea and looked warily at her father.

'Any fisticuffs broken out over illicitly acquired dentures? Anyone keel over dead from watery hop poisoning?'

'Not lately.'

'Pity, I could have used a cheap laugh at the expense of my neighbours.' He frowned. 'I don't like that place, Lulu. Is there any other news on the employment front?'

Lulu sighed, heavily.

'No, Dad,' she said. 'No news. None whatsoever. Not even a whisper. OK?'

'Nothing at all?' he asked. 'Not even something from the vet's office, which would at least be an improvement?'

'Nope.'

'Any possible other thoughts of something else you might be thinking of doing?'

'Absolutely none.'

David sighed in his turn. 'Any other question I might ask that wouldn't lead to a dead end?' he asked.

Reluctantly, Lulu smiled. 'Probably not,' she said.

'Poor Lulu,' said Fee. 'We're always bugging her about her work — let's talk about something else. I heard from Aunt Amy, Lulu. The exhibition opened and it seems to be going well, even without Grandma Cissie's recipes. And she loved the photograph of Grandma Jo — she does remember that day, although she hadn't known there was a photograph of it. Have you found anything else interesting up there?'

'This and that,' said Lulu. 'I found some pictures of you at the Collective. You looked scary.'

'You don't know the half,' said David. 'She was terrifying. We met at a party in Boston. She walked in wearing dungarees and boots, she'd just had her head shaved to make a point about something or other and I turned to the person I was talking to and said, 'I'm going to marry that girl.' And I did.'

The story, one of David's favourites, had long acquired its comfortable niche in family lore; but now, with her mind awakened by Grandma Jo's romance, Lulu wondered for the first time what her mother's experience had been of falling in love.

'Did you know you were going to marry him, Mom?' she asked.

'I don't know.' Fee looked across the table at David and smiled. 'All I knew was that there was this eccentric English guy following me around who talked like someone out of Monty Python, and we started to spend time together, and the next thing I knew I was marrying him and moving to England.'

Between Fee and Grandma Jo, thought Lulu, it seemed to be a family trait to marry a foreigner. She looked at her father, trying to see him as a stranger might — although presentable, she thought, he was no Herr B.

'Was he handsome?' she asked.

'Sort of.' Fee thought. 'He had nice teeth, for an Englishman. But it was more that he made me laugh than anything about the way he looked.'

'Don't mind me,' said David. 'Just ignore me

211

and carry on talking as if I weren't there. Oh, wait, you already are.'

'He was very dry,' said Fee. 'Very sort of deadpan, a classic witty Brit. And he was kind, too, which is important, and he respected me, which is essential, and we seemed to want the same sorts of things out of life. Anyway, I married him. Lulu, won't you have something to eat with us? There's raspberries for dessert if you can wait around.'

'I can't,' said Lulu. 'I really do have to get back to the pub, Mom, I'm late already and they're short-staffed tonight.'

'Oh, bugger the pub,' said David. 'I hardly ever see you these days, Lulu. Tell you what, why don't you give up the bloody Hat and Stick and come and meet me in Santorini at the end of the week? Get away from things and get yourself some beach time?'

'Great, Dad, thanks.' For all of David's daughters, the charm of joining him on his travels had long worn thin. 'And what am I supposed to do, stuck alone in the hotel while you're off checking out the state of the local public toilets?'

'I've been led to believe that people can give themselves a good time in Santorini,' said David. 'And oddly enough, you wouldn't be alone, either. My friend Jane will be joining me — remember Jane, Rob's mum? She's not been very well, so she's coming out for a break. Maybe you and she could keep each other company a little bit.'

'Oh, score, Dad,' said Lulu. 'You and your

middle-aged invalid college friend, it's the weekend I've always dreamed of.' She stopped. 'Is this your friend Jane?' she asked.

'Well, yes, Lulu,' said David. 'I'd say that, all things considered, my friend Jane is pretty much the category that my friend Jane would fall into.'

'Your college friend Jane, who lives in Cambridge.'

'That's the one,' said David. 'Jane.'

'The one,' said Lulu, 'who works as a careers counsellor.'

There was a silence, while David and Fee exchanged glances.

'She does other things, too,' said David, after a moment. 'She listens to music, she votes in elections, she watches films. I'm not going to ask her to wear a bell around her neck and shout 'unclean' because of what she does for a living — you wouldn't even have to talk about careers if you don't want to.'

'Right, Dad.' Lulu swallowed her tea and stood up. 'Have a nice time in Greece. I have to go back to the pub now, which is my job, which I work hard at, and which I wish you'd just occasionally show a shred of respect for. Bye, Dad. Bye, Mom. Bye, Toby. Thanks for not bugging me, Toby. I'll bring you a nice catnip mouse next time I come to show my appreciation.'

★　★　★

'I'm not kidding.' Lulu brandished her coffee mug indignantly. 'Five minutes into the conversation. Five. Tops. And he was pushing a careers

213

counsellor on me. Can you believe it?'

'What I can't believe,' said Emma, 'is just how many hours a person is capable of lolling in bed on a Saturday morning when she knows there are people waiting to talk to her. Doesn't the little brat understand the seriousness of the situation?'

It was the day after Sophie's big scene with Dr Broody, and Emma had presented herself at the flat at an early hour, expectant for gossip. Sophie, however, had yet to put in an appearance.

'She was out late last night,' said Lulu. 'Celebrating with Rupert. He does a killer trick with a beer bottle and a five pound note, which must be emotionally draining.'

'And she's probably quite tired anyway,' said Charlie. 'She's been working really hard on this, rehearsing with Jamie till all hours.'

'It's eleven fifteen.' Emma looked at the clock on the kitchen wall. 'She has till eleven thirty. Then I'm going up there to get her.'

At 11.29, Sophie yawned in, in white T-shirt and faded pink pyjama bottoms, yellow hair rumpled, smiling sleepily into the sunshine.

'How tall?' said Emma.

'Hmm?' Sophie squinted uncomprehending at her sister. 'Morning, everyone. Nice to see you, Emma, have you left me any coffee? Ooh, marmalade.'

'You seem unclear on my needs,' said Emma. 'I need to know how tall Dr Broody is. I need to know many things about him, actually, but most of all, I need to know how tall.'

'What's she talking about?' Sophie accepted a plate of toast from Charlie. 'Thanks, Charles. Did you enjoy the play last night? I heard Brenda Blethyn's amazing but Sir Anthony Absolute's been so drunk all week they've been threatening to send the understudy on.'

'Sophie.' Leaning forward, Emma waved a hand in front of her sister's eyes. 'Hello, Sophie. My name is Emma, and I'm your elder sister, you might remember me from the maternity ward, where I was dragged to see you at the age of six hours, even though it meant missing *Jackanory*, which, believe me, would have been a very great deal more interesting. We don't live together any more, but I've come to visit you because . . . Do you know why I've come to visit you, Sophie?'

'Actually, no,' said Sophie. 'But it's nice to see you anyway, Emma. Nice marmalade, Lulu, it's different from the usual sort, isn't it?' She swallowed an enthusiastic mouthful. 'Chunkier,' she commented. 'Nice.'

'I told you,' Lulu said to Emma. 'She's been like this all week. You mention the word gossip, and she turns into a fourteenth-century Mongolian peasant confronted with an iPod.'

'Leave it to me,' said Emma. She turned to her sister. 'Sophie, I have a question for you.'

'Yes?' Sophie looked up, helpfully, from her second slice of toast.

'What,' said Emma, 'is Dr Broody really like?'

Sophie pursed her lips, thinking. 'He's a very good actor,' she said at last. She thought some more. 'Very reactive,' she added.

215

There was silence, while Emma stared at Lulu, and Charlie smiled quietly into her coffee.

'Reactive,' said Lulu, then.

'It's very important,' said Sophie. 'You don't want someone who just sits there and doesn't react. That's the kiss of death. Ask Brenda Blethyn.'

'OK.' Emma tried again. 'How tall is he?'

'Tall?' Sophie frowned her puzzlement at the question, but shrugged tolerantly. 'Tall enough, I suppose.'

'Yes, but *how* tall? I can't express to you strongly enough how essential this information is.'

'I don't know!' said Sophie. 'He's probably a couple of inches taller than me. It really isn't important. If you're a halfway decent actor, you can make yourself as tall or as short as you like.'

'Sophie . . . ' Emma leaned further across the table, dangerously clutching a butter knife.

'I'll tell you something that *is* important about your *Dr Broody*, though,' said Sophie. She finished her toast, and reached for a piece of kitchen roll to wipe her fingers. 'Which is that after we'd wrapped the scene, I went to the loo. And when I came out I overheard Colin talking to the director. And he was talking about me. He was asking where I'd come from. He said I had — and I quote — 'definitely something that was worth watching'. *And* . . . ' Bunching up the kitchen roll, she tossed it triumphantly into the air. 'He said he thought he and I had had good chemistry and he looked forward to working with me again!'

'Sophie!' As one, her two sisters descended on her with hugs, while even quiet Charlie gave a whoop of delight.

'That does it,' she said. 'We're going out to dinner tonight, somewhere nice, my treat, and you're neither of you saying no. That's fantastic, Sophie! You're really on your way now.'

'It gets better!' Attempt at cool abandoned, Sophie had leaped from her chair and was performing pirouettes in front of the stove. 'He came up through small parts himself and, because he really does seem to be a nice guy, he occasionally does pick people he likes and puts in a word for them. And he obviously has some say-so, too, because the last person he picked was Miranda Fentiman, you know, the girl who plays the social worker? Well, she originally only came on for one episode, just like I did, but Colin liked her, too, and now she's a semi-regular. And it gets better still because *St Luke's* give you time off to do more serious stuff, too — she did *The Seagull* last year at the Orange Tree, and I hear that now she's even talking to the people at the Vagabond, which is only like the best theatre in the entire universe and the whole of world history, so not too bad to look forward to, is it?' She finished a pirouette, and spread her arms wide in an elaborate curtsey. 'Behold, Dame Sophie Atwater, legend of the Vagabond Theatre!'

'Sophie, this is amazing.' Lulu rose to join her, turning the solo into a stately minuet. 'We'll be boasting about you before the year is out. You'll be our sister, the famous actress.'

'I knew Dr Broody was a nice guy!' said Emma. 'And he's right, too, you *do* have something worth watching.' She raised her brow, hopefully. 'When you say he was asking about you . . . '

'Purely professionally,' said Sophie. 'I don't think I'm his type.' She twirled solemnly past Lulu, and swept her gaze around the room. 'I don't think anyone here is, if you know what I'm saying.'

'Dr Broody?' Emma's jaw dropped: Colin Hobbes was rarely out of the gossip columns, and almost never without a pretty girl on his arm.

'Well, what do you think they're going to do, take out an ad in the papers?' Sophie dropped to a chair, suddenly serious. 'And none of you are allowed to mention this, by the way. Not a word to anyone, not any of you, and I'm specially looking at *you*, Emma Gossipykins Atwater. If I get on in this profession, I might be telling you things sometimes that you can't talk about ever to anyone, and I have to be able to trust you about it, because if I can't trust you, I can't talk to you any more. Do you understand?'

'I understand,' said Emma, reluctantly. 'Lips are sealed about Dr Broody, I promise. What I don't understand is why you'll tell us something like this about him, but you won't tell me how tall he is.'

★ ★ ★

It was strange, thought Lulu a couple of days later, mopping a beer puddle from the

218

countertop, how much lonelier she could feel at the Crown & Sceptre than she ever had at Goncharoff's. At Goncharoff's there had been long periods when little had happened, drowsy afternoons when the sun hung heavy in the air and there had been no sound but the rustle of papers on Mr Goncharoff's desk or the flicking of Sasha through his catalogues; but there had been peace there, too, Lulu thought, and pleasantly unspoken companionship. Here, where customers spilled cheap beer and vinegary wine and Michelle watched her relentlessly, avid for a cause for criticism, there was neither.

Then give it up, suggested a corner of her mind. It was certainly not what she was going to do for a career, so walk away. Find something else to do, and let them find another relief barmaid.

But she had committed to work until the end of September, and if she quit before then, she would leave both Michelle and Jasmine in a difficult situation. Which Michelle was sure that Lulu was going to do anyway. And one thing that Lulu was not about to do was prove Michelle right.

'Are you bored?' Michelle herself was standing over her, her frown mark more pronounced than ever. Lulu realized that she had stopped mopping, and was standing with the cloth idle in her hand.

'Sorry,' she said. 'I just got distracted for a moment.'

'I'm sorry you have to come to work, love,' said Michelle. 'Sorry Daddy doesn't make quite enough to give you a private income. It must be terribly hard for you.'

You don't have to do this, her mind reminded her.

But if she gave it up before the end of September, then Michelle would be right.

'Give me a kiss.'

'What?' Startled, she looked up. A plump young man wearing an Arsenal shirt was leaning over the counter, smiling confidently.

'It's my birthday,' he said. 'You've got to give me a kiss.'

'Excuse me?' She stared at him, incredulous.

'You've got to give him a kiss.' Another young man, thinner and ferret-faced, leaned forward to explain: it was clearly not their first pub visit of the day. 'It's his birthday.'

Lulu sighed. Although not a threatening situation, this could shape into an extremely irritating one. From the corner of her eye, she saw Michelle settle with interest to see how Lulu would handle it.

'What do you want to drink?' she asked.

'Oh, go on, love,' said the plump young man. 'Just a little kiss, just for my birthday.'

Lulu gritted her teeth. 'I'm not going to give you a kiss,' she said. 'I'll pour you a drink, though. What do you want to drink?'

'Give him a kiss,' said the thin young man. 'What's the matter with you, love? It's his birthday — be nice to him.'

'What do you want to drink?' repeated Lulu. 'Because that's all that's on offer here, believe me.'

'Oh, awl that's orn orfer,' repeated the thin young man mincingly. 'What's wrong, love — think you're better than we are, do you?'

'Of course she's bleeding better than you.' Jasmine, swiping cheerfully from the other end of the counter. 'My gran's budgie's better than both of you two put together.'

This was the language the young men understood. They relaxed over the counter, laughing and making mock-kissing noises.

'Piss off,' she said, smiling. 'What d'you want to drink?'

'Your tits,' said the plump young man, dissolving into giggles.

'Don't mind him,' said the thin young man. 'It's his birthday. Show some respect, Gavin, eh? We'll have two pints of bitter, my lovely, if you would be so good.'

'Here you go.' Jasmine quickly pulled two pints and slapped them on the bar. 'And we'll have no more cheek from you, or I'm calling the manager.'

'How do you do that?' said Lulu when the young men had shambled cheerfully to a table. 'Talk to them like that and not make them hate you?'

'You just do.' Jasmine, who had never fallen prey to introspection in her life, shrugged. 'You've just got to be firm, haven't you? Show them who's boss.' She smiled, kindly, at Lulu. 'Don't think so hard about it, Lulu. Just do it.'

But how do you do it? wondered Lulu, returning to her mopping. How do you talk to people without alienating or confusing them, in the way Jasmine so easily did, and Sophie, and Sasha Goncharoff, and, yes, young Herr Bhaer, whose genes Lulu had inherited every bit as much as had Sophie, but, unfairly, not, it seemed, that part of them? How do you manage to be charming?

'You look lost in thought,' said a voice. It was Charlie, glossy-haired and elegant in a red silk top and dark linen skirt, looking as out of place in the Crown & Sceptre as a long-stemmed rose in a cabbage patch.

'What are you doing here?' said Lulu.

'I went to my hairdresser on Upper Street, so I thought I'd come and see your new place of employ.' She looked around at the beige walls and stained and patterned carpet. 'It's not exactly the Palais-Royal, is it? Can I have a glass of wine?'

'I really wouldn't,' said Lulu. 'I'm off in a couple of minutes, let's go to the Albion.'

As the two young women walked out together, Lulu caught the eye of the thin young man, who nodded to himself with the air of a mystery solved.

★　★　★

'You did not,' remarked Charlie mildly when they were ensconced in the garden of the Albion in a shady spot under the wisteria tree, 'look like you were having the time of your life in there.'

'It's honest work,' said Lulu. 'We can't all cater to people who are rich enough to stay at The Fitzcharles.' Then relented: alone with Charlie, she was able to let down the wall of defensiveness that so many others found impenetrable. 'But it's not really what I'm cut out for,' she admitted, 'looking after people and spreading good cheer and such.' She looked across the table, thoughtfully, at her friend: it occurred to her that, although the scale of expenditure at the Crown & Sceptre was hardly that of The Fitzcharles, still, what Charlie did for her living was not so very far removed from what Lulu was currently doing for hers. The difference was that Charlie, unlike Lulu, seemed to enjoy it. '*You're* quite good at it, though, aren't you?'

'It seems to be in my genes,' Charlie nodded. 'I do like arranging things so that people are happy, it's the old Irish hospitality in me, I think. And of course, it's been so easy for me with my dad and the hotels, so I'm lucky there.'

'It's a funny thing, luck, isn't it?' It had been too long, Lulu thought, since she and Charlie had sat alone together, as they used to when they were at university, undistracted by Charlie's career or Lulu's sisters, turning over the world and its workings. 'You've got your career and lots of money so you're lucky there, but you lost your mum, which is really unlucky. Do you miss her?'

'Mum?' Charlie twirled her wine glass thoughtfully: she had been hardly more than a baby when her mother had died, and rarely spoke of her. 'I can't say I really miss *her* as such, because I don't really remember her. There's always been Maeve in the background, although she's always been sort of off in her own world of cookery. It's really been my dad and my brother Liam and me, and we all get along really well, even though Dad and Liam are always off travelling the world. I know we're unusual, but it's the way it is, and it's what seems normal to me. That's why it's so interesting for me to watch you and your family, so many women, and all living so close to each other, and talking things over all the time; it's something I don't know. It feels sort of exotic somehow, like living in a foreign country.'

'Well, make sure you keep taking your anti-malaria pills.' Lulu pushed at her glass, wondering how Charlie would have dealt with the two young men in the pub. More gracefully than she had, doubtless, as her great-great-grandfather Bhaer had dealt gracefully with the annoying young Lucy. 'How's Javier?' she asked then, her mind turning to romance. 'You haven't talked about him lately.'

'Oh.' Charlie grimaced and sighed, pushing a puff of air through her cheeks. 'I don't know what to do about Javier. We get close and then we get non-close, you know? I know he likes me, but something seems to stop him.'

'Indecisive guys.' Lulu nodded sympathetically. She had been plagued at university by boys who did not know their own mind; stylish and beautiful Charlie had always been popular, and with men who had long outgrown the indecisive phase. 'Remember that awful Will, who kept on telephoning me to ask whether I'd mind if he telephoned me and then not telephoning? It's the worst, you just want to shake them.'

'Well, it's not so much that he's indecisive, actually,' said Charlie. She looked down, blushing a little. 'We really do have a little bit of a genuine problem here, because I am . . . well . . . I'm sort of the boss's daughter.'

'Oh.' This was an aspect which had not occurred to Lulu.

'And he's obviously a decent enough guy that this matters to him,' said Charlie. 'Which of course complicates it further.'

'Oh.' Lulu looked down into her glass. Each element of the situation Charlie described to her was so far outside her own realm of experience that she did not know what else to say.

'I don't know what to do, Lulu!' Now having opened the floodgates, Charlie for once was the one doing all the talking. 'It obviously really is an issue, and I don't know whether to talk to him about it or not to talk to him. I'm not good at talking to people, you know that. And besides, if I did talk to him, what would I say? 'Hi, Javier, I have reason to believe you fancy me, and, since I know that I fancy you quite probably more than I've ever fancied anyone in my whole life, do you think we might leave aside for a few minutes the minor fact that your employer just happens to be my father, who just happens to be one of the most powerful hoteliers in the world and in a position to make or break your entire chosen career with a single phone call, in order that you and I, his daughter, might get together to discuss the question of whether we both might want to start a relationship?' How romantic is that? What if he just turns in terror and runs away? And . . . if he does say yes, where does that leave the romantic part for *me*? Don't I have a right to want to be pursued? But on the other hand, I do also know that this is an unusual situation, and if I do hold out for him to make the first move, then am I doing myself out of a possibly wonderful relationship, which I think this really could be? I've thought about this and thought about it, and I just don't know what to do.' She stopped and looked down again at her glass. 'I think,' she added quietly, 'that the answer to your earlier question, is that, yes, there are times when I miss my mother very much indeed.'

'Oh, well.' Now able at last to make a helpful contribution, Lulu drained her glass, stood, and pulled her friend to her feet. 'If a mother's what you need, that's very easily sorted. Come along.'

★   ★   ★

Fee was sitting in the small, lush garden behind the family home, reading a book under a climbing white rose bush, its flowers beginning to gleam in the gathering dusk, a dish of plump black olives to her hand. She looked up when her visitors arrived, and her face lit.

'How lovely,' she said. 'Charlie, don't you look pretty, red is definitely your colour. Lulu, my darling, you look pooped, I'm tempted to report that place to the Slave Labour Board. Sit down and have an olive, I decided your father needn't be the only one gorging on them this week.'

Lulu perched on a bench and sampled an olive.

'A bit too much oregano, but otherwise very nice,' she pronounced. 'Mom, Charlie has a boyfriend problem.'

'Lulu!' Charlie, who had been hoping for a more gentle introduction to the topic, blushed crimson.

'Well, you have,' said Lulu. 'That's why we're here. And we could spend the next quarter of an hour being polite and talking about olives and colour schemes, or we could get down to business. So go ahead.' She took another olive, and nodded encouragingly. 'Mom's really good at this sort of stuff. She does it for a living, remember.'

'I know she does,' said Charlie. 'And I'm thinking that maybe she's been doing it all day long and doesn't necessarily feel like doing it all over again in the evening.'

'What are you talking about?' said Lulu. 'It comes naturally to her. Like painting to Picasso, or chasing mice to Toby.'

'Lulu,' said Charlie. 'I really don't think — '

'Lulu, honey,' said Fee. 'I have an idea. Why don't you go to the bathroom, run yourself a nice long shower and change into some of your old clothes? Then maybe go into the kitchen — we have cheese, eggs, spinach, all sorts of good things — and fix us something delicious for supper? We'll open a bottle of wine, have ourselves a nice meal and then I'll send you girls home in a taxi. Sound good?'

★   ★   ★

A week later, Charlie came home from work with pink in her cheeks and a smile on her face.

'What's Fee's favourite flower?' she asked Lulu, busy about roasting a chicken.

'Mom's?' Sophie looked up from her latest *Stage and Screen*, and snorted. 'Try anything with petals and a stem. That should just about cover it.'

'Why do you ask?' said Lulu, narrowing her eyes hopefully. Charlie had not told her what she and Fee had said in the garden that evening, and Fee had privately forbidden Lulu to ask.

'Well.' Charlie sat down at the table, the colour in her cheeks deepening. 'I talked to him.'

'Who?' Scenting a story, Sophie abandoned her paper. 'Who did you talk to? What am I missing?'

'Shut up, Sophie, this is grown-up stuff.' Lulu closed the oven door on the chicken and joined Charlie at the table. 'And?' she asked.

'And what?' said Sophie. 'What are you two talking about?'

'It's over your head, little snot-nosed sister. Go on, Charlie, spill. What happened?'

'I talked to Javier, Sophie,' said Charlie. 'The business manager at work?'

'She knows who Javier is,' said Lulu. 'What happened?'

'Well,' said Charlie, 'I was getting a bit confused, Sophie, about whether he wanted to ask me out or not, so Lulu very kindly took me to chat to your mother about it, and we sat in the garden and talked it over, and she did a funny sort of thing, really, in that she didn't actually give me advice as such about what to do, but she kept on and on asking me questions about all sorts of things, what was going on, what I was feeling, what would I feel if this happened, what would I feel if that happened, until in the end I found I was coming up with the answers all by myself.'

'She does that,' nodded Sophie.

'I know she does that,' said Lulu. 'We all know she does that. Charlie, I am dying from suspense here.'

'So she and I talked it over for quite a long time, actually, and she kept on asking questions, and I kept on figuring things out, and in the end, we both agreed that, although it would be difficult and possibly embarrassing, it was probably the best thing in the long run if I at least tried to have a conversation with him, and find out what was going on.'

'Finally,' said Lulu. 'At last we're up to a bit which is news to me, too. So you talked to him today.'

'So I talked to him today,' agreed Charlie. She looked down at the table, and smiled. 'And . . . he's taking me to see flamenco on Saturday.'

'Yes!' Sophie sprang up and flung her arms in the air, clacking imaginary castanets. 'Let's hear it for Carlita y Javier, lovers for the ages!'

'That's wonderful, Charlie,' said Lulu, more quietly, as Sophie stamped and twirled through the kitchen in triumph. Then remembering their earlier conversation, 'It *is* wonderful, isn't it?'

'Oh, yes.' Charlie nodded, ducking her head a little shyly, as she did when excited. 'He said he's been wanting to have the conversation for ages, but didn't know how to. We cleared the air about Dad, we agreed that we know it's going to be complicated, but we . . . well, we said lots of things, but the most important thing is, we agreed that we both really — really — want to give this a try.' Breaking her reserve for a moment, she grinned at the table, wagging her head in glee like a little girl. 'God, Lulu, I can't believe it's actually happening! And, you know, we'd never have done it if I hadn't talked to him, and I'd never have had the nerve without talking to your mum that night. She's amazing, she really is.'

'Ha.' Dancing past, Sophie stopped in mid-stamp to toss her head. 'Even I'd figured that one out by now.'

★　★　★

The next day was Friday, and Lulu found it even harder than most Fridays to go into work. It was not, she thought, dejectedly polishing glasses, that she was not pleased and excited for Charlie's good news, as she had been delighted and proud for Sophie's; but sometimes she wondered, too, if it would ever be Lulu's turn to come home with good news, to be exclaimed over and danced around in triumph, to wake up in the morning and feel a smile beginning as she woke, spreading warmth through her body from the top of her scalp to her toes, instead of a grimly cold sinking in her stomach as she thought of the day ahead.

'Watch out!' Michelle pushed past her, carrying a tray of empty glasses. Then, 'Oh, for heaven's sake!'

Startled, Lulu had jumped, dropping her own glass to the floor, where it shattered into pieces.

Michelle sighed heavily, leaned against the counter, and watched while Lulu went for the dustpan and brush to clear up the pieces.

'You've missed a piece,' she said, when Lulu thought she was done.

'Sorry.' Lulu bent to pick up the remaining shard. 'Ow.' She had picked it up clumsily, and it had grazed her finger.

'Oh, poor ickle fing,' said Michelle. 'Hassums cuttum-self?'

'Not badly,' said Lulu.

'I can see that,' said Michelle. 'And there's no need to look so put-upon, either. You don't have to do this job, you know, if it's so awful for you. You can always quit early and leave me and Jasmine in the lurch here, which I know you're dying to. I bet if you asked Daddy nicely, he'd send you back to university for another year.'

Lulu located the faintly unsavoury first-aid kit under the counter, bandaged her finger in silence and returned to her glasses. When her lunch break came, she thought, she would go back to the attic: it seemed to be where she was happiest these days.

★ ★ ★

231

Fee had adopted Emma's earlier suggestion of placing a notice on the front door at times when she felt it necessary, and the family now knew that a small sticker in the shape of a rainbow signified that she was seeing a client in particular need and requested quiet in the house. There was one such there today, so Lulu opened the door with particular care, laying a finger to her lips at Toby, curled contentedly on a chair cushion beside the hall table, who greeted her with a sleepy silent yawn and outstretched paw, and promptly returned to sleep. From her father's study on the left of the house came David's voice, talking quietly to someone on the telephone, and she stood, irresolute, for a moment, wondering whether to go to speak to him. She had not seen him since he had returned from Greece, and was by no means sure that she had forgiven him for their last conversation.

Whoever he was talking to seemed to need some reassurance.

'It's going to be OK,' he was saying, his voice quieter and more serious than any he was accustomed to use with his family. 'It's going to be fine, I promise. It's all going to be fine, sweetheart.'

Still in the hall, Lulu froze. Her father, she knew, had curious nicknames for some of those close to him. He called Fee ball and chain and blight of his existence; he called his sister, Lulu's sweet-natured Aunt Katy, Attila the Hun; he and his best friend Phil, in legacy of a joke long since passed into the mists of forgotten hilarity, had for many decades addressed each other as

232

honey-bunch. He did not call anyone whom she knew of sweetheart.

'Me, too,' he said now. 'Me, too, sweetheart, oh, me, too. No, Fee hasn't noticed. Fee doesn't seem to notice very much of anything about me these days. I'll see you tomorrow, then. Bye, sweetheart. Bye, Jane.'

More quietly than she had ever done in her life, Lulu opened and closed the front door, and stole silently down the front steps to the street outside.

★   ★   ★

Lulu had always thought — on the rare occasions when she had thought about her parents' marriage — that that marriage was a happy one. Her parents made each other laugh and did not appear to fight unduly, functioned happily during their time apart but seemed pleased to see each other when they reunited. It was true that her mother, with her American vowels and outspoken opinions, hardly fitted the stereotype of the middle-class English wife; but then her mother made it plain that she had never aspired to fit any sort of stereotype anywhere. It was true, too, that her father was in the habit of making jokes about a fantasy wife who was as different from his real wife as it was possible to be; but then her father made jokes about most things. Or rather, thought Lulu now, walking away from the house and down the streets that she had known all her life but that were now subtly changed, tilted on a different axis as if she were drunk or in a fever, her father made jokes about most things when he was talking to his wife and to his daughters; apparently, when he was talking to the woman called Jane whom he also addressed as sweetheart, he did not make jokes at all.

Lulu tried to summon to mind all that she knew about her father's friend Jane. She was a friend of her father's rather than of the family's, an old friend from his university days, short-legged and slight, with dull brown hair, a mild manner, and the air of someone who expected to be disappointed. She had had a hard life, Lulu had always been told: her husband had abandoned her several years into their marriage, leaving her alone to raise their son, a slightly unpleasant boy, who had once stolen Sophie's Mars bar and later denied it. She lived in a poky house in Cambridge, was a good cook, and had once served a bread made with cheese and rosemary which Lulu a little shamefully remembered considerably more vividly than anything Jane had ever actually said to her. Lulu had met Jane maybe half a dozen times in her life, and each time she had Fee had reminded all her daughters in advance of the meeting to be kind and polite because of Jane's hard life. Fee had always been pleasant to Jane, but Lulu realized now that she had no idea of whether or not she genuinely liked her. And now David was making telephone calls to Jane when he thought he could not be overheard, sitting downstairs in his office while his wife was upstairs giving counsel to a stranger, calling Jane sweetheart, and confiding to her about his marriage.

Fee hasn't noticed, he had said to Jane. And then, sadly, *Fee doesn't seem to notice very much of anything about me these days*. Lulu wondered now exactly what it was that Fee hadn't noticed that she presumably should have. She wondered — since her father, at least, was apparently not as happily married as she had until now supposed him — exactly how unhappy he was and for how long he had been so. She remembered a Sunday a couple of weeks previously when she had walked into the house to hear her parents arguing and her father shouting, 'For Christ's sake, Fee, will you for just once in my life let me finish a whole sentence without interrupting me!' and remembered that she had been mildly amused at the time, but wondered now if she should rather have been concerned. She wondered if David's jokes about Claire had really been jokes at all, or whether they had been the only way he could find to express that he would rather spend his life with a less assertive sort of woman than her mother, a woman more like, yes, Jane. She wondered, if her father were now deciding he would rather deal with Jane, who was so very different from Fee, whether he would have preferred to have daughters who were different, too.

A car horn sounded, urgently, and someone grabbed her by the arm, startling her. It was Tom.

'You OK?' he said. 'You were about to walk into the street.'

Lulu looked up to see the car, a light blue

Volkswagen, whose driver, a pleasant-faced middle-aged woman, raised infuriated hands at her as she shot past.

'Sorry,' she said. 'I was thinking about something.'

'I guess so.' Tom looked at her in concern. 'Did something happen?'

'Sort of,' she said. She checked her mind; hoping for a moment that this might be simply a nightmare: but, no, it was not a dream. 'Yes, I suppose it did.'

'Want to talk about it?'

'No!' The force with which her response shot out startled even her.

He smiled. 'I'll take that as a negative,' he said. 'But you look like you could use some food. Want to come to Carroll's?'

They walked together to the cafe in a silence that was surprisingly companionable.

'How's the job hunt going?' he said, when they were seated over their meal. 'Did you find anything with animals yet?'

'I'm on various waiting lists,' she said. 'But it seems to be quite a popular field. Right now, I'm working at the Crown & Sceptre. It's a bit depressing there, but it was all I could find.'

'I kind of like the Crown & Sceptre,' he said. 'They do a good cauliflower cheese.'

'They do?' Lulu thought of the watery white florets encased in vivid orange sauce.

'Well.' He seemed to consider it. 'When I say it's good, I probably mean it's better than the way my Aunt Pam in Wisconsin used to fix it, which is the only way I've had it before. But to

236

tell you the truth, most things I eat as an adult are better than the way my Aunt Pam in Wisconsin used to fix them. The real reason I like the place is because it's quiet in the afternoons and I can read there.'

It was quiet all right, thought Lulu.

'The reason it's quiet,' she told him, 'is that not many people go there because it's not very nice.'

'Huh.' He raised an interested eyebrow; this apparently was an element of the pub that had not previously struck him. But he himself had commented that he was not an observant man. He had also commented that it was a characteristic that had driven his ex-wife crazy. She frowned at him, thoughtfully.

'You're divorced, aren't you?' she said.

'Five years ago,' he nodded. 'Back in California.'

Divorce did happen, she thought, feeling a little sick. It was a common consequence of infidelity.

'Why?' she asked.

'Wow.' He had taken a sip of tea, and choked a little. 'You get straight to the point, don't you?'

'Sorry, was that rude?' Lulu and her sisters had grown up watching Fee ask direct questions of people she knew and people she did not, and not thought twice about it. Now that Lulu was older, she was becoming aware that this was an American habit rather than a British. She bit her lip: Jane, she would lay bets, did not ask questions.

'No, it's fine,' he said. 'It's good, in fact, makes

me feel like I'm back home. English people are so discreet I sometimes miss a bit of good American curiosity.'

'Good,' she said. 'So — what happened with your wife?'

'Well.' He thought for a moment and then grinned, suddenly looking years younger. 'I guess the honest answer to that is that I miss being asked the questions much more than I miss having to answer them.'

'Oh.' That made sense, she thought; she had not cared to tell him why she had just nearly walked under a car, and nor had he pressed her.

'It's kind of a long story,' he said. 'I might tell you about it one day, when you have an hour or two to spare. But you can ask other questions if you want. You look like you have quite a few of them in your head right now.'

'Just one, if that's OK,' she said. 'Was one of you . . . unfaithful?'

'Hmm.' He frowned, reached for sugar, and added it to his tea, seeming to forget that he had already done so. 'Unfaithful is sort of a tricky word, because most people take it to mean adultery, and there are many other ways of being unfaithful than by having an affair. Obviously one of us did break faith with the other, or we'd still be married, I guess.' He stirred his tea and then looked up at Lulu. 'I don't want to pry,' he said. 'But I'm kind of guessing that someone has broken faith with *you* today, am I right?'

'I think they have,' she said. Yes, her father, whatever he had done or not done, had quite clearly broken some faith with her mother; now that she thought about it, he had definitely broken faith with her, too. 'Yes, I'm sure they have.'

'Tough.' He nodded, sympathetically. 'I'm sorry for you.'

'What do you do?' she asked him. 'When someone breaks your faith?'

'Well, it's a difficult one,' he said. 'It's going to hurt for a while, and you just have to know that and steel yourself to hang in there till it gets better. It does get better, though, so long as you haven't broken any faith yourself. I always, feel that if you can look yourself in the eye, most things do get better.'

It was surprisingly easy, she thought, talking to this strange and quiet man almost a generation removed from her: easier by far than talking to many boys of her own age.

'This person,' she said, 'who's broken faith with me. Will *they* be able to look themselves in the eye afterwards?'

'Whoa.' He puffed air through his cheeks. 'As many answers to that as there are people in the world and situations between them. It depends on how badly they've broken faith, I guess, and how well they deal with it, or don't deal with it, afterwards. The only person you can be in control of is you. And in the end, that's the only person whose conscience you have the right to care about.'

'OK,' she said. She thought. 'That makes sense, actually,' she added.

They sat in silence for a moment.

'Want to talk about something else?' he said.

'Yes,' she said firmly.

'OK,' he said. 'Then maybe there's something you can explain to me about the Crown & Sceptre, which is something I've been wondering about for some time. Now, even I'd noticed the woman who hangs out behind the counter there, the one with the hair who's kind of witchy-looking, and always looks at you as if you've murdered her pet tarantula. Know the one I mean?'

'Yes,' said Lulu. 'Oh, yes, I know the one you mean.'

He leaned forward across the table, his brow furrowed in bafflement.

'What is her problem?' he asked, interestedly.

* * *

Later that afternoon, Lulu's mother telephoned her at the pub.

'You have to come home,' she said. 'As soon as they let you out of that awful place. That terribly wicked and reprehensible young friend of yours Charlie has sent me the most enormous bunch of ridiculously over-the-top flowers, which she had no business doing, and I'm most upset with her, but they are completely beautiful and you just have to come home to see them.'

'Is Dad there?' said Lulu.

'Oh, honey,' said Fee. 'You're not still upset with him about the Jane business, are you?' It took a frozen moment for Lulu to realize that her mother was talking about the invitation to Santorini. 'Oddly enough he's gone off to see her .

240

tonight. They had such a good time catching up last week that she's organized a mini-reunion weekend with Neil and Helen. He'll be home on Sunday.'

'He's gone to see Jane?' she said. 'Didn't he invite you, too?'

'No, thank God! Can you imagine the reminiscences? I get to stay home instead and have marvellous flowers delivered to me from a beautiful young woman. Come and see them.'

'OK.' Lulu wanted to see her mother; more, she now realized, she needed to see her mother. 'I'm off in an hour, I'll be there then.'

★   ★   ★

The flowers were in a jug on the hall table, an explosion of colour and fragrance, roses and lilies, hydrangeas and larkspur.

'Aren't they glorious?' said Fee. 'But she's a very bad girl, and I want you to tell her so, this is completely unnecessary. All I did was ask her a few questions — she came up with the answers all by herself.'

'Well, she's pretty pleased with the outcome,' said Lulu. 'She's going out with him tomorrow, and I dread to think how much money she's spending on hair care products probably right at this very moment.'

'Well, good.' Fee smiled, led them into the kitchen and poured tea. Then looked a little wistfully, at Lulu. 'I only wish I could be as useful to my daughter, too.'

'Mom,' said Lulu. 'If you are going to start

241

talking about my career yet again . . . '

'Don't shoot me, I'm not!' said Fee. 'You just look so sad these days, and I wish there was something I could do to help. A mother's allowed to wish that, isn't she? Let's talk about something else, then. How's the attic going? Have you found anything interesting up there?'

'A couple more photographs of Grandma Jo,' said Lulu. 'At least, I think they're of her, the family do tend to look alike. Do you think I look like her?'

'I think you're prettier.' She reached across the table to lift a lock of Lulu's curls. 'If only we could see you behind all the hair.'

'Mom!'

Fee sighed. 'It was worth a try,' she said.

'Well, consider it tried,' said Lulu. 'It's too hot for tea, can I have a Coke?'

She got up, and went to open the fridge. 'Who is Jane, anyway?' she asked from behind the door.

'Oh, sweetie,' said Fee. 'Can't you get over that, please? It was an ill-judged suggestion on your father's part, but it's not as if he drugged you, dragged you onto the plane, and forced you to meet her. He meant well, and he's sorry, OK?'

'I should hope he is.' Lulu hoped her father was sorry for many things, right now. She returned to the table, and opened her can of drink. 'Was it your idea, too?'

'That's between me and your father.' Which meant no, thought Lulu: Fee and David had always provided a united front to their children.

Or rather, she reminded herself, had always used to.

'I just want to know who Jane is,' she said. 'He's spending most of the weekend with her, so I'd like to know.'

'OK.' Fee squeezed lemon into her tea, and stirred, thinking. 'There's not very much to know, really. They were at Oxford together. I think she might have read English with him, but I'm not sure. She married a man who left her for another woman which I think is a wicked thing for a man to do to his wife, and an even more wicked one for a woman to do to another woman. She plays bridge, she's active somehow in local politics, and she has that unspeakably terrible profession we're not allowed to mention. Oh, and she's had a rough year, poor thing, some sort of romantic break-up, which is particularly hard when you get older, and she's also been in the hospital with a stomach ulcer, although it seems to have cleared up now. And that's about it, really. She's not the most interesting woman in the world, to tell you the truth, but your father's fond of her.'

'Was she ever his girlfriend?' asked Lulu.

'I don't think so,' said Fee. 'He was with that nice Finnish girl for most of the time at Oxford, and I think Jane married quite young. I suppose they might have had a fling at one point — we were always having flings in those days — but he's never mentioned it. Why do you ask?'

'Just wondering,' said Lulu. Then, 'Does he have a nickname for her?'

'I don't think so. I think he just calls her Jane.'

Her attention at last aroused, Fee looked up at her daughter in curiosity. 'What a funny question, Lulu, why on earth would you want to know that?'

Lulu did not answer; but, looking into her mother's eyes, she saw everything suddenly change for Fee, too.

'Lulu,' said Fee. 'Is there something you want to tell me?'

'Absolutely not,' said Lulu. 'I have to go home now, Mom. I'll see you for brunch on Sunday, OK?'

★ ★ ★

But Sunday brunch at her parents' house, for once, did not happen. On Saturday evening, Fee telephoned Emma to tell her that David would be setting out early from Cambridge, and she would be meeting him for lunch alone.

'She sounded a bit mysterious,' said Emma when they were gathered at Charlie's flat where Lulu had offered to cook brunch instead. 'I think they were planning to do something romantic.'

'Ewww.' Sophie pressed her palms to her eyes and shook her head. 'Sick, sick, sick. That is the single most disgusting image I can imagine.'

'You don't have to get gross about it,' Emma told her. 'I think it's nice that they get romantic. I hope Matthew and I still do after thirty years.'

Lulu grunted from the counter where she was chopping tomatoes, peppers and aubergine for a ratatouille. She had not told either her sisters or Charlie the thing she had heard in her parents'

244

hallway during the week; nor had she slept particularly well during the intervening nights. 'So long as it's still each other you're getting romantic with,' she said.

'Lulu!' Emma looked up at at her in shock. 'That's a terrible thing to say.'

'You never know,' said Lulu. 'That's all I'm saying.'

'Ignore old Grumpypants,' said Sophie. 'She's been like this all weekend. I blame the pub, they're horrible to her there.'

'Well, there's no need to take it out on us,' said Emma. 'And talking of being romantic, which we were before my gorgeously optimistic and idealistic sister spoilt the moment, you're looking quite glowy and pleased with yourself, Charlie. Did you have a nice time last night?'

'Very nice, thanks.' Wandering in with bath-steamed skin in a dark pink cotton dressing gown, Charlie looked down at the table with a quiet smile. 'Yes, you could say it was very nice indeed.'

She sat down, and poured herself coffee from the pot.

Emma waited.

'Well?' she said at last. 'What happened?'

'We had a nice time,' said Charlie. 'We saw flamenco, we talked, he told me about Madrid, I told him about my family, we had a nice time.'

'Well, yes,' said Emma. 'But what *happened*?'

'Charlie's not like us, Emma,' said Lulu. She stirred the vegetables, set them to simmer, and joined the others at the table. 'She doesn't have sisters. She's allowed to have a private life. It must be quite nice, actually.'

'And now that I've got *your* attention,' said Emma, turning to Lulu, 'who was the guy you had lunch with on Friday?'

'Excuse me?' Briefly forgetting her parents' trouble, Lulu glared at her sister in disbelief. 'What are you, the head of the Secret Police, North London branch?'

'Rosie from work had an optician's appointment on Friday, and she saw you from across the street coming out of that disgusting transport caff place you're so fond of with a tall man who was making you laugh. She tried to wave to you, but you didn't notice because you were so busy laughing. So — who was he?'

'Ooh — gossip!' Sophie clapped her hands in excitement. 'Lulu's been on a secret date!'

'Imagine it, Charlie,' said Lulu. 'Living with this, week after week, year after year. Are you sure you'd have liked to have had sisters?'

'I'm waiting, Lulu,' said Emma. 'Rosie said he was tall, with glasses and lightish brown hair, wearing jeans and a blue shirt. Who was he?'

Cornered, Lulu sighed. 'Tom,' she said. 'Happy now?'

'I knew it!' Emma slapped the table in triumph.

'Who's Tom?' said Sophie.

'The lodger, Sophie,' said Lulu. 'He's still living in Emma's old room, and Emma is just beside herself with delight to have discovered that he and I had lunch together on Friday.'

'The lodger?' said Sophie. 'Isn't he a bit old for you?'

'Thank you, Sophie,' said Lulu. 'At last, some words of sense, and from you, no less. Yes, you are correct, he's a nice guy, but in terms of going on a date, he is not a bit old, but very much indeed too old for me.'

'He's not that old,' said Emma. 'He's twelve years older than me.'

'Twelve years older than *you*?' said Sophie. 'He's older than God.'

'Keep talking, Sophie,' said Lulu. 'Maybe Emma will listen to you, because she's made it plain that she won't listen to me.'

'But it does happen,' said Sophie, then, thoughtfully. 'There was Emma and Mr Knightly. And Maria and Captain Von Trapp. And did you see that movie with Scarlett Johansson and that really old comedian?'

'Will you all shut up?' said Lulu. She ratted her hands through her hair, sending it spiralling in wild curls. 'Since you're all so interested about this, I happened to bump into Tom when I was walking down the Caledonian Road, and as it happened to be lunchtime, we happened to have lunch together at Carroll's. I had a bacon sandwich, he had the full English breakfast, and he puts Tabasco sauce on his scrambled eggs, which I still think is weird. It's entirely possible that in the course of the forty minutes tops that we spent together, he said something that made me laugh, because he's actually quite an amusing person once you get to know him. But he's not my boyfriend, OK? I don't have a boyfriend, and, to tell you the truth, right now, I don't even want one, because as far as I can make out, relationships are more trouble than they're worth. I'm happy for you, Emma, and I'm happy for you, Charlie, and, Sophie, if your grinning, beer-bottling Rupert keeps you happy and out of my hair, then I'm happy for all of us. But I am really — really, truly, and seriously — not looking for a boyfriend, and I really wish you'd all accept that. OK?' She got up from the table and returned to the oven. 'Now, who wants me to start sausages with their vegetables, and who wants to wait for poached eggs?'

★ ★ ★

The next afternoon, when Lulu was finishing her shift at the pub, her mother called her.

'I think there's a conversation you and I need to have, honey,' she said. 'Can you come home?'

'Is Dad there?' said Lulu.

'I've sent him out with Phil,' said Fee. 'Unless you want him to be here, in which case he'll come home directly.'

'God, no,' said Lulu.

'Everything's fine, sweetie,' said Fee. 'We still love each other, and it's going to be OK.'

'It doesn't feel fine,' said Lulu.

'Just come home,' said Fee. 'We'll talk about it then.'

★ ★ ★

'Thank you for not telling your sisters about this,' Fee said, when they were sitting at the kitchen table, a pot of tea between them. She looked tired, and lines seemed overnight to have sprung up around her eyes and mouth. 'Your father and I appreciate it greatly.'

Your father and I. How many countless times, thought Lulu, had she heard the phrase from her mother's mouth; and how impossibly luxurious had been the days when it had not occurred to her to question it.

'Has he been unfaithful?' she said.

'That's a complicated question,' said Fee. 'And not one I'd ever hoped to be having to answer to any of my daughters. But . . . he hasn't been physically unfaithful, no. I'm not going to go into details of the precise way in which he's screwed up because that's between him and me, but he hasn't actually been physically unfaithful.'

'Is he going to be?' said Lulu.

'I'm pretty sure not,' said Fee. 'He says he won't — he's been told pretty plainly by me that if he does sleep with Jane, or with any other woman come to that, then our marriage is over, and he says he wants us to work on getting it back, which is a huge relief to me. But you can't be certain of anything about another human being, Lulu, as I'm learning to my cost.' She stopped and sighed. 'I'd kill for a cigarette,' she muttered. 'Lulu, I don't have all the answers, honey. I sometimes think you girls think I do, and, to tell you the truth, I sometimes like to make out that I do because it feeds my ego. And, to tell you another truth, I sometimes get so into myself that I even believe I have the answers, too, but the fact is that I don't. I will say that, Number One, your parents will always love you and that's something that will never change, and, Number Two, it seems you've already figured out that your father and I have found ourselves in an unfortunate place that we need to work our way back from. But that means both of us working, not just him, because I've messed up here, too, in my own way, almost as much as he has.'

'I don't see how,' said Lulu.

'Probably not,' said Fee. 'But, take my word for it, I have. Lulu, you've stumbled on a situation here that is much more grown-up and complex than I'd have chosen for you to be exposed to at this stage of your life. But I didn't raise stupid daughters, and particularly not my middle one, and since you obviously have found out — damn your inconvenient sharp eyes and ears — something about what's going on, I'd like to try to begin to explain it to you by telling you a story. Can I do that, please?'

'Well, that sounds grown-up, Mom,' said Lulu. 'Does it have three bears who lived in the wood?'

'No.' Fee smiled a little, and then sighed again. 'It doesn't have three bears who lived in the wood. It has a very, very nice and kind-hearted young man who lived in London, who fell in love with a girl who lived in Boston. And the girl in Boston was living in times that were particularly interesting for women, when everything was changing, and all sorts of opportunities were opening up for her that just hadn't been there for her grandmother or even for her mother, and, she being an independent sort of a girl, she just loved it. This independence was so exciting for her that for a long time she thought she'd never even get married, but the young man who was in love with her was so kind and so attentive to her that she found herself falling in love with him, too, so she married him and followed him to London, and found — after a few hiccups and a couple of false starts — that she was able to be just as independent there as she had been back in Boston, and they were very happy together.

'And pretty soon they had babies — three gorgeous, beautiful, adorable little daughters — and rather to her surprise, the independent young woman, who hadn't thought she was much of a maternal sort at all, found she just loved taking care of them. She particularly loved talking to them, teaching them, helping them with their problems. She discovered she loved helping people with problems in general, in fact, and as soon as the little girls were old enough to look after themselves a bit, she qualified as a family therapist so that she could carry on helping people with problems, even people she didn't know. And meanwhile, the girls were growing up into the wonderful new world for women that the young woman from Boston had helped to create, and the young woman was helping them to grow, and over the years the three girls just blossomed into the most amazing, strong, independent, self-reliant young women you could ever hope to meet, and the woman from Boston, who was middle-aged by this time, thought that life just couldn't get any better.'

Fee stopped for a moment, and smiled, wryly.

'What the woman from Boston had forgotten,' she continued after a moment, 'was that the man from London liked to take care of people, too. He'd been very active in winning her heart during their courtship, and when she first arrived in London, she'd needed all sorts of help and guidance to find her way around and figure out the new life. When the babies were small, he'd been a wonderful father, pitching in with the cooking, the cleaning, the nappy-changing, and when the woman had been studying round the clock for her therapist exams he'd fixed family meals, run her baths, done all sorts of kind and thoughtful things to make her life easier. But gradually, all that changed. The girls grew up into those beautifully strong and independent young women, who loved him, certainly, and who he was proud as Punch of, but they no longer needed him as they once had. The woman, who had been so anxious to preserve her own independence, had taken very great pains to make her own life, forge her own career, have her own concerns. No one, it seemed, needed the man any more.

'Then, by chance, he spent a weekend in a place far away from London with an old college friend. Now, this woman was not someone who was strong, or independent. She'd had a rough life, in fact, had been badly treated by her husband, and recently left by another boyfriend, and needed to be cheered up a little bit. She'd also been sick, and needed to be tended to somewhat, physically. She needed . . . it seemed . . . him.'

'But he's ours,' said Lulu.

'Oh, yes.' Fee nodded vigorously. 'Well, he's

not *ours*, in the sense that people don't belong to other people, although he'll always be your father, Lu, and he'll always love you as one, no matter what happens. And I'm quite sure that if Jane Caldwell were to sit down with her own friends or her therapist or whoever, she could describe what happened from her side in a way that would make sense, too. But I'm not interested in her side of what happened, Lulu. I'm interested in what goes on in this family. And that includes trying to help you to see a little of what your father was going through to make him act the way he did.'

'I'm not sure that I do see, though,' said Lulu. 'If Dad felt like that about things, shouldn't he have come to talk to you and tried to put it right?'

'I'd obviously have preferred that,' said Fee. 'But he's a man after all, and men aren't so good at talking about these things, and English men are even less good than most. This was a lack in me as much as in him — I'm a therapist, I should have tried to open up better communication.'

Lulu looked down at the grain of the wood on the friendly worn table.

'Is Claire just a joke-type joke?' she asked then. 'Or is she the sort of joke that means he'd really secretly like us all to be sort of more like that?'

Fee smiled. 'She's just a joke, sweetie,' she said. 'Part of your father's dry British sense of humour, which was one of the parts of him I fell in love with all those years ago. I can't say she's an especially funny joke right now, but she's a joke all right . . . Make no mistake, Lulu, your father has messed up big-time, and I am more angry with him and hurt by him than I have ever been in all our marriage. But marriage isn't perfect, any more than the rest of life is. I'm sure that you'll be married, too, one day, and when you are you'll find out that it isn't a tidy little picture of one person meets another and they live happily ever after. It's two imperfect human beings coming together and scrambling and struggling and rough-and-tumbling their way through a lot of obstacles — whether it's crossing an ocean in my case, or being the boss's daughter in Charlie's. It's years of commitment and loving and making decisions and making jokes and cooking supper and saying the right thing and saying the wrong thing and making mistakes and forgiving each other for mistakes until over the years you find that, together, you've formed a great, big, wildly coloured tapestry of a whole shared life. And, in your father's case, the last couple of weeks or so are an unfortunate part of the tapestry that he and I have created, and one that I certainly wish weren't there, but it's by no means the whole piece, and it's by no means big enough to ruin it completely.'

'Do you forgive him?' said Lulu.

'I will,' said Fee. 'It's going to take some time, because what he did was pretty big, although it could have been much bigger. But I'm working on it, and he says he'll wait till I do, and he's also been pretty frank with me about which bits of the tapestry *he* doesn't like and needs me to work on — and, yes, there are some quite big ones — so I'm fairly confident we'll get there. And, if things go as they should, we'll both have learned from this a valuable lesson about what we each need from the other, how we each need to go about asking for it, and — in my case — how I must learn never to be careless with love, and never ever to take for granted someone I love and value. Many experts say that, if your father and I approach this in the right way, then one day we'll be the stronger for it, and that's what I'm aiming for, and what he says he's aiming for, too.'

Lulu thought for a moment.

'Do you forgive Jane?' she asked.

Fee, too, thought.

'I hope,' she said then, evenly, 'with every inch and fibre of my being, that that bitch contracts an excruciatingly painful and slowly fatal illness and then roasts in hell for all eternity.'

'Good,' said Lulu.

'I should say 'wait a minute' here,' said Fee. 'Because it's not an OK thing to hope for. But I'm not going to. On the other hand, there is one other thing I'm hoping will happen that is OK to want. Which is — will *you* forgive your father? He's put you through some pain in the last few days, and we're both hoping you'll forgive him, although I know we don't have a right to demand it.'

'I don't know,' said Lulu. 'I need to think. Can I go up into the attic? And will you not ask me why?'

'I think the very least your father and I can give you now,' said Fee, 'is the right to privacy.'

★　★　★

It was much easier, thought Lulu, settling into the armchair in the attic on legs that were suddenly shaky, to think about the past than the present these days. The past was safe and held no surprises; the past, she knew, had a happy ending. It was much easier, for instance, she thought, reaching for the letters, than contemplating her parents' marriage to reflect on how relatively few letters Jo seemed to have written to Meg during 1868, compared to how many she had written to Amy in that time. It made sense, of course, she reflected, sinking with relief into the now familiar world of her great-great-grandmother's life, since after Jo had returned to Concord from the New York trip, she and Meg had obviously lived close enough to see each other regularly in person, while Amy was still off travelling in Europe. However, it was frustrating that the five from New York were the only letters that remained addressed to Meg from that trip, because they apparently held all the information there was to be read about the youthful Herr Bhaer. After those — apart from the brief mention to Meg in that sad letter about Beth of the Shakespeare he had given Jo for Christmas — he simply disappeared from the correspondence, resurfacing several years later as fully fledged Professor Bhaer, with whom Jo had founded the school for boys. Presumably, they had agreed to keep their engagement secret for some reason until he had completed his studies: but it must have required some self-restraint for Jo not to have mentioned him at all in all that time. Maybe in the fifth letter, there would be an explanation: but Lulu would not open the fifth letter, not on this strange and disturbing evening when so many things she knew had been thrown into the air. She would reread through the letters to Amy instead, to see whether, despite herself, Jo had let slip some clue to her younger sister of the feelings she must surely be discussing in person with her elder. She curled her legs beneath her in the armchair, and set herself to the task, until one letter, in particular, stopped her.

Concord, June 1869.

Dearest Amy,

I have just been again to Beth's grave and laid upon it two roses, a fine and cultivated one from Mr. Laurence's conservatory from you, and a thorny wild one I plucked from the hedges from me. I'm glad you've agreed not to shorten your visit to all those splendid places, although I miss you — it's too late for you to say good-bye to Beth, which must grieve you, but she's well and happy now, and she blessed you with her last breath, which must give us all what comfort it can in these sad days.

Dear, has Laurie yet arrived to see you? And has he, by chance, made mention of me? I ask because we've had one of our silly quarrels, and I want to make up with him. I wrote him a letter earlier this year and made a joke about his music, which offended him. Then he wrote back and made a joke about my writing, which offended *me*, and — you know how hot-tempered we both are — I made no bones about telling him so, and told him never to write to me again. So there we sat for many weeks like two stone statues, half the world apart, and each too proud to unbend. And then when Beth failed, so many things went out of my mind, and suddenly I looked up and saw that Bethie was gone, and Laurie and I had been sore at each other for weeks, and both too stubborn to ask pardon.

I wrote him a note to say I was sorry for my harsh and hasty words, that I forgave him for his, and hoped we could be friendly again, but haven't heard a word from him since, and knowing how letters can be delayed, I wonder if he's received it? So when he comes to you, as I know he will, will you please send my boy my warmest love and ask him to forgive me? It don't feel right to be at odds now, with the house so still and quiet as it is. Grudges are dreadful things, Amy. And life is so short, and sometimes we don't have the chance to make peace with those we love until it's too late. Do you remember the time when we were children, and you and I had that quarrel over my book and you near drowned in the lake? It weren't easy to forgive you for that, for it *was* a dreadful thing you did to burn my dear little book that I loved so and had worked so hard over, and to tell the truth, I think of it sometimes to this day and mourn for it, for that was the work of years and I can never write it again. But, dear, I *did* contrive to forgive you, with Marmee's help, and I thank God daily that I did, for a life spent bearing a grudge to one close to me would be a sorry one.

A happier piece of news, dear, is that I have *at last* rebelled against going to visit the Hummels! You know how Marmee has always insisted that we take care of them, and of course I don't mind *giving* to them because it's right that we share what we have, little though it be. But Mrs. Hummel has always been such a sourpuss, and that cross little Lotty grows more disagreeable with every week that passes. I'm sorry for their hard lot in life, but it ain't fair to grudge us what we have, especially if we try to share it, and I don't understand why they do. We may have more than the Hummels, but Laurie has more than we do, and if we can be happy for him, why can't they be happy for us? But they can't, it seems. I took them a pot of soup and some other tid-bits last week, and just for a relish added at the last moment some sunflowers from my plot, for they always make me smile with their long stalks and broad, friendly faces. But Lotty took the food without a word of thanks, cast a glance at my poor beaming sunflowers, then pointed to those two sickly daisies that still struggle to survive beside their wall, and said, 'Do you think, Miss March, that we are so low we cannot grow our own flowers?'

I had had enough. I went home and told Marmee that *she* was free to visit the family as often as she chose, and that I would even help to make up parcels for others to take there for they are souls in need, but that I, for one, had had enough of visiting them, and would do so no more.

I leave you to imagine the lecture I got. 'Privilege brings duty.' 'We must love our neighbor better than ourselves.' 'A kiss for a blow is always best.' 'That I should see a daughter of mine refuse charity to the poor.' All these and more of the familiar adages rained like hail about my head until I felt as buffeted as the brave boys at Gettysburg, but to no avail — I stood firm like a true Union soldier and stuck to my guns.

To everyone's surprise, it was Hannah who rode to my rescue. She'd 'seed how that sour little creeter Lotty spoke to Jo when Miss March warn't watchin'' and she'd 'seed Jo a-frettin' her brow on the ways out to that place, and onste she'd seed her cryin' her pore heart out on the ways home.' (So I once did — thought no one had seen — won't tell you why, so don't bother to ask, miss.) Quite a speech she made, and in the end — partly through sheer astonishment — even Marmee was forced to concede defeat.

It *is* a comfort not to have to go there again, Amy. They are *so* mean of spirit, and so envious of what we have, that visiting them had become more of a burden than I could bear to carry. Time is so precious and if my poor Bethie had so few years of it, I am not going to squander whatever I have left in attempting to be pleasant to people who make no such effort with me. There is perplexity enough in making peace with those I value, such as Laurie and a certain fine young lady when she's home from her travels, without wasting my trouble on those who don't deserve it.

Your loving sister,
Jo.

When Lulu came down from the attic, she met Fee on the stairs.

'I was just coming to call you,' said Fee. 'Your Dad's in the kitchen. He hopes you'll go in and talk to him. Will you?'

Lulu sighed. *A life spent bearing a grudge to one close to me would be a sorry one.* 'I suppose I'll have to sometime, won't I?' she said.

'Good girl.' Fee patted her arm, and went upstairs to her bedroom.

★   ★   ★

Lulu's father was sitting at the long kitchen table that the family had had since before Lulu had been born, a glass of wine in front of him, looking exhausted. She glanced at him but did not greet him, seated herself opposite, and they two sat in silence for a while.

'I regret every part of all of this,' said her

261

father at last. 'But by far and away the part I regret most is that I have caused you distress.'

'You scared me, Dad,' said Lulu. 'You really, really scared me.'

'I know,' he said. 'And I will live with that knowledge until my dying day. An apology seems pretty feeble after that. But, for what it's worth, I do apologize most profusely and wholeheartedly. I'm really sorry, Lulu.'

'Hm.' Lulu screwed her mouth, frowning at him.

'I love your mother very much,' he said. 'You do know that, don't you?'

'I thought I did,' she said. 'And I thought she had reason to love you.'

'Ouch.' He winced. 'I deserved that,' he said then. 'But I do love her, and, believe it or not, she does still love me. We clearly have issues that we need to address, and we've talked about them and we've agreed that we're going to work on them.'

'Good,' she said.

'We're going to go to therapy,' he said. 'Your mother knows someone who specializes in cases like ours. Your mother says she's the best there is. We're going to go to see her and keep on going to see her until we've come out at the other side of this, which we intend to do.'

'Good,' said Lulu again. 'I'll look forward to it.'

'Do you want to come with us?' he asked.

'God, no!' Lulu was not a fan of her mother's profession. 'Sit in a room and tell my secrets to someone like Mom who's not Mom? I don't think so, Dad, thanks for the very generous offer.'

'I didn't think you would,' he said. 'But I thought I'd ask.'

She looked at him, and for the first time a faint smile crept onto her face.

'I bet *you're* really looking forward to it, too, aren't you?' she observed.

He met her eyes, and, tentatively, smiled back. 'Every iota as much as you can imagine,' he agreed.

'Serves you right,' she said.

'You're right,' he said. 'It absolutely does serve me right. But I'd do more than go to therapy to get my marriage back. I'd do anything, Lulu — anything — to get my marriage to your extraordinary, wonderful mother back.'

'OK then,' she said.

There was another silence.

'You can't ask me about jobs,' she said.

'OK,' he said. 'I accept that.'

'Never, ever, ever, not a question, not a joke, not a word, not even a single syllable until I decide what I want to do and decide that you're allowed to talk to me about it. It's really annoying and you're not allowed to annoy me now.'

'You have a point,' he said. 'No talk about jobs then.'

'And you'll never talk to that Jane person again, will you?'

He smiled, a little wryly.

'I think we can confidently say,' he said, 'that I won't be talking to Jane again.'

'OK, then,' she said. *A life spent bearing a grudge would be a sorry one.* 'I suppose I'd better forgive you, hadn't I?'

'I appreciate that.' With an odd formality, he bowed his head. 'Your mother and I are going to the Drapers Arms for dinner. Would you like to come with us?'

'I don't think so, Dad,' she said. 'To tell you the truth, I've had quite a lot too much of you two over the last few days.' She thought for a moment. 'Besides, there's something else I have to do this evening.'

'Oh, yes?' said her father. 'What's that, if I'm allowed to ask?'

Lulu stood up.

'I have to go back to the Crown & Sceptre,' she said. 'And tell them exactly where they can put the Sceptre.'

7

Concord, October 1867.

Dearest Amy,
Your letter has arrived from London, and I leave it to you to imagine how it was exulted upon and pored over; how Meg was in bliss to hear of the shopping on Regent Street, and Laurie convulsed with laughter to read of your picturesque trip through the countryside; how Beth turned bashful to learn that Frank Vaughn had asked for her, and how Marmee smiled at the story of the lovers with the rose-buds, while adding quickly that she 'was happy to trust that her own daughter could be depended upon to behave with prudence at all times;' how father tore through the letter to find whether uncle had, after all, contrived to have you all pay a call upon Mr. Darwin and his family, and, finding (a little more to his disappointment than to yours, I fancy) that he had not, contented himself at the last with as hearty an enjoyment as any of us of all the things you *had* done.
Dear Amy, I know that for you, the 'pineapple' of the trip (as you would once have called it) will be the paintings and statues of Rome; but I confess that, if I were

265

the one traveling instead of you, it would be London that I would relish the most. Ever since I read the words of wise old Sam Johnson that 'when a man is tired of London, he is tired of life,' I have burned to go there, and if ever I were so fortunate as to do so, oh, Amy, what a time I should have. I should see it all, from the green parks and the broad avenues to the little winding lanes that lead down to the great sweep of the river; from the tombs in Westminster Abbey to the high dome of St. Paul's, to the dreadful Tower of London where poor Princess Elizabeth was confined in such terror; from the round church in the City where the knights prayed before going on to do splendid things in the Crusades, to the Curiosity Shop where Nell and her grandfather worked and toiled their days, and all the way out to the Angel at Islington where wicked Fagin taught the orphan boys to pick pockets. I should meet every fine and interesting person, and attend every lecture and concert, and visit every spectacle at every theatre, and when at the end aunt and uncle had decided they really must move on, they would be reduced to hiding a sleeping potion in my pot of tea, or binding me with ropes and stuffing me, shrieking, into the Dover coach before they could tear me from such richness as London holds.

In consideration of which, dear Amy, it is no doubt for the best, for the sake of good sense, propriety, and the good name of

Americans abroad, that *you* are the one
crossing the sea with aunt and uncle and not
   your dreaming, fancy-stricken sister,
   Jo.

'Wotcher, Josephine, you're looking pleased with
yourself.'

It was a crisp Saturday morning in autumn,
and Nigel-Manolete, coming out of a newsagent
a couple of hundred yards above his shoe shop
on Upper Street, fell into step with Emma, who
was, in fact, feeling altogether pleased both with
herself and with life in general. She had just been
to the stationer's on the particularly agreeable
errand of placing the order for her wedding
invitations, a set of plain but elegant cream-
coloured cards, stating simply that Emma and
Matthew requested the pleasure of their friends'
company to join them in celebrating their union.
In a couple of hours, she and Matthew would be
meeting their friend Dominic, a journalist with a
seemingly endless supply of gossip from the
House of Commons, for lunch at an Ethiopian
restaurant on Edgware Road that they had all
been promising themselves to try: that evening,
they two had tickets to the Old Vic to see Kevin
Spacey in *The Merchant of Venice*. As
Saturdays went, Emma thought, this particular
one would be hard to improve on.

'I like autumn,' she said. 'It reminds me of
going back to school in my new winter uniform
with fresh exercise books and different teachers.'

'Being kicked around the football pitch and
called Fatso is more like it,' he said. 'But I do

have my autumn line just in, there are some lovely shoes, if I do say so.' He stopped, and clutched her arm. 'Oh, Josephine, you're not walking past my shop, are you?' he asked.

'Well, yes,' she told him. 'It's sort of on my way home.'

'Then you'll have to take a detour,' he said. 'I'm taking no chances here because you and my autumn line'd be a disaster waiting to happen, and I'd never forgive myself. Tell you what, I'll buy you a cup of coffee, you can tell me about your wedding plans, and then we'll split up. It's for the best, believe me.'

They were standing outside Ottolenghi, and he led her in, past the crowds of people clustered around the trays of prepared food that Fee found so difficult to resist, and into the coffee shop behind.

'Manolete! Darling!' A rich voice hailed them. It was Alice Weathers, the actress, sitting in a corner, having coffee with a dark-haired young man. 'How marvellous to see you, do come and join us.'

'Depends on what you're wearing,' said Nigel-Manolete. 'Stand up and let's see 'em.'

'I'm wearing you, darling,' said Alice. She stood up and cocked a leg on which a skirt of chocolate-coloured wool fell over a knee-length boot of softest russet leather. 'I've hardly taken them off since Tuesday.'

'And quite right, too,' said Nigel. 'Doesn't she suit a boot, Josephine?'

Unseen by the others, he poked Emma, firmly, in the back.

'Absolutely,' said Emma. 'I always think you have to have a sort of dashing flair to be able to carry off boots.'

'Well, thank you, Josephine,' said Alice. 'We've met before, haven't we? Was it at Fashion Week? This is Colin.'

Sophie's acting partner Dr Broody, standing politely to shake hands, was tall enough, Emma was gratified to note. Not quite as tall as Matthew, which was of course more gratifying still; but certainly tall enough.

'Josephine here is planning her wedding,' said Nigel when they were seated. 'Tying the knot in February and half the young men in London will fall on their swords of a broken heart when she does.'

'What fun!' said Alice. 'You'll have a wonderful time, I adored my wedding day. Are you doing it in London or the country?'

'London.'

'Good choice, darling!' She clapped her hands approvingly. 'Just like me.'

Alice had been married in the Jesuit church in Mayfair, with the reception afterwards at the Connaught Hotel: half of Hollywood had attended, and the photographs had circled the globe.

'We're a London family,' said Emma. 'We don't really do the country very much.'

'Nor me, darling.' Alice shuddered, delicately. 'All those trees and fields, I nearly went mad when I was shooting *The Trumpet-Major*. You can give yourself a perfectly nice time on good firm pavements with a taxi rank nearby, and if you really must look at some grass, there's always Gibson Square, isn't there? Now let's see.' She tapped her chin with a shapely finger. 'What can I tell you about your wedding day? Oh, I know! Have you booked your honeymoon yet?'

'We're doing it this week, actually.' They had debated, luxuriously, for several weeks between Barcelona and Athens, and finally settled as a compromise on Marrakech.

'Good, then I'm in time.' She leaned forward towards Emma, and lowered her voice. 'Now I want you to listen to me very carefully because this is very important. You may go where you like for the honeymoon, you may do what you like. You may do anything or you may do nothing. You may go white-water rafting in the Fiji Islands or you may go shrimp fishing in Southend-on-Sea.'

Shrimp fishing, thought Emma, entranced. She actually said shrimp fishing.

'But whatever you do,' continued Alice, 'don't — do not — travel on the day after the wedding.'

'Um . . . ' Seeing a response was expected, Emma blinked obediently. 'No?'

'Absolutely not.' Alice shook her head, and wagged the finger reprovingly. 'No, no, no, no, no. Think about it, darling. You'll have all your very favourite people in the whole world all in the one place together and probably only for the one time in your entire life, well, except for your funeral, which isn't really your life any more anyway, is it?' She took Emma's arm, and looked earnestly into her eyes. 'You must promise me

270

— you must *swear* to me — that you won't go leaping onto a plane the next day and leave them all alone without you. It'd make you all so terribly sad I just couldn't bear to think about it.'

'All right, then,' said Emma. She must pay close attention, she thought, in order to repeat each word to Matthew when she got home. 'I won't.'

'And besides,' continued Alice, 'you'll be far too tired when you wake up even to think of getting up and onto a plane anyway. You'll be exhausted, darling. Depleted. Drained. More tired than you've ever been in your life, more than if you'd just read the whole of *War and Peace* to a theatre packed entirely with old-age pensioners after lunch. And Colin here can tell you a thing or two about pensioners after lunch. The snores can be deafening, can't they, Colin?'

Colin only smiled. On the screen, his features were famously sullen, even menacing: off it they seemed to diffuse and rearrange themselves into an expression so pleasant that it bordered on the vacuous.

'Which reminds me,' said Alice. 'Have you decided about your hen party?'

'Not yet,' said Emma. In fact, now that she thought of it, Lulu had not so much as mentioned a hen party.

'Keep it relaxing.' Alice lifted a forestalling hand. 'I know, I know, you're about to say, 'Oh, but Alice, my bridesmaid has such a marvellous idea, so amusing and original, she wants to go bungee jumping or organize a tiddlywinks tournament.''

She must particularly remember, thought Emma, to tell Matthew about the tiddlywinks. He would like the tiddlywinks.

'Don't let her, darling,' said Alice. 'Be firm. Demand something that is pure relaxation, like a weekend at some wickedly self-indulgent hotel with a lovely, lovely spa and lots of beauty treats. Hot stones, or maybe mud. Oh, for heaven's sake, will you listen to me.' Suddenly she stopped, and slapped herself firmly on the hand. 'You must forgive me, darling. I'm an eldest and frightfully managerial. You probably have the most wonderfully organized chief bridesmaid who's got everything sewn up quite perfectly for you already.'

'Actually, I haven't,' said Emma. 'My chief bridesmaid is my younger sister, and I love her to bits, but she's a bit, well, absent-minded, really.'

'Younger sisters!' Alice cast her eyes to the heavens. 'I'm sure we could swap war stories all day long. I have three, heaven help me, how many have you?'

'Two.' It was pushy, Emma knew, but she could not look Sophie in the eye if she failed to mention her now. 'Oddly enough,' she said to Colin, 'my youngest sister is an actress who recently worked with you.'

'Oh, yes?' Colin raised a politely wary eyebrow, and Emma began to regret having spoken. It had been two weeks since Sophie's episode of *St Luke's* had aired, and she had not, after all, been called back to the show; it occurred to Emma now that she had only had Sophie's account of Colin's conversation with the director. But having raised the subject, she could hardly abandon it.

'It was the episode about the law suit,' she said. Then, giving him a polite escape should he feel the need for one, 'She only had a small part, but she made a point of saying how kind and welcoming everyone was, which I gather isn't necessarily the case on all sets.'

'The blonde girl?' he said. 'Sophie something? Tall and sort of . . . '

He stopped and spread his hands, waggling his fingers in the air.

'Effervescent?' suggested Emma. It was encouraging that he remembered her, at least. 'That'll be Sophie.'

'But whatever happened to her?' he said. 'She was wonderful.'

'What do you mean what happened?' said Emma.

'I thought we were going to get her back on the show. I know I suggested it, but she never appeared again. I supposed she'd gone out of town or something.'

'No, she's still around.' Emma smiled. 'And I have the idea that if she had been asked back, she'd have got around to mentioning it.'

'She's *very* — what was your word — effervescent, isn't she?' he agreed. 'Well, I don't know what happened there, maybe Tim lost her number or something. I'll make a point of reminding him. Sophie — what's the name again?'

'Atwater,' said Emma.

'Atwater.' He produced his BlackBerry and

typed it in, carefully. 'I'd love to work with her again. You'd like her, Alice, she's a really nice girl, and once she's had some experience I think she'll be a very fine actress.' He nodded, approvingly. 'She's very . . . I suppose the word would be reactive.'

'You all right, Josephine?' said Nigel.

'Sorry,' said Emma. 'I just choked on my coffee a little, but I'm OK now.'

★　★　★

She would not tell Sophie about the conversation, Emma decided later, having been firmly directed by Nigel into the side streets behind Upper Street to find her way home. It was clear to her from the purposefulness with which Colin had written Sophie's name that her sister would be hearing from *St Luke's* very shortly; however, she would let the telephone call come as a surprise, and let it come, too, untainted by the idea of big-sisterly meddling. If Sophie were indeed to be asked back to the show, and if Colin happened to mention to her that he had had coffee with Emma, then she could find out that way. Although, of course, Colin would not refer to her as Emma, but as Josephine.

In the few weeks of her budding friendship with Nigel, Emma had become rather fond of being Josephine. She was not, of course, the richly overdrawn Josephine of her earlier fantasies, nor did she have the least serious desire to be; however, she was, somehow, subtly, a different person with Nigel than she was with her sisters, a person who was just a little younger than Emma was usually, and just a little less sophisticated. She was also a person who could be bossed. Emma had discovered that — in small doses and under controlled circumstances — she rather liked being bossed. She had not, for instance, even thought to explain to Nigel that the side street he had pushed her onto was on the other side of Upper Street from the side where she lived — but that only gave her a chance to walk down some different streets from usual, she thought, happily strolling the small squares and crooked side lanes under leaves that were just starting to turn scarlet and gold, and London was so very lovely under the October sunshine.

Alice was right, she told herself, secretly savouring the fact that she had just come from coffee at a fashionable restaurant with a famous actress, you didn't need the countryside. Except for their honeymoon in Marrakech, she would be happy never to leave London as long as she lived. She stopped at Chapel Street market to buy a bunch of fluffy-headed yellow chrysanthemums, and crossed Upper Street, at a safe distance past Manolete's, to carry them behind the Tube station and home.

★ ★ ★

'I was about to send out a search party,' Matthew remarked mildly when at last she returned to the flat.

'Sorry, was I a long time? You should have

275

telephoned.' She smiled at him, feeling rather glamorous as she rummaged for a vase, carrying flowers home from coffee with two actors and a fashion designer to a man who had missed her, whom she would marry. 'How was your boys' night out? Did you get roaring drunk and gamble all our money away?' The night before, Matthew had been for a drink with his manager, which had turned into dinner: Emma had taken the opportunity for an early night.

'No, we mostly talked shop,' he said. 'Sit down, Emma, there's something I have to tell you.'

She sat, suddenly wary. 'Something good, I hope?' she said.

'That's the thing,' he said. 'I'm not quite sure. *I* think it's good, but I'm not sure how you'll feel about it.'

'Then you'd better tell me,' she said.

'OK.' He took a deep breath, and stared downwards at the table. 'There's a project that I've been asked to head next year. It's quite a big installation of quite a complex system, and it's actually quite a big thing that they've asked me to head it. It'd take a year to complete, possibly longer than one, but not more than two, and after I'd done it, which I'm confident I could do successfully, then I'd have made myself quite an impressive reputation, and we could look forward to a very nice career for me.'

He stopped talking, and continued to study the table.

'Well, so far,' said Emma, 'that all sounds pretty good to me. But I'm interested to know the reason why you're not looking at me when you're talking about it.'

He did look up at that, and straight at her.

'Because it's in North Dakota,' he said.

'Oh,' she said.

Emma had lived in London for all her life. She also knew Boston quite well, of course, and New York less well, although she liked it, and had visited California once, where she had preferred San Francisco to Los Angeles. She was not entirely sure that she would be able to find North Dakota on a map.

'It's a place called Closker College,' he said. 'It's in a farm-country town called Lamott about a hundred and fifty miles north of Bismarck. The president went to Cambridge with our big boss, and they've kept in touch ever since — it seems he's always liked us because, well, because we're rather good, actually. Anyway, he wants this installation, and he wants us to do it, and he asked Mark to pick someone he could trust to head it. And Mark chose — me.'

'To go to North Dakota,' she said.

'I know,' he said.

North Dakota was farmland. Stretches of roads with gaunt houses at thousand-acre intervals, where monosyllabic men with weather-beaten faces would climb into their battered trucks to drive to places that Emma could not imagine, to do what Emma was not entirely sure, except that she knew it would not involve either Ethiopian food or the Old Vic.

'And what would I be doing with myself,' she asked, 'while you're out installing the computers in Closker College, Lamott, North Dakota?'

'Well, that's the problem,' he said. 'You might be able to find work at the college — of course you already have citizenship because of Fee. I don't know what sort of work it would be — to be honest, I don't really know what's available out there for you. But you really wouldn't have to work at all if you didn't want to, they'd be paying me enough that you could take time off if you wanted.'

'In Lamott, North Dakota,' she said.

In a small town in a rural district a hundred and fifty miles north of Bismarck.

'I know,' he said. 'In Lamott, North Dakota.'

She thought for a few moments.

'*You'd* be quite enjoying yourself, though,' she said. 'Wouldn't you?'

'I would,' he said. 'I can't say the prospect of a year in North Dakota makes me want to turn cartwheels for joy, but the work itself would be certainly interesting enough that I'd be involved in it and looking forward to going to work every day. Look, there's no way around this one, Emma. If I took this job, it would mean a huge change in our lives for a year or so, and more so for you than for me because your work would change more than mine would — which is why I want you to be the one to decide what we do here. I'll take the job or not take the job — you can come with me or stay in London, whatever feels best to you. It has to be your decision, and whatever you decide I'll support fully. I don't even want to talk to you too much about it because I don't want to try to talk you into anything you might regret. All I will say is that opportunities like this don't come along every day, that the job would last probably a year and certainly no more than two, and that afterwards, my career prospects would be very rosy indeed. Which would obviously be good for us, and would be even better when the children come, because we might be able to give them quite a nice life in material terms.'

'We're not exactly planning to send them out cleaning chimneys as it is,' she said.

'That's true,' he said. 'And I'd far rather they had a happy mother than a slightly richer father. But it is an element of the situation that I thought I should point out.'

'Let me think about this,' she said. 'I need to think.'

'Take all the time you want,' he said. 'The job doesn't start till March, so we have time.'

'Time.' She looked at the clock. Time to be getting ready for lunch with Dominic. Time to be going out into the sparkling London day and descending into the tunnel of the Underground to emerge in Edgware Road and eat African food with a good friend, while talking theatre, and politics, and music, and books. It was too much stimulation, too much London, to be taking on board the thought of a life in Lamott, North Dakota.

'Do you mind if I stay at home?' she said. 'I don't feel I can face going to lunch right now.'

'Of course not,' he said. 'Do you want me to stay with you? We can fix a sandwich or go to the pub, and go to Nyala another day.'

'No, you go ahead,' she said. They had always been considerate with each other about social arrangements, and she had been, quietly, proud of that. But how on earth could she stretch the consideration for a lunch date in Edgware Road to encompass a year in Lamott, North Dakota? 'Say I've got a headache or something, and tell him I'm sorry.'

'Take your time,' he said. 'And don't agree to do anything that you're going to hate or resent. It's easy for me to say it's only for a year or so, but it's a year we'd be remembering for all our lives.'

From somewhere, she found a smile. 'No pressure, then,' she said.

★　★　★

Fee was planting bulbs in the garden, frowning thoughtfully over the newly turned earth. She stopped frowning when she saw her daughter arrive, and smiled and waved a companionable trowel.

'I'm getting the ranunculus in for the spring,' she told her. 'It's wonderfully therapeutic to plant bulbs; it gives you something to look forward to and reminds you of all the calm and stable parts of home life. Oh, Emma, honey, whatever is the matter?'

★　★　★

'I have always said,' she said later when Emma had finished her story, 'that Matthew was a particularly intelligent sort of young man.'

'Well, I knew he was good at his job,' said Emma. She balled up her Kleenex, picked a ranunculus bulb from the bag beside the flower bed and twirled it in her fingers. 'These are such funny things, they always look like little bunches of bananas for garden gnomes. But if this is where his intelligence leads us, I'd frankly be as happy to give some brain cells back.'

'I'm not talking about that sort of intelligence,' said Fee. Gently but firmly, she rescued the bulb. 'Although he obviously has that as well. But plenty of young men in the world are brain smart — Matthew is wise, too. He understands that if this is going to happen, it can only happen on the basis that you go along with it willingly and without feeling you're making too much of a sacrifice. That's very wise of him.'

Which was all very well, thought Emma, for Fee to say, whose marriage was so impervious to change or challenge.

'But aren't you supposed to make sacrifices?' she said. 'Isn't that what marriage is supposed to be about, two people doing for each other things they don't necessarily want to do for themselves?'

'It's about two people compromising,' said Fee. 'It's about two people caring for each other and wanting to do as much as they can to make each other happy while still maintaining their own self-respect, which can sometimes get complicated and which, believe me, Emma, is something your father and I are still figuring out together and still sometimes surprising each other by.'

She turned to set the rescued bulb into the ground, and covered it, carefully, with earth. She was moving a little stiffly, Emma noticed: maybe her yoga instructor was on holiday again. 'Of course we all want to make compromises for our spouse,' she said then, turning back to her daughter. 'That's part of the bargain of marriage after all. But when compromise gets into sacrifice, then that's when the territory becomes dangerous because that's when resentments build up. And the problem with navigating this territory is that there is no map, because what's compromise for one person might be the most terrible sacrifice for another. A year in North Dakota is obviously something you wouldn't have chosen for yourself, but only you can decide whether to agree to it would be a compromise or an out-and-out sacrifice. And Matthew understands that, which makes him a very wise young man, and you a very wise woman for having chosen him.'

'I don't feel wise right now,' said Emma. 'I feel thoroughly confused. I feel that whatever decision I make I'm hitting my face against a brick wall, and I don't know what to do.'

'Well, we've been through the possibilities,' said Fee. 'You say you don't want to be parted in your first year of marriage, which I applaud and think is very sensible of you. So either you both go to Lamott or you both stay in London. If you stay, then Matthew misses out on an opportunity he'd like to take advantage of, although if he's good enough to be suggested for this job then I'm sure another opportunity would come along for him in time. If you both go, then you make him happy, as well as getting the opportunity to have a year in a new place, experience a different culture and have a little bit of an adventure, although it would be . . . '

' . . . in North Dakota,' said Emma.

'North Dakota isn't so bad,' said Fee. 'I think most places can be interesting to live in if you find a way to make them so. You've only ever lived in London, after all. It might be good for you to experience living somewhere else. And I believe there are some parts of North Dakota that are extremely pretty.'

'I don't believe you've ever been there,' said Emma. 'I don't believe even Dad's ever been there.'

'I'm pretty sure he has,' said Fee, then frowned. 'Or was that Alaska?' she wondered.

'Oh — hi.' Tom was coming from the french windows that led to the sitting room, a book in his hand. When he saw the two women, he stopped. 'I was going to read in the last of the sun here, but if you're in the middle of something, I'll go back indoors.'

Emma looked up at him, thoughtfully.

'You're American, too, aren't you?' she said.

'Last time I looked,' he said.

'Do you know anything about Closker College in North Dakota?' she asked.

'As a matter of fact, I do,' he said. 'A friend of mine taught literature there for some years. It's a good school. I even visited him there once — he asked me over to give a talk on Dr Johnson.'

'What's it like?' she said.

'It's your classic American college town,' he said. 'Quite an interesting place to visit from a sociological point of view. There's not too much going on in the town itself; it mostly caters to the farmers, who tend not to have too much in common with the college folk, so the college folk are kind of thrown back in on themselves. So you have a collection of highly educated academic types, all pretty much fishes out of water in a rural town, all rubbing shoulders with no one much but each other. I guess the best way to describe it would be like a kind of grown-up version of your old university campus.'

'Not my old university campus,' said Emma. 'I went to London. King's College. On the Strand.'

'Ah,' he said.

'But what's the town like?' she said, after a moment. 'Are there bookshops? Nice restaurants?'

'I don't recall a bookstore,' he said. 'As for restaurants, there's probably a Chinese — there generally is. And I remember a diner which did a good coconut cream pie.'

Coconut cream pie, thought Emma, sadly.

'Is there a theatre?' she said.

'A small one,' he said. 'But it's pretty much for the local kids, so it mostly just shows the latest action movies. It'd be mostly about ordering DVDs from Netflix if you wanted something more interesting.'

'No,' she said. 'Not a cinema theatre. A theatre theatre. With real actors doing plays. On a stage.'

'Oh,' he said. He thought. 'I'm pretty sure there's one in Minneapolis,' he said then, helpfully. 'That's only three hours if the traffic's good.'

★   ★   ★

'But you can't go to North Dakota,' said Sophie the next day over brunch. 'How can Matthew fix my computer if he's half the world away?'

'Thank you, Sophie,' said Emma. 'I'd miss you, too.'

'Take her with you,' said Lulu. 'She spilled a bag of sugar in the kitchen that hot day last week and then left for work. We've been wading through an inch of goo ever since.'

'I replaced the sugar,' said Sophie. 'And at least I don't bring in dog hairs and bits of twig every time I come home. It's like living with the Hound of the Baskervilles.'

For the last few weeks, Lulu had been working for a dog-walking agency in Hampstead: the pay was negligible but, as Fee was given to cheer herself, at least it got her into the fresh air.

'You'd have an easier time of the separation than we did in my day,' said Fee now. 'We didn't have email or Skype or any of the things you girls take for granted now. When I first came to London, I used to write letters home to my mom once a week.'

'We know, Mom,' said Lulu. 'With a quill pen under a guttering candle before dining on roast dinosaur and poached pterodactyl eggs.'

'Did you like London?' said Emma. 'When

you first came here?'

'It was a challenge at first,' said Fee. 'There weren't so many non-English people living here back then, and at first I felt quite out of place as a foreigner. But your father, who really is a very kind and wonderful man . . . '

'He's a marvellous man,' Sophie told Lulu. Fee had lately adopted the habit of taking every opportunity to remind her daughters of David's good qualities.

'He's an OK sort of man,' conceded Lulu.

'He's a spectacular man,' said Sophie. 'He's a magnificent man. He's a — '

'Will you two shut up?' said Emma.

'Your father was a great help,' continued Fee. 'He showed me around, helped me find my feet, didn't expect me to fit in perfectly straight away. He knew, Emma, that I was making quite a compromise in moving here. But he was also smart enough to know that once I'd got the feel of London, I'd very much enjoy it, and, as it turned out, I do. It's a wonderful city, and I love my life here.'

'Well, you would,' said Emma. 'It's London.'

'You know, I might come and visit you in North Dakota,' said Sophie. 'I've seen all the movies about American small towns. I'll let my hair grow long and wear tight jeans and skimpy tops and have affairs with all the married men.'

'You will not,' said Fee, sharply.

'Just joking, Mom.' Sophie stared at her mother in surprise.

'Well, don't.' Collecting herself, Fee tapped Sophie lightly on the top of the head with the newspaper. 'I've seen rather too much of that lately in my work, and I'm afraid I've misplaced my sense of humour about it. It's only temporary, I'll have it back by Christmas.'

'OK, Mom. No accepting the lead in *The Scarlet Letter* before then, I promise. Ooh.' She gulped at her coffee, and waved a hand for attention. 'That reminds me, I might have some news. Jamie's friend Rhys, who is an awesomely creative guy who runs an experimental theatre company in Coventry, telephoned him on Friday. They want two talking skateboards by next weekend, so we're going up to talk to him about it tomorrow.'

'Excuse me.' Emma shook her head, as if doubting her hearing. 'Did you just say talking skateboards?'

'They were rehearsing all yesterday,' said Lulu. 'You'd be amazed at the range of emotions recreational planks of wood are capable of.'

'It's a very interesting play,' said Sophie. 'And Rhys is really nice and awesomely creative, so it'll be an amazing experience. And you needn't worry, Mom, they're both very happily married skateboards, although not to each other, they're more sort of colleagues.'

'Colleagues,' repeated Emma, fascinated. Then, 'Did you say it's in Coventry? What would you do if the *St Luke's* people wanted you?'

'*St Luke's*?' Sophie sighed, and shook her head. 'You don't understand, Emma. Television is all very well for getting my name and my face out there, but it isn't really anything much like acting, which is what I really do.'

'They never called,' said Lulu.

'And in many ways it's a relief,' said Sophie. 'Just imagine if I'd been committed to do something with *St Luke's* right now. I'd never have been able to take up this opportunity, which would be tragic, really, because it'll never come along again.'

'They're paying her less than the coffee shop,' said Lulu. 'And she and Jamie are sleeping on Rhys's floor.'

'Jamie's sleeping on Rhys's floor,' Sophie corrected her. 'I'm sleeping on his girlfriend's futon, they're supposed to be very good for the posture. It's only for three weeks, but it should be an awesome experience.'

'But, just out of curiosity,' said Emma. 'Just supposing, only hypothetically of course, that all of a sudden you got a call from *St Luke's* offering you more work. You would take it, wouldn't you?'

'Well, of course I'd take it,' said Sophie. 'I'm not completely mad, whatever you and Lulu seem to think. And that's the good thing about going to Coventry, I can always come back for a day. It's not like I'm going to Khartoum, or Kathmandu, or the Sahara desert. Or North Dakota,' she added, reaching across Emma for the scrambled eggs.

⋆ ⋆ ⋆

'You'd hate America,' said Rosie at work the next day. 'It's full of Americans. They're always smiling, they say things like tom-ay-toes and bay-sil, and they keep ordering you to have a nice day.'

'Actually, my mother's American,' said Emma.

'Oh, God, yes,' said Rosie. 'Sorry. I was only joking.'

She had been: Rosie had not a malicious bone in her body. But then, thought Emma, there were jokes and there were jokes. There were jokes like Sophie's about seducing married men, which had no connection whatsoever to reality and about which Fee had so inexplicably jumped down her throat; and then there were jokes which were sidelong ways of expressing a genuine opinion. Rosie did not, on the whole, like Americans. Just as Emma did not, in any sense, want to go to North Dakota.

'It might be an adventure,' she said now. 'I've only ever lived in London, after all. This might be a chance to experience living somewhere else.'

'If you want an adventure,' said Rosie, 'you should do something exotic. Go trekking in the Andes or take the Silk Road through China. Don't go to bloody North Dakota.'

'Well, the problem with that,' said Emma, 'is that Matthew hasn't been asked to go to work in the Andes or in China. He's been asked to go to work in North Dakota.'

'And that's the real problem, isn't it?' said Rosie. 'This is all about Matthew's work. It's not about you at all. It's the same old story all over again. They say times have changed for women, but they haven't, not really. When it comes down to it, it's the man's job that's the important one, not the woman's. They don't care about your life at all.'

'I don't know that I'd agree with that,' said Emma. 'Matthew's made a point of asking me if I'd be OK about this.'

'Asking you!' Rosie snorted. 'I know that sort of asking. 'Hello, darling, I've been given this wonderful opportunity for *me* which would be really interesting for *me* and lead to amazing things for *me* and, oh, by the way it would be completely hideous for *you* but you don't mind if we do it, do you, because it would be so marvellously good for *me*.''

'That's not how he's saying it,' said Emma. 'I mean, he says he wants to do it, because he obviously does. But he also says that it has to be my choice, too, and he's not going to do it unless I'm fully in agreement.'

'Well, that's even worse,' said Rosie. 'That's emotional blackmail. He's making you make the decision for both of you, and if you don't make the decision he wants, then he'll sulk.'

'I don't think he would,' said Emma. 'I know Matthew pretty well, and he's not a sulker.'

'Well, then,' said Rosie. 'If you really hate the thought of it, and he wouldn't sulk if you didn't, then why would you do it?'

* * *

'I just wish,' said Emma to Matthew the following Saturday morning, 'that you'd stop being so bloody *reasonable* about this.'

290

Matthew poured more coffee into his mug and sighed.

'If you'd rather,' he said, 'I hit you on the head with my club and dragged you to North Dakota by your hair, I'll go out and buy one for the purpose. But you can't go to the hairdresser for a few weeks because I'll need it a little longer to get a really good grip.'

Emma looked wistfully at the bowl from which he was helping himself to sugar; but reminded herself, sternly, that four months before her wedding was no time to start putting on weight.

'It would just be much less complicated,' she said, 'if you could find it in your heart to find a way to be even the smallest little bit obnoxious because that would make the decision very much easier for me.'

He thought.

'You can't sing,' he offered. 'You hog the duvet, and you look really silly when you've got a cold.'

'Nice try,' she told him.

He laughed a little, then stopped.

'I'm sorry, Emma,' he said. 'I know how difficult this must be for you. If I were you, I wouldn't want to go to North Dakota just because I'd been sent there. I don't even know what decision I'd make about it if I were in your place, so I really feel for what you're going through now.'

'I preferred you obnoxious,' she said.

'Sorry,' he said. He drained his coffee, and stood up from the table. 'How about this. Let's both of us go away and find something separate to do for a couple of hours and then meet at the pub for lunch. I'm going to get the car washed. And if you don't have anything else you'd rather do, you might want to walk up to Herringe's because I was in there the other day and I saw some possible handles for your drawers.'

'Handles?' Emma perked up a little. When she had moved in with Matthew, Fee had given her a small chest of drawers that had once belonged to Grandma Jojo, its prettiness marred by the fact that it lacked two of its original handles: she had been hunting ever since for a set of suitable replacements.

'They're nickel, like you're looking for,' he said. 'About the right size, and I thought looked rather suitable. Why don't you go up there and take a look?'

'I'll see you at the pub at one,' she said. 'But I'm afraid your obnoxiousness quotient has just fallen crashing through the floor.'

'Sorry,' he said again.

★   ★   ★

He was a nice man, Emma thought gloomily, walking through the sleepy Saturday morning to Herringe's Hardware, a small shop tucked away in a back street between Canonbury Road and Highbury Corner. Not many men visiting a hardware shop would think to look for their girlfriend's furniture accessories. He was a very nice man indeed, in fact, and not only to her but to her family, which all boyfriends were not. But was fixing her sister's computer and keeping his eyes open for drawer handles worth twelve months and more in rural North Dakota?

Herringe's was another relic of the old Islington, a meticulously ordered place with brooms outside the door and within a gleamingly regimented array of tools and electrical goods neatly aligned under the stately and impassive eye of Mr Herringe. Emma loved Herringe's, where her family had been shopping for all of her life. Mr Herringe greeted her now with the magisterial nod which was his customary greeting for high and low, and directed her to the card hanging on the wall which showed the array of drawer knobs and handles. She saw immediately the ones that Matthew had seen: they were three inches long and reassuringly solid, with a subtle scalloping at the ends. They would be perfect, she thought. Perfect for her chest of drawers which had travelled from America to be in London. Which now sat happily in the bedroom of the small and cosy flat that she and Matthew shared and that she loved so, whose windows trapped the elusive London light and turned it silvery and pale.

'Ron! Darling!'

Emma looked up in surprise: she had not even known that Mr Herringe had had a first name. But clearly he did because here he was, ducking his head and smiling a little bashfully as Alice Weathers light-stepped in, wearing a long black coat and the merest hint of Chanel, and bestowed on him an enthusiastic double kiss.

'You are a magician!' she proclaimed. 'A sorcerer. You are one who can raise the dead,

293

because that's what I truly thought it was. Is it really mended, darling?'

'Fixed her like new, Miss Weathers,' said Mr Herringe. He produced from below the counter a small brown bag, and patted it, proudly. 'She won't be giving you any more trouble, I fancy.'

'You are a lifesaver, Ron,' said Alice. 'I'm going to erect an enormous bronze statue to you right in the middle of Canonbury Square and hire a sky-writer to write in the sky 'Ron Herringe Saves Lives'.' She turned to fling a dramatic arm across the shop and caught sight of Emma by the drawer handles. 'Josephine! What a lovely surprise!'

If Mr Herringe had observed that Emma was being addressed by a name other than that which her parents, her sisters and her friends had called her for most of her life, he betrayed not one flicker of reaction.

'What a stroke of luck running into you two Saturdays in a row,' continued Alice. 'Don't you just love the way London always throws the nicest people together? I wonder if it happens in other places? No, of course it can't, because all the nicest people live here, don't they? I've been having the most wretched drama, darling, I'm a positive nervous wreck and if Ron here hadn't ridden so gallantly to my rescue like the knight in shining armour that he is, I'd have toddled off to the zoo and poisoned myself with an asp like Cleopatra.' She collapsed onto a chair and fanned her hand across her chest. 'I broke my iron,' she announced.

Emma decided she could use a jolt of Alice in

her day. She sat down on the chair next to her, and adopted an expression of suitable sympathy.

'Your iron,' she said.

'And it wasn't just any old iron,' said Alice. 'It was positively my dearest, my best iron in the whole wide world, and if my wonderful, wonderful Ron here hadn't fixed it for me in time for ironing tonight, I just shudder to think what I'd have done.'

Saturday night ironing, thought Emma. By an Oscar winner in a Georgian house in Canonbury Square. Well, the rich were famously eccentric.

'Ironing can be quite therapeutic,' she remarked politely.

'Do you think so?' said Alice. She wrinkled her nose distastefully. 'Well, each to her own, darling, but I personally find it the most tedious occupation known to mankind. Standing like a soldier over that great pile of shirts with your arm going *in* and *out* and *in* and *out*, and you keep having to splash water everywhere or they'll dry out, and you can't have a drink because you'll spill it, and you can't have a chat because you'll get distracted and get the creases in the wrong places, and you can't watch telly because you'll get terribly cross with the actors — I can't begin to tell you the shirts I have ruined over *Doctor Who* — no, you just have to stand there concentrating and getting so bored you just want to shriek in agony.' She stopped, and looked at Emma, thoughtfully. 'But if *you* find it therapeutic, darling, then maybe it can be if one puts one's mind to it. That's a very good idea, in fact. I'll definitely think about it.'

She fell silent, looking pensively into space.

After some resistance, Emma cracked.

'If you don't like it,' she said, 'then . . . why do you do it?'

'What?' Alice looked up at her, puzzled. Then, 'Oh, for Johnny,' she said. 'He loves it. Always has.'

Johnny Genovese was Alice's husband, a much-feared director of action movies. Emma wondered just how deeply Sophie would disapprove if she were to spread the word that he kept his glamorous wife chained to the ironing board on Saturday nights.

'Poor lamb,' continued Alice. 'He lost his mum was he was only twelve — can you imagine, poor little mite — and he's generally frightfully brave and manly about it, well, you know Johnny, no talking about emotions *there*, thank you very much, but he did let slip just the once that the smell of ironing reminds him of her, and it does cheer him up so wonderfully when I do it. It makes *me* want to tear my hair out, but it means so much to him, that it's worth it.'

Suddenly, Emma felt ashamed of herself and rather small.

'That's nice of you,' she said, quietly.

'Well, you want to do things for them, don't you?' said Alice. 'They're so nice to us, after all, and there's really not much point if we can't be nice back. And, poor darling, Johnny goes through hell sometimes, well, can you imagine being married to *me*? Think of your sister, then imagine her after ten years of being spoilt rotten on film sets and with no elder sisters at home to slap her down. Yes. Quite.'

Despite herself, Emma had winced.

'But you know, Josephine,' said Alice, slowly, 'if *you've* found a way to find ironing therapeutic, then you've hit on a really very good idea. I find a lot of things can be therapeutic if you find a way to make them so, don't you? Darlings, look at the time, I must fly!' She leaped to her feet and swiftly kissed both Emma and Mr Herringe, who blushed like a boy. 'I wonder where we'll run into each other again?' she said to Emma. 'Isn't it fun to guess?'

Emma paid for the drawer handles, walked out of the shop and turned left onto Upper Street. She walked past the stop for the 19 bus, which for the flash of an Oyster card would take her clear across town, down Rosebery Avenue, and past Grays Inn, through Holborn to Charing Cross Road, around Piccadilly, along past Green Park to Knightsbridge and all the way beyond Kensington Gardens to Chelsea; she went past the graceful white façade of Islington Town Hall with a brightly coloured party gathered on the steps for someone else's wedding, and the small side street beside it that until recently had held a small farmers' market, now swallowed into the larger market in Chapel Street, where the cookery columnist for the *Guardian* had shopped and where Matthew had sometimes gone to buy a meat pie for Sunday supper; past Ottolenghi, where last week she had had coffee with Alice and Colin and Nigel and where next month she planned to buy *Ottolenghi: The Cookbook* for Lulu's birthday present; past the pub by the corner where, on a dusky winter afternoon in their childhood, she and Lulu had once found a five-pound note in the gutter and wondered what to do with it, since it was not theirs but did not appear to be anyone else's either: they had finally taken it into a bakery shop and stuffed it into the charity jar, which she now thought had been honourable of them.

Passing Manolete's, she saw Nigel through the window in full Manolete mode, swooping a stoutly elegant boot past the face of a sturdy middle-aged woman: turning to see her, he winked and then made a shooing motion to move on. She smiled and obeyed, crossing the street just before the Green to walk past the Screen on the Green, where Matthew had taken her on an early date to a screening of *My Fair Lady*, past the coffee shops and the wine bars and the small florist where she always bought lilies to take to Fee on Mother's Day, to the section across from Camden Passage where the pavement was elevated behind all the bus stops, where she had once unexpectedly come across Matthew and Sophie deep in conversation, Sophie laughing and gesticulating, Matthew listening with that quiet smile of his, and, seeing them briefly as a stranger might, had thought what a kind and gentle face he had, and how much she loved him.

At the bottom of Upper Street and on the other side of it was the side street that led behind the Angel Tube station to the Charles Lamb, the 180-year-old wood-panelled pub where she was to meet Matthew for lunch. But before crossing the street she turned right, through a small crack between buildings and into a gleaming shopping centre built around a giant steel sculpture of angel wings, where you could procure anything from jeans and T-shirts to Japanese noodles, from almond-oil soap to your choice of a dozen new films to see in the cinema complex. Emma walked to stand under the sculpture, and looked around at the teeming, chattering mass of humanity of Saturday morning London, at the liberated office workers and business moguls and schoolgirls, the students and tourists and young professionals, the actors and politicians, artists, bank clerks and, no doubt, pickpockets, at the light brown skins and the dark, at the mottled pinks, the smooth ambers, and the coffee-coloured, at the blue jeans and the saris and the dashikis, the pale pink cardigans on grannies and cream-coloured cashmere on glamorous young mothers, the cotton and silk, corduroy and crimplene, the shopping bags and the parcels, the satchels and the handbags and the pushchairs. She walked on through the crowd towards the Liverpool Street end of the shopping centre where there was a bookshop, three bright floors crammed tight with knowledge on every subject under the sun. She stopped outside, and smiled, and sighed. Then she went in.

'Can I help you?' said the assistant lurking near the door. He was young and pale, with a Londoner's sallow skin, pierced eyebrows, and a spark of mischief in his eyes.

'I'm looking for the travel section,' she told him. 'I need to buy some books about North Dakota.'

8

Concord, November 1869.

Dearest Amy,

We have had our first Thanksgiving without Bethie, and though we *tried* to be gay, it was uphill work, I fear. Marmee got herself up in her silk and looked as splendid she always does with grandma's comb in her hair and a knot of winter roses in her bosom; Meg and John were there, too, Meg such an elegant matron now in her new winter suit, with the 'babbies' as cherubic as it is possible for them to be while still remaining human children. Hannah outdid herself with the turkey and the stuffing and the pies, father and John talked of books, Marmee and Meg talked of babies, and at the end of the feast father read to us, as he always does, the story of the brave men from whom we spring, who dared to cross the seas for freedom, and founded our great country. But there was one little chair that was empty now and always will be, and, although its occupant was a shy little soul who never said much and hid her face in the sofa-cushion whenever anyone praised her, oh, Amy, now that her quiet voice is silenced, how great is the void she has left behind.

Oh, ain't Jo dismal! I *won't* sadden you

further on your trip, Amy, not while you are so far away from all of us, but will tell you something comical instead, for there is always something comical in our family, it seems. Demi has discovered the delights of apple tarts. He has also decided that he likes the 'apple' portion a great deal better than he likes the 'tart'; and, being a boy of admirably practical bent, he addresses this by the simple expedient of sucking all the fruit out from the shell and discarding the remains in whichever spot he happens to have finished eating it, with the result that we have all of necessity acquired the habit of checking any chair most carefully before we sit upon it for fear we will find ourselves on rising adorned about our person with a damp circle of sticky pastry. Daisy, meanwhile, who most pleasingly combines feminine knack with a good Yankee detestation of waste, has discovered in those pastry shells the perfect source of new bonnets for her dolls. It is 'quite a landscape,' as Teddy would say, to see her rows of dollies all with their crumbling pastry headwear, this one decorated with a little daisy, that one with a tiny bow, for she has inherited all the good taste in dress of both her Mama and her Aunt Amy. Can you think how Bethie would have delighted in them, dear? Do you remember those poor invalid dolls she cared for so tenderly when we were all children? We laughed at her then, but I can only weep now to remember what a big and generous heart beat in the breast of that little girl while we had her with us.

I long for you to be home, Amy, for it is so quiet here without you, and I do get cross and lonely at times. Well, I'll comfort myself with the thought that you are the sister I *will* see again, when at last you have returned from your travels, and, oh, the stories you will have to tell then, and the jolly times we'll start to have once more.

Kiss my boy Teddy for me, and tell him to behave himself or he'll have me to answer to as well as you.

Ever your loving,

Jo.

On the morning after Sophie had arrived home from Coventry, Emma telephoned her at Fulla Beanz.

'How was Coventry?' she said. 'I heard about the floods.'

'It was amazing,' said Sophie. She swiped a towel over a coffee machine and perched herself against the shop's counter. 'The most awesomely creative experience of my life. We took the parts to places you would not believe. We were even able to use the rain because we found ourselves sincerely worrying about warping, it was really evolutionary.'

'Evolutionary,' repeated Emma. Then, 'Did you get any interesting phone calls while you were away?'

'Well, Mom was always on the phone to check I'd remembered to close all the windows — she'll never let me forget that time, although it was years ago and the bed did dry out eventually.

Lulu claims I took her brown jumper but Lulu's mad, she just won't get it through her head how pathetic her clothes really are. I haven't heard from Rupert, so I suppose we're not going out any more, but that's OK, we were starting to get on each other's nerves, actually. Oh, and Esme's found someone new, I hope he's more sensible than Jack, who I always thought was a bit sort of suspicious. He goes salsa dancing, which you really shouldn't if you look like Prince Harry.'

'Anyone else?' said Emma. 'Anyone I might want to know about, for instance?'

'Well, you've met Esme lots of times,' said Sophie. 'And I know you've met Jack because you were the one who noticed about him and Prince Harry. And if you must have it all about you, she and I were thinking of coming to see you in North Dakota during the summer. But not before June because her parents have their silver wedding anniversary in May, and — '

'I think,' interrupted Emma, 'that we have exhausted the subject of Esme, much as I love her. I was wondering whether you'd had any telephone calls about work lately.'

'No, Emma,' said Sophie after a moment. 'I haven't had any telephone calls about work lately, thanks for reminding me. If I had, I'd have told you about them.'

'Well, that's odd,' said Emma. 'You haven't heard back from *St Luke's*?'

'No again, Emma,' said Sophie. 'For the ninety-nine-and-three-quarter-millionth time, no, I have not heard back from *St Luke's*. It seems I need to explain to you that it seems they didn't like me as much as I'd thought they did. What is this thing about you and *St Luke's* anyway? You keep on asking me about it, and it's getting really annoying.'

'If you must know,' said Emma, 'I happened to have coffee with Colin Hobbes three or four weeks ago. And he told me quite specifically that — '

'Wait a minute,' said Sophie. '*You* had coffee with Colin.'

'Well, not with *him*, as such,' said Emma. 'I was having coffee with a friend, and we happened to bump into another friend who was with him, and we all had coffee together.'

'What friend?' said Sophie.

'Just a friend,' said Emma. 'I do know people you don't know about, strange as it may seem.'

'No you don't,' said Sophie. 'We know everything about each other, Lulu's always complaining about it.'

Emma sighed. 'Do you seriously think,' she said, 'that I have nothing better to do with my time but sit around inventing imaginary friends to impress . . . no offence, but . . . *you?*'

She had a point, thought Sophie.

'I wasn't going to tell you about this,' continued Emma, 'because I wanted it to come as a surprise. But I obviously mentioned you during my conversation with Colin, and when I first started to talk about you I could see him doing that actor thing of preparing a diplomatic answer to brush me off without hurting my feelings, and then when he realized it was you I was talking about, he got genuinely interested,

304

said he'd particularly asked for you to come back on the show and had wondered why you hadn't, and then he wrote your name down on his BlackBerry, and said he was going to follow it up.'

There was a silence.

'Did he?' said Sophie, then.

'Yes,' said Emma. 'So if you haven't heard back from them four weeks later, I think there's a little bit of a mystery here, don't you?'

'Yes,' said Sophie. 'Wow. Yes. Did he really say he was going to follow it up?'

'Yes, he did,' said Emma. 'And I'm not like you, Sophie; I don't get carried away and imagine things, I only talk about things that really happened. And this most definitely did happen. So I think you need to talk to your agent — Maggie? — to find out what's going on.'

'Wow,' said Sophie. 'Yes. Wow. I'll find an excuse to go to see her today. I'll go on my lunchbreak, I'll just casually drop by. Should I take her some chocolate? She likes chocolate, but sometimes she goes on a diet. Would it be good to take her some chocolate or would she think I was encouraging her to get fat?'

'I don't know, Sophie,' said Emma. 'Because, you see, I've never met the woman. But I do think you should talk to her.'

'Wow,' said Sophie again. And again, 'Yes. Wow.'

There was another silence.

Then, 'What else did Colin say about me?' she asked.

'He said you were a grubby little nightmare,'

305

Emma told her. 'But once we'd both agreed on that, he said you were quite a nice sort of grubby little nightmare. And he said he thought that once you'd had some experience, you'd be a very fine actress. Ow.' She held the phone out at arm's length, and massaged her ear with her free hand. 'I hope you're saving your money,' she said after a moment. 'Because when I go deaf at fifty, I shall expect you to pay for my treatment.'

★　★　★

Maggie Gallagher, Sophie's agent, was a small-framed woman in her forties, with a whispery voice, flowing light brown curls and a fondness for ruffled dresses. She was known in theatrical circles as the Pit Bull.

'Choccies!' she cooed delightedly when Sophie handed her a gold-ribboned box. 'What a lovely thought, how clever of you! All for me!' With a dainty hand, she swept them firmly into a drawer. 'How are you, my precious? How was Coventry? Did you manage to keep your tootsies dry in all that rain?'

'It was really good.' Sophie sank herself into one of the over-stuffed chintz armchairs with which Maggie decorated her office. 'Rhys is amazingly creative, and it was an awesome experience. But something a bit, well, weird has happened, and I want to talk to you about it.'

'Something weird?' Maggie wrinkled her brow sympathetically. 'That'll never do, my precious. Tell Mummy.'

'Well, a couple of weeks ago, my sister had

coffee or something with Colin Hobbes, you know, the one who plays Dr Brodie on *St Luke's*?'

'Colin.' She smiled fondly. 'Such a sweet boy.'

'Yes, that's what my sister said. And she mentioned my name to him, and he told her he'd really liked working with me and that he'd asked them to ask me back to the show, and he was wondering why he hadn't seen me since. But you haven't mentioned them calling, and I'm just wondering what's happened. *Have* they called?'

'Oh, dear.' Maggie's smile faded, and she tapped her brow lightly to stave off a frown. 'No, my precious, I'm afraid they haven't called.'

She picked up a china shepherdess that adorned her desk, and began to examine it closely.

'But isn't that a bit strange?' said Sophie. 'My sister doesn't make things up, and she was very clear that that's what he said.'

'Oh, dear,' said Maggie again. She sighed, replaced the shepherdess, and looked at Sophie compassionately. 'I think there's just a teeny little something here that you and your sister don't quite understand. Colin's a sweet boy. A sweet, sweet, darling poppet of a boy, and a lovely actor, too. But he hasn't got what we might call the most enormous of brains, bless his heart, and meanwhile he's such a lovely little sweet darling of a poppet that he apparently hasn't yet noticed that since he brought Miranda Fentiman into the cast not a single one of the other actresses he has recommended who has been prettier than

Miranda has ever once been called back.'

'Oh,' said Sophie, feeling suddenly very young and somewhat foolish.

'I'm so sorry,' said Maggie. 'I thought that everyone knew about that.'

'No, I didn't,' said Sophie. 'I didn't know that at all.'

'Awfully sad for you, of course.' Maggie pursed her lips sympathetically. 'But there's your explanation, I'm afraid.'

But there was a bit of the story missing, thought Sophie.

'It doesn't really explain it, though,' she said. 'She's only Miranda Fentiman — she's barely even a regular. And he's Colin Hobbes. He's the top actor on the show.'

'And, my precious little girl,' said Maggie, 'since about five minutes after Miranda arrived on the set, she's been sleeping with the director.'

'Oh,' said Sophie again. She hadn't known about that, either.

'She's a popular sort of girl, is Miranda,' said Maggie. 'And I've noticed that she's been even more popular than ever since she took that lovely little holiday in Thailand a couple of years ago. She had such a useful time there, the clever girl. You can learn a lot in Thailand.'

But this was Miranda Fentiman, thought Sophie. Miranda Fentiman who cared enough about acting to have taken time off from television to do Chekhov at the Orange Tree. Miranda Fentiman who was talking to the people at the Vagabond.

'But she was in *The Seagull*,' she said.

'Oh, she's a lovely little actress,' said Maggie. 'Just lovely. And Lord knows dear sweet Colin would have had no reason to notice her if she hadn't been good. She's also just a very, very popular sort of girl.'

'Oh,' said Sophie, feeling younger and more foolish than ever.

'But I'll tell you what, my precious,' said Maggie. 'Now that we've got the *St Luke's* episode to show around, perhaps I can send you to meet a couple of new casting directors. Let's see.' She thought for a moment, squinting her eyes at a silver-framed photograph of herself as a child. 'I know,' she said then. 'I'll send you to see Hughie. Hughie Brown, he's a good friend of mine, and he knows lots of awfully good and clever people. He's a little bit of a naughty boy, but I think it's time we introduced you to some naughty people, isn't it?'

★ ★ ★

'I swear to you that that is what she said,' said Sophie later, drinking tea at the kitchen table with Lulu and Jamie while the November dusk fell outside. 'Cross my heart and hope to die, it's a word for word direct quote.' She cocked her head like an arch little bird and pursed her lips prettily. '"He can be the eensiest weensiest little bit of a naughty-waughty boydie, but I think you can deal with him, my precious.' And that is exactly how she talks, isn't it, James?'

'I wouldn't know,' said Jamie. 'She refused to take me on, didn't she?'

'Well, she doesn't do boys. She says they're loud and rude, although I can't see that they're worse than girls, I'm much louder than you and I'd say that bloody Miranda Fentiman is about as *rude* as it's humanly possible to be. But never mind, I'll go and soften up naughty Hughie Brown and once I've made friends with him, I'll take you to meet him and you can both be naughty-waughty boydies together. And talking of boys, Lulu, I spoke to Mom today and she says Tom says thanks for the invitation and he'd love to come.'

Lulu, brushing a piece of Hampstead Heath from her sleeve, looked up, puzzled.

'What invitation?' she said.

'You invited her to bring him here for Thanksgiving,' said Sophie. 'Remember?'

One of the American habits that Fee had brought with her to London was to celebrate Thanksgiving in November: for the last two years, Lulu had assumed the role of family cook.

'I didn't invite him,' said Lulu. 'He's welcome to come, but I didn't invite him. Maybe Mom did and forgot.' Her face darkened. 'No, she didn't. I bet bloody Emma did.'

Emma had not mentioned Tom to Lulu lately, and Lulu had supposed that with all her preparation for North Dakota, she had forgotten her matchmaking plan. Apparently not.

'Awww.' Sophie smiled. 'She wants you to be happy. She wants you to be in loooooove. Like her and Matthew, and Charlie and Javier.' Since the summer, Charlie and Javier had slid so seamlessly into a relationship that people were

310

starting to forget they had ever not been together. Sophie linked her arm through Jamie's and dropped her head sentimentally onto his shoulder. 'And Jamie and me,' she added.

Jamie smiled weakly. His skill in looking other than wistful when Sophie joked that they were boyfriend and girlfriend had not improved; and by this stage, thought Lulu a little sadly, it probably never would.

'She can want all she likes,' Lulu said now. 'If she's so fond of him, why doesn't she leave Matthew and run away with him herself? I hope we've got enough chairs for all these people who're coming, by the way. How many are we?'

'Ten, I think,' said Sophie. 'Mom and Dad, Emma and Matthew, Charlie and Javier, you and your smoochie-woochie cuddly-wuddly boy-friend Tom — '

'And if you don't cut that out, you'll be walking down to McDonald's for Thanksgiving dinner,' said Lulu. 'And don't think I don't mean it. How do you get ten? So far there's eight and maybe you, if you behave yourself.'

'Well, there's him.' Sophie nodded to Jamie. 'He eats enough for three, but he only actually uses one chair, although it should probably be the big one.'

'Are you coming, Jamie?' said Lulu.

'I don't know,' said Jamie. 'Am I?' he asked Sophie.

Lulu looked at her sister, and shook her head.

'Is this how you invite him?' she said. 'Your manners are terrible, Soph, you should take a course in etiquette from Miranda Fentiman.

311

Jamie, since it seems to be the family tradition this year for us all to invite people on behalf of each other, would you like to join us for Thanksgiving a week from Thursday?'

'I think that would be OK,' said Jamie. He had not learned how to pretend to hesitate before accepting dinner invitations, either.

★   ★   ★

Hughie Brown was a wirily built man in his mid-thirties, with a shock of black hair, rakish eyebrows and an expression of amusement.

'I liked your *St Luke's* reel,' he told Sophie when she visited him in his office high above Wardour Street.

'Thank you,' said Sophie. 'I thought Colin and I had a good connection. He's very nice to work with, actually.'

'So I hear,' said Hughie. 'And I thought that *you* looked very nice in the nurse's uniform.'

Sophie blinked in surprise. She was casually aware that she had a nice figure; however, this was the first time that she had had it complimented so directly in a professional context, and she was by no means sure that she welcomed it. But Miranda Fentiman, it seemed, was able to be a popular girl and a serious actress at the same time. Miranda Fentiman, in fact, was a quite successful serious actress. It was time, Sophie thought, that she grew up a little.

'Thank you,' she said. 'I really liked doing *St Luke's*. I was hoping to be asked back but it didn't happen.'

'The Fentiman Factor.' Hughie nodded. 'She's a problem, that one. Hard-faced number to play a social worker, I always think. But then there's a reason Tim decided to put her in baggy jumpers instead of a nurse's kit.'

Sophie was not usually unkind; but this was Miranda Fentiman, after all.

'Shouldn't that be two reasons?' she asked demurely.

He laughed; then looked at her with increased interest.

'I think we can do better for you than *St Luke's*, can't we?' he said. 'Are you up for meeting people? Going out and putting your face around a few parties and so on?'

'Absolutely,' said Sophie. 'That sounds like fun.'

'It helps if people know you,' said Hughie. 'Let's face it, there are dozens of pretty young actresses walking through a director's door every time he opens it — no matter how talented you are, it's hard to get yourself noticed. If you're not just pretty blonde Sophie Atwater but pretty blonde Sophie Atwater who made that witty comment at the party last week, that might just make all the difference. Now, let's think.' He frowned at her thoughtfully. 'Do you know Johnny Genovese?' he said after a moment.

'Of course,' said Sophie. 'Well, I don't *know* him, but of course I know who he is.'

'Used to be a great party man, did Johnny,' said Hughie. He smiled, reminiscently. 'God, we'd get wrecked and get into trouble, we made Ollie Reed and Richard Harris look like Little

Red Riding Hood and Little Bo Peep. Then he married that awful shrieking Weathers woman and all the fun had to stop. But she does let him give parties occasionally, I will say that for her, and they're pretty damned popular parties, too. Want to come to one?'

A party with Johnny Genovese, thought Sophie. A pretty damned popular party with Johnny Genovese and Alice Weathers and all their director and actor friends.

'Do I!' she said.

'Good,' he said. 'And we're just in time because he's off to Hollywood at the end of the month to make the Rocky Marciano thing. But he's giving just the one last bash before he goes, if you'd be free for it?'

'I'll make myself free,' said Sophie, carefully refraining from pinching herself for joy. She sat up straight and saluted, smartly. 'Private Atwater reporting for party duty, sir.'

'That's what I like.' He winked at her approvingly. 'A girl with dedication to her craft. Let's see. The party's on Thanksgiving. And Thanksgiving is . . . when is it?' He reached into his pocket for his BlackBerry.

'A week from today,' said Sophie, quietly. 'My mother's American.'

'Is she, now?' said Hughie. 'Yes, you do have that wholesome corn-fed look going for you. Yes, there we are, Thursday of next week, Johnny's place in Canonbury Square. Do we have a date?'

'I suppose we do,' said Sophie.

★ ★ ★

314

'But you can't go!' said Lulu later that cold and windy night as they warmed themselves on a supper of thick vegetable soup and bread and cheese. 'You've asked Jamie to come here.'

'Well, he can still come to dinner,' said Sophie, although a little uneasily. 'It's not like he doesn't know the rest of you, is it?'

'And I'm sure he'd just love to travel halfway across London to spend the evening with Emma and Charlie and me while you're out chatting up directors. Tell her, Charlie. It would be really unfair to Jamie, wouldn't it?'

'If he did come alone, I know Javier would like to see him,' said Charlie. 'He's still a little nervous of the rest of you, but Jamie makes him laugh.'

'Don't drag Charlie into this, Lulu,' said Sophie. 'It isn't her problem, and it isn't your business, either. It's between Jamie and me, and Jamie will understand.'

'Will he?' said Lulu. 'I wouldn't if I were Jamie.'

'Well, you're not Jamie, are you?' Sophie poked with her soup spoon at a piece of carrot. It was obviously not an ideal situation as far as Jamie was concerned, but it had become apparent to Sophie that, in order to succeed as an actress, she needed to work a little harder than she previously had on her popularity. Sophie had certainly no intention of going so far as Miranda Fentiman apparently went in her quest for friends; and if and when Sophie became successful then she was certainly not going to block other young actors from sharing in her success. But if popularity were a pathway to success, then it would be foolish of Sophie simply to ignore it. 'Jamie and I are in the same profession,' she said. 'We know there are certain things you have to do that you might not have done otherwise. We both want to be successful, and we've both made a pact that when we get opportunities we'll share them with each other. And who knows what opportunities this party might lead to? It could end up being good for both of us.'

'It could end up,' said Lulu, 'that he gets you an awesomely creative opportunity to go to Coventry to play a surfboard . . . '

'Skateboard,' corrected Sophie.

' . . . skateboard, and the way you repay him is by standing him up for Thanksgiving dinner. Have you talked to Mom about this?'

'She and Dad have gone away,' said Sophie. 'Remember?'

Fee and David, who had taken lately to going on trips together, had left that morning for a long weekend in Washington DC.

'That's the second time they've gone away since the summer,' said Sophie now. 'I don't know what they find to say to each other when we're not around.'

'They have stuff they want to talk about,' said Lulu.

'Oh, like you know all about it,' said Sophie. 'I suppose you're their personal marriage guidance counsellor now.'

'If I had been,' said Lulu, 'I'd have told them to stop the family at two children.'

★　★　★

Walking a large retriever down the hill behind Flask Walk the following bleak and chilly day, Lulu found herself wondering with a certain detached curiosity whether she were currently more irritated with Emma or with Sophie. Sophie was the more obvious choice, she thought, because she was close at hand and the wealth of material was great, from Lulu's missing brown jumper, which had been found stuffed into a pocket of their father's spare suitcase, which Sophie had borrowed for her trip and at last got around to unpacking, with Sophie claiming she had mistaken it for the lining for Toby's cat carrier, to her latest idea for Thanksgiving, which Lulu thought so unfair to Jamie and which Sophie apparently did not. On the other hand, Emma's irritant factor was more personal. It was one thing to walk off absent-mindedly with an item of Lulu's clothing; quite another to try to meddle in her romantic life.

However she might protest to the contrary in public, Lulu did feel lonely at times without a boyfriend, and particularly so since Charlie had taken up with Javier, a quietly handsome young man who looked at Charlie with such naked love that Lulu sometimes felt a corner of her heart would burst with longing to have someone look so at her. But that did not, she thought now crossly, by any means lead to the inevitable conclusion that the man she wanted to look at her must be Tom. Or did it? She thought about

Tom now, trying to see him as a potential girlfriend might. He was certainly not an unattractive man — if not exactly handsome, then good-looking enough, in a sandy American way, with broad shoulders, strong, freckled hands, and a kind smile. Lulu had always liked a kind smile. She liked his company, too. They shared both a sense of humour and a mild eccentricity, and it was true that, either despite or because of their age difference, she felt at ease with him in a way she felt with few younger men. But did that mean she could feel romantic about him? He was older than her, she thought, doubtfully, and, in some ways, too similar to her to be intriguing to her; she enjoyed his company, but he did not thrill her as Herr Bhaer had thrilled Grandma Jo all those years ago. And surely, thought Lulu, she deserved to be thrilled as her ancestor had.

She shivered through the cold air to the house of the banker who owned the retriever, delivered the dog and wandered back up the hill, wondering what to do with the couple of hours that remained before her next appointment. It was a mean-spirited day, she thought, with a pinched white sky and a spiteful wind that rattled the bare branches of the trees, not a day to be outdoors for longer than one could help. But Sophie was at home today, on her day off from the coffee shop, and had stated a clear intention of moving no further than the chair by the fire in the living room; and on the whole, Lulu thought, she would rather face the wind than her younger sister right now. It still left two

318

empty hours though, she thought disconsolately, huddling her coat closer around herself for warmth.

She could, of course, she thought then, go to her parents' house. She examined the idea, and the closer she looked at it the more attractive it became. She could be there in twenty minutes and have more than an hour to spend in the attic with the letters; she could even, she thought, with a faint but perceptible lifting of her heart, give herself at last the pleasure she had withheld for so long and read the last of the New York chapter, the letter in which Grandma Jo would at last win Herr Bhaer's heart. It would be the perfect time to do it, in fact, she thought. Since her parents were away — off in a snug hotel in Fee's country's capital, rediscovering their own love which had been so threatened — there would be only Lulu in the house for Grandma Jo's love story, Lulu and the spirit of the long-dead young woman who had been odd and eccentric and whom her older sister had tried so unsuccessfully to make matches for, and who at last, and all on her own, had won the love of a handsome young man with thick yellow hair. Oh, yes, she thought, it was unquestionably time that she allowed herself that particular treat. She would, in fact, buy herself a celebratory bar of chocolate to accompany it. She quickened her step, and when she reached the end of Flask Walk turned, not left towards Belsize Park, but right towards the Tube station.

★ ★ ★

319

Nearly an hour later, she sat in the attic, staring in surprise at the piece of paper in her hand.

New York, January 1868.

Dearest Meg,

By now you will have guessed from my silence that my plans for the New-Year's eve party did not turn out as I had hoped. I made myself sound cheerful in my letter to the family, but the truth is I'm anything but cheerful, Meg. My heart is hurt, I'm sad and lonely, and feeling more foolish than ever before to have dreamed that any gentleman so handsome as Herr Friedrich Boormann could ever have cast sweet glances at one so thorny and plain as me.

The parts of the party that I told in the family's letter are true, Meg — never told fibs to anyone, ain't going to start now. I *did* rig up as Mrs. Malaprop, and I *did* dance, and joke, and make play, and I enjoyed it, too, and I did make Herr Boormann laugh at me harder than anyone else did — I'm good for making sport, it seems. But when midnight struck and we all unmasked, I looked across the room to him and saw him standing beside the mantelpiece with stupid little Lucy's hand on his arm in that detestable way she has. I walked towards him eagerly, thinking to claim my prize, and drew into earshot just in time to hear Lucy say to him, 'What capital fun that queer Miss March can be when she unbends. It quite makes me yearn to be an old maid, too.'

'You vill nefer be as plain as old Mees Marsch,' he replied, looking at her with a meaning in those beautiful blue eyes that even I could not mistake, and so, arm in arm, unseeing of me, they strolled together out of the parlor and into the garden.

I made myself look gay for an hour, for my pride made me hold my head high. But as soon as I could creep away, I went to my room to weep my heart out for my foolish hopes and stupid regrets. I *am* plain, and awkward, and old, Meg, and it was nothing but vanity and imagination to think Herr Boormann might look at me; if I rig myself up to be a guy and make people laugh at me, then that don't mean they'll love me. I know that now.

Well, if I am to be an old maid, at least I shall make sure to be a useful one. Professor Bhaer is still in his delight about the pipe holder I gave him for Christmas, and it does me good to see it. I'm still plugging away at my German lessons with him — shan't let a little thing like a broken heart stop me from the pursuit of knowledge — and even beginning to fancy I am making some progress, so *one day* I shall be able to read Schiller and even Goethe in the original, see if I don't. The Professor is a fine teacher, even though he does resemble a middle-aged Struwwelpeter!

With love from your sadder but wiser sister, Jo.

Lulu turned the paper in her hands, absorbing this unexpected turn to her great-great-grandmother's love story. So she had not, after all, married the handsome young student with the thick yellow hair and the charming manner; and meanwhile, and quite by coincidence, the real Professor Bhaer had been present all along in the correspondence, and from Jo's description was a middle-aged man with a wild beard, and a capacity to be delighted by something so simple as a pipe holder. Lulu laid down the last letter and went back to read them all from the beginning, examining them for mentions of him. Yes, there he was, homely and stout, with a propensity to pull at his beard until it resembled a great towzled brown bush, and a resemblance to someone with a curious name which she must find out about. What a far cry he was from the handsome young man with the rich blue eyes and the gallant manner.

But the story had had a happy ending at last, Lulu reminded herself, quickly. If not handsome, Professor Bhaer had apparently been a kind man; Jo had mentioned his good nature more than once. And he was intelligent, too, and apparently skilled at his profession of teacher, since by the end of the letters he had obviously managed to arouse in Jo a genuine interest in German. And you didn't need thick yellow hair to be a good husband, Lulu added sternly to herself; in fact, it seemed that handsome Herr Boormann had revealed himself in the end to be very far from a prize, a nineteenth-century equivalent of one of Sophie's passing boyfriends, looking for little beyond blue eyes and a pretty smile. The family had always said how happily married Grandma Jo had been, how she had adored her husband every bit as much as he adored her. It was just a surprise, she told herself, that Jo's husband was not handsome and young after all; it just took a little getting used to. She read the letter again, wondering about the person with the odd name, Struwwelpeter, to whom Jo had compared the Professor, who seemed to be a character from history or literature. She had never heard of him, but would look him up. It might turn out that, whoever he was, he had been interesting in his own way. Maybe, in his own way, even a little dashing.

She replaced the letters in the box and climbed down the ladder to the landing by the stairs. As she set the ladder in the corner, the door of Tom's room opened.

'Hi there,' he said. 'I thought I heard the dancing squirrels again.'

'Hi,' she said. Then remembered that he was a scholar of literature. 'Have you heard of someone called Streuelpeter?'

'Struwwelpeter,' he nodded, correcting her pronunciation. 'A nineteenth-century German children's book.'

Yes, thought Lulu, that would make sense. It might even be hopeful: there were some adventurous types, she remembered, in nineteenth-century children's books.

'What was it about?' she said.

'A collection of cautionary tales,' he said. 'Struwwelpeter was a kid who never, ever combed his hair and everyone hated him because of it.'

And so went the last of Lulu's hopes for a shred of glamour to attach to Great-Great-Grandfather Bhaer.

'Untidy hair,' she commented with some dignity, 'does not make you a bad person.'

'According to the guy who wrote Struwwelpeter it does,' said Tom. 'It's a real feel-good work, is Struwwelpeter. It also has a little girl who plays with matches and burns to death and a little boy who sucks his thumbs and someone comes to cut them off. You should read it next time you need cheering up.'

'I'll bear that in mind,' she said. 'Thanks for the suggestion.'

He tipped his finger to an imaginary hat. 'Happy to oblige, ma'am.'

She began to smile; then, abruptly, stopped. Tom, like Professor Bhaer, was a foreign-born scholar, with a kind heart. He was some years older than Lulu, and, although clean-shaven, had thick brown hair. To Lulu's alarm, she found herself noticing that Tom, at least, was apparently in the habit of employing a comb.

'You're coming for Thanksgiving, aren't you?' she said, reaching desperately for something to divert her mind from the unwelcome pathway upon which it had set itself.

'Looking forward to it.' He smiled that kind smile. 'What can I bring?'

'I don't know,' she said. 'Maybe some wine if you want it. Is there anything I should know about you and food? Are you allergic to anything?' And he was, of course, she now remembered, Californian. 'Are you a vegetarian?'

'I order the full English breakfast,' he reminded her, gently. 'At Carroll's.'

'Oh, yes. Sorry, I wasn't thinking.'

'He's really absent-minded,' she had told Emma at some point during the summer. 'He said it drove his ex-wife crazy.'

'Well, there you are,' Emma had replied. 'You're like two peas in a pod — you can drive each other crazy.'

'Speaking of Carroll's,' he said, 'I'm on my way there now. Do you want to come?'

Two peas in a pod, she had said. Driving each other crazy.

'God, no!' she said quickly.

He smiled. 'You know your own mind, don't you?' he said.

'Sorry,' she said. 'I was thinking about something else. I can't come to Carroll's, unfortunately — I have to be somewhere for a dog. I don't want to be rude, but I really, really can't come. Truly.'

'It's OK,' he said. 'We'll do it another time, maybe.'

They parted at the front gate, and she watched his broad, surprisingly athletic back as he walked down the street and around the corner.

★ ★ ★

That evening, Sophie presented herself at the greetings-card shop in Chelsea where Jamie had been working late. He was selling a birthday card to an elderly customer, and when he saw her his face became alight.

'What are you doing here?' he said. 'I thought this was the day you were staying by the fire all day.'

'I have a craving for Thai food,' she told him. 'And you're the only person I know who likes it as hot as I do.'

'You didn't have to come all this way,' he said. He looked at her, beaming in unconcealed joy. 'It's freezing cold out, I'd have met you somewhere.'

'Well, I wanted to see where you work,' she said. 'I've been indoors all day and it was starting to drive me mad, and Lulu's come home in the worst mood you can possibly imagine. And we've been to all the Thai places near me, I want to try one around here. A hot one.'

All of which statements were perfectly true, she reminded herself. Perfectly true, and ample reason for her having made the journey across London. She was not feeling guilty about what she was about to tell Jamie over the Thai meal, which was one of his many favourite sorts of food, for the simple reason that there was no reason to. She had made a professional decision about how to spend her Thanksgiving, which, yes, was a little bit unfortunate for him, but which would benefit her more than it would inconvenience him, and might in the future benefit him, too. Jamie would understand this. Any reasonable person would.

'There's a place round the corner,' he said, his smile, impossibly, broadening at the prospect of an evening involving both Sophie and Thai food, 'where the chili blows the roof of your mouth all the way through the top of your skull.'

'James Roderick MacNichol,' she announced, 'you are my kind of man.'

As they walked down the dark London street, she slid her hand through his arm.

'Are you warm enough in that?' he asked, plucking at her black cloth jacket: Sophie rarely wore as many clothes as other people. 'You can borrow my coat if you want, it's bloody cold.'

'I'm fine,' she said. 'I'm half Bostonian, and we're pretty hardcore.'

'Well, it looks like we're getting some Boston weather to celebrate Thanksgiving,' he said. 'I'm looking forward to that, by the way. I've never had a Thanksgiving dinner. What do you eat besides turkey?'

'Lots of things,' she said. 'But let's not talk about food till we get to the restaurant, because I'm seriously hungry and the thought only makes it worse. I'm going to order that spicy mixed seafood thing. Do they have it there? Hope they do, because my mouth's all ready and sort of tingling for it.'

'Thought you didn't want to talk about food,' he said. 'Hey, how did it go with the naughty-waughty boydie? Did he say anything interesting?'

'Actually he did,' she said. 'He said some really good and useful stuff, and I want to talk to you about it when we get to the restaurant. But I can't talk till I've got some food in me. I've just realized I forgot to have lunch.'

He tapped her on the head with his knuckles. 'Well, you were a wally-ette, then, weren't you?' he said.

The spicy mixed seafood, when it arrived, was both substantial and fiery.

'Delicious,' pronounced Sophie, forking a hefty mouthful. 'The most seriously delicious food that anyone has ever tasted in the history of the world, and I'm not exaggerating. Jamie, I need to talk to you about Hughie Brown.'

She paused, marshalling her thoughts and feeling suddenly anxious. But there was no need to, she told herself then. Jamie would understand. Jamie always understood.

'We had quite a long talk,' she said. 'And he said some really interesting things.'

But that was odd, she thought. She felt very anxious indeed, more anxious, now that she thought of it, than she had ever been in her life. Her heart was racing and the inside of her mouth felt what could only be called strange.

'He said — ' she began, but she never finished the sentence. Instead, she felt her throat close up and the table rush towards her, and caught a brief glimpse of Jamie's terrified face before she fainted.

★ ★ ★

When Lulu arrived at the hospital, Jamie was in the waiting room, looking relieved.

'They've taken her away,' he said. 'But it turns out it's nothing serious, just an allergic reaction.'

Actors, thought Lulu, irritated. Their heads so

far up in the clouds they could talk to the man on the moon.

'What do you mean?' she said. '*Just* an allergic reaction?'

'Well, just an allergy,' he said, surprised. 'I have them from strawberries. It itches a bit and then it goes down; it's uncomfortable but it's no big deal.'

Lulu sighed. She had occasionally wondered just what was taught at drama school; apparently, it had not involved science lessons.

'For your information,' she said, 'anaphylaxis is a potentially serious medical condition. I'm overcome with relief to learn that in *your* particular case it's just a little bit of an itch which goes away, but in fact it comes in all sorts of forms and can go to all sorts of degrees, and if it's serious enough — which it quite often is — it can make your throat swell up so that it blocks the breathing and you die.'

How could he not know that? she thought. Everyone knew that. Really, he was every bit as scientifically illiterate as Sophie. Then she remembered where they were and why they were there; and then she noticed that his face had turned very white, and that she herself felt suddenly very sick.

'Are you the sister?' A small man was at her elbow, with a kindly face and a mop of baby-fine silver hair.

'One of them,' she said.

He extended a small, warm hand. 'Dr Chisholm. Shall we sit down to talk?'

Gently, he led them both to a couple of chairs

in the corner of the room.

'Your sister,' he said, 'is having an anaphylactic reaction. She's gone into shock, and we're doing everything we can to reverse the effects. It seems that she ate something this evening that she's allergic to — her boyfriend says she had shellfish for dinner, so it's probably that.'

'Shellfish?' There flashed into Lulu's memory a picture of Sophie, aged sixteen, on a family trip to France, finishing an enormous dish of mussels, then dipping her face ecstatically into the bowl to slurp the broth.

'It can't be shellfish,' she said. 'Sophie isn't allergic to shellfish.'

'People can be allergic to some shellfish and not to others,' he said. 'But that's not the point now. The point is that she is having a reaction, and we're trying to counteract it. What typically happens in these cases is that after a few hours the reaction will subside; and if your sister survives that — which we are making every effort to make sure that she will — she'll be fine. She's a strong young woman, which is in her favour.'

He was being reassuring, thought Lulu, her mind suddenly floating in and out of her body in the strangest way. Doctors were trained to be reassuring. Unfortunately, Lulu had a degree in biochemistry and understood the situation.

'You can't know for sure, though?' she said. 'Can you?'

He looked at her for a moment, then shook his head.

'We can't know for sure,' he agreed. 'If she

330

survives, she'll be fine. But — no, we can't know for sure.'

If she survives. 'If wishes were horses, beggars would ride.' Sophie, aged fourteen, lugubriously mimicking a now-dead elderly aunt who had been fond of the expression.

'We're doing everything that we possibly can for her,' said Dr Chisholm. 'She's strong and young, which will help greatly.'

'I'm dyyyyyiiiing.' Sophie, sometime in the spring, flinging herself onto the kitchen sofa in imitation of Great-Great-Great-Aunt Beth, who had died young.

'There's reason to hope,' he said. 'She's a strong young woman after all.'

He had said that twice before, thought Lulu. And the only reason that people ever said there was reason to hope, was when there was also reason not to.

The doctor patted her knee. 'Where are your parents?' he asked.

Oh, God, thought Lulu. Her parents. Renewing their love in Fee's country's capital.

'On holiday,' she said. 'In America. We should telephone them.'

Oh, God, she thought. Telling her parents.

'Not necessarily,' he said. 'It's the middle of the night there, and by the time they got here the crisis will have passed, one way or the other.' Lulu winced. 'You might want to spare them in the expectation that your sister's going to be fine.'

She looked up and into his eyes. 'If it were *your* daughter in there right now,' she said, 'would *you* want to be told?'

He looked at her with such kindness that she thought she could hardly bear it.

'Yes,' he said, softly. 'Yes, I would.'

When Emma arrived a few minutes later, the two sisters ran and clung to each other as if they were clinging to Sophie's life itself.

★ ★ ★

'I can't believe they've both let the batteries run down again.' Standing shivering in the hospital's car park, Emma pressed the 'end' button of her mobile phone and shook her head in frustration. 'I've told them again and again. What if an emergency happened?'

'Well, we're finding out now, aren't we?' said Lulu. 'Can't you remember the name of their hotel?'

'I'm not sure if they told me,' said Emma. 'It wasn't one of the big ones. I wonder if Tom knows. Have you got his number?'

'Of course I haven't bloody got his number!' said Lulu. 'Why the bloody hell would I have bloody Tom's number?'

'I'm just asking, Lulu,' said Emma. 'I think we're stuck on this one. Dr Chisholm said there was nothing they could do anyway, didn't he?'

Lulu closed her eyes.

'He said,' she said, 'that by the time they got here, the crisis would have passed. One way or — '

'You don't have to repeat that bit!'

'Sorry, Em.' But they couldn't just do nothing,

Lulu thought. 'I'll call the home phone anyway and leave a message there. Dad sometimes remembers to check.'

She punched in the number. Her father's voice answered, rich with the luxury of carefree ignorance. 'You've reached the Atwaters. Leave a message after the tone and we'll get back to you.'

But when the tone sounded, she could not at first speak. How to voice to her parents, off on a romantic weekend in Washington DC, snug in a hotel room with warm lighting and a deep and comfortable bed, the most terrible news that any parent could ever dread to hear?

'Daddy?' she said at last, hearing and barely recognizing her own voice. 'Daddy, would you phone me? It's quite important, Daddy, it really is. It — '

'Hello?' The machine clicked off as a voice broke into her message. Tom's voice. 'Is that you, Lulu?' he asked. 'I was just passing through the kitchen. What's up?'

'What's up?' 'The sky.' Sophie, aged five, prone on her back in a blue summer dress in the grass, convulsed with hilarity at the cleverness of it all.

'Sophie's dying,' she said. No, that could not be right. Sophie could not be dying. Sophie was too irritating to die. 'She had an allergic reaction to something and we're waiting to see if she'll make it. Do you know where my parents are? Both of their mobile phones have gone dead.'

'I'll find a way to track them down,' he said. Something in his voice had changed: it had become sharper, and somehow firmer. 'Sit tight

333

and wait. Which hospital are you at? I'll be there in under an hour.'

★ ★ ★

We are not whole without her, the letter had said, *and never shall be. We are a family of cripples who have lost a part of us that was more precious than any ordinary limb. If I could have my Beth back for only a day I'd trade places with blind, maimed Billy for life and think myself the richer for it.*

'I'm going to kill her,' said Lulu, biting at her thumb while Jamie fidgeted, Matthew paced, and Emma sat staring silently into space. 'If she pulls through, I'm going to kill her for what we're going through now.'

'Don't make jokes,' said Emma. 'Not about this.'

But what was she supposed to do? thought Lulu. Sit quietly as Emma was, and contemplate, seriously, a life without Sophie? A family of two sisters where once there were three? Photographs on the kitchen wall without a person attached, an empty chair at Thanksgiving? No, there could not be an empty chair at Thanksgiving, it was only days away; it was impossible that life could change so unimaginably and so soon.

'Hi.' The door to the waiting room opened and there was Tom, looking rumpled and carrying a battered Marks & Spencer's bag. Lulu astonished herself by flinging herself on him like a child.

'It's OK,' he told her, patting her a little

334

awkwardly. 'OK, now, it's OK.'

He did not, she somehow noted gratefully, tell her that it was *going* to be OK. Because, of course, it so very well may not be.

'I made some telephone calls,' he said, sitting on a chair. 'Good news is I've tracked down Fee and David's hotel — I did some detective work on the Internet and found his assistant, Jenny. Not such good news is there's a storm in Washington right now and the hotel seems to be having a power outage. No idea when it'll be back on, but Jenny's calling them every twenty minutes and as soon as she gets through she'll have David call Emma. Which leaves us with you guys.' He looked around at all four of them. 'Have any of you eaten?'

'Eaten?' said Emma. 'I can't even think about food right now.'

'Wrong.' He pointed a stern finger at her. His bearing had changed as his voice had on the telephone, Lulu thought: he had become older than all of them and had taken control. 'We all might be here for a long time and we need to get some fuel in. You two.' He switched the finger to Matthew and Jamie. 'Go to the cafeteria now, get yourselves some nourishment, and come back.' He rummaged in his bag for a couple of small parcels, and turned back to Emma and Lulu. 'As for you two, I've brought you peanut butter sandwiches and chocolate to keep you going for the time being — you can have either or both but you have to have something. And now.' He returned to the bag and drew out a large red cardboard box. 'We three are going to play Scrabble.'

There was a silence.

'Scrabble,' said Emma.

'Scrabble,' he assented. 'I've been in hospital waiting rooms before, as might be apparent by now. There's nothing you can do but wait, and while you're waiting there's nothing you can do but think, and that can get ugly at times like this. We want something to distract you, and I find Scrabble works as well as anything's going to. So how about it?'

There was another silence.

'Actually,' said Lulu, 'that sounds like a really good idea to me.'

Emma shrugged, weakly.

'Why not,' she agreed.

It was years since Emma and Lulu had played Scrabble together. In that time Emma had discovered opera, shared a flat with a girl who had subscribed to *Yachts and Yachting*, and fallen in love with a computer professional; Lulu had acquired a degree in biochemistry.

'I do not believe,' said Emma shortly into the game, 'that isomer is a word.'

'It's as much a word as applet,' said Lulu. 'An isomer is a compound that has the same molecular formula as another one but in differing proportions. Everyone knows that.'

'If everyone knew it,' said Emma, 'then you wouldn't need to be explaining it, would you? I didn't understand a word of what you just said, and I think you made isomer up. I think you're cheating.'

'No, I'm not,' said Lulu. 'I don't cheat. I think you're confusing me with Sophie.'

The name hung shivering in the air for a moment.

'Does Sophie cheat?' said Tom, then.

'Cheat!' said Lulu. 'She forges vast new territories and claims them for her own. She's both fearless and legendary. She's the Christopher Columbus of the invented word.'

'Remember koalish?' said Emma. 'Not quite a koala bear but something that reminded you of one.'

'I liked elmee,' said Lulu. 'A person who has been knocked down by a falling elm tree.'

When Matthew and John returned from the cafeteria, they were surprised to find the sisters engrossed in a dispute over forestay.

'The food's not gourmet,' said Matthew. 'But it's not as bad as it could be. They have chicken, Emma, and some OK-looking salad.'

'I'm not going down there,' said Emma. 'I've had some chocolate, and I'm not going anywhere.'

'Nor me,' said Lulu. 'When Dr Chisholm comes through the door with the news, I'm going to be right here.'

'You probably should eat something,' said Jamie. 'It probably won't make you feel any better, but it probably would do you good.'

'I'm not leaving.' Emma shook her head. 'Not negotiable. I'm staying here until it's over.'

'You should eat something, Emma,' said Matthew. 'There's a cafe just down the road, shall I go and buy some chicken sandwiches?'

'Honestly, Matthew,' said Emma. 'I really don't care.' Despite herself, her voice had risen. 'I can cope with Scrabble,' she said, 'but that's about it. Please don't make me think about food or make decisions about anything because I can't. I just know that I'm staying here until I don't have to any more.'

'Why don't you both go for chicken sandwiches,' said Tom to Matthew and Jamie. 'And you might bring some coffee, too — the hospital stuff is terrible.'

After the men had gone, the Scrabble resumed, and Emma was surprised at how quickly she felt calmer. It was a good idea of Tom's to bring Scrabble, she thought, and a kind one, too; he was obviously a wise man as well as intelligent. It was strange, though, she added to herself, her mind skittering from subject to inconsequential subject in its effort to avoid the unavoidable one, that a successful professional man should choose to live cramped into a room in their parents' house instead of in a home of his own; and she had noticed that sometimes, when she looked at him when he did not know she was looking, he seemed a little sad. The next time her turn came, she looked at her tiles and spotted an opportunity which pleased her.

'*Lodge*,' she said, fitting the letters around the O of the disputed isomer. 'Like I wish a little sense of honesty would in my sister's non-existent conscience. And it's a double word score, which makes eighteen.'

'Interesting.' Tom looked at the board, and smiled, quietly, to himself. Then dropped five

338

tiles of his own. 'I have *query*. Q. U. E. R. Y. On the triple word score, which makes, yes, I do believe it's fifty-four. And I also get a few more on top of that for making *lodge* into *lodger*. Which is kind of what I am at your parents' house, isn't it, Emma?'

In any other circumstance, Lulu would have been delighted to see Emma blush for the first time in a dozen years.

Tom leaned back in his chair and looked over at Emma, his lips curling in amusement.

'You know, Emma,' he said, 'I have to say I'm sort of disappointed in you.'

'Sorry,' said Emma. 'I didn't mean to be crass.'

'I expect that kind of polite dodging around the subject from British women,' he said. 'I've lived here for a couple of years now, and I've even almost gotten used to it. But you, Emma — you're Fee's daughter, just like Lulu here. And if you want to know why I'm renting a room at your parents' house instead of living in my own place, I'd expect you to come out and ask me directly, rather than having your subconscious sacrifice a good game of Scrabble.'

'I am sorry,' said Emma. 'This all just feels so unreal and so strange that I hardly know what's going on in my mind right now.'

'I'll tell you what happened if you like,' he said. 'It's not a secret. Lulu asked me once before and I didn't feel like talking about it then, but if you're really interested I could tell you now.'

'You don't have to,' said Emma. 'I'm really sorry. I feel terrible now.'

339

'Don't,' he said. He smiled his kind smile at her. 'It's not like we have too much else that's pleasant to think about, right? OK, here's my story.' He reached to pick a couple of tiles from his shelf, sat back in his chair, and began to examine them.

'I've always been what I guess you could call a dreamer,' he said then, slowly. 'I come from a family of them. Both of my parents were college professors, and I guess we all three of us pretty much tended to live inside our heads. I remember bringing a friend home from high school once for dinner, and afterwards he asked me kind of strangely, 'Are your parents, you know, OK?' 'What do you mean?' I said, because they seemed OK to me. 'Well,' he said, 'they're nice enough people and everything. But . . . do they always sit at opposite sides of the table reading books to themselves through dinner?' First time I'd realized there was anything strange about it. We were a happy family, though. We used to make each other laugh and my parents were very happily married — they both died within a year of each other, which they say is a sign of a great love. That's when I found out about hospital waiting rooms . . . '

'When I grew up, there was never any question but that I should become an academic, too. So that's what I did. Went East to get my degree, bounced around the Midwest for a while, and then ended up back in Los Angeles again, partly because my dad had gone, and my mom's health was starting to fail, and I wanted to be around for her. I was able to read to her during the last few days of her life, I'll always be happy about that. Funny thing, she was a brilliant woman, spoke multiple languages, able to read Plato in the original, had once translated *Macbeth* into Latin just for fun, and what did she want to have read to her on her deathbed? *Anne of Green Gables*. She was no literary snob, my mom, I'll say that for her.

'Well, she died, we had the funeral, I did a good bit of crying, and then life started to begin again. And one evening, I was at a barbecue at a friend's house and there was a girl there who was an actress. And we started talking and she seemed to like me, and then we started dating and I figured out that I really liked her a good deal — she was blonde and sweet and prettier than any other girl I'd ever dated — so one day I took it into my head to ask her to marry me, and what do you know, she said yes. So we did, and we were very happy at first. We made each other laugh the way my parents had, we were young, and, God, she was pretty.' He stopped for a moment, and looked absent, as if remembering. 'We were very happy indeed,' he said then. 'And for a while I thought life just couldn't get any better.'

Slowly, he reached the tiles down to the shelf, and replaced them.

'Unfortunately, the happy times didn't last. Sarah thought it was amusing for a while to be married to a professor, but the novelty pretty soon wore off, and she was left with a guy who didn't notice if she cut her hair or if she grew it or if she dyed it blue, a guy who didn't go to the movies, didn't watch TV. Plus, I don't much care for parties, and she loved them. It was part of her job, she said, to go to parties and be charming and meet people; I fairly soon had had enough of the sort of people she met at the sort of parties she liked to go to, and maybe I didn't make as much effort as I could have to try to get along with them, so pretty soon she started to go to the parties without me. After a while, and over the course of a couple of years, we just kind of drifted apart.'

'But that doesn't have to be a bad thing,' said Emma. 'Matthew and I do lots of things separately, and we still manage to get along.'

'But I know you do things together, too,' said Tom. 'Sarah and I got more and more into the habit of not doing things together, so much so that we ended up not doing anything together, and I'm such a dope about these things that I didn't even notice what was going on, until one day I happened to look up from the book I was reading over dinner, and realized that I'd been reading alone at dinner for several weeks straight. And by that time, Sarah had gotten into the habit of doing the things she did with another guy who she decided she wanted to be with instead of me. And, you know something, it was only then, when it was too late, that I realized that living in my head as I do, and neglectful of our marriage as I'd been by that stage, that I really couldn't fault her for wanting out.'

There was a silence.

'That's a sad story,' said Lulu.

'Very sad,' said Emma; but there was a frown of puzzlement on her brow.

'Good point, Emma.' Tom nodded at her. 'You're quite right. It explains why I'm single, but not why I'm living like a student in one room of your parents' house when most London University lecturers of pushing forty can afford a place of their own. Well, see, all these parties that Sarah liked to go to, they were quite the fancy parties, film premieres and award shows and such. And it seems you need fancy clothes for all of those parties, and you need a different set of fancy clothes to each one, because it seems that in the film world, to be seen wearing the same clothes twice is a fatal sign of poor acting skills. So every time Sarah went to a party, she'd buy herself a fancy new dress and add in some shoes and a new brand of make-up for good measure, and, because she wasn't very often working herself, despite all those parties and all those clothes, she'd put the cost of them onto all the credit cards that I didn't notice kept turning up at the house in my name. And here's where it's dangerous to be not so good at noticing things, because it wasn't until we were good and divorced that I finally got around to noticing that she had run my credit cards down to the tune of several hundred thousand dollars.'

'*What?*' said Emma. 'That's awful.'

'I wasn't pleased,' he agreed, smiling wryly. 'I could have gone bankrupt or just skipped out on the debts, but I didn't want to do that. I contacted the credit card companies and I managed to set up payment plans with all of

343

them, and then I did some sums and I worked out that if I lived very simply indeed for a few years, I could pay the debts in full and begin again. So that's what I'm doing.'

'But that's rather noble,' said Emma.

He thought about it for a moment.

'I don't think so,' he said, then. 'I think it's more a case that it was something that happened to me when I was young and dumb, and I don't want to be defined by it for the rest of my life. And even though these debts weren't my doing, still, if I didn't pay them, they'd be following me around always. I can't say the last few years have been fun, but this way, in a couple of years' time, I'll be fully free and able to start over. And poor little Sarah will be racking up a whole new set of credit-card debts on her own card or on someone else's, so I guess I've come out of it ahead after all.'

'Well, I still think it's noble,' said Emma. 'Don't you, Lulu?'

Lulu opened her mouth to reply, but as she did, the door to the waiting room opened, and Dr Chisholm stood leaning against the jamb, looking exhausted and old. He stood there for a moment that felt like an eternity, looking at them all with his kind, kind eyes. Then, very slowly, he raised his thumb.

At the same moment, the men returned with sandwiches and Emma's mobile phone rang feebly, crackling against the spotty reception of the waiting room.

★ ★ ★

'I'm going to kill you,' said Lulu a few minutes later, standing at the foot of Sophie's bed. 'We've been here half the night drinking disgusting hospital coffee, and Mom and Dad have had to cut their trip short.'

'Sorry,' said Sophie mildly. She was pale, and still a little groggy from the sedation, but apart from that was looking and sounding, impossibly, as Sophie had always looked and sounded before the world had changed forever. 'Was it very dramatic?' she asked hopefully. 'Did I nearly die?'

'You're going to be fine now,' said Emma, firmly. 'That's the main thing. You're going to be fine.'

'You nearly killed *us*,' said Lulu. 'Emma and I have lost half our lives with worry this evening. But *you*, it seems, are going to be just fine. Which is just almost too typical, isn't it?'

'They're going to keep you here for a day,' said Emma. 'But I gather that's just a formality. After that you'll be able to go home, and it'll all be over. You'll have to stay away from shellfish from now on, that's all.'

'No shellfish?' said Sophie, aghast. 'No mussels? I love mussels.'

'If you ever so much as look at another mussel,' said Lulu, 'I shall personally ram it down your throat, shell and all. You nearly died tonight, Soph.'

'So you said,' said Sophie. She blinked dazedly at Jamie, who had possession of the hand that Emma had not.

'You look awful,' she said.

'Of course he looks awful,' said Lulu. 'We all look awful. We've been through hell.'

'I feel fine,' said Jamie. 'Better than I've ever felt in my life. I feel really, really great, Sophie.'

'You see?' said Sophie to Lulu. 'Did you call an ambulance?' she asked him then.

'You had the works,' he told her. 'Flashing lights, wailing sirens, people rushing round with stretchers shouting things like *vital signs* and *stat*. It was all the most incredibly dramatic thing I've ever seen.'

'Cool.' She smiled, and then frowned. 'I'm going to be OK, right?' she asked Emma.

'You're going to be fine,' Emma said.

'I'll be out of here by Thanksgiving?'

Lulu sighed and shook her head.

'Yes, Sophie,' she said. 'You don't have to worry about that, you'll be out of here by Thanksgiving.'

'Good,' said Sophie. 'Because someone has to make sure that Jamie leaves some turkey for the rest of you.'

★   ★   ★

'I think,' said Fee the following Thursday as they sat over the feast of turkey and trimmings that Lulu had created, 'that we all know what we have to give thanks for this year.'

She raised her wine glass to Sophie who sat at the other end of the table, a little pale and quiet, with Jamie glued devotedly to her side while wolfing his meal with enthusiasm.

'I'm not giving thanks for her,' said Lulu.

346

'She's just annoying. She's been annoying me ever since she was born. I didn't even think it was possible for her to be more annoying than she already was, but last week she managed it.'

'She kept saying she was going to kill her,' said Emma. The sisters were still telling the story of the evening, to their parents, to Charlie and Javier, and to each other, repeating the events, trying to adapt their minds to what had happened and to what had nearly happened. 'I kept trying to tell her to shut up, but she just wouldn't. It was driving me mad.'

'I am going to kill her,' said Lulu. 'Not today, not tomorrow, but I'll pick a time. And now I know the method I'll use, too.'

'You can make as many jokes about this as you like,' said Fee. 'Just not in my hearing, please.'

'Sorry, Mom,' said Lulu. She turned her head away from her mother and towards Sophie. 'Bouillabaisse,' she mouthed.

'I'd like to propose a toast to Tom,' said Emma. 'The man with the magic Scrabble board who kept us all sane.'

'To Tom,' agreed everyone, while Tom looked embarrassed.

'And next,' continued Emma, 'I'd like to propose a toast to Lulu, who is seriously the most amazing cook I know.' She smiled at Tom, and then at Lulu. 'Isn't the food amazing, Tom?'

She might, thought Lulu then grimly, just find herself killing Emma before she got around to killing Sophie.

'Excellent,' said Tom. 'I didn't know you were a cook, Lulu.'

'She's an amazing cook,' said Emma. 'Have you tried the stuffing? Isn't it amazing? She cooks like this all the time.'

She would definitely kill Emma first, thought Lulu. Possibly before the evening was over.

'Is Thanksgiving in California the same as in Boston, Tom?' asked Charlie. 'My brother lives in San Francisco, and he says the West Coast is as different from the East Coast as New York is from London.'

It was as well, thought Lulu, kicking Charlie gratefully on the shin, that there were people in the world who were not her sisters.

★ ★ ★

'Amazing meal,' said Jamie some time later, wistfully patting his replete stomach. 'Everything was fantastic, Lulu. Everything.'

'Wasn't it?' said Emma. 'Is it time for coffee yet? Do you like coffee, Tom? Wait till you taste Lulu's, it's coffee perfection.'

'It's coffee, Emma,' said Lulu. 'Get a grip, please.'

'It is good coffee,' said Javier. His gaze flickered to Charlie with teasing affection. 'My girlfriend is half Italian, but when she makes coffee, she uses her Irish half, unfortunately. You will like Lulu's coffee, Tom. It's strong, like Spanish coffee.'

Lulu sighed. 'Who wants coffee?' she said. 'Who wants the mind-blowing tsunami of taste sensation that is a cup of bloody coffee? Everyone? OK.'

348

She ground the beans, measured them into a pot and set the machine to percolate. Then she opened the door of the fridge.

'And we've run out of milk,' she announced.

'You can't have run out of milk,' said Emma. 'I can't drink coffee without milk. How can you run out of milk?'

'Easiest thing in the world,' said Lulu. 'Share a flat with Sophie.'

'I'm a convalescent,' said Sophie. 'I need building up.'

'You need something, all right,' said Lulu. She positioned her back to her mother, and mimed winkling a prawn out of its shell.

'Want me to run out and get some?' said Tom. 'There must be a late-night store somewhere near here.'

'Oh, would you?' said Emma. 'There's one just round the corner, actually. I'm sorry to be picky, but I just can't take coffee without milk.'

'No problem.' He stood, and, to Emma's unutterable delight, looked down at Lulu. 'Come and show me the way?' he said.

* * *

The night was milder than it had been on the night of Sophie's accident, and the wind had dropped. Lulu and Tom left the house under a clear sky, turned left, and made their way together to the main road.

'It seems to me,' said Tom after a moment, 'that you and I are kind of what we Americans call odd ducks, wouldn't you say?'

'Probably.' Lulu looked up at him warily through the comforting curtain of hair that waved at the edge of her vision.

He nodded. 'I'd say we are,' he said. He paused. 'Your sister Emma, on the other hand,' he added, 'now, she's not an odd duck at all, is she?'

Lulu smiled into the darkness. 'Emma,' she said, 'is just about the un-oddest duck I know.'

'Mm-hmm.' He nodded again, quietly, to himself. 'She's a nice girl, Emma, I like her. But . . . I kind of have the impression that she thinks that every single odd duck in the world belongs in a tidy little pair with any old other odd duck, no matter what.'

In the dark of the night, Lulu began to feel relief spreading like hot tea through her body.

'I think she thinks,' she said, 'that after night falls, someone comes knocking on our doors and leads us back gently to the Odd Duck Enclosure to keep us all safe till morning.'

'Don't get me wrong, Lulu,' he said. 'You're a great girl. Really.'

'And you're a nice man,' she agreed. 'And you were amazing at the hospital. Really.'

'And it doesn't mean we can't keep on going to Carroll's,' he said. 'I hope we will, in fact, because I enjoy your company. It just doesn't mean it has to mean anything else, either.'

Lulu thought about this. 'I suppose,' she said after a while, 'that once you learn to go with it, there are some advantages to being an odd duck.'

'Big advantages,' he told her. 'Stick around

me. I'm the sensei master of duck oddity.'

'Humble Lulu-san at your feet and ready to learn, master,' she told him.

They bought the milk and walked back to the flat in companionable silence. When they got to the gate, Tom stopped, and laid a hand on Lulu's arm.

'Want to have some fun?' he said.

Lulu looked at him, and slowly began to smile.

'Oh, yes,' she said. 'Yes, I do believe I would love to have some fun.'

* * *

'How did you two get on?' said Emma when they entered the kitchen.

Tom and Lulu exchanged glances and refrained from smiling at each other.

'Fine,' said Tom.

'Fine,' said Lulu.

'What did you talk about?' said Emma.

'Nothing really,' said Tom. 'Did we, Lulu?'

'Nothing much at all,' agreed Lulu.

Emma looked at them both, and beamed.

'Oh, good,' she said.

Concord [undated]

Dearest Meg,

Thank you for your invitation. I felt quite the fine lady to be receiving so proper a letter, and on such good thick paper, too.

I rejoice to learn that Mrs. Brooke would be pleased to receive Miss March at a supper for

Mr. Brooke's birthday at Mrs. Brooke's house on Saturday. Miss March would be happy to grace the occasion with her presence, on the strict understanding that, if Mrs. Brooke produces so much as a whisker of Mr. Scott's brother, Mr. Scott's cousin, Mr. Scott's cousin's bootmaker, or Mr. Scott's cousin's bootmaker's apothecary, and pushes him towards Miss March with a meaningful smile and a hopeful glance, Miss March is turning directly on her heel and marching straight home.

If Mrs. Brooke accepts these conditions, then Miss March looks forward to attending and having a capital time.

With love,

Jo.

9

Concord, June 1870.

Dearest Amy,

Such goings-on! Aunt March has visited the Dovecote! Demi is to visit Plumfield! John is convulsed with laughter, and Meg don't know where to put her face! But I'm telling the tale all topsy-turvy, so will settle down and 'begin at the beginning,' as the King advised the White Rabbit in that nonsensical English book you sent us about the little girl who fell down the rabbit hole.

You know that Aunt March had not visited the Dovecote since Meg and John moved in there. Having told Meg on her wedding day itself that she 'thought she'd be sorry' for marrying John, she could hardly come a-calling like a plain friendly neighbor; and though they had all three been civil enough when they happened to meet at our home, still, there was a coldness between them that did not decrease, and — since John is every particle as stubborn in his way as Aunt March is in hers — if something hadn't happened to break it, it looked set to stay. I don't know for sure what did happen, but *had* suspected that father might have had a quiet word with Aunt; although, upon reflection, am now moved to wonder whether perhaps the old lady had received a wheedling letter from a certain favored niece who is spending her summer in Trouville? Whatever the cause, the post arrived at the Dovecote one morning last week bearing a note announcing the intention of Mrs. Henry Joseph March to pay a call in three days' time.

You have never witnessed such a commotion as that little house saw while it was being prepared for Aunt's visit. Meg flew around like one distracted, sweeping corners, wiping windows, moving this vase of flowers here to that table there and changing this picture on this wall with that looking glass on the other, then trying a different effect with an alternate composition, then deciding upon another, until at last she had arrived upon the perfect arrangement for her little nest, which was the very same one she had always had from the beginning, with the only difference being that its owner was now half perished from exhaustion. John looked upon all of this with quiet amusement — he's too good a man to have ever said an unkind word about the dreadful things Aunt March said of him, but there was a pucker about his mouth as he watched her activities, and all of her invitations to him to join her were met with a calm; 'Thank you, my dear, but I'm just as content to sit with my book and improve my mind, which always needs it, rather than the house, which doesn't.'

At last, the Dovecote was deemed fit for its

visitor, and the next matter to be turned to was the conduct of its younger inhabitants. Daisy, thought Meg, posed no cause for alarm, for, as you know, she 'loves evvybody,' and can generally be relied upon to be an ornament to the finest of society. Demi, however, was another matter. He has lately acquired the habit of repeating everything he has heard to everybody he meets, and sometimes to devastating effect. It was not his mother, nor his father, but no less an authority than Dranpa himself who took him aside for a discussion. He was not, he was instructed firmly, to inquire of his august Aunt the meaning of the words 'crotchety' or 'cross-patch'; he was not to ask what it meant to 'hoard like a magpie' or 'have a face so sour it could curdle the milk' (this last reprehensible expression, I confess, having fallen into his receptive little mind from the unwary lips of his Aunt Dodo); he was to be quiet, and respectful, and bear in mind that she was not only his Aunt March, but his Great-Great-Aunt March, and as such must be accorded all deference. He listened carefully to this oration, several times nodded his curly little head, and at last declared himself schooled in appropriate behavior. Meg was less than convinced, but as she herself said, 'Father had spoken — and what more could any of us do?'

The day arrived, and Aunt March descended, fatter than ever and splendid in new silk with an imposing rustle of petticoats. She lumbered into the house like a great purple elephant, and

355

leaning on two canes not just one, for her lameness grows worse and she *won't* have it that it is in any way a result of the fact that she spends her days sitting in a chair eating bon-bons and drinking lemonade. Meg and John greeted her hospitably, took her bonnet, gave her the easy chair, and at last produced for her inspection the twins, all scrubbed up in their Sunday suits, and — as Hannah said — 'fit to be shown to the Empress of Chiny herself.'

Alas for both appearances and maternal hopes of good behavior. And on this occasion it was not Demi who confounded his mother's expectations, but angelic little Daisy, the child who loves everybody, who took one glance at Aunt March and straightaway opened her mouth to let loose so dismal a wail of distress and terror that you would have thought she was being held captive by a tribe of banshees who were using her plump little form for a pin-cushion.

'What on earth ails that child?' demanded Aunt March, her imperious tones happily drowning from her own hearing Daisy's piteous cries of 'howwid lady,' and 'fwighten Daisy.'

'She has the stomach-ache,' I assured her, sweeping Daisy quickly into my arms and up the stairs into the nursery, there to comfort her with chocolate drops and cuddles until the poor little soul had forgotten her fright, and fallen asleep in my arms, quite worn out by the ordeal of the encounter. A comfort for her, but a sore loss for *me*, for I later learned that while I was attending to Daisy, I missed the best spectacle of the afternoon. It seems that after we had left, Demi stood for some time in front of Aunt March, examining her gravely, wearing his 'philosopher's face,' which makes him look so much like a little miniature version of father.

'Is you my Great-Great-Aunt?' he inquired at last, tugging thoughtfully at his collar, which *won't* lie flat no matter how Meg fixes it.

'I am,' she replied in her most magisterial of voices, bestowing upon him the famed 'Aunt March gaze,' that made us all quake so in our boots when we were children.

He continued to peer at her with furrowed brow and meditative air, and then interestedly asked, 'Is that because you has such a great great belly?'

Meg says she wished a tornado would strike, or an earthquake engulf them all into the bowels of the ground. But imagine her astonishment when, after a moment, the old lady actually burst out laughing, and declared, 'No, child, I have a great belly because I like my food far too well, and *you* are the image of your grandfather when he was your age. Would you like to sit upon my lap?'

Some time later, when I myself descended the stairs to rejoin the company, I was transfixed by the sight of Master Demi Brooke sitting at his ease upon the lap of the one he now calls his 'fluffy aunt,' and showering her with crumbs of sugar cake as he exposited to her most carefully the means by which 'cattle-pillars' turn into 'buttle-flies.' He is to visit her at home next week to be shown Uncle March's collection of rare insects. He is to stay with her when she goes to Plumfield next month. And he has assured her, to such of her relief as you may imagine, that she is not to bother herself unduly about Daisy, for, as he explained to her, girls are the oddest creatures, he and Parpar have agreed that they can never predict how Marmar will be from one day to the next (this causing shot-up eyebrows from Meg and a sudden fascination from John in the condition of his fingernails), but if she'll leave it to him to have a word with the little woman, he's confident that she'll 'come wound.' Who — except, I now more than suspect, for my most sly puss of a sister in France — would have ever thought we'd see the day?

All is well here otherwise. Marmee's tooth-ache is better; she did go to the dentist at last, and says she is glad she did, though she had dreaded it so. Father's shipment of books has arrived, which pleases both him and John, who still loves to read as dearly as he ever did, and can happily lose himself in a book through the noisiest of household din. And I saw little Mr. Parker in town the other day and asked him if he minded very much about you and Teddy; for he *did* care for you a great deal, for all that we laughed at him for it, and it ain't pleasant to be passed over, as I know too well by now — might tell you about that one day when you're not too busy billing and cooing with your lover. Mr. Parker looked sober for a moment, but then said that he had always known he would never merit a goddess such as yourself, and that it was a consolation to know that the man who *had* had the immense good fortune to win you was so capital a fellow as Teddy. Wasn't that sweet?

I will bid you — not *adieu*, which is how you've taken to signing your own letters, Mademoiselle, but a plain American good-bye, and leave you to go back to your 'lovering' with the capital fellow, to whom I send my best respects. And if ever I suggest to you again, Amy, that miracles do not occur in this world of ours, I give you full liberty to silence me with the two simple words, 'fluffy aunt.'

Your loving sister,

Jo.

★ ★ ★

It was a bleak morning in early December, and Lulu was walking up Hampstead High Street under a darkly swollen raincloud, wondering how she was going to be able to buy Christmas presents. She had been walking dogs for three months now: it was part-time work at best, and in spite of her frugality her severance pay from Mr Goncharoff was all but used up. Charlie had forbidden her to think about paying rent until she had found a more lucrative occupation; and Fee had adopted a habit of mysteriously finding herself on Sundays with more food than she could possibly eat and begging Lulu to take it home with her and off her hands. Even so, Lulu knew that she could not go on like this — she must find a job, if only for the sake of buying Christmas presents. Lulu was not a young woman who cared a great deal for material things: but Christmas would not be Christmas, she thought, if she could not give presents.

She would not, she thought, squinting warily up at the sky, be sorry to see the end of the year which had just passed. It had been a year of too many questions and too few answers: a year when something unthinkable had nearly happened to her parents, and something unspeakable had nearly happened to Sophie, and Emma had announced she would be spending the next year half the world away; a year when, once again, she had failed to identify a career path that attracted her enough for serious consideration. The only bright spot had been the discovery of Grandma Jo, the strange, spiky, uncomfortably intelligent girl who had grown into the woman the family had loved so. Unfortunately, Grandma Jo was unable to step out of her letters and tell Lulu how to identify her own road to happiness in this world which had shown itself capable of changing so suddenly and so completely; that task was for Lulu alone.

There was a crash as the raincloud opened, pelleting water from the heavens. Caught without her umbrella open, Lulu ducked into the nearest shop for shelter, a children's toy shop, its inside yellow and inviting against the steel-grey downpour without. She smiled at the proprietor, and for politeness pretended to peruse the shelves, turning over dolls and plush stuffed animals, idly remembering the time when such items had been a part of her own world. When she had been a child, she recalled, she had longed to be a grown-up; but now, in memory, childhood seemed a rather pleasant and privileged state, a fairytale existence in which food and clean clothes appeared as if by magic, nobody ever asked her about her career, and a giant incarnation of Mom or Dad would read her a story in bed each night. Lulu had liked to have stories read to her. She noticed now a shelf of books on one wall of the shop, and wandered over to examine them, wondering which of her own childhood books were still being read to children today. There was one she remembered with particular fondness, about a witch who had boarded a bus at Paddington Station and worked a charm, causing an originally drab and straightforward tale suddenly to erupt into an explosion of colours and unexpected pop-ups, bright flowers and exotic animals. The book was not on the shelf now, she noted with disappointment; maybe it had gone out of print.

'Want a toy.'

A child's voice came from behind her, a cacophonous cocktail of whine and menace. Lulu set her teeth; she had never had time for spoilt children.

'Now, we've already discussed this, haven't we, Oliver?' The adult's voice held the brightly placating tones of one who knew her place in the pecking order. 'We haven't come here to buy a toy for you — we've come here to buy a toy for

Rufus, because it's his birthday. Do you remember that it was your birthday only last week, and you got all those lovely toys, didn't you? Well, now it's Rufus's birthday, so it's his turn, isn't it?'

'Want a toy.' The voice had risen, slightly, but perceptibly.

'But we've been through this, haven't we, darling?' said the adult. 'Rufus gave you that lovely car for your birthday, and we're going to buy him this lovely robot that — look, Oliver, isn't it fun? — turns into a plane that turns into a submarine. And I'm sure that Rufus will let you play with it too, darling, because Rufus is a very kind boy, and kind boys let other boys play with their toys, don't they?'

'Want a toy.' The voice was definitely louder now, and the threat in it unmasked.

'No toy today, darling.' Without turning to look, Lulu could see clearly the desperation in the adult's smile. 'Now, you're going to be a very good and patient little boy, aren't you, darling, and stand there quietly while Mummy waits for nice Joanna to wrap up the present in the lovely way she always does. Thank you so much, Joanna, you are marvellous. And you can't have another toy, darling, because you've got all those lovely birthday toys at home already waiting for you, haven't you?'

'Want. A. *Toy*.'

'Ohhhh . . . ' The adult's voice wavered into a sigh. 'Oliver, darling, you are such a grumpy little boy sometimes. But I'll tell you what, darling. If you'll just stand by very, very patiently, and wait very, very quietly while Joanna wraps up Rufus's present, then perhaps, now just *perhaps*, mind you . . . '

'Ow!'

The boy Oliver, executing a triumphal war dance of victory, had careened into Lulu, knocking his head against her stomach and sending the book she had been examining flying to the floor.

'Excuse me.' Frowning, Lulu looked down at the child. He had a long head with hard dark eyes and a fierce expression. He reminded Lulu a little of the Jack Russell terrier she walked on the Heath on Monday afternoons.

'I think you need to pick that book up, don't you?' she said.

The boy looked up at her, and uttered a snort of derision.

With the Jack Russell, thought Lulu, it was all in the tone of voice.

'Pick that book up,' she said. 'Now.'

The boy's eyes widened in surprise, and from the corner of her own gaze Lulu saw his mother beside the till brace herself in dread. He looked at her for a long moment, and then, suddenly and without a word, bent to retrieve the book from the floor, and handed it to Lulu.

'Thank you,' she said. She looked the book over: happily, it seemed to be unharmed. 'Now you need to say sorry for running into me.'

The boy looked at Lulu.

Lulu looked at the boy.

'Sorry,' he said, then.

'That's all right,' she said. The Jack Russell,

363

she remembered, was actually quite a nice dog once you had established who was boss. 'Just watch where you're going in future. You'd better go to your mother now, hadn't you? She's waiting to go home.'

As mother and child left the shop, they both stopped in the doorway and turned to cast on Lulu an identical gaze of the purest astonishment.

'That was brilliant!' Joanna the shop owner was staring at Lulu, her mouth open in wonder. She had long salt and pepper hair pulled back into a ponytail, and a toothily pleasant face. 'Simply brilliant! How on earth did you do it?'

'I walk dogs,' said Lulu. 'It seems to be good training.'

'Well, I'm going to start walking dogs myself if that's the effect it has. That child is a nightmare. A beast. He's horrid.'

'I felt a bit sorry for him,' said Lulu. 'It's obvious that no one's taking the trouble to discipline him, so he doesn't know how he's supposed to behave.'

'Oh, aren't you sweet!' said Joanna. Lulu blinked in surprise: it was very many years since anyone had described her as sweet. 'Please forgive me for being so vile about him, I've become the most awfully jaded old thing lately, I'm afraid. I'm usually much nicer than this, but I'm run ragged at the moment, because my marvellous assistant has gone off on maternity leave — so selfish of her to want to have a life of her own, isn't it? He's a sweet little boy, though, one of those just squishably delicious babies and wonderfully smiley already, and she's very intelligently asked me to be godmother, because what better godmother could any child ask for than a lady who owns a toy shop?'

Lulu laughed, then looked around at the bright, warm room filled with books and toys, then back into the good-natured face of its owner.

'Have you found a replacement yet?' she asked.

*　★　★*

'You, in a toy shop?' said Emma, warming her hands on an oversized mug of coffee at Sunday brunch. 'Does she know what she's taking on? You didn't leave a single one of my possessions unscarred for thirteen years.'

'Three years,' Lulu corrected her. 'After that it was Sophie, and it was both of our things. I've got my story all ready for when the gossip magazines come calling now that she's a big TV star.'

Despite Sophie's having missed the Thanksgiving party, Hughie Brown had been active on her behalf. He had already secured her a small part in a television adaptation of *Vanity Fair*, and was talking confidently of more substantial television roles in the year to come. Emma and Lulu had privately discussed both the efficiency and the speed with which Sophie's head had been turned by this.

'We've been over this, Lulu,' said Sophie now, shaking her head with a patient sigh. 'I don't want to be a big TV star. I've told Hughie quite plainly, I don't mind doing a bit of TV to get my name and my face out there, but what I really want to concentrate on is the stage.' She took a bite of bagel, and stared dreamily into the distance. 'I can feel it *here*, you know?' she said, pounding on her chest with the hand that was bagel-free. 'I want a huge, fabulous meaty role to sink my teeth into, and chew to little bits. I want to own the stage, to feel the audience in my hand. I'm hungry for it, like a starving person wanting a big, fat, juicy steak.'

'I thought you said Hughie didn't deal with theatre,' said Emma.

'He doesn't,' said Sophie. 'But at a certain point I felt it was only fair to let him know that was where my real focus was. It's not right to lead people on to think you'll be dealing with them forever, so I told him my feelings and asked him if he could maybe introduce me to one of the artistic directors at one of the big theatres, Kevin at the Old Vic, say, or Marcus at the Vagabond, but he doesn't seem to want to for some reason. I don't think he's ready to give me up to the competition.'

'More likely he doesn't want to subject them to the horror,' said Lulu.

'I can see the headlines now,' said Emma. 'Kevin Spacey and Marcus Wickham found cold and stiff in respective offices, having been talked to death by rising young actress.'

'I think it's all very exciting,' said Charlie, reaching across Lulu to pass a bagel to Javier. 'Don't you, Javier? Almost nobody makes it as an actress, Sophie, and here you are with two television roles within six months, and promise of more next year. You're really on your way, aren't you?'

'Thank you, Charles,' said Sophie. 'It's nice that somebody appreciates me at least. Javier, have some of the blackcurrant jam before Emma hogs it all. When my Rosalind opens at the Vagabond, you two can come to the after party, and those two can't. They're completely horrible old bags.'

'Ah, the sweet sound of birds in their little nest agreeing.' Fee, who had been on a telephone call, sat herself down at the table. 'Sorry about that, folks, I had to take the call. Have the girls been looking after you, Javier? Do you have enough coffee, Charlie?'

She pronounced the name Chah-lie with a broad 'a' in the Boston fashion, which her two younger daughters pounced on with delight.

'Mom's gone native,' said Lulu. 'Which means she's been talking to Aunt Amy. How is the old de-ah, moth-ah?'

'Amy Pah-kah has gone down to the Chahles Rivah,' said Sophie. 'For a bah-eld beef dinn-ah and a trip to the theat-ah.'

'Havin' pah-ked her cah in Hah-vahd.'

'It keeps them happy,' Fee told Charlie and Javier. 'It's not illegal. And they do run down eventually. Are you two ready yet to hear what Aunt Amy said in this telephone call you're giving yourselves such a good time making fun of?'

'Ceh-tainly, moth-ah.' Sophie lowered her

voice to a dowageresque growl, and sat up ramrod straight in her chair. 'We're ve'y, ve'y grand,' she told Charlie. 'And we have peh-fect post-ure.'

She was also, thought Lulu suddenly, a descendant of one of the women Grandma Jo had sent letters to a century ago and half the world away.

'How are we related anyway?' she asked. 'I've never known.'

'She and I share the same great-great-grandparents,' said Fee. 'I'm the great-granddaughter of Grandma Jo, and she's the great-granddaughter of Jo's sister Amy, if you want to work that one out.'

Amy Parker, thought Lulu, then. As in lovelorn little Parker who had known he had not merited a goddess such as Amy March.

'So Amy's daughter married a Mr Parker,' she said, thoughtfully.

'It was her granddaughter in fact,' said Fee. 'My Aunt Margaret — I think her name was Lamb — married Uncle Ted Parker. The families had been friends for years and the story was that Ted had actually been called after Aunt Margaret's grandfather, who was quite a colourful character, they used to say. He was a sweetheart, Uncle Ted. Half Aunt Margaret's size and couldn't take his eyes off her. He used to say he'd been in love with her since she beat him in a pillow fight when they were five.'

'Oh, good,' said Lulu. She thought about it, and smiled: yes, Amy's granddaughter and Mr Parker's grandson would be a particularly pleasing couple. 'I think that's lovely.'

'What's so lovely about it?' said Sophie.

'It's just a nice story,' said Lulu. 'You wouldn't know about it, not having a heart, but it is nice when people who like each other get together.'

'Well, well,' said Emma, hopefully. 'A romantic sentiment from my sister Lulu. Is there anyone *you* like, by any chance?'

'Yes,' said Lulu. 'The head of the North Dakota League For Protection Against Bossy Brits. He contacted me when he heard you were coming, and what can I say, love bloomed.'

'Much as I hate to interrupt this touching display of sisterly devotion,' said Fee, 'I have to talk to you girls about something. The reason your Aunt Amy called today was to tell me that she's coming to London next week.'

The sisters exchanged glances.

'Oh,' said Emma.

'I'm not cutting my hair,' said Lulu.

'I've given up asking,' said Fee. 'But I am going to ask you all to do something else for me, please. Thursday of next week is the last day of her trip, and the only night she can come to dinner, so I'm going to ask you all to come here to see her.'

'Thursday?' said Sophie. 'Sorry, Mom, I can't. Esme's in that thing at the Bush and a group of us are going to see her, it's all planned.'

'I'm afraid I'm going to have to ask you to change your plans, honey,' said Fee. 'Amy has dinners on Monday and Tuesday, and on Wednesday she has tickets to see *Hamlet*, so Thursday's the only night she can do.'

'*Hamlet*?' said Sophie. 'At the Vagabond? No! I can't bear it! Tell me it isn't true, Mom, or I'll kill myself!'

The Vagabond Theatre's current production of *Hamlet* was a much-talked-about affair with spine-chilling spectral effects, a powerful and furious Ophelia and erotically charged scenes between unexpected characters. It had been running for two months and tickets were all but impossible to come by.

'I'd sell my soul to see that *Hamlet*,' said Sophie. 'I'd kill my sister. And I *deserve* to see it, too. I love the Vagabond, it's my absolute favourite theatre in the whole world, it's *my* theatre, the one I really, really, really want to work with once I've got myself established, and this is supposed to be the best thing they've ever done ever. I've tried all sorts of ways to get tickets, and not been able to, and Aunt Amy gets to see it just because she's rich and knows people on boards. Aunt Amy! She never goes to the theatre. She doesn't know *Hamlet* from a cheese and mushroom omelette. This is disastrous. It's the ultimate unfairness. It's so annoying it's left me literally speechless.'

'Welcome to the world, honey,' said Fee. 'She has friends who got her tickets, it seems. Anyway, she's coming here to dinner on Thursday of next week, which frankly isn't all that convenient for me either, as your father will still be in Africa, and it's the day I have that all-day workshop at the Royal Free. So what I'll do is make a casserole on Wednesday, and I'll ask you, Lulu, to heat it up with some side dishes on Thursday, and I'll join you all as soon as I can, probably in time for dessert. OK?'

'Why don't you ask her to come to our place?' said Lulu. 'It's closer to the Royal Free and I can easily cook something.'

'Oh, would you?' said Fee. 'That would make my life easier, I must say. If it's OK with Charlie, of course.'

'Actually, I'd like it,' said Charlie. 'I'm sort of strangely intrigued with Sophie's impression, and I want to compare it to the original.'

'It's dead-on accurate,' said Sophie. 'Isn't it, Lulu? You just wait, Charles, you won't be able to look her in the face.'

'Well, so long as you don't start doing it in front of her.' Fee narrowed her eyes at her youngest. 'And you're not going to show her that tattoo, either, are you, honey?'

'It's barely three degrees outside, Mom,' said Sophie. 'Even I'm not taking my socks off for anyone. Not even the ghost of Hamlet's snobby old aunt from Boston.'

★　★　★

'Exactly who is this aunt?' said Joanna the following week, as Lulu prepared to go home early to cook a dinner of roast pork with apple sauce, mashed potatoes and green beans — Aunt Amy disapproved of exotic flavours.

'She's my mother's distant cousin.' Lulu smiled at Joanna, who had already begun to feel like a friend. 'She's quite rich and very sort of commanding. She's on the board of various

371

charities and things, and she's used to bossing people around. She's the only person I know who makes my mother nervous.'

'She sounds rather alarming,' said Joanna. Joanna liked quiet and serenity, and was given to wondering aloud just how it had come about that she had ended up owning a toy shop. 'Maybe you should use your Rottweiler-walking voice on her.'

'I don't think anyone's ever used a Rottweiler-walking voice on Aunt Amy,' said Lulu. 'If they did, she'd bite them back and probably give them rabies.' She climbed into her coat, wound her scarf round her neck against the chill of the winter night, and struck an attitude of bravery at the shop's door as she looked back into the bright, inviting interior. 'Goodbye, Joanna,' she said. 'If I don't make it through the night, it's been really nice working with you. Think fondly of your former assistant who suffered the horrible fate of being Aunt Amified.'

★　★　★

Aunt Amy was a tall woman, with soft gold hair framing a hawk-like face, and a fondness for well-cut tweed skirt suits.

'I've never been to this part of town before,' she told her nieces when she arrived at the flat. 'The cab went through some questionable parts on the way here, I must say, but this part seems safe enough.'

'Actually, it's quite a popular part, Auntie,' said Emma. 'They have a film star living around

372

the corner and one of Paul McCartney's daughters is just a couple of streets down.'

'Movie stars. Musicians.' Aunt Amy shuddered faintly: she was not of an artistic bent. Then smiled at Emma, who was the niece she approved of most. 'How are your wedding plans coming along?' she asked.

'Very well indeed, thank you,' said Emma. 'And these two are being an amazing help. They're my bridesmaids, of course, Lulu's baking the cake, Sophie's made the bridesmaid dresses, and she's also rounded up some friends who have a steel band for the music, so we'll have a little touch of the Caribbean in rainy old London.'

Aunt Amy raised her eyebrows.

'Bohemian,' she murmured. 'Just like your mother. Lulu, have you found a job yet, or are you still catching rats, or whatever you were doing?'

'I was walking dogs, Auntie,' said Lulu. 'And I'm not doing that any more, no. I'm working in a toy shop up in Hampstead with a really nice woman called Joanna. It's a very friendly sort of place and I'm actually quite enjoying myself.'

'A toy store,' said Aunt Amy. 'With a brain like yours.'

There was a silence while Lulu served bowls of black bean soup.

'How was *Hamlet*?' asked Sophie, after a moment.

'It was good enough,' said Aunt Amy. 'Everyone remembered their lines at least. But I never did understand why Hamlet and his uncle didn't just sit down and talk things over sensibly. Then none of the rest of it would have been necessary.'

Sophie closed her eyes.

When Charlie arrived, everyone turned to greet her delightedly.

'Sorry I'm late,' she said. 'The meeting went on.' She went to Aunt Amy and extended her hand. 'I'm Charlie,' she said. 'Alfreda Fitz-charles, but they call me Charlie.'

'How do you do, Charlie,' said Aunt Amy. 'We've already started eating, as you see. It seems my nieces don't believe in putting dinner on hold just for the sake of politeness.'

'I called and asked them not to,' said Charlie earnestly; she was carefully avoiding Sophie's eye. 'I had a meeting and knew I'd be late. Is the soup on the stove, Lulu? I'll help myself to some.'

Behind Aunt Amy's back, the sisters saw Charlie briefly lean against the sink, her shoulders shaking, before she collected herself.

'And how do you know my nieces?' said Aunt Amy when Charlie was seated.

'Lulu and I were at university together. We stood together in the queue for our student cards on our first day, and we've been friends ever since.'

'Did you study chemistry, too?'

'No.' Charlie smiled across the table at Lulu. 'Lulu's the brainy scientific one. I studied English literature and sat around reading books all day.'

'Humph.' Aunt Amy's eyebrows expressed her

opinion of a degree in English literature. 'Fitzcharles,' she said, then. 'Irish?'

'I am. My father's from Limerick, although I was brought up all over the place.'

'Your people do tend to travel,' commented Aunt Amy. 'There are a lot of them in Boston, of course. Some of them have even worked their way into good society these days, and are doing a fair amount of charitable work, I will say that for them, so I suppose they've learned something from us in their time there. Are you related to the Fitzgeralds?'

'I don't think so.' Charlie cast a surprised glance at Lulu.

'Maybe the O'Neills?' Aunt Amy thought and then snorted. 'I'm supposing you're not related to those dreadful Kennedys — a pack of crooked Catholics making the world think that's what Boston's about. They should have gone back to where they came from, and we'd all have been better off.'

'Actually,' said Charlie, quietly, 'I don't know who I'm related to. The name Fitzcharles is a made-up name. My father was dumped into an orphanage, along with his twin sister, when he was a baby, and no one ever found out where they came from. So for all I know I might be one of the Kennedys after all.'

'Your father was a foundling?' Aunt Amy's eyebrows went up again. 'But I thought your family owned this apartment.'

'We're doing OK now,' said Charlie. 'My father and my aunt were both very clever, got scholarships to schools and university, and worked their way up from there.'

'Extraordinary,' said Aunt Amy. 'We can trace our family back to the *Mayflower*. And you have no idea who your grandfather was.'

'None whatsoever,' said Charlie.

Aunt Amy drew in her breath. 'Well, I suppose that sort of thing will happen,' she said, 'in a place with all those pubs and no responsibility about birth control. I must say you're quite nonchalant about it. You don't even try to keep it a secret.'

'Excuse me!' Suddenly snapping, Sophie slapped her glass down on the table. 'Would you please stop being so bloody rude to our friend Charlie? It's rude to be rude to people anyway, and what you're saying is just stupid. If my father had been born with the disadvantages Charlie's father had and got himself to where he has, I'd be incredibly proud of him. I thought Americans were supposed to admire self-made people. If you're looking for what you'd call good society, you've found it, actually, because even though Charlie's pretty much the richest person I know, even richer than you, believe it or not, she never, ever puts the rest of us down or patronizes us, which gives her perfect manners in my opinion, and much better than yours, quite frankly. And if you want to talk about charitable works, she's actively invited Lulu and me to live in this fabulous flat — just look at it; it's awesome — more or less rent-free, for as long as we need, which is an amazing example of charity, I'd say, and she didn't need to live in Boston or know who her grandparents were to learn how to do it either. You should be looking at her to see how you could be more like her instead of insulting her, and you can put that in your stuck-up Bostonian pipe and smoke it.'

There was a pause which lengthened and shivered over the kitchen table.

At last, Aunt Amy rose from her chair. 'I think,' she said slowly, 'that this visit is at an end. Please tell your mother that I shall be writing her from Boston. Good evening.'

'Wow,' said Lulu after she had left. She was looking at her sister with a new-found respect and even admiration. 'All right, Soph. Really good one.'

'I should have been the one to say that,' said Emma. 'Not you, and I apologize for not speaking up earlier, Charlie. But if I had said it, I couldn't have said it half as well as that. Congratulations, Sophie, that was amazing.'

'Well, she was being rude to Charlie,' said Sophie. She shook her head, firmly. 'Not acceptable. Are you all right, Charles?'

'I'm fine,' said Charlie. 'Thank you, Sophie, for standing up for me.'

Sophie snorted. 'Very least any of us could do,' she said.

For a moment, the sisters looked at each other, their eyes shining. Then, as one, they sank back into their chairs.

'What are we going to tell Mom?' said Emma.

★　★　★

377

'If that's really what she said, then you did the right thing, Sophie,' said Fee when the story had been told. 'Although I'd very much rather it hadn't included the part about the stuck-up Bostonian pipe. But I warn you she'll be quite angry with you. Aunt Amy isn't used to people standing up to her, and she doesn't like it when they do.'

'Then she can learn not to talk to people like that,' said Sophie. 'Not to any sort of people. And this is *Charlie*.'

Fee sighed. 'You're absolutely right,' she said. 'She shouldn't speak to people like that. But I'm going to take some time out here, because I think I need to have a bit of a talk to you girls about Aunt Amy. I'm very fond of your Aunt Amy, as you know. I know she isn't a saint and I know she isn't always the easiest person in the world for you to deal with, but — because, just as Sophie feels loyalty to Charlie, I feel a certain loyalty to her — I'd kind of like to explain to you that in many ways she hasn't had life all that easy.'

'Not easy!' said Lulu. 'She doesn't have to work, she travels the world, and every time she opens her mouth someone runs scurrying. What's not easy for her?'

'Getting the point of *Hamlet*, for one thing,' said Sophie. 'And behaving like any sort of recognizable human being, for another.'

Fee sighed again.

'I don't think you girls realize,' she said, 'exactly how different the world was for women just fifty years ago.'

'Oh, God.' Lulu slumped across the table. 'Here we go. Oppression of the patriarchal society. Fishes and bicycles. More than a rose in a man's lapel.'

'I know, I know,' said Fee. 'I know you think I talk endlessly about the Collective, and the fact is, I probably do, because it was a very important time in my life. But I'm not talking about me now, I'm talking about Aunt Amy, who is fifteen years older than me, and grew up in a much more conventional family than our branch of it ever was. Which means that whatever struggles I had in finding my place in the world, she had far, far worse. You girls have no idea — absolutely none — of the expectations that were placed on girls at the time and place where she was growing up. They were supposed to sit in a corner, look demure, keep their voices quiet and their hands folded in their lap, and not express a single opinion about anything but which brand of washing powder they preferred — and washing powder, by the way, was something they were expected to take very seriously indeed. It was an impossible time for any woman who had an ounce of spark or intelligence. None of *you* would have lasted five minutes, quite frankly.'

'Well, but neither did Aunt Amy,' said Emma. 'She doesn't exactly fit into that category today, does she?'

'No, she doesn't,' agreed Fee. 'And she didn't back then, either, which was something I used to admire immensely about her when I was growing up. She was the girl in the room, you see, who didn't sit quietly in the corner with the other girls. She was the one who dared to get out of her chair and live her own life in the way she chose. The one who followed baseball, and talked to men about politics, and never learned to cook, because she was too busy taking over her father's business when he died, and running it at a profit, I might add. The one who shocked her friends' mothers to bits and made the more conventional girls laugh at her and make fun of her behind her back, and didn't give a damn. She was a huge influence on me, and she was someone I'll always be grateful to, because she was the one who showed me it was all possible.'

'OK,' said Lulu. 'I get that part. But I don't see what about this made her life so very difficult.'

'She was odd,' said Fee, flatly. 'She was unusual. She was ahead of her time, which meant that for much of her life she was doing these interesting things that she did all alone. And I don't know if any of you have ever felt odd or unusual, but it can be quite lonely and it can be quite hard. When I started waking up to women's rights, I had my friends in the Collective, and a whole community of women out there to back me up and be friends with. Aunt Amy had no one. It's not easy to have other women disapprove of you when you're not even doing anything wrong. And those men who liked talking politics and baseball and doing business with her? I don't think that fifty years ago it so much as occurred to any of them that a girl who liked talking baseball and politics was also a girl who might welcome a little bit of romance in her life. She never married and she told me once that she'd have loved to. And she never had children, and she'd have loved that, too.'

There was a pause.

'Bet she's changed her mind about the last part,' said Sophie, quietly.

Fee looked around the table, and sighed again.

'I'll give her the weekend to get over her jet-lag,' she said. 'And then I'll call her to talk about things. She shouldn't have said what she did, but I don't want to be at loggerheads with her, because she doesn't have much in the way of family, poor soul. You three — four, actually, because, Charlie, you're certainly part of the family by now — are lucky to have each other, because you never have to be lonely. Amy's known a lot of loneliness, and that's been hard for her.' She stopped speaking, and smiled at Sophie. 'But it doesn't excuse bad manners and I'm glad you stood up to her, Sophie,' she added. 'It was the right thing to do, and it must have taken some doing, because I know how intimidating she can be.'

'It was amazing,' said Sophie. She gulped at her coffee and waved a spoonful of baked pear. 'Just amazing. I don't know where I found the courage, actually. I just suddenly felt this tingling inside me, like a sort of fountain of passion welling up. It was like I was possessed, like I was someone like Lulu who just didn't care what people thought of me. And it'll be really useful to me later on in my career, because next time I have to play the part of someone who's rude and tactless and goes around offending people, I'll know where to find it.'

'You know,' said Lulu to Sophie, 'for about two minutes there you actually managed to stop being annoying, and it was really nice. But the two minutes are up now.'

Concord, December 25, 1870.

Dearest Bethie,

We have had our second Christmas without you — and, dearie, please don't be hurt, or think for a moment that we love you any the less, or that we will ever stop missing you even for an hour, but the truth is, dear, that it *is* getting just a little easier for us all to bear your loss at last, and I know that my tender-hearted Bethie will rejoice to hear it.

You would have liked to see us, I think, as we sat at Christmas dinner today, Marmee a little thinner and graver than when we were children, and father a little more stooped, but both as full of love and wisdom as it is possible for two human beings to be; Meg, all womanly grace as she tended to the little ones, and John, as always, with his head half buried in a book; and, best of all, my lady Amy and my lord Teddy, she the height of elegance in her blue silk Parisian dress trimmed with a becoming little collar of Brussels lace, he so completely captivated by her that he can't take his eyes off her for more than a minute. She has such a good effect on him, dear, for he grows more steady and sensible under her soft hand than he ever could under my rough one, and already they smile and nod at each other for all the world like 'old married folks' at the peaceful end of life's shared journey instead of newly-weds at its beginning — it is altogether jolly to see them.

Even so, I confess I felt a little low when the day began, for Fritz was so far away at his college in the West, and I hadn't had a letter from him for days, which was hard to bear, especially at this time of festivity. But I quickly chided myself for my selfishness when I saw old Mr. Laurence come in, for, dearly as Amy and Teddy care for him, *his* beloved has long been in that place from where letters are never, ever sent. 'Fie upon you, Josephine,' I told myself, using that hated sentimental name to perform a penance, 'thinking only of your small burden when others have loads to carry that are so much heavier. You will make it your special endeavor this day to tend upon that good old man, and give him comfort in his loneliness.' And my virtue was rewarded at last, for, as we were drinking toasts over the cake and the ice cream, suddenly there came a knock at the door, and there in the porch stood my Fritz himself, beaming like Santa Claus, with his arms full of parcels of oranges, lemons, dates and raisins, and nuts of all kinds, all from the grounds of his college.

'So much fruit they haf in the West, I must share with my dear friends in the East,' was his greeting. Or rather it was the greeting that he told me later he had planned to deliver, for he hadn't got but two words into this prettily prepared speech when his betrothed, showing a dreadful want of propriety I fear, uttered an unearthly shriek and flew at him with kisses, causing him to scatter the fruits and nuts clear over the floor, to the delight of Daisy and Demi, who promptly fell to foraging and nibbling like two young squirrels on this unexpected bounty.

It *was* a happy Christmas, Beth, for all that you were not there in person, for we all felt your dear spirit there among us, as we do each day and always will; death cannot break the bounds of love that tie us, and, though we can no longer see your tranquil face smiling at us from the little chair by the hearth, still, we know you smile always on us from the other home where you now are, and now, at last, we feel the shadow of your earthly loss begin to lift, and ourselves begin to be able to smile back at you.

With love from us all, dear, this merry Christmas Day,

Jo.

Lulu smiled, too, as she wrapped herself closer into the moth-eaten quilt that protected her from the worst of the attic's chill, and, just for pleasure, began to read the letter again. It was the Saturday afternoon following Aunt Amy's visit, and quite soon she, Emma and Sophie would be meeting in the living room to trim the Christmas tree over tea and gingerbread; but Lulu had arrived at the house early, to give herself time to slip up to the attic and the letters.

She liked the few letters that Jo had written to Beth's memory after the worst grief of her bereavement had passed; she liked to know that Jo had found peace at last in her loss; she liked, too, that Jo had found love. And it most clearly had been a real love, and a passionate one, for all that its object was stout and middle-aged rather than young and handsome; Lulu, too, she thought now, would like to have someone in her life to fly at with kisses and send parcels scattering. It would not be Tom, for all of Emma's hopes and hints; but someone, she thought, still smiling as the last pale-yellow drop of winter sunshine trickled through the attic's window and onto the more than hundred-year-old paper in her hand, would be nice.

★ ★ ★

'It's been a funny sort of a year,' said Emma an hour later when the sisters were gathered around the tall tree in the bright living room. She looked dreamily out of the window at the blue-grey dusk that was falling in the garden outside, the warm glow of the lamps shining pools in its gloom. 'I started it as a single woman living in London, and now I'm almost married and on my way to North Dakota.' A little wistfully, she touched a lop-sided papier mâché star that Lulu had made when she was nine. 'I wonder where I'll spend next Christmas.'

'You can always come home,' said Sophie. 'There's Fitzcharles's Bed and Breakfast if there's no room here.'

'I don't think I'll be able to,' said Emma. 'They're going to be working Matthew so hard, I don't think he'll have time. And I want to spend Christmas with him, which is the point of it all, after all.'

Unseen by the others, Fee squeezed her daughter's hand.

Emma was quiet for a moment, and then collected herself.

'And talking of my wedding,' she said, turning sternly on Lulu, 'I'm still waiting to hear what my brilliantly efficient chief bridesmaid is thinking of organizing for the hen party. And don't say you've had the most marvellously amusing and original idea of taking us all on a cookery course, because thank you very much but I happen to think my cooking is just fine as it is, and so does Matthew.'

'I was going to talk to you about the hen party,' said Lulu. She placed a carved wood angel with flowing gold curls from a German Christmas market next to a pink reindeer on roller skates that Sophie had bought from a street stall in Brighton, and evicted Toby from the decorations box. 'Toby, this isn't a game we've invented for your amusement, it's a very serious business. I've been thinking about it, Emma, and I remember you said you wanted to do something relaxing. So I've had a word with Charlie, and she says she can get us a deal on a weekend at Granville House, you know that posh hotel spa place in Oxfordshire? Would you like that?'

'Oh,' said Emma, surprised and pleased:

Granville House had recently been featured in *Vogue's* list of Top Ten Luxury Hotel Spas. 'Well, yes, I'd say that on the whole I'd like that very much indeed. Granville House, huh? Wow, Lulu, that's a really amazing idea, thank you.'

'I do listen,' Lulu told her. 'And occasionally I even remember what I hear. And it is supposed to be a very good place. Not sure if they'll let Sophie in, but if they don't we can always dump her in a field to frighten the cows in the morning.'

Sophie, carefully placing gold and silver glass balls, extruded her tongue with dignity.

'How's your year been, Lulu?' said Fee. 'You've had some ups and downs, I think.'

'I suppose I have.' Once again, Lulu thought back over the year and all that had happened in it, from the Goncharoffs, to the Crown & Sceptre, to Joanna in the bright and friendly toyshop; from the new and surprising knowledge she had acquired about her parents, to the terrible thing that had nearly happened to Sophie last month. There had been some bad things, she thought, but they seemed mostly over now, and the worse things hadn't happened after all. And maybe next year some good things would start to happen instead. 'It hasn't all been great, but I'm liking the toy shop better than I've liked any work yet. And I've cooked some nice meals and made a couple of new friends, which is nice.' And, of course, she added, but only to herself, it had also been the year she had made the acquaintance of Grandma Jo. That in itself had made it worthwhile. 'It's been an OK year, actually.'

'You've spent an awful lot of it in the attic,' remarked Sophie, exhibiting a faintly disturbing tendency she sometimes showed towards mental telepathy.

Lulu contemplated a comment about spiders, but discarded it. The fact was that she had spent a lot of time in the attic, and it would be unrealistic of her to expect her sisters not to have noticed. And one day, she thought now, she would bring down from the attic to share with them the treasure that she had discovered there. Not yet; not quite yet. But one day.

'I'm working on something up there,' she said. 'I'll bring it down soon, maybe for the wedding. It's not ready yet, but I'll bring it down soon.'

Watching her middle daughter's face, Fee moved quickly to distract the others from further questioning.

'What about you, Sophie?' she said. 'How do you feel about this year?'

'Well, I'm still alive,' said Sophie. 'Which *I* think is a plus, whatever Lulu says. And apart from nearly dying I've had a good time on the whole: I generally do. Work's coming along — at least I'm not working at Selfridge's like I was last year. And, who knows, maybe next year will be the year I get to have a go at the stage.' She stood back and regarded her distribution of the balls with a critical gaze. 'I would like to get onto the stage,' she added quietly. 'I know you all laugh at me for it, but it's much more like real acting than television is. And I do quite like acting, actually.'

From the hallway, the letter box rattled as a sheet of paper fell through.

'If that's the pizza place again,' said Fee, 'I'm going to start dropping flyers through their letter box saying 'Leave Me Alone', and see how much they like it. Which reminds me, I haven't yet opened the Christmas cards.' She got up, went to the table where the day's pile of post lay, and began to sort through it, murmuring to herself.

'Cousin Susan in Boston, looking forward to the wedding, nice girl. A nice one from Malcolm, I can never remember whether he's David's publisher or the man who runs the off-licence. A photograph of my friend Bobbie from the Collective — good lord, when did we turn into old ladies? Your Aunt Katy, I owe her a phone call, oh, and a lovely one from Charlie, how sweet of her. And . . . oh.'

There was that in her tone that made her daughters stop what they were doing and look at her. From the pile she took an envelope and held it out to Sophie.

'This is for you,' she said.

The envelope bore the address of the Dorchester Hotel, and the handwriting was Aunt Amy's.

'Better sit down before you read,' advised Emma.

'I don't care what she says,' said Sophie. But she had gone a little pale and was biting her lip nervously. 'I meant what I said to her, and I'd say it again.'

'Take a deep breath,' said Fee. 'Remember that she's an older woman and that the fact is that you were quite disrespectful to her. But remember too that we're here and we're on your side.'

'OK.' Sophie flashed her mother a brief, shaky smile. 'Here goes.'

With a hand that trembled only slightly, she opened the envelope and read.

Dear Sophie,

It's late at night in my hotel room, and I am unable to sleep, as I am still recalling your words to me of this evening. It was not pleasant to be called 'stuck-up,' or 'stupid,' especially by someone who is so very much younger than me.

However, I have given the matter some serious consideration, and have come to the conclusion that — although your manner certainly left a great deal to be desired in the way of politeness or of respect for your elders — still, on the whole, you were correct to say what you did. I *was* wrong to dismiss your friend so thoroughly, and I did exhibit a great want of manners in my dealings with her. It is, as you so accurately stated, rude to be rude, and you did the right thing in pointing it out to me. Our family has always been loyal to its friends and has never hesitated to speak up on the side of right. I'm proud to see that you are following on in this tradition. Would you please send me your full address so that I can write Charlie a letter of apology?

Your mother tells me that you are a talented young actress, and interested in getting some experience on the London stage. I wonder if, when I visit London in February for your sister's wedding, you would care to be introduced to my friend Marcus Wickham? He has a connection with a theatre called the Vagabond, a popular theatre, apparently, where, thanks to him, I saw a production of *Hamlet* on Wednesday — despite the theatre's unfortunate name, I can assure your mother that it is a perfectly respectable place. I believe that Marcus is its artistic director or some such — he's a new friend of mine, and surprisingly sensible for a theatrical person.

Take care of yourself, my dear, and keep speaking up for what's right — although, as a concerned aunt, I might just suggest that in future you consider taking a leaf out of what is unfortunately *not* your aunt's own book, and throw a modicum of diplomacy into the mix!

Merry Christmas from your affectionate aunt,

Amy.

10

Concord, November 1870.

Dearest Bethie,

It is a year and a half since you left our little home to go to the other home so far away, and not a week has passed since but I've picked up my pen to write to you of what we were doing and how we were faring, and always burned the letters later for they were so full of grief and despondency that I couldn't bear to keep them. But I think I *shall* keep this one, dearie, for I write to tell you that, for the first time since you left us, I am truly happy again. Amy and Laurie arrived back from their travels this week, and, oh, Beth, the difference in Amy! The silly little goose with all her childish affectations has quite gone, and the fine young lady we knew before she went to Europe has grown into a woman of good sense and real kindness. It does me good to see the tenderness with which she cares for old Mr. Laurence, and she has asked Meg to teach her how to cook and housekeep, for, she says, however many servants there may be in a house, it is a poor home if its mistress don't know how the work should be done, too. And such a kindness she did me last night that I can never fully thank her for, and I must tell you the story, for it's a comical one.

Do you remember old Miss Crocker, who worried us so when we were girls with her fussing and prying and gossiping? Well, she'd left us alone for a while, mercifully, having decided that a house holding nothing but a quiet old couple and their spinster daughter must provide so little material for gossip that they weren't worth the trouble of a visit. But lo and behold, no sooner do Amy and Teddy arrive back home from their travels, than there she is at the front porch, right around dinner-time, eager as can be to see all that is going on and report her findings all around the town. Of course, we couldn't but invite her in, so in she comes, yellow and sharp-nosed as ever, and starts to cast her eyes around.

It happened we had another guest that day. Do you remember Professor Bhaer, the German teacher I met at my lodgings in New York? It happens that he's in town, for he has business in the city that is keeping him here for a few days; and, since he chanced to be passing our door on his way home from his business to his lodgings, he had stopped to pay a call, and you know how hospitable Marmee is — she *wouldn't* have it but that he'd agree to stay to dine.

Down we sit, mother and father, and Amy and Laurie and old Mr. Laurence, for they are dining with us until their own house is settled, and the Professor and Miss Crocker, the latter all the time casting her eyes over Amy's Parisian clothes and jewels, while Amy's trying to hide behind Laurie, for she never could abide the gossiping old creature, and certainly don't want to have to deal with her in her first week back home. Hannah brings the veal, we all fall to talking, and of course we tell the tale of that dreadful dinner I served Miss Crocker all those years ago, with the terrible lobster and the strawberries covered with salt not sugar — mercy me, how long ago that seems. Now, Laurie's in his glory here, for he's had many years to perfect the story, and the justice he does by it now is nothing short of handsome.

Professor Bhaer, who's the only one of the company who hasn't heard it before, is reveling in it, which is a delight to witness, for it *is* a good joke, when told at this distance, and the Professor has a splendidly hearty Teutonic laugh, which is truly a tonic to the ears. He listens, and laughs, and then when the story is done, he turns to me — for the Germans are a courteous race and can none of them abide to have a person feel slighted in their presence, and especially not a man so good-hearted as the Professor — bows gravely to me, and adds, soberly, 'I hope that Mees Marsch does not think that we make fun of her, for I am sure that on that day she worked hard and wished only to make a wholesome dinner for all.'

I thought that Miss Crocker's eyes would pop out of her head! Bethie, I was in despair, seeing her look from the Professor to me and back to the Professor again, fabricating all manner of nonsensical notions, which I knew she'd then go tattling and telling around to all. But before she could even properly pinch up her nose to draw conclusions upon this, I saw a whisk of silk as Amy mysteriously contrived to change places with Laurie, putting herself at the old lady's elbow, and looking up at her with that pretty look in her blue eyes that no one can resist.

'Dear Miss Crocker,' she said, 'please do tell me truly what you think of my dress here. It's cut narrow in the sleeve, as you can see, in the Paris fashion, but now that I am home, I think I like the fuller American style best. What do *you* think?'

Now, this was magnanimity, for not only was Amy at the old lady's mercy for the rest of the meal, but she knew quite well that 'Croaker,' as we used to call her, was all the while running her sharp and spiteful eyes over every last inch of Amy's fashionable dress and European air, storing up each detail of Amy to report back to her cronies far and wide, and, blessedly, quite forgetting *my* stupid little affairs while she was about it. It was perfectly noble of Amy to sacrifice herself so for me, and I told her so after Croaker had departed.

'Why, Jo!' she said innocently in reply. 'It was only what you'd have done for me if the circumstances had been reversed and Laurie and I still courting.'

Bless the child! She still gets her 'vocabilary' muddled at times. If the circumstances she referred to were able to be *reversed*, then that would mean that the Professor and I were not merely passing friendly acquaintances, but a courting couple! But I was too pleased with her to correct her, so simply kissed her and sent her on her way.

Your loving sister,

Jo.

'Yes, Mum.' Matthew rolled his eyes at Emma when she walked into the kitchen and glared in exasperation at his mobile phone as he paced in front of the sink. 'Well, no, Mum, I don't know the answer to that question, because I wouldn't, would I? And I don't know the answer to that, either, you know how vague Dad is.' He waved desperately to Emma with his free hand, and made a slashing motion across his throat.

'Matthew!' she shouted at him obligingly, as from a distance. 'Matthew, are you ready yet?'

Matthew raised his thumb. 'Hold on a second, Mum, Emma's just calling, and . . . No, Mum. Not really, no. Well, I'll try to find out but I can't promise anything. Yes, I do understand that, but I hope you understand, too, that . . . Yes, Mum. Of course, Mum.' He gaped in silent anguish, and lolled his head as he hanged himself from an imaginary noose.

'Matthew!' Emma shouted again, more sharply now. 'We've really got to go. We're going to be late!'

'Just coming!' he called back. 'Sorry, Mum, I've really, really got to go now. I'll phone you later, OK? Bye, Mum, I love you.'

He pressed the off button on his phone and

sagged into a chair.

'Thank you,' he said quietly, 'for saving my mother's life. If you hadn't come in just then, I was seriously about to reach down the telephone line all the way to Bath and throttle her.'

She tousled his hair gently as she went behind him to the coffee-pot to pour him a cup. Matthew's parents' divorce ten years ago had been a bitter one. Matthew's father, having stayed dutifully married to his wife until Matthew had left university and begun to make his way in the world, had moved out of the family home exactly one day after Matthew had moved into his first adult flat. Matthew's mother had not spoken to Matthew's father since the divorce had been finalized. When Emma talked to Matthew about the situation, she tried, out of female solidarity, to take Matthew's mother's side. It was not always easy.

'What's the fuss about this time?' she asked.

'Her hotel,' he said, grimly. 'The one where she usually stays is full up with a urologists' convention, of all things, and her friend Trish, The Woman Who Knows, has told her that the single only other hotel where it's possible to stay in this crime-ridden and dangerous city without being robbed and murdered in the night by drug-addicted foreigners is in Westbourne Grove, which is far too close for Mum's liking to where Dad will be impossibly selfishly staying with his friend Ian, a mere hop and a skip of three miles away in Shepherd's Bush, and what on earth would she *do* if, perish the terrible thought, she happened to walk past her ex-husband on the street and was forced to undergo the dire and horrible torture of saying hello to him?' He ran his hands through his hair and groaned. 'And we've got four more weeks of this to look forward to before the wedding.'

'I feel sorry for Caroline,' said Emma. 'I know she's difficult, but you and Andrew are so close, and she must feel quite left out a lot of the time.'

Matthew and his father, a sweet-natured semi-retired general practitioner living in York, had always been very good friends; Emma sometimes wondered how it must have been for Caroline to have spent all those years outnumbered by men, and how much that might have shaped the way she was today.

'And Andrew's got a friend to stay with in London and she hasn't,' she continued. 'He'll have been here for a week, having a great time catching up with Ian, and Caroline's only coming for the wedding. She's all on her own, she hates London anyway, and she's having to stay in a hotel, which must be lonely. I'd offer her Lulu's old room at Mom and Dad's, now the ceiling's fixed, but my cousin Susan's got it.'

'I wouldn't let you,' said Matthew. 'I wouldn't do it to Fee. She doesn't even like Mum.'

'Well, she doesn't *dis*like her,' said Emma. 'She just hardly knows her, that's all.'

'She hardly knows her,' said Matthew, 'because Mum hasn't made the slightest effort to be sociable. Dad's gone out of his way to make friends, and I know that both of your parents appreciate that.' Andrew and David, indeed, had bonded to what Lulu described as an alarming degree, over a shared sense of humour and what all their offspring agreed were disproportionately happy memories of the music of the Woodstock era. 'Fee really doesn't like Mum, you know,' he said. 'Her eyes do that glassy thing every time I mention her and she sort of sets her cheeks to look polite. It's OK, Emma, I've known for ever that I've got a difficult mother. Dad's fine, and one out of two is better than none.'

'I feel sorry for Caroline,' repeated Emma. 'She's coming all alone to a city she hates just to see her only son get married, and she's going to spend the wedding day in the same room as a man she has all this resentment about, watching him be much friendlier with our family than she is. I'd be feeling terrible if I were her. We'll have to make a big fuss of her when she comes, to make sure she feels special. Have you asked her yet to Mom and Dad's on the Friday?'

On the night before the wedding, Fee was giving a family dinner for Aunt Amy and their cousin Susan from Boston.

'Ohhh.' Matthew sighed. 'Are you sure you want her there? She'll complain about London, and make comments about Lulu's hair, and get that disapproving look when Lulu and Sophie start to crack jokes, and I know she'll find a way to work in her All Americans Are Hopelessly Superficial speech, and it'll be a mess. Don't get me wrong, Emma, she's my mother and I love her, but let's not sugarcoat the fact that she can be pretty much a pain sometimes.'

'Two words, Matthew,' she told him, 'on the subject of pain-like relations. Aunt Amy.'

He thought, and then smiled. 'You've got a point,' he agreed. 'And I suppose we can't exactly let Mum fend for herself for the night. OK, I'll do you a deal. You do damage control on Mum, make sure she's happy and taken care of and doesn't misbehave too terribly, and I'll do the same for Aunt Amy, and with a bit of luck we might avoid bloodshed.'

'Deal,' agreed Emma. 'I do think we work well together,' she added, reaching across the table for a coffee-flavoured kiss.

★　★　★

'I hope you don't mind,' she said to her mother the next day over Sunday brunch. 'But Matthew and I have invited Caroline to dinner the night before the wedding. She's not the easiest woman in the world, but she'll only be here for Friday and Saturday night, so we sort of have to see her.'

'Of course you'd invite her,' said Fee. 'I was already planning on it.' How observant Matthew was, thought Emma, watching her mother with a tangential burst of quiet pride in her fiancé: Fee's eyes did change when Caroline was mentioned. Fee squinted appraisingly now down the long, narrow dining table, its surface comfortably nicked and worn with circles. 'Ten at the table's no stretch,' she remarked. 'Remember all those birthday parties when you were little? And it'll be a full family affair, then, Emma, because your father talked to Andrew yesterday, and invited him, too.'

'He hasn't.' Emma stared at her mother in horror. 'But we'll have seen plenty of him by then — he'll have been here all week, he's coming to brunch on Sunday, he's taking Matthew and me to dinner on Monday, we're all going to the theatre on Wednesday, and those are just the plans we've already made.'

'Well, I didn't know we'd set a limit on how much time we spent with him,' said Fee. 'I thought you liked Andrew, Emma. David and I think he's terrific.'

'I love Andrew,' said Emma. 'He's lovely. I would spend as much time with him as I could. It's just, well, Caroline.'

'What about Caroline?' said Fee. Yes, her eyes did definitely change, thought Emma: she wondered now how she had not noticed that before.

'Well, she really hates him,' she said. 'It was a really bitter divorce, and she's still angry about it.'

'Oh, for heaven's sake,' said Fee. 'That was years ago now and it's their son's wedding. Surely we're all grown-up enough that they can put their differences aside for just one weekend.'

There were times, thought Emma, when she wondered just what her mother chose to hear when she was counselling clients in Sophie's old bedroom.

'She hates him,' she said. 'She'll go ballistic if he's here. She can hardly bear to be in the same hemisphere as him.'

'She'll be fine,' said Fee. 'There'll be lots of other people there, she'll hardly notice him.'

'She will,' said Lulu, looking up from the crossword puzzle she was sharing with Sophie, 'when he and Dad start shouting at each other about Protocol Harem.'

'Procol Harum,' Fee corrected her. Then, less certainly, 'Maybe Caroline liked them, too, when she was young.'

'I've seen photographs, Mom,' said Emma. 'She wasn't a Procul Harum sort of person.' She set down her coffee mug and groaned, her heart sinking. 'This is going to be terrible,' she said. 'She really hates him, you know, and she'll be furious to find herself at the same dinner as him. Can't we find a way to uninvite him?'

'Of course we can't,' said Fee. 'Caroline can deal with it, Emma, she's a grown woman. What's she going to do, lie on the floor screaming and drumming her heels?'

'She'll do worse,' said Emma. 'She'll get pinched and nasty and lurk at the table with a face like a thundercloud, not enjoying herself and making sure no one else does either. I've seen her do it — she can be awful.'

'Then she should be ashamed of herself,' said Fee. 'And if she pulls anything like that in our house, I've more than half a mind to tell her so.'

'Mom!' Emma's heart sank further. There was a certain sort of Englishwoman with whom Fee had never learned to have patience: Emma wondered now how she could have failed to see before precisely how squarely into the category her future mother-in-law fell. 'You wouldn't really, would you?'

'Why not?' Fee set her jaw, and Emma noticed

402

despairingly that her Boston accent had suddenly grown more pronounced. 'If one of my guests is being unpleasant to another under my roof, I think I'm allowed to comment.'

'Cool!' said Sophie, her attention diverted at last from the puzzle. 'Family drama, I love it. I'm going to stand in the hall, selling T-shirts, Team Caroline and Team Andrew.'

'I'll bring some mascots from the shop,' said Lulu. 'A big teddy bear for Andrew, and what do you think for Caroline? A tarantula, or maybe a nice slithery snake?'

'We can make it an event. The Battle Of The Exes, the fight of the year.'

'Sell tickets to help pay for the honeymoon. I could sell loads at work; kids love a bit of violence.'

'Will you two shut up!' said Emma. 'This isn't a joke, you know, it's serious.'

'Sorry,' said Lulu. 'Just trying to help you out with your wedding costs, weren't we, Soph?'

Sophie shrugged. 'There's no pleasing some people,' she observed.

'I wouldn't worry too much, honey,' said Fee. 'I'm sure it'll all be fine. These things have a way of working themselves out.'

With some people they did, thought Emma. With Caroline, she was not so sure.

★ ★ ★

'If you tell her Dad'll be there,' said Matthew later on that evening, 'she'll think you're asking her not to go.'

403

'That's ridiculous,' said Emma. 'Of course I want her to go. I just feel I should warn her that he'll be there too, so that she can prepare herself. I wouldn't want to walk into a room, and meet my ex-husband unexpectedly. Not that I'm planning to have one, by the way.'

'I know why you want to warn her,' said Matthew. 'Any normal person would understand that. But I also know how Mum's mind works. Which is that if she knows Dad will be there she won't want to go. And because she knows that everyone knows that, she'll blame the person who told her because she'll think they were telling her in order to keep her away, because that's the way she'd behave herself in that situation. That's why I'm recommending not telling her. I'd frankly rather face the atmosphere on that evening and just deal with it, than live with weeks and months of recriminations for having tried to warn her.'

'But this is terrible,' said Emma. 'Either we warn her and get blamed, or we don't warn her, which feels just wrong. It's an impossible situation.'

'Welcome to Mum,' said Matthew. 'I love her, but I didn't choose her. And you'll notice I'm not rushing to marry someone like her, either.'

Emma looked at him, and shook her head.

'I can't do this,' she said. 'I can't let another woman walk into a trap like that. I don't care if she gets angry with me, and if she does choose to stay away, that's her decision not mine. I'm going to phone her.'

'Be my guest,' said Matthew.

Caroline Morrison answered her telephone on the second ring. Emma pictured her sitting upright in the spick and span living room of her house on the outskirts of Bath, where never a paper was misplaced by a careless hand, or a coffee cup set hastily down to cast a friendly circle on the polished wood table.

'Hello, darling,' she said, when Emma identified herself. Emma knew that Caroline liked her; even so, she occasionally reflected, when they spoke, on the surprising degree of chill with which it was possible to infuse the word 'darling'.

'I'm just calling for a chat,' said Emma. 'It's not too long till the wedding and I felt we hadn't talked for a while, so I thought I'd see how you were doing.'

'Well, I'm glad *someone's* interested.' A brittle laugh tinkled down the telephone line. 'I was beginning to wonder if my son even remembered he had a mother.'

Not for the first time, Emma found herself wondering whatever had possessed Matthew's kind and jocular father to marry Caroline Morrison.

'Did you hear the drama about the hotel?' said Caroline.

For Caroline, the smallest inconvenience was a drama.

'I heard they were booked up, yes,' said Emma.

'With bloody urologists!' said Caroline. 'You'd

405

have thought it was bad enough to have to do that sort of work at all, without getting together to hold a convention about it. And Trish tells me the only possible other hotel in London is in Westbourne Grove. *Not* an area I care for, but Trish seems to think it's OK so long as you stay inside the hotel. So I suppose I'll be under house arrest for the duration.'

'Westbourne Grove has come up quite a lot over the years,' Emma told her. 'And the good thing is it's closer to Paddington than Piccadilly is.'

'If we ever manage to get out of the train station!' said Caroline. 'The taxi queues are always endless, and Matthew's refusing to bring the car when he comes to meet me, because he says he won't have time to go home and get it. Oh, well, at least it'll give us time while we wait to catch up on our news, because I gather that's as much as I'm going to see of him. He'll deign to come into the hotel to check me in, but he says he can't stay for the afternoon because he'll be too busy.'

'Well, he will have a hundred things to do,' said Emma. 'But I'm sure he'll have time for a cup of tea before he rushes off.'

Across the room, Matthew stared at her in protest: she faced him sternly down.

'And then of course, you'll see him again at dinner at my parents' house,' she continued.

'Oh, yes,' said Caroline. 'Dinner at your parents' house.'

'They're really looking forward to seeing you,' said Emma. 'They really love Matthew, and they were so disappointed you couldn't make it last time you were in town.'

'Yes,' said Caroline. 'Remind me again where they live.'

'Islington,' said Emma. 'Sort of north and east of Westbourne Grove, and not too far from us, in fact. Matthew will write the address down, and you'll just show it to the taxi driver. It's a very simple trip across town, it shouldn't take you too long.'

'I hope not,' said Caroline. 'Although let's not forget that your and Matthew's ideas of a simple trip across town are rather different from mine. London's a little bit of a zoo for a mere provincial like me.'

She tinkled the laugh again; but Emma had heard the tremor in her voice, and her heart was touched.

'I'll tell you what,' she said. 'Why don't you and I do something naughty together. Shall I come to meet you at your hotel and we'll have a glass of champagne first, just the two of us, to get us in the mood? Then we can both grab a cab and arrive at my parents' together.'

'Oh,' said Caroline. 'Well, that would be rather fun, I must say.' Her voice had lifted, become almost girlish. 'Yes, let's do that,' she said. 'My treat.'

'I'll hold you to it,' said Emma.

'Congratulations,' said Matthew when they had hung up. 'You've just landed yourself with yet another task on the day before your wedding.'

'I'm glad I thought of it,' she told him. 'She

407

needs to be made a fuss of. I know she's Caroline, but there are so many of us and we're all so close, and she's all alone.'

'Mm-hmm.' He regarded her with a gaze of bland contentment. 'How did she take it,' he enquired mildly, 'when you told her about Dad?'

'Oh, God,' said Emma. She had forgotten about Andrew. 'I'll tell her in the taxi, then she'll have to come to dinner after all.'

'I wouldn't bet on it,' he said. 'She won a medal at the last Olympics for leaping out of doors at traffic lights.'

Emma laughed; then thought of the evening and groaned.

'When I get to Granville House,' she said, 'I'm going to check straight into the massage room and not leave it for the entire weekend.'

★ ★ ★

Granville House Hotel and Spa, where the sisters went the following weekend for Emma's hen party, was a graceful old manor house of yellow stone, set in acres of rolling grounds, with four-poster beds in the rooms and a roaring fire in the lobby.

'It's sort of suspiciously nice, actually,' said Emma as they lay in the steam room, massaged, manicured and replete with excellent food, on the Saturday afternoon. 'For what we're paying. I hope Charlie isn't sneakily subsidizing this.'

'If she is,' said Sophie, 'she'll be doing it because she wants to. She's really cool about having all that money, she's sort of casually

408

generous but says she only spends what she wants to spend on what she wants to spend it on. She's a bit of a magical person, actually. God knows how she ended up friends with Lulu.'

Lulu, half dozing under her towel, waved a dismissive hand at her sister. 'She says she likes us all,' she murmured, 'because we're so noisy, she's able to stay quiet under the din. She even likes Sophie, mysteriously.'

'Well, if she is paying for some of this, it's incredibly kind of her.' Emma frowned, worriedly. 'Maybe we should have asked her along, too. Damn, I didn't think of that.'

'I did,' said Lulu. 'And I knew you'd think of it too late. But she says she has plans with Javier. Which don't involve hanging around with other women, if you get my drift.'

'They're really happy, those two, aren't they?' said Sophie. 'I wonder what it's like, to be someone as quiet as Charlie having a relationship with someone as quiet as Javier.'

'Well, that's something *you* won't know about,' said Emma. 'Your boyfriends are as noisy as you. I think quiet men are nice. Matthew's quiet, and I like it. It's sort of restful.'

'It's lucky you like it, then,' said Sophie. 'Considering that in exactly three weeks' time you'll be walking past everyone you know to marry him.' She stretched herself, proudly. 'And *I* shall be being the ultimate bridesmaid.'

'Watch it.' Stirred, Lulu opened an eye. 'I'm the chief bridesmaid, and don't forget it.'

'And that's the point,' said Sophie. 'The bride takes centre stage, and the chief bridesmaid's busy handing tissues and fixing bouquets and such. The smart money's on being the junior bridesmaid because all you have to do is skip around enjoying yourself and spreading an atmosphere of celebration, which I'm actually rather good at.'

'You're certainly good at enjoying yourself,' agreed Lulu before closing her eyes again.

'I think it's going to be lovely,' said Emma. 'It's going to be lovely and it's going to look lovely, too. The bridesmaid dresses are beautiful, Sophie, I can't thank you enough. And I think that when we're all scrubbed up, we're not a bad-looking threesome, are we?' She sat up and squinted in the mirror on the wall at their shared reflection. 'We're quite an interesting group, actually,' she observed. 'Like enough that you can tell we're sisters, but different enough that it's not just the same old face all over again. I think we'll look really good in the photographs. I know it's shallow, but it is nice to have nice photographs.'

'I think we'll look gorgeous in the photo-graphs,' said Sophie. 'Radiant. Exquisite.'

'It's all coming together beautifully,' said Emma. She closed her eyes and stretched her arms, dreamily. 'The first wedding. I can't believe how beautiful it's all going to be.' Suddenly remembering, she groaned. 'At least, it will be beautiful if we all manage to survive the dinner the night before.'

Sophie sat up and frowned at her sister.

'Are you seriously worried about that?' she asked.

'No,' said Emma. 'I'm looking forward to it so much, I can hardly stand it. Of course I'm seriously worried! This is the night before my wedding, we'll be sitting around the house with my mother who doesn't like my future mother-in-law, my mother-in-law who really, really hates my father-in-law, and my father-in-law who everyone else loves, which is going to infuriate my mother-in-law, and there's going to be bad feeling. And I really and truly can't tell you how much I don't want bad feeling on the night before my wedding.'

'Well, we can't have it, then, can we?' said Sophie. 'What are we going to do about it, Lulu-belle?'

Lulu stretched herself luxuriously under the towel. 'Simple scientific solution,' she yawned. 'We sit Caroline at one end of the kitchen table next to Dad at the top, and Andrew at the other end of the same side next to Mom at the bottom. Caroline and Andrew can't see each other without craning, Caroline and Mom are too far away from each other to revisit the War of Independence, and the same goes for Dad and Andrew and The Incredible Melting Strawberry Buttercup Band, or whatever they're called. Sophie and I sit in between, one of us makes extra-special best friends with Caroline, the other with Andrew, and we both keep them talking so hard to us that they each barely notice the other.'

'Brilliant!' said Sophie. 'Problem solved. My sister's a genius, first prize for Lulu.'

'Actually,' said Emma, slowly, 'that's not half a

bad idea, Lulu. If you could keep them both happy and distracted, so that Caroline feels spoilt and stays in a relatively good mood, and Andrew's kept too busy to join in the general conversation and remind her that he's there, then maybe it might just be OK after all. It'd be quite hard work for you, though, especially the one who has Caroline. Would you two really do this for me?'

'We'd do more than that for you,' said Sophie. 'We'd walk through fire for you. We'd dance on knives for you. We'd snog poison snakes for you. Bagsy Andrew.'

Lulu shook her head and sighed. 'You can't have Andrew,' she explained. 'He always flirts with you and that'd send Caroline into meltdown. You'd probably better avoid him for the whole weekend, in fact. I'll have to have Andrew, I'll wear my paisley shirt and bombard him with scientific questions. You can take Caroline.'

'That's not fair!' said Sophie. 'A whole evening of Caroline? She's horrible. Sorry, Emma, Matthew's lovely, you know we all think that, but she's really awful.'

Lulu sat up and regarded Sophie benignly through the steam.

'That's what you get for being the charming one,' she told her. 'The tough cases.'

Sophie sighed.

'Wow,' said Emma, quietly, after a moment. 'If you two would do that for me, I'd be more grateful than I could say.'

'Special luxury wedding weekend package,'

Lulu told her. 'Champagne on arrival, chocolates in the room and well-behaved sisters over dinner on the first night.' Looking past her sisters, she caught sight of herself in the mirror, her hair a mass of curls that were wilder than ever in the steam. 'God, is that my hair? I didn't realize how much of it there was, I look like an overgrown privet hedge.'

'You could get topiary work,' said Sophie. 'Have it cut like a swan for the wedding, that'd get Andrew's attention.'

Lulu continued to look at herself. It was some time since she had had a haircut, she realized; she had grown so accustomed to fielding comments on it that she had stopped noticing just how bushy it had become. She looked at herself for a while, and then looked, thoughtfully, at Emma.

'There's a hairdresser in the hotel,' she said. 'Would you like me to have it cut? For the wedding?'

'I'd like you to be you,' said Emma, immediately and firmly. 'I hate brides who ask people to be in their wedding and then want them to change things about themselves. It's so insulting — if I want you to be there, it's because I want *you*, not some idea I've made up all in my own private head of my personal opinion of how you should be. So all I want, please, is you to be there with me and wishing me well. That's all I have the right to ask and it's all I do ask.'

Lulu waited patiently until she had finished.

'But you wouldn't mind me having it cut,

413

either, for the photographs?' she said, then. 'Would you?'

'I think you'd look nicer,' said Emma, cautiously, after a moment, 'if it was just a little bit tidier. But that's just my opinion, it's your hair not mine.'

Lulu looked into the mirror, and sighed a little.

'I'll do it,' she said, 'if you'll promise never, ever to nag me about Tom again.'

'I do believe,' said Emma, taking care not to speak too quickly, 'that we have ourselves a deal.'

★ ★ ★

When Lulu walked into the hotel bar an hour and a half later, a couple of young men turned to look at her.

'Oh, my God!' said Sophie, already sitting over a bottle of champagne with Emma. 'You're pretty!'

'Thanks for the vote of astonishment, Soph,' said Lulu. 'I wish I could say you'd grown a working brain, but it's wrong to tell lies.'

Before she sat down, she turned to look in the mirror above the bar at the new and surprising Lulu who met her eyes there. She was just a little taller than the old Lulu and already seemed to carry herself with just a little more grace; she had big brown eyes and unexpectedly neat features under a close-cut curly crop. She was different, though, Lulu thought, a little uncertainly, the cut was shorter than she had expected, or, now that she thought about it, had asked for. She would reserve judgement, she decided, on whether or not she preferred the new self to the old.

'You look lovely,' said Emma. 'Really lovely, you can see your face at last. Don't you feel wonderful?'

'Not sure.' Lulu ran an experimental hand over the new texture of her head. 'Don't you think he took off a bit too much?'

'Well, that's the good thing about having it shorter,' said Emma. 'You can experiment and find your best length. I think it looks lovely, Lulu, Mom's going to be delighted. Oh, let's not tell her. Let's drop in on her when we get home tomorrow and surprise her.'

'Um, bit of a problem there.' Sophie waved her hand over her glass. 'She already sort of knows. She wants a photograph in fact. Hold still.'

She pointed her mobile phone at Lulu and clicked.

'You've told her?' said Lulu. 'You little ratbag. I can't believe you told her before I did.'

'Well, one of us was going to,' said Sophie. 'It's not like we've ever had secrets.' She looked a little anxiously at her sisters. 'Have we?' she asked.

Emma smiled at her kindly. 'No, Sophie,' she said. 'We don't have secrets. We don't need them.'

'Well, not for long,' amended Lulu, thinking of the letters in the attic.

'And speaking of secrets, Sophie,' continued Emma, 'for about the seven thousand five hundred and third time, have you decided yet who you're going to bring to the wedding as your date?'

Sophie shrugged. 'I expect probably Jamie,' she said. 'He's my best boyfriend and I'm not really seeing anyone else.'

Lulu looked at Sophie, then drew her brows down and inspected her champagne glass; she had grown fond of Jamie over the last year.

'You sure you should be leading him on like this?' she asked quietly. 'Since he's in love with you, and everything.'

'Jamie?' Sophie stared at her in astonishment. 'In love with me?'

Emma and Lulu exchanged glances.

'Well, yes, Sophie,' said Emma. 'Jamie in love with you. Hadn't you noticed?'

'*Jamie?*' repeated Sophie. 'Don't be silly, we've been friends for years.'

Lulu shook her head. 'And people never fall in love with people they're friends with,' she said. 'It's a scientifically proven fact.'

'Well, Jamie and I don't,' said Sophie. 'This is Jamie, for heaven's sake.'

'When you die,' said Lulu, 'I want you to leave your brain to medicine so that we can all find out what it's made of. Everyone knows Jamie's in love with you. Even I know that, and I never know these things.'

'Had you really not noticed?' said Emma. 'The way he looks at you with those great sad eyes, all yearning and puppy dog?'

'Oh, that's just Jamie,' said Sophie. 'He looks at everyone like that.' Then frowned a little. 'Doesn't he?' she asked.

'No,' said Emma. 'He doesn't.'

'Oh,' said Sophie. She blinked a little, and stared into the distance.

Lulu narrowed her eyes at her.

'Have you actually formally asked him to the wedding?' she asked. 'It's in three weeks' time, and if you're really planning to take him, I should think he'd probably like a little bit of advance notice.'

'I can't remember,' said Sophie. Whatever she was looking at, appeared to be holding her attention.

Emma picked up Sophie's mobile phone from the table and handed it to her, Still absent-mindedly, Sophie began to punch in a number on her speed-dial.

'I've invited Tom, by the way,' Emma told Lulu while Sophie was talking.

'Excuse me,' said Lulu. 'I believe we'd made a deal.'

'I'm just telling you,' said Emma. 'Tom's family now, even if you're too pig-headed to make him part of it officially. After that night with Sophie at the hospital last year, he's definitely family.'

'Oh,' said Lulu. She thought. 'OK, then,' she said. 'If you want to invite him on that basis, it'll be nice to see him.'

'I think so, too,' said Emma. 'I like Tom. Have I mentioned how nice your hair looks? Ow.'

'I'll do it harder next time,' said Lulu.

★ ★ ★

The following Wednesday, knowing that both of her parents would be out, Lulu paid a visit to the attic. After some searching, she had finally decided on the box she would present the letters in when she showed them to the rest of the family, a capaciously elegant rectangle of sturdy cardboard with a hinged lid, its surface patterned a little like an old book's cover in warm deep brown with a faint cream mottling and edges of discreet gold. It was plain, but she thought that Grandma Jo would have approved of its simplicity; when she took it to the attic, she was gratified to see that the letters fitted in quite perfectly.

Lulu knew — and over the last few weeks had become increasingly aware of the fact — that Grandma Jo did not belong to her alone. She knew that she belonged to Emma and to Sophie as much as to her, and to Fee, possibly, even more than to any of them; she knew, too, that the drawings in the battered leather case that had been done by Amy belonged to Aunt Amy, and that the letters from Meg belonged to their cousin Susan, and that it was very nearly time for her to share what she had found with the rest of the family. She would not do it quite yet, she thought, with a funny little pang of loss at the prospect, she couldn't quite bear to give up Grandma Jo quite yet, but she would do it soon. She closed the lid on the box of letters, and sat for a while, looking at it a little wistfully, realizing that she knew its contents now more or less by heart. She had grown to know Jo, she felt, almost as well as she knew Fee or Emma; in a profound and instinctual way that she could not fully explain but that was tied up in some fashion with shared blood and inherited habits, with shapes of hands and falls of hair, with sets of shoulders and expressions of eyes, she felt she knew Jo as well as she knew herself. She squinted at the top of the box, wondering if it might be just a touch too severe to house such a treasure as it did. Maybe she would find a red rose made of silk or velvet to decorate it before she showed it to the family, she thought; she had the idea that Grandma Jo had liked red roses.

She left the attic, and went down the stairs to the front door. Coming out of the kitchen and into the hall, was Tom.

'Hi,' he said. Then stopped, and looked at her. 'There's something different,' he said.

Cocking her newly shorn head, she smiled at him, teasingly.

'It's a noticing test,' she told him. 'You've got to guess what it is.'

'OK,' he said. 'A noticing test, huh? I'm man enough to give it a shot.' He squared his shoulders, and studied her, frowning. 'I'm pretty sure you haven't shaved off a beard,' he commented after a moment. 'You look good, anyway. Have you maybe lost some weight?'

She shook her head. 'Nope.'

'No weight loss,' he murmured. He frowned some more. 'Are you wearing different clothes?' he asked. 'No again? Used to have glasses but switched to contact lenses? . . . You *haven't* shaved off a beard, have you?'

'Sort of,' she said. 'I've had my hair cut.'

'Oh, right!' he said, his face clearing. 'So you have, it looks really good. Are you pleased with it?'

'Mostly,' she said. 'Although it feels a bit short.'

'Well, it looks great. Buy you a cup of coffee at Carroll's to celebrate?'

'I'd love to,' she said. 'But I have to get back to work. I'll walk with you to the corner, though.'

'How is work anyway?' he said as they fought the wind to the corner of the street.

'Quite good, actually,' she said. She thought about the happy toyshop with its friendly owner, and nodded. 'It's not my life's career, but I am enjoying it. You should come and check out the book section. We're not too strong on Dr Johnson, but we're pretty good on Dr Seuss.'

He laughed. 'I might just do that,' he said. 'Next time I get a craving for higher literature.'

They had reached the corner. When they parted, to Lulu's surprise, he reached down and kissed her, lightly, on the cheek.

'You look really good, Lulu,' he said. 'It's nice to see you looking so happy. I have a feeling something good is going to happen for you soon.'

★ ★ ★

The following Sunday afternoon, in the dark last weekend of January, Lulu was standing alone in the kitchen of the flat, experimenting with Emma's wedding cake. She had made the traditional heavy fruit bottom tier several weeks before, and it sat now in a cupboard, wrapped in foil, and happily soaking up a very great deal of brandy. She had tried various combinations for the other two tiers, and had at last decided on a middle tier of the buttery cake that she called Madeira cake and her mother called pound cake packed with glacé cherries, and a top tier of a lighter sponge flavoured with coffee and walnuts.

She set out the ingredients on the table, neatly arranged for optimum access, and began to chop the walnuts for the top cake. Lulu liked baking. You knew where you were, she always thought, with baking. There were no questions with baking, like what was she going to do with her career, or how could she afford new winter boots if her old pair completed their disintegration before the spring, or how could Matthew's mother Caroline have once apparently been in love with Matthew's father Andrew and now hate him so intensely, or how could Emma know she was in love with Matthew and Sophie not know that Jamie was in love with her, or might or might not Emma just know better than both Tom and Lulu after all, and be right about Tom being the man that Lulu should fall in love with. Baking was simple, she thought, and certain. You just lit the oven, prepared the ingredients and followed the rules.

So absorbed was she in her chopping that she failed to hear the door to the flat swing open and shut, and footsteps mount the short flight of stairs past the downstairs bathroom. She didn't hear anything, in fact, until she looked up and saw framed in the doorway to the kitchen a tall young man holding a bottle of wine.

Not for nothing was Lulu a child of the modern metropolis. She quickly picked up the knife from the chopping board, and pointed it directly at him.

'Who are you and what do you want?' she snapped.

The young man stepped back, and raised the hand that was not holding the bottle.

'Sorry,' he said. 'I didn't mean to frighten you. I'm looking for Freddie.'

Lulu jerked the knife a little forward in his direction.

'There's no Freddie here,' she said. She flicked the knife towards the wine bottle. 'You must have the wrong address for the party, so I suggest you leave. Now.'

'I think there's some mistake,' said the young man. 'This is Maeve Sullivan's flat, right? Well, I'm looking for Freddie Fitzcharles.'

Anyone could read a name by a doorbell, thought Lulu.

'There is no Freddie Fitzcharles,' she said. 'And in case you're wondering, I'm not afraid to use this, and it's bloody sharp.'

'I can see that from here,' he said. 'Honestly, I'm not going to hurt you. I'm looking for Maeve's niece, Freddie? She's about this tall . . . dark hair . . . sort of not bad-looking if you like that sort of thing?'

'Oh!' Of course, Lulu remembered then, Charlie's first name was Alfreda. She lowered the knife. 'You mean Charlie.'

'Do I?' he asked.

'That's what we call her,' she said. 'Short for Fitzcharles, you see.'

'Well, that wouldn't narrow the field much where I come from,' he told her. 'I'm her brother.'

'Oh. Hello.' Setting the knife on the table, and coming forward to shake hands, Lulu saw now that he did, indeed, resemble Charlie. 'Liam, right? I'm Lulu. Sorry about that, I'm all alone in the flat, and you never know.'

'It was good, actually.' Liam Fitzcharles smiled down at her. 'Female empowerment and all.' He picked up the knife and ran a thumb along its blade. 'Sharp,' he said. 'You could really have hurt me.' He nodded, approvingly. 'I see you like a good knife.'

'It's your Aunt Maeve's knife,' she said. 'Not mine.'

'Well, you keep it up very well, which is where too many people fall down on the job.' He nodded again, set the knife down, and looked over at the cake ingredients on the table. 'Is it someone's birthday?'

'It's my sister's wedding in a couple of weeks. I'm practising for the tiers, one batch with glacé cherries, the other with coffee and walnuts.'

'Do you have ground almonds for the cherries?' he asked. 'It stops them from sinking to the bottom of the batter.'

'I usually just dust them with flour before I put them in the mix,' she said. 'But ground almonds sound nice, I might try another batch tomorrow. Are you a cook like Aunt Maeve?'

'No, it's just a hobby. I work for a wine

merchant's. That's why I'm here, actually — they've sent me to check out their London office for a few weeks, and if we all like how it works out, I might even stay here.'

'Really?' This was news to Lulu. 'Charlie didn't say.'

'*Charlie* doesn't know.' He smiled, happily. 'One of my missions in life is to spring myself on her when she least expects it. She never wants to admit she's pleased to see me, so if she has some warning she's all cool and laidback; but sometimes if I surprise her, she'll be shocked into demonstrating affection.'

'Ah.' Lulu nodded. 'She said you were weird.'

'Did she?' He looked gratified.

'Actually, she said you had weird friends. She's gone out shopping, but she should be back soon. Are you hungry? There's some cheese and stuff on the counter there.'

'What've you got?' He inspected the cheese plate and raised his eyebrows hopefully. 'Cheddar,' he said. 'Sadly underestimated in England, but a good one is the king of cheeses. It's surprisingly difficult to come by in California.' Reaching for a knife, he carved himself a slice. 'This,' he said, quietly, after a moment, 'is a truly excellent Cheddar. Where'd you get it?'

'A place near Borough Market. It's a bit of a hike but it's worth the journey. Do you want some crackers? There are some in the cupboard.'

'This one?' He opened the door, and scanned the selection of dried beans and pasta, oils, vinegars and spices. 'This cupboard,' he said firmly, 'was not stocked by my sister.'

Lulu failed to repress a snort. 'Hardly,' she said.

'She's a sore disappointment to the family, you know,' he said. 'Maeve once sent her into the garden to pick spinach and she came back with rhubarb.'

Lulu laughed. 'She's good to cook for, though,' she said. 'She really enjoys her food.'

'Oh, enjoyment has never been her problem,' he agreed. 'And she's a lovely — lovely — person. It's not her fault that she has a palate like a ping-pong ball.'

There was a silence for a while as Liam munched on the cheese, contentedly watching Lulu beat, cream and stir.

'Excellent cheese,' he said again, after a moment.

'It's a Cheddar,' she told him. 'The king of cheeses, although it's sadly underestimated in England.'

'I wonder if you can get it in California,' he mused.

'Hi, Lulu-belle.' Sophie trooped in, a whirl of vivid colours against the January afternoon, dark coat, white shirt, scarlet scarf, golden hair, carrying in her hand a small bunch of snowbells. 'These are from the garden. Mom sends her love and we're to wrap up warm tomorrow because it's going to get colder.' She turned and noticed Liam. 'Wow,' she commented succinctly.

Looking properly for the first time at Liam, Lulu noticed that he was handsome, as of course Charlie's brother would be, with dark eyes, a clear olive complexion, and a sculpted mouth and chin. And with the observation came a pang of loss, because if he was handsome, he would doubtless prefer now to talk to Sophie, and Lulu had been enjoying talking to him.

'Wow yourself,' he returned to her amiably, standing to shake hands. 'I'm Liam, Freddie's brother.'

'Nice for Freddie,' she said. 'Whoever he is. I'm Sophie, Lulu's sister.'

'Nice for you,' he said. 'Are you the sister who's getting married?'

'No, I'm the one who's still available.' She perched herself on the kitchen counter and swung her legs. 'So it's your lucky day, isn't it?'

'Do you know,' he said, slowly, 'I'm beginning to think it is.'

It was the sort of thing that men were always saying to Sophie, but not, thought Lulu a little crossly, the sort that generally made her gape and goggle at Lulu like a demented hen who had just won the lottery. It was a couple of moments before she realized that Liam was looking, not at Sophie, but at her.

Before she could react to this unexpected and disturbing development, there came a wordless howl of joy from the door and the sight of unflappable Charlie hurling herself across the room to bury her face in her brother's jacket. Liam returned her embrace with enthusiasm, only detaching himself to wink conspiratorially at Lulu and stab a triumphant index finger downwards towards the top of his sister's head.

After a moment, Charlie drew back.

'I'm not pleased to see you,' she told him. 'I

426

haven't missed you, and I never think of you.'

'Too late,' he said. 'I have witnesses. You told Lulu I was weird.'

'I didn't. I said you had weird friends.'

'What weird friends?'

'Ohhh . . . ' She drew a breath and began to count on her fingers. 'Anton. Stefan. Edward. Luke — hello, Luke? And what about that guy who — '

'I've brought you some wine,' he said. 'And it's the good stuff, so no knocking it back from plastic beakers.'

'Good,' she said. 'It'll take the edge off the pain of your presence. Why are you in London anyway?'

'The brothers sent me. For six weeks, possibly longer — aha! Just couldn't quite stop that smile, could you? You're pleased, aren't you?'

'That was a rictus of agony,' she said. 'Do you want a cup of tea?'

'I have to go meet my new boss, unfortunately. I just looked in to give you traumatic shock syndrome. Take you to lunch tomorrow?'

'If you must. Why don't you come back tonight for dinner to meet Javier? Lulu's cooking lamb, we're celebrating because Sophie got paid.'

'Doesn't happen often.' Sophie hung her head dolefully. 'Actress.'

'Bad luck,' he commiserated. 'Afraid I can't do that either, Freddie, Dad's sending me on recon. That's food reconnaissance,' he added to Lulu and Sophie. 'There's a chef in a restaurant in Stoke Newington he wants me to check out before anyone else gets to him.' He looked at

427

Lulu. 'Come with me,' he said.

From the corner of her eye, Lulu saw Sophie's hand snake to grab Charlie's wrist — she avoided looking at Sophie's expression.

'Don't you want to take your sister?' she asked, coldly.

'I'm not taking Freddie on food recon! Dad would bust a gut, I'd never hear the end of it. But you look like you'd be up to the challenge. Do come, it'll be fun.'

It was all very well, thought Lulu, for handsome, world-travelling Liam Fitzcharles to decide he wanted to spend the evening with Lulu. She herself, however, might have other ideas.

'I have things to do,' she said.

'No you haven't,' said Charlie. 'We were going to watch *Friends*, and explain to Javier about Ross and Rachel and Monica.'

'I have to cook dinner,' she said.

'Of course you don't,' said Charlie. 'We're capable of feeding ourselves, you know.'

'If you think,' said Lulu, 'that I'm letting either of you two anywhere near my lamb . . . '

'We won't touch your precious baaaaah-lamb, Little Bo Peep,' said Sophie. 'I've heard tell from them as know that there are places out in the big wide world these days serving something called pizza. I do believe they even have a couple right here in London town.'

'Do come to dinner,' said Liam. 'Even if you think I'm awful, the food in this place is supposed to be good. And even if it isn't, at least it's a spot of secks.'

'Excuse me?' Incredulous, Lulu turned to Charlie.

'Secks,' explained Charlie. 'Someone Else CooKS. It's his little joke. I've been covering for him all along, but the jig's up now. He's as weird as his friends.'

'Someone Else CooKS,' said Lulu. 'Got it.'

'And you like it!' exulted Liam. 'Don't pretend you don't, because I can tell. Are we on, then? Pick you up at seven?' He stopped. 'If that's OK with you, of course,' he added.

'Seven thirty,' said Lulu. 'Contrary to what your sister thinks she knows about my every waking hour, I really do have some things I have to do first.'

As soon as he had gone, Lulu turned on her flatmates. 'Don't say a word,' she warned them. 'Not a word.'

'I don't intend to,' said Charlie. 'The idea of you and my brother is so close to incest, it makes me feel all grubby just thinking about it. Sophie, can I show you something in my bedroom, please? I've torn a shirt and I think it can be mended, but I'm not sure.'

'Then I'd better take a look at it,' said Sophie. 'You never know with shirts. And your luck just happens to be in, Alfrederesco, because I just happen to have some time to spare right now.'

'And there's no time like the present, is there?' Charlie observed.

'None whatsoever,' Sophie agreed. 'We might be a while,' she added to Lulu, pausing as she passed to snatch an unopened package of ginger nuts.

A few hours later, dressed in a chocolate-brown skirt and a cream shirt that flattered her colouring, and smelling lightly of Jo Malone's lime, basil and mandarin bath oil, which Emma had dropped off earlier on the grounds that anything of Sophie's was too girly for Lulu and anything of Charlie's would remind Liam of his sister, Lulu looked at herself in her bedroom mirror, missing her hair. Everyone who had seen her new hairstyle had complimented her on it, from Tom, to her mother and Joanna, to a couple of the more regular mothers at the toyshop, to Maureen Carroll's father Sean, who had winked and told her she was a gorgeous girl and he wishing he were fifty years younger by God; but Lulu herself was still not so sure. She had liked having hair at the edges of her vision; it had comforted her and hidden her just a little from a world which at times seemed to change with a suddenness that was little short of alarming.

Take, for instance, the entrance into it this very afternoon of Liam Fitzcharles. It was not, she thought, squinting thoughtfully at herself in the mirror as she tried to process her feelings about this evening, that she had not enjoyed talking to him earlier. She had liked it, in fact, she reminded herself, encouragingly: they had talked about food, and about Charlie, and he had made her laugh, and obviously loved his sister, which would have been an important point in his favour even if his sister hadn't been Lulu's closest friend. But whether that meant that she had welcomed the way he had looked at her just before he had left to meet his new boss, she thought, was another matter entirely. It was one thing, she thought, to sit safely alone in the attic, reading the letters of happily married Grandma Jo and think how pleasant it would be to have someone to give her own heart to; it was quite another to be confronted with the risk of actually opening up her chest to give it.

Down below, she heard a door open and close, and Sophie's voice calling her name. She crossed her eyes at herself, stuck out her tongue childishly and opened the bedroom door to go downstairs and meet her date.

★ ★ ★

'The thing is,' said Liam in the taxi while they were speeding through the darkened streets of the winter London night, 'we can't do anything to draw attention to ourselves.'

'They do let me out,' she said. 'Every other Sunday, with a suitable companion.'

'No, you idiot.' The playful nudge he gave her was reassuringly unromantic. 'We can't do anything to let on we know about food. We don't want this guy to figure out who we are and pull out anything special for us — we want to know what he cooks for everyone. So no food talk in front of the waiter, OK? No suspiciously informed questions. No letting on we know the difference between cilantro and parsley. Act like we don't have palates. Act like we're Freddie, OK?'

'OK,' she said. Maybe this might not be frightening after all, she thought. Maybe, if they kept the conversation light and joking, it might even be fun. 'Can I be Sophie instead of Charlie?' she asked. 'I've had lots more practice being her.'

'I'd rather you were you,' he said in a tone which was very far from reassuring, but caused instead a positive flotilla of butterflies to swoop and circle down to the very pit of her stomach.

⋆ ⋆ ⋆

The restaurant was dimly lit, with comfortably solid chairs around dark wood tables. Liam touched her lightly on the waist as he guided her to her seat, and her body leaped in response in a way she did not care for at all.

'Can I tell you something?' he said, when they had ordered their food.

She looked across the table at him.

'What?' she said. She missed her hair, she thought, oh, how she missed her hair.

'I have to confess,' he said, slowly, 'that I find you very attractive indeed.'

She stared at him, frozen in fright. Her hair, was all that she could think, her glorious, missing, irreplaceable hair.

'Oh,' was the best she could say, after a moment.

'You're incredibly pretty,' he said. 'But you're not just pretty, you're also sort of wonderfully familiar somehow. I'm a bit, well, kind of eccentric, as I'm sure Freddie's told you, and I promise you I've never said this to anyone else before, but as soon as we started talking, I felt as if I'd known you for years and years and years. You make me laugh, and I think I make you laugh, too; we seem to look at the world in the same way, and I have the feeling that, if we let it, something really, really special and wonderful and magical could start to happen between us.'

He stopped, and looked directly at her. He was so handsome, she thought miserably, he was so impossibly, so terrifyingly handsome.

'And can I tell you something else?' he asked.

Rigid with dismay, she could only nod.

He leaned towards her, confidentially, across the table.

'I'm scared out of my wits,' he said.

And suddenly, beautifully, it all became possible.

'You are?' she said. She too leaned forward, and, unconsciously, grasped his wrist. 'Me, too,' she said. 'I'm terrified.'

'Horrified,' he said.

'Petrified,' she agreed. 'It's awful.'

'Terrible,' he said.

'Hideous,' she said.

There was a pause.

'But don't you think it's also sort of a little bit nice, too, at the same time?' he asked, then, a little hopefully.

'No,' she told him firmly. She released his wrist, and tapped a finger on it, reprovingly. 'It's unalloyedly horrible.'

'Sorry,' he said, humbly. The wine arrived, and

he poured her a glass. 'You're right,' he said. 'It really is awful. I'll make sure to remember that. I suppose we should start telling each other who we are and such, shouldn't we, if we're going to do this whatever it is we're doing? You go first, I'm sure you're more interesting. Where did you grow up?'

The food arrived when she had got herself as far as university, and she tasted her pork loin, crunchy outside and meltingly tender within.

'Fennel,' she identified approvingly.

He reached over and forked a mouthful.

'Rosemary, of course,' he said.

'And just enough pepper and garlic.'

'But not too much. My venison's amazing, too, want to taste?'

Lulu accepted a forkful.

'Good,' she said. 'I like the little back taste of vinegar.'

'He is good.' Liam nodded. 'Word's getting out, too — I'll have Dad give him a call tomorrow before someone else gets there. He's supposed to be a bit eccentric, but that sort of goes with the territory, and he obviously knows his way around a kitchen.'

Lulu looked at him, thoughtfully.

'You mean people get jobs doing this?' she said. 'Cooking in restaurants?'

'Well, yes, Lulu,' he said. 'They're called chefs.'

And the world tilted on its axis for the second time that day, and suddenly for the first time fell into place.

'How do you train to be a chef?' she asked.

434

'I'm not going to ask you in for coffee,' she said, after dinner, while they were waiting for a taxi.

'It would be weird, wouldn't it?' he agreed. 'With my sister and all. But we'll work something out. We have time. Can I ask you a question?'

She looked up at him, suspiciously, in the night.

'Depends,' she said.

'Well, this might sound strange,' he said. And reached out and gently touched her hair. 'You have such beautiful hair, and I don't want to offend you because it looks just wonderful exactly the way it is, but I can't help but wonder . . . have you ever worn it longer?'

Leaning against his arm, she began to laugh.

'Stick around,' she said.

'I intend to,' he said.

Concord, December 8, 1870.

Dearest Bethie,

Such news I have to share with you, dear, that it cannot wait a single moment. My Professor and I are in love and plan to be wed as soon as his boys are settled! My heart's in a flurry and I am bubbling over with such happiness as I had never dreamed of; I had not known this bliss was possible until I met my Friedrich in the rain today and he gave me his heart and I gave him mine.

Friedrich is *such* a handsome man, Beth.

His forehead is like Jove's, his features are manly, he has beautiful teeth, and his hair is as thick as a haystack; but more important than these attributes is the kindness that shines from his heavenly eyes, the good-will towards his fellow-man that informs each aspect of his being, and best of all, the real love that lights up his face whenever he looks at *me*, your cross and thorny topsyturvy old sister!

I never thought I'd find love, Bethie. Odd and plain-spoken and too tall as I am, I'd supposed that love was reserved for happier souls like Meg and Amy, and resigned myself to the notion of living my life as a literary spinster with a pen for a spouse and a family of stories for children. But then I turned around, and there was Friedrich, and suddenly — I can't explain it but it felt as if I'd been lost and wandering for all of my life and then suddenly come home. Never thought I'd feel this way — but I do, and Friedrich says he feels the same.

He ain't a rich man, my lover. We won't wear elegant clothes or live in a splendid house with a horse and carriage, and I'll never be a fine lady, ordering servants and quirking my finger over tea all day long, but you know how little I care for that. I think that poverty is a beautiful thing if it is nobly borne, and you know I've always been happier when I could carry my share of the load, for it suits me so. My Friedrich comes to me as I to him, with a heart full of love, which is worth more than all the gold and jewels in a sultan's treasury. If

436

only you could have met him, dearie, my happiness would be complete . . . but I like to think that you can see him, at least, from where you are, and are able to rejoice for me.

With love from your brim-full of happiness sister,

Jo.

11

Concord, October 1872.

Dearest Bethie,

This is the last time I shall write to you from this home where we all once shared so much laughter and so many dreams, where I grew from a wild girl to a happy woman, where Meg was courted by John, and Amy made her mud pies and fretted about her nose, and you were our angel and still are. Dear, tonight my Professor returned from the West, and tomorrow, all in a day, I am to marry him, and move to Plumfield to start the school!

Here's how it all came about. Do you remember Aunt Carrol's friend Miss Crabbe, who lives out across the river? Well, she don't talk about it, but she had a younger sister who went astray, poor soul, and had gone to New York to hide herself in the big city. And last week word arrived at Miss Crabbe's that the sister had died of a fever — poor forlorn creature, I hope that someone kind was with her at the last — and left behind her a little fatherless boy that no one knew what to do with. A kind lady in the building had cared for him for some time, but she had been sent for by her brother in St. Louis who had no room for the lad, and finding Miss Crabbe's address

438

among her sister's few papers, had written to throw herself on her generosity for assistance.

Miss Crabbe is a good soul as you know, but she's old and feeble and unable to take care of anyone, let alone a boy of twelve, and at first it seemed there was no help for it but to send him to the poorhouse. It was Aunt Carrol, bless her, who had the happy thought of starting Plumfield, even though the repairs on the house ain't but half finished, the barn needs a new roof, and until last Sunday, when his work with the college came to an end, the school's Professor was still teaching out in the West. But you know how I like adventures, Beth. We have beds and rugs enough for three, and a fine new stove in that great kitchen where stern old Hepzibah used to frighten you so — Fritz and Jimmy and I can make ourselves a capital nest in the part of the house that's already finished, and as for the repairs still happening in the rest of it, I can't think of a happier or more wholesome amusement for a boy, when he is not at his books, than to watch skilled carpenters and plasterers at their work, and maybe take up an idea for an honest trade for when he is grown himself.

Our wedding is to be tomorrow, for of course we can't delay. Fritz arrived home last night (and, oh, it was joy to see him), he goes into town in the morning for the marriage license, and then father will join us, quite plainly, in the parlor, and our life together will begin. Amy's in her despair, for she *had* been planning a grand ceremony with musicians and a splendid breakfast and I know not what else besides; but to tell *you* the truth I've been keeping from her to spare her feelings, I like it better this way. Grand shows ain't my style or Fritz's either: we're plain folk and a simple wedding will suit us best.

I think I shan't write to you again, Bethie. I'm leaving this home where for so long I have lived so quietly with mother and father and your memory, and going to a different place, to start a busy new life whose activities will leave me little time for writing letters to you. But don't think, dearie, that I've forgotten you or ever will, even for an hour. Death cannot part us, for our love can never die, and nor can my changing home, for I feel your presence always watching over me, and wherever I go, I know you are there. Dear, *such* an adventure as I am embarking on in my life with Fritz! But please know that, no matter what happens to me from now on, no matter what joys or sorrows befall, no matter where my life takes me, or how many years of it may be given to me to live, I will take you with me, in my heart, always.

With love, dearest Bethie, from

Jo.

On the Tuesday before the wedding, Emma telephoned Sophie, who was still working at Fulla Beanz.

'Mom says Aunt Amy got in safely,' she said. 'I'm summoned for tea on Thursday, three sharp at The Ritz. Has she been in touch with you about this Marcus person?'

'He's taking us to lunch tomorrow,' said Sophie. 'At The Ivy. Or maybe Aunt Amy's taking us, anyway, we're going, which is quite exciting, isn't it? I've never been to The Ivy. We're having a fashion show tonight at the flat to decide what I'm going to wear, do you want to come? There'll be Lulu and Liam and Charlie and Javier, so you could be the carrying vote in case of a tie.'

'I'm a little bit busy this week,' said Emma, 'since I'm getting married at the end of it. But thanks for thinking of me anyway. Sophie, what do you know about Marcus Wickham?'

'Ohhhh . . . ' Sophie drew a breath. 'Only that he's the best artistic director in the entire history of the theatre. He did the *Hamlet* that Aunt Amy got to see and I didn't, and the awesome *Pygmalion* a couple of years ago, which I did see and I'll never forget — I'd love, *love* to do Eliza Doolittle — and of course there was all that amazing stuff he did in the eighties and the nineties, and he's won three Tonys and a shedload of Laurence Oliviers, and he pretty much single-handedly discovered Alice Weathers while she was still at RADA, and Vanessa Redgrave once said he was one of the three most intelligent theatrical directors she'd ever worked with. Stuff like that, you know?'

'OK,' said Emma. 'But what do you know about him personally?'

'Well.' Sophie thought. 'He was born in London, but his family moved to Dorset when he was a child. He's quite posh, went to Harrow and Cambridge, and then sort of dropped out to be a fashion photographer, of all things, in the seventies, but he says that's been good training for when he finally did find the theatre because it's given him a visual sense. He lives in a flat just off St Martin's Lane and walks to work every day. He's good friends with Emma Thompson and Ian McKellen, and pretty friendly with Kevin Spacey, too, although they pretend not to like each other but everyone knows that's just for publicity. He — '

'What,' interrupted Emma, 'about the women?'

There was a silence.

'What about the women?' said Sophie, then.

'Well, I read an article about him the other day,' said Emma. 'And it seems there have been quite a lot of them.'

'Well, there probably have,' said Sophie. 'He's been around since the seventies, remember.'

'And this article was suggesting there still were,' said Emma. 'There was half a page of photographs, in fact, and some of them were quite young. And there was something else I noticed about them, too.'

Sophie sighed. 'What was that?' she said.

'They were blonde,' said Emma. 'All of them. Without exception. All the way back to Princess Diana.'

There was another silence.

'Do you want me to wear a black wig?' said Sophie. 'I have one for emergency purposes.'

'No, I don't want you to wear a black wig!' said Emma. 'I'm just saying be careful, that's all.' Then, despite herself, 'What do you mean,

442

emergency purposes?'

'Well, in case someone wants me to play dark-haired at the last minute,' said Sophie. 'What do you think I mean?'

'I never know with you,' said Emma. 'Anyway, watch out for yourself, OK?'

'I'm twenty-two,' said Sophie. 'Not twelve. And Aunt Amy will be there, which I think should be passion killer enough for most. Do you think I look like Princess Diana?'

'No,' said Emma.

Sophie sighed again. 'I didn't think so,' she said, then. 'But she always said they were just friends anyway.'

When she had hung up from Emma, Sophie stood for a moment, looking a little wistfully at the telephone in her hand, and wishing she could report the conversation to Jamie. It was not, she reminded herself carefully, that she had been in any sense avoiding Jamie since the conversation with her sisters during Emma's hen weekend. She had answered the telephone each time he had called her, had met him for drinks on the couple of occasions he had suggested, and had promised, faithfully, to telephone him the following afternoon to report on the lunch with Marcus Wickham. Nevertheless, she had started to feel just a little less comfortable with him than she usually was. It was true, she admitted, now thinking about it, that she and Jamie were particularly good friends; and true, too, that they had a habit of being affectionate with each other. It was even possible, now that she thought further, that they might tend to be a little more

443

affectionate with each other than many platonic friends, but then, Sophie reminded herself, she and Jamie were actors, and that was how actors were. Sophie had had a teacher at drama school who had a slightly florid habit of referring to non-actors as 'civilians', which many of her class-mates had mocked but she herself had found secretly just a little thrilling. And the problem with Emma and Lulu, she reflected, now and not for the first time in the last couple of weeks, was that they were, after all, civilians. And the prob-lem with civilians was that they just didn't understand the relationships between actors.

★ ★ ★

The next day, Sophie dressed herself in the agreed-on outfit, a black sweater borrowed from Charlie, a not-too-short black wool skirt and thick black tights, with a blue and black cotton scarf knotted at her neck to provide a hint of colour.

'You look gorgeous,' said Charlie, when Sophie dropped by The Fitzcharles for a fortifying cup of coffee on her way to the restaurant.

'Not too gorgeous, I hope,' said Sophie. 'I wasn't going to say this in front of Lulu, because she'd only go and tell Emma, but he does have a bit of a reputation.'

'I think he should be able to control himself at lunch,' said Charlie, mildly. 'He's probably had some practice by his age. And, after all, you'll be in a public place.'

'And Aunt Amy will be there,' said Sophie.

'*Don't* tell either of the others, but I'm a bit relieved by that part.'

★   ★   ★

As a young man, Marcus Wickham had been legendarily handsome, and was still striking at sixty, with a mane of white hair and piercing blue eyes. He was sitting alone at the table when Sophie walked into the restaurant, but stood up as soon as he saw her, waving enthusiastically.

'I'd know you anywhere,' he said, pumping her hand in greeting, 'because you're the image of your aunt. I'm sure everyone tells you that, but the similarity is quite striking. I'm Marcus, and it's the most complete pleasure to meet you.'

'Sophie,' murmured Sophie, sliding a little disconcertedly into her seat. Beyond the blonde colouring, which showed itself in the family occasionally, which Amy and Fee shared and Sophie alone of the sisters had inherited, she had never been aware of a physical resemblance to her aunt, and was by no means sure that she was flattered by the observation. But she quickly shelved the thought — this was Marcus Wickham, after all, sitting across from her at The Ivy, smiling at her, talking to her, offering her a glass of champagne from the bottle that stood cooling in ice in a silver stand beside the table.

'Or would you rather have what my god-mother, rest her soul, used to call a ginny thing?' he added. 'No? Quite right, I always think champagne is so civilized for lunch, don't you? Now.' He raised a large, white hand. 'I know you want to talk about theatre, and of course we will, we will, but we're not going to start talking about it yet, because I forbid us to say a word about it before your aunt arrives. Not a word. We'd only get talking, and, really, what would be the point of attempting to have a conversation about the theatre without having Miss Amy Parker around to set us straight?'

There was a pause, while he looked at her with interest.

'Um . . . Aunt Amy?' said Sophie, then, cautiously.

'Your Aunt Amy,' agreed Marcus. 'A woman of extraordinary intellect and intuition, who has somehow managed to live her life to this point with almost no exposure to good theatre whatsoever. She is unshaped by experience. She is unsullied by familiarity. She is, in short, the ultimate civilian, and as such, possesses an astuteness of insight that is nothing short of remarkable. Have you ever *been* to the theatre with your Aunt Amy, Sophie?'

'Not,' said Sophie, carefully, 'as far as I can remember.'

'Then you must,' he said. 'I insist on it. It's quite an experience, I assure you.'

There was another pause, during which he continued to look at her.

'OK,' she said, after a moment. 'I'll, um, bear it in mind.'

'Do that,' said Marcus. He was still watching her, Sophie noticed, and with what she now realized to be a faintly disturbing degree of attention. 'Has anyone ever told you, Sophie,' he asked then, 'what an unusually attractive young woman you are? When I look at you, I can quite see how your aunt must have been when she was your age. She's told me a lot about you, you know.' He smiled, appreciatively. 'It seems you're one to be reckoned with.'

'Oh.' Sophie grimaced. Family anecdotes, she thought, were one thing: it would not do, however, to be thought difficult to get along with. 'We're a bit of a feisty family, I'm afraid,' she said. 'It sort of runs in the blood. But I can put it aside if I have to.'

'Never apologize.' Marcus raised his hand again. 'I adore a feisty girl. Some men like the meek and mild sort, but that's not for me and never has been. Give me a touch of the spitfire, please, and I'm a happy boy, and if the spitfire comes with blonde hair, well, what more could a chap ask for, really? Now let's see. What shall we talk about if we're not to talk about the theatre?' He paused, narrowed his eyes, and raised his chin, pursing his lips thoughtfully. 'I know!' he said then. 'Let's talk about . . . love.'

'Love,' said Sophie. Marcus Wickham or not, she was beginning not to like the way the conversation was going.

'Love,' agreed Marcus. ''Why love?' you ask. The answer is, quite simply, because love is everything. It is the beginning and it is the end and it is everything in between. It has impelled poets and playwrights and writers of songs. It has created tragedy — look at poor little Juliet and her Romeo — and the most ecstatic pinnacle of happiness — think of darling

Cinderella living happily ever after with her prince. The Beatles said it was all you need, and it was, let us face it, an act of love between our parents that brought about our very existence in this world in the first place. The question we should be asking ourselves, Sophie, is not, 'Why love?' but 'Where on earth would we be without it?'' Reaching across the table, he tilted Sophie's chin with a finger, and fixed his piercing blue gaze deep into her eyes. 'Are you in love, pretty blonde Sophie?' he asked, softly.

'Um.' Sophie tried subtly to extricate herself, but his finger was surprisingly firm. 'Not right now. Not really, I mean no.'

'You mean not yet,' he corrected her, gently. Grimacing regretfully, he loosed her chin and sat back. 'And I shouldn't have expected you to be, yet, because the young are so hard-hearted, bless them. Darling Emma Thompson, wonderful woman, always says that a heart's no use as a heart unless it's been broken a few times, and she's right, of course, she's right. But you will be in love, one day, I hope. I hope, one day soon. You'll meet someone special, or maybe in a week or a month you'll take a look at a chap you already know and think, I say! *He's* rather splendid! It can happen just like that, you know.' He snapped his fingers, producing a surprising volume of sound. 'Just . . . like . . . *that.*' Still gazing at her with that unsettling intensity, he leaned back across the table to her. 'I'm in love now, Sophie,' he whispered to her. 'I'm in love and it happened just . . . like . . . *that.*'

He raised his champagne glass, and tilted it towards her.

'To your health,' he said, 'pretty young Sophie with the butter-yellow hair, whom I'm hoping to get to know very well indeed.'

It occurred to Sophie for the first time to wonder precisely what words Aunt Amy had used when describing her to Marcus, and exactly what sort of girl she had somehow led him to believe her to be.

'We'll have to prepare for some talk, you and I,' he said, 'when we go public. It's so completely ridiculous on so very many levels, there's the age difference apart from anything else, and, 'Oh, Marcus,' they'll say, I can hear them already, 'Oh, *Marcus*, not another blonde, you silly, silly sausage.''

Aunt Amy would be there soon, Sophie told herself. Aunt Amy would be there, she would take control, and normal life would resume. And there was nothing actually wrong with television after all, she added to herself. There were actually some very good parts for women on television.

'But here's the thing, yellow-haired Sophie,' Marcus continued. 'I *like* blondes. Now you girls are much more imaginative than us chaps. You can fall for all sorts and shapes and colours and ages, and aren't we blokes lucky you can, because it gives so very many more of us a chance with so very many more of you. Us poor boys, we're an uncomplicated bunch, and the fact is that some of us like dark hair and some of us like blonde, and that's the long and the short

449

of it, and I'm a blonde man, always have been. And tell me, Sophie, is that so very wrong?'

It wasn't just hospital dramas and period adaptations on television, Sophie reminded herself. There were some good and, yes, gritty new plays that were being written specifically for television, plays that would be a real challenge to appear in.

'Is it breaking the law of the land to like blondes?' asked Marcus. 'Is it a sin? Was there an extra commandment on the second tablet Moses brought down from the mountain, that said, 'Thou shalt not prefer fair hair to dark?' I don't think so, do you, Sophie? Anyway, you'll stand by a chap, won't you, Sophie, when they start talking about us? Show some of that wonderful fiery family spirit — what your aunt would call moxie — and stand up for me?'

And if you were lucky enough to land a recurring role on a series, she continued to herself, then you could have the chance to explore the same character over a period of time, in a way you never could on the stage. Really, she concluded, when you thought about it, there were very many ways in which television was actually preferable to the stage.

'Good girl, Sophie,' said Marcus. 'I knew I could count on you. I have a feeling that we're going to be very great friends, you and I.'

Suddenly, his eyes shifted to a spot above Sophie's shoulder, and his face broke into a broad smile of the purest delight.

'And here she is,' he said, rising to his feet. 'The ripely beautiful woman I've been tracing in the unformed face of the pretty girl these last ten minutes while we talked of love. The one and positively the only Miss Amy Parker, the golden-haired goddess who holds the whole of this poor fool's heart in the palm of her delicate hand.'

'Oh, Marcus,' said Aunt Amy as he bent to kiss her square, manicured fingers. 'You do talk the most dreadful nonsense sometimes.'

★ ★ ★

'So let's get this straight,' said Liam to Lulu, that evening over dinner. 'We have your Aunt Amy, who's hated the Irish ever since the cook burned the potatoes on the *Mayflower*. We have your cousin Susan, who's really, really nice but so scared of Aunt Amy that she gets hiccups whenever she's around her. We have your mother, who's as likely to ask me at what age I lost my virginity as she is to offer me a glass of wine. We have your father, who's completely lovely until he gets together with Matthew's father, Andrew, when they both take to smashing air guitars over each other's heads and starting stories about going clubbing with Keith Richards, which they can never remember the endings to because, obviously, you wouldn't if you've been clubbing with Keith Richards. And we have Matthew's mother, who is agreed by everyone without exception to be the single most difficult woman on the face of the planet. Correct?'

Lulu nodded. 'Correct,' she said.

'And this is the occasion,' he continued, 'you've chosen to introduce me to your parents.'

451

'There hasn't been time before now,' she said. 'I've told you. Either Dad's been away or you've had to work.'

He thought for a moment.

'There are only two reasons why a man would agree to this invitation,' he said. 'Either he'd be insane. Or he'd be falling very hard in love. Hmm, I wonder which I am?'

She pointed to his wine glass. 'You'd better drink up,' she said. 'The nice man will be here soon to help you back into your jacket.'

* * *

When Lulu and Liam arrived at Lulu's parents' house, Aunt Amy, cousin Susan, Sophie, Matthew and Andrew were already seated at the kitchen table, Andrew at the furthest end from the door.

'Welcome, Liam,' said Fee, kissing him on the cheek. 'I hope you don't mind, but your sister feels so much like another daughter to me that it's hard to be distant and polite. Come in, come in. Normally, we'd relax for a little in the living room before dinner, but my daughters tell me it's good luck to spend the night before a wedding sitting around a table, so that's what we're doing. Would you like a glass of wine?'

'You know, Fee,' said Liam, slowly, 'I have huge admiration for Lulu here and I'm hoping that you and I can be friends, too. But there are certain questions that you just don't . . . ' He stopped. 'Did you just offer me a glass of wine?' he asked.

'Yes,' said Fee, a little surprised.

'Oh,' said Liam. 'Sorry. Yes, please, that'd be marvellous.'

Before he sat down, he shook hands with the other guests.

'Liam Fitzcharles,' he said.

'I believe I've met your sister,' said Aunt Amy. 'Most charming girl, and very attractive. I thought she had a look of the Kennedys.'

'There's a family rumour we might be related,' he said.

Lulu kicked him, not gently, on the shin.

The front door opened and closed, and Emma, wearing a smile that was slightly frozen, ushered in Matthew's mother, Caroline.

'Is this the difficult one?' Liam muttered to Sophie.

'You don't know the half,' she told him.

'Shift over,' he said. 'I'm good at this. They breed 'em tough in the Napa Valley.'

Standing to shake hands, he nudged her down a seat and took his place next to Caroline.

Sophie, displaced to the chair next to Lulu, dug her in the side.

'Keep him,' she whispered. 'Nail his foot to the floor if you have to. He's gold.'

★　★　★

'How was the journey?' Matthew asked Emma when they were seated. 'I was starting to wonder where you were.'

'It was OK,' said Emma. 'Except the taxi driver insisted on taking Marylebone Road.'

'Oh, God.' Lulu shook her head in sympathy.

'I hate Marylebone Road,' said Sophie. 'I want to kill myself by Madame Tussaud's. I always make them go above the park, it's much quicker.'

'Now, that depends on the time of day,' said Matthew.

Liam turned to Caroline, smiled and rolled his eyes.

'Londoners,' he commented quietly. 'They're as bad as New Yorkers, assume everyone's as interested in their city as they are. My father travels the world for his work, and he always says that the people from big cities are far more insular than the people from the smaller places *they* call provincial. You're from Bath, aren't you? This is a terrible confession, but I've never been there, although I hear it's an amazing place. Is it?'

Caroline looked at him for a moment, and then allowed him a thin smile.

'It's beautiful,' she said. 'The most beautiful city I know. I grew up there, but then I lived away from it for far too long. I didn't know how much I'd missed it till I moved back.'

'Then I must make a trip,' he said. 'Now that I'm in England for a while. What should I see there?'

Watching from across the table, Emma saw Caroline's face soften as she began to talk.

★ ★ ★

'So how's life, Lulu?' said Andrew. 'I like the hair, by the way, it suits you.'

'Thank you,' said Lulu. 'And I've got some news, actually, which is that I've decided to go to cooking school this autumn. I've been cooking as a hobby for ages, and I think I'd enjoy it professionally.'

'What an interesting idea,' said Andrew. 'Yes, I can see you doing that. How do you go about training for it?'

Starting to tell him about the cooking schools she had begun to research, Lulu thought fleetingly how extraordinarily pleasant it was to have some good news at last to contribute to a conversation.

* * *

'Marcus wants you to call him at the theatre,' Aunt Amy told Sophie. 'I've told him not to give you a very big part, because I shouldn't think you could remember all those lines, could you?'

'I'm quite good at remembering lines, actually,' said Sophie, after a moment. 'It's remembering other things I sometimes have trouble with.'

Aunt Amy looked unconvinced.

'Well, you can always carry the script around with you,' she said, at last. 'Pretend it's a book or something.'

* * *

Andrew leaned across the table to cousin Susan.

'I'll tell you a trick,' he said, quietly. 'Put your finger at the bottom of your throat, just above where the two collarbones meet, yes, right there. Feel that little hollow? Well, go down a little over that hump of bone, press into the slight indentation beneath it and those hiccups will go away.'

'Oh, my God,' said Susan after a moment. 'That's amazing.'

Andrew winked at her. 'It's also good for self-defence,' he said. 'Push there, and you can send a strong man flying off his feet.'

$\star$ $\star$ $\star$

'Are you enjoying your stay?' Lulu asked Andrew.

'Having a marvellous time, thanks,' said Andrew. 'There's always so much to see in London. I went to Shepherd's Bush market today, do you know it? It's fantastic, a real slice of the immigrant city, with the railway line running past, stalls selling West Indian fruit and veg that have been run by the same family for generations now. It was completely charming and somehow Sixties-ish.' He turned to peer hopefully towards David at the other end of the table. 'Almost like walking into a Beatles song.'

'Can I ask you a medical question?' said Lulu. 'Talking of, um, fruit stalls. You know we had that drama with Sophie last year. Well, that was an allergic reaction to shellfish and she nearly died, and yet another friend of ours is allergic to strawberries and he only gets a slight rash on his skin. Why were Sophie's symptoms so much worse than Jamie's? Is it because they're allergic to different foods?'

456

'Well, that's an interesting point,' said Andrew: although semi-retired, he prided himself in keeping up with the latest news in medical research. He laid down his knife and fork, and prepared to explain carefully to Lulu the intricacies of the pathology of anaphylaxis.

★   ★   ★

'I think,' said David, 'we need some more wine at this end of the table.' He rose and went to the kitchen counter, picked up the bottle that Liam had brought, and raised his eyebrows.

'I think you're going to be a rather useful sort of chap to have around,' he told him. He sat down again, poured a splash into his glass, sipped, then leaned forward to Liam and Caroline.

'I think,' he whispered to them confidentially, 'that we're going to keep this particular bottle a little secret just between the three of us.'

Caroline actually giggled.

★   ★   ★

'If you want to change places,' Sophie muttered hopefully to Lulu as they cleared the plates from the main course, 'you can play footsie with Liam and I can talk to Andrew instead of Aunt Amy.'

Unseen by the others, Lulu jabbed her sister, hard, in the ribs.

'Don't push your luck,' she hissed, sternly.

★   ★   ★

457

'Marvellous food, Fee,' said Caroline to Fee at the end of the evening.

'Thank you,' said Fee.

The two women looked at each other, and, as one, decided not to prolong the conversation.

★　★　★

'Stick around,' said David to Andrew when the guests had departed and Fee and Susan retired to bed. 'Nobody cares if *we* get beauty sleep or not.'

'I suppose I'd better,' said Andrew. 'Someone has to help you finish all this wine.'

'Bunch of lightweights, the younger generation,' grumbled David, reaching for the corkscrew.

★　★　★

Looking back on her wedding day, Emma always thought how simple it all had been.

She and her sisters had gone back from dinner at their parents' house to spend the night in Belsize Park, where they had sat for one last delicious hour around the kitchen table with Charlie, gossiping sleepily, drinking chamomile tea and eating chocolates from the shop in Camden Passage, which Lulu had urged upon her, pointing out that it was a medical impossibility to gain very much more than half a stone between ten on one evening and two the following afternoon. She had slept in Lulu's bed, and the next day woke to a morning of pale February light, to her last breakfast as a single woman of toast and apricot jam and not too much coffee, followed by a walk to wake her up and a visit from Fee's masseuse, a gentle Brazilian woman with kind hands.

She bathed in Jo Malone's bath oil, smelling of lotus blossom and water lily, wrapped herself in a dressing gown, and ate her last single lunch, chosen after careful consultation with Lulu, of broccoli quiche with spinach and walnut salad and a large fruit plate of melon, pineapple, strawberries and grapes. She dressed herself in the slippery silk garments in the lovely indescribable pinky-creamy-champagne colour, which had been waiting so patiently in the closet for her for almost a year, fastened the pearl buttons, and clasped around her neck the single strand of pearls that Aunt Amy had given to each of the sisters on their eighteenth birthday, which all three were wearing today.

Then she went to the mirror and sat while Sophie, pretty as a picture in her own sweet-pea-pink bridesmaid dress, her lower lip caught in her teeth with concentration, fastened in her sister's hair a comb of white silk flowers with silver seeds, then, at last, she opened the box containing the Josephine shoes, and, at last, slipped them onto her feet.

Then all three sisters, laughing together, clutching each other, feeling a little dazed and as if they were dreaming, went out to the street, where a friend of Jamie's, who worked for a vintage car company, awaited them in a capacious and gleaming black Rolls Royce. They drove through the streets of North London, where people who saw them drive past either smiled, or waved, or looked nostalgic, or thoughtful, to the oblong cinnamon and cream brick pumping station by the reservoir, which was looking exactly as Emma had hoped it would that day, with great blocks of silver light reflecting from the water and pouring through the long windows, bouncing off the iron pillars, and onto the shining wood floor, where Mom and Dad were waiting for them: Mom elegant in tailored maroon and pink and clutching a tissue, Dad unrumpled and wearing a suit and tie, with his smile a little wistful today, offering her his arm as the steel band struck up a reggae version of the 'Trumpet Voluntary', to walk her through the long, light room past the eighty people she loved best in all the world, to meet the man she loved better than all of them.

The ceremony was brief and free from fuss, with simple readings and traditional vows: Emma had worried that she would cry during the vows, but as it turned out it was Matthew who faltered, although he collected himself quickly and threw at her a glance of alarmed relief. The next thing she knew, the vows were over, the registrar pronounced them husband and wife, Matthew — her quiet, contained Matthew — launched himself upon her with a kiss so fiery that it took her breath away, the room burst into laughter and applause, and Emma was married.

★   ★   ★

After the ceremony and the photographs, the guests were offered a buffet meal from a catering company recommended by Charlie, which they ate at tables decorated with pots of paperwhites. Aunt Amy, sitting at her table near the buffet waiting for Susan to bring her a plate, was joined by Jamie, his plate heaped high with chicken, salmon and beef.

'Shouldn't you have some vegetables with that?' she asked him, looking with interest at his selection.

He frowned at her in faint surprise. 'I'm a bachelor,' he explained.

Aunt Amy, unusually, was silenced.

★　★　★

Javier and Charlie waited at their table next to Aunt Amy's until the line had diminished before going for their food. 'This is a phenomenal wedding,' said Javier, quietly, to Charlie. 'All this light, and everything so clear and simple, I have never been to a wedding like this before. My parents would not like it so much, because they are quite conventional and they prefer things to be Catholic, but, for me, I like it.' He frowned, a little anxiously. '*You* are Catholic, aren't you?' he asked.

She smiled at him and laid a hand on his knee beneath the table.

'I'm half Italian,' she reminded him, 'and half Irish. I think we can safely say that I'm Catholic.'

He smiled back, and set his hand on top of hers.

461

On Aunt Amy's other side, she was joined by Nigel-Manolete with his partner, a very large, very handsome young man from the West Indies.

'I'll tell you something you won't often hear me say, Auntie,' he told her. 'And that's that if anyone in the world could tempt me from my lovely Winston here, it's your corker of a niece.'

'Excuse me.' Aunt Amy favoured him with one of her more chilling stares. 'Have we been introduced?' she asked after a moment.

'No,' he said. 'But I know you're family, and do you know how?' He winked. 'The legs. They're unmistakable. The minute you walked in, I thought, Aha! So that's where the bride gets her gorgeous gams.'

People very rarely addressed Aunt Amy thus. Watching with interest from the safety of the next table, Charlie was surprised to see her pinken a little and toss her head. 'I've been told they aren't bad,' she admitted. 'For an old lady.'

Nigel nudged her. 'Oh, go on,' he said. 'You're in your prime, and you know it.'

Aunt Amy looked pensive. If she had had a fan, thought Charlie, she would have rapped him with it at that point.

★ ★ ★

Tom filled his plate and found a place at a table by a window next to a woman in her thirties with dark hair and deep brown eyes set in a long face.

'Tom Doyle,' he said. 'From California. I'm

Emma's parents' lodger.'

'Susan Brooke,' she said. 'From Boston. I'm Emma's thirty-third cousin, or something like that. I think I saw you on the stairs yesterday, but I couldn't introduce myself because Sophie was telling me a story about her roommate and our Aunt Amy and it was kind of like being hypnotized by a very friendly blonde windmill.'

'And I think I saw you walking through the hallway the day before, but Lulu had caught me recycling a teabag and was showing me the correct way to make a proper pot. Who knew it was so complicated? Hello, Susan Brooke from Boston. How are you liking London?'

'I'm loving it,' she said. 'I always do. I love London. The person who's tired of London is tired of life.'

He looked at her with interest. 'You've read Dr Johnson,' he said.

'I grew up with him,' she said. 'We have a very good copy in the family. My great-great-grandfather was tutor to a rich man's son, or nephew, or something, and when he married my great-great-grandmother the rich man gave him his own copy for a wedding present.'

'Interesting wedding gift,' he said. 'Not very practical, but interesting.'

'Story is, my great-great-grandmother wasn't too pleased, but my great-great-grandfather was delighted. He was a big reader, and it passed on down the genes. My parents used to sit and read to themselves over dinner.'

'Did they?' he said. 'Wow.' Then, softly, almost to himself, 'Wow.'

'How are you feeling?' Fee asked David, watching as Emma glided from table to table, graceful in her silk dress and Josephine shoes, talking, kissing, being admired.

He smiled. 'Old,' he said. 'And tired. And incredibly stupid for what I nearly did and incredibly lucky that you've given me a second chance. But most of all more proud than I've ever been of Emma, which I didn't think was possible. You've raised a good woman, Fee.'

She shook her head. 'We,' she corrected him. '*We've* raised a very good woman indeed.'

She looked down at her plate for a moment, and then back up at him.

'It's kind of a pity,' she said slowly, then, 'that Claire couldn't be here, too.'

His eyes lit, hopefully.

'She did come, in fact,' he said. 'You know I don't allow her to have money but she hitchhiked. I sent her away at the door, told her today was for you and me.'

'Well, we'll see her at home,' said Fee. 'How's her breath these days?'

'Much better,' he said. 'She had all her teeth out — well, both of them — so that cleared that up. Her foot's turned gangrenous, though, but at least it's a different sort of smell.'

'Ewww.' Sophie, floating past with a glass of champagne, wrinkled her nose in disgust. 'Can't you two keep your spotted old hands off each other at least for a few minutes, *at least* when we're out in public?'

'This is really good stuff,' said Lulu, when Emma stopped at the table where she was sitting with Liam. 'Really good. Although if it had been me, I'd have used just the very smallest little bit more paprika on the chicken.'

Emma stared at her. 'This is my wedding day, Lulu,' she reminded her. 'I cannot believe that you have just criticized the paprika on my wedding-day chicken.'

'Neither can I,' said Liam. 'The paprika's perfect, any more would be too much. I'm surprised at you, Lulu. There *is* rather a lot of sage, though, which might have confused your taste buds.' Looking up, he caught Emma's eye. 'Although it's quite delicious,' he added hastily. 'And you probably shouldn't listen to me about the sage, I've always happened to prefer thyme with chicken myself, but that's just me.'

'Oh, God,' said Emma. 'Two of you.'

★ ★ ★

'Are you OK to dance?' whispered Matthew to Emma as the applause died down on Cheng's best-man speech. 'Those shoes are pretty, but can you dance in them?'

'They're not pretty,' she corrected him. 'They're beyond heavenly. And just watch me.'

★ ★ ★

After Matthew and Emma had danced, the floor was thrown open and Lulu and Liam danced together for the first time.

'Thanks for inviting me,' he said. 'This is a great wedding. I like weddings.'

'It is a good one, isn't it?' she agreed. 'But it was always going to be — Emma's so efficient.'

'Isn't she,' he said. 'I like weddings.'

Lulu said nothing.

'Weddings,' he said after a moment. 'Funny things, but I like them.'

Lulu stopped dancing and drew back to look up into his eyes.

'If you say that one more time,' she said levelly, 'I won't take you to the Cheddar-cheese shop.'

'Sorry,' he said quickly. 'I like funerals, too, if that's any help? We do marvellous ones in Ireland, we're famous for them.'

*   *   *

While Emma danced with David, Matthew danced with Caroline.

'She'll make you a good wife,' she told him. 'I don't care for the mother and the younger sister is an odd sort of girl, but her boyfriend's surprisingly normal.'

Which, coming from Caroline, was praise so stratospherically high that Matthew tripped on his step, kicking himself in the shins.

*   *   *

After Emma had danced with David, she danced with Andrew.

'Look after my boy,' he said to her. 'Give him a happy place to come home to, always.'

'I plan to,' she told him, fumbling for the emergency tissue tucked discreetly into her pearl-buttoned sleeve.

★　★　★

At the end of Matthew's dance with Fee, Liam cut in.

'It's so very good to meet you at last, Liam,' Fee said to him as they danced. 'I'm immensely fond of your sister, as you know, and I know how close you both are. I don't want to pry, and please do say if you don't want to talk about it, but how old were you when your mother died?'

'You know, Fee,' said Liam, 'I have huge admiration for Lulu, and I'm hoping that you and I can be friends, too. But . . . ' He stopped. 'Did you just ask me about my mother?' he asked.

'Yes,' said Fee.

'Oh,' said Liam. 'Sorry. I was five and Freddie was three.'

'Poor little babies,' said Fee. 'Five and three, that must have been so hard on all of you. It's a huge credit to your father that you've both grown up so beautifully. Can I ask you another question, Liam?'

A little nervously, Liam cleared his throat. 'Ask away,' he said.

'What on earth,' said Fee, 'has Lulu been telling you about me?'

'You know what you'd look good in?' said Nigel to Aunt Amy as they danced. 'My duchess line. Not many girls can carry it off, but you could. Come into the shop tomorrow and I'll fix you up — the Malfi, I think, or maybe the Marlborough in a nice classy chestnut, show off those ankles. And I'll bet you a pound to a penny there's someone who'd like to see that, isn't there?'

'There might be,' said Aunt Amy.

'It's a date, then,' said Nigel. The music ended and he escorted her to her chair. 'Now, if you'll excuse me, I'm going to go and wrestle my boyfriend back from the band's drummer and propose to him.'

★ ★ ★

Sophie danced with Matthew, with Winston, with Cheng, with David, and with Liam. Jamie danced with Emma, with Fee, with Rosie, with Lulu and with Emma's best friend from university. At last, Jamie saw Sophie sitting alone at a table, looking thoughtful, and went over to her.

'Do you want to dance?' he asked her a little shyly.

Sophie looked up at him and smiled.

'I suppose it would be silly not to, really, wouldn't it?' she said.

★ ★ ★

Tom and Susan did not dance. They were too busy talking. And talking.

★ ★ ★

'Mom, I have something terrible to confess to you,' said Emma the next day when she and Matthew arrived at her parents' house for brunch. 'I've started an affair with a married man. Can you ever forgive me?'

'Only if you promise to continue it,' said Fee, smiling. Emma had never looked so pretty, she thought, as she did today in faded jeans and a loose red jumper, with no make-up and her hair hanging softly around her face. She turned to kiss Matthew. 'Welcome, son-in-law. Did Caroline catch her train OK?'

'She did,' said Matthew. 'And she even admitted to having had a good time this weekend, for which I think we can largely thank Liam. Thank you, Liam.'

''Twas me Oirish charrm, sure,' said Liam. ''Twas the blarney, d'ye see, the blarney.'

Lulu looked at him over her coffee mug.

'Never talk like that again,' she said.

'Sorry,' he said, returning to his scrambled eggs.

'You looked beautiful, Emma,' said Charlie. 'I know all brides are beautiful, but I see lots of them at the hotel, and you were really something a bit above and beyond.'

'Well, thank you,' said Emma, 'although I'm sure it helps that we're friends. We all always think our friends are special.'

'Well, *I* hardly know you at all,' said Liam, 'and I still thought you looked pretty good. Not that I'm a connoisseur of bridal fashions, mind you. Lulu, do you have any Tabasco sauce? Everyone eats it on scrambled eggs in California and I sort of got into the habit.'

'Californians.' Fee, who was standing by the kitchen cupboard, shook her head sadly at Liam as she took out the bottle and handed it to Lulu.

'Aha,' said Lulu. 'That explains it, then.'

'Explains what?' said Liam.

'Nothing,' she said. 'Have some sauce. Actually, can I try a bite? I thought it would just taste weird, but now that I think about it, it might be quite interesting.'

'This is amazing food, Fee,' said Jamie, who an hour before had appeared at the door at Sophie's side, looking, Lulu later said, like the cat that had swallowed the caviar. 'Really awesome. I can see where Lulu gets her talent.'

Lulu looked at Jamie's plate.

'Are you all right, Jamie?' she asked. 'Because I notice you've only had a normally enormous sized portion and yet you seem to be slowing down. Are you not feeling well or something?'

'It's his second breakfast,' said Sophie. 'I wasn't going to unleash the full appetite on you all without proper preparation, so we stopped on the way at Carroll's, in your honour, Lulu-belle. Oh! And you'll never guess who we saw coming in when we were going out! Only Tom and Susan looking all pink and happy, and I think they'd been holding hands!'

'I knew it!' said Emma triumphantly. 'I knew

470

they'd get on! I was hoping for that all along — they're like two peas in a pod! What on earth's the matter with you three?'

From the sofa where Lulu, Sophie and Charlie had collapsed in a heap of merriment, Lulu raised a weak head.

'Nothing,' she croaked, feebly. 'Nothing at all. Carry on eating and ignore us.'

'I think,' said Javier to Liam and Jamie, 'that there are matters about our girlfriends that we will never understand. And I think it is better if we do not try to.'

'And I think,' said David, raising a coffee mug to him in salute, 'that you're a very wise young man.'

'What's it like to be married, Emma?' said Sophie. 'Does it feel different being somebody's wife?'

'In a funny kind of way it does,' said Emma. 'Not different with Matthew, he and I are the same as we've always been, which is good because I wouldn't have wanted that to change. But I do feel different about myself somehow. Yesterday I was a woman who lived, very happily and faithfully, with my boyfriend. Today, I'm not just me any more. I'm a wife, which means I've become part of a line of women in the family who fell in love and got married, a whole long line that goes back through history, past Mom and Grandma Jojo, and even past Grandma Jo and Grandma Jo's mother and Grandma Jo's mother's great-great-grandmother, all the way back to the women we don't know anything about and never will, but who we look like and walk like and think like in more ways than we can ever guess, because they were the ones who made us. Mom's always saying that times have changed for women, but this is something that's stayed the same, this falling in love and promising to be together forever, even when the romance has worn off and we're old and busy and tired, and we've raised babies and fixed houses and changed jobs and heard each other's jokes and stories a hundred thousand times, and Matthew's got a paunch like his dad and I can never find my car keys like Mom. He'll be my husband and I'll be his wife. And that feels ... just ... amazingly wonderful, really.'

'Come here, you,' said Fee.

'Mother-daughter moment,' Sophie told Jamie as Fee and Emma hugged. 'Sorry about that, those two are full of them lately.'

'I think they look sweet,' said Jamie, rummaging in the pocket of his jeans: happiness had made him sentimental.

'Then you're a silly old thing,' said Sophie, handing him a tissue. 'And we'll have to stock up on these, because it's going to get much worse before she leaves for North Dakota.'

It was time, thought Lulu, then. Time to share the secret she had guarded for nearly a year now, time to bring the letters from the dark of the attic and into the light-filled house to show them to her mother and sisters, time to extend to them, too, the pleasure that had been hers of meeting Grandma Jo. She sighed a little, then smiled to herself, took a deep breath, stood up, and rapped a spoon on her coffee mug for attention.

'I want you all to listen,' she said. 'Because I've got something to say, OK? Now, I know you know I've been spending a lot of time in the attic lately, and I'm sure you've all been wondering what I've been doing up there, and now I'm going to tell you.'

Emma looked at her through narrowed eyes. 'If you've found Grandma Cissie's recipes,' she said, 'and you're going to bring them down here to criticize them, would you please do me a special wedding favour and wait till after we've left for our honeymoon?'

'It's not the recipes,' Lulu told her. She had never found the recipes, in fact. They were gone with Grandma Jo's books, it seemed, vanished into the void where some once-cherished items do eventually go, left forgotten on a shelf somewhere, or fallen behind a bookcase, or carelessly stuffed into a bag for a charity shop; Cissie Bhaer Fraser's recipes were gone forever, and no one would ever know now what foods she had liked to cook in her kitchen nearly a hundred years ago, or how she had liked to cook them. But parts of the past would always disappear, and Lulu was luckier than most; Liam did not even know who his grandfather was. And, missing or not, the recipes had proved their worth and more, because it was searching for them that had brought her to find Grandma Jo.

'I never did find the recipes,' she said. 'But I did find something else. It's something that's sort of amazing and a little bit magical, that's about all of us. I've probably been a bit selfish in keeping it to myself for all this time, but it's something that I needed to do for a while, and when you see it, I hope you'll understand why I needed it all to myself, and also understand why I don't need it so much now, not any longer. Anyway, I'm not going to say any more, I'm just going to go up there and get it now and bring it down to show you.'

'Do you want some help?' said Liam, rising.

'No, thanks.' She smiled at him, the man without a past with whom she was falling in love, and shook her head. He could help her later, she thought, when she brought down the larger boxes, the big box with the theatre programmes and school yearbooks, and the little leather case that held the fans and the sketches and the pieces of needlework. But first, she would go alone to bring down the letters; it would be the last time she would have Grandma Jo to herself. 'Thanks, but I want to do this on my own.'

'Independent family, aren't they?' Liam grumbled to Matthew, sitting down again.

'You don't know the half,' said Matthew.

★   ★   ★

Lulu went up the stairs of her parents' house, as she had so many times in the last year, up past the seventh stair that creaked on the left side but not the right, and the twelfth stair, where there was a yellow paint stain on the carpet that had never washed out, past her parents' bedroom and Fee's consulting room, up the stairs, past

474

Tom's room — its door closed, its occupant out eating breakfast with cousin Susan — and up the rickety ladder into the attic. She went to the bookshelf, picked up the box with the letters — she had never found time to attach a rose, but maybe Sophie could make a decoration that would be even prettier — turned to go down the ladder again, and then stopped.

It was true that she had been selfish, she thought, keeping such a treasure so secret for all this time; it would be a nice gesture now to bring down, not only the letters, but just a couple of items from the little case of souvenirs to give her sisters a taste of what was there. Nothing big — she had the box and couldn't carry a lot more — but maybe just four small things, one to represent each sister.

She set the letters box down, switched on the light, and went to open the case. The kid gloves, she now knew, had belonged to Meg; the piano music to Beth; the drawings to Amy. But what would have been Jo's? Jo had not been good, Lulu had gathered, with possessions; there had been frequent references in the letters to objects broken or lost, and looking through the collection Lulu realized now how few surviving items seemed to have belonged to her great-great-grandmother. The copy of *The Pilgrim's Progress* would have to do, she decided at last, impossibly battered and broken as it was, with the inscription on the flyleaf all but faded away, its words more or less indecipherable but for three: 'Jo', 'Marmee' and what had apparently once been 'Christmas'. At least its state demonstrated that its owner had enjoyed reading it. She lifted it, very gingerly, from the leather case, and set it carefully on top of Amy's sketch of Marmee.

As she did so, another envelope fell from the book's back cover. Lulu bent to pick it up: it was thicker and more modern than those in the box, and addressed in a far shakier writing, but Lulu could tell from a glance that this, too, was Jo's hand. She took it to the window for light, looked at the front of the envelope, and blinked in astonishment. It was addressed 'To My Great-Great-Granddaughter'.

Lulu placed the sketch and the piano music carefully on the shelf by the letters box, sat down on the armchair and turned on the lamp. Then she opened the envelope — it seemed to have been opened before — and began to read.

Boston, November 1945.

My dearest great-great-granddaughter,

I dreamed about you last night. Now some may say the old dame's gone crazy at last, that the second glass of wine with the cake and ice cream at her hundredth birthday bash yesterday, the one which caused Cousin Henry to frown so ominously and shake his head in foreboding, has sent her clear bananas, and who's to say but that they're right? Nevertheless, I *did* dream of you, and the dream was so strong and so real that I can't help but pick up my pen — a stout sturdy Waterman, a far cry from the flimsy quill pens I used to run through at such a rate when I was a girl — to send you a greeting. And if anyone who isn't you should chance to pick this letter up to read after I'm gone, and shake their head and think, The old dear's nutty as a fruitcake, then I'd remind them that the letter weren't addressed to them in the first place, and add that I'd thank them kindly not to go snooping through other people's correspondence because it ain't polite. (Ha! The old girl may be crazy, but she's no more dumb than she ever was — sprinkle *that* on your Thanksgiving turkey and chew on it.)

Here's what I dreamed. I dreamed that my granddaughter Jojo married that decent fellow Bob Chamberlain who's lately come a-courting — always liked that family, you knew where you were with them — and that Jojo had a daughter who was like me, and that the daughter had a daughter who was like her. Couldn't get a name, couldn't get a face, had the feeling you lived somewhere far away — our family always did like to go adventuring — but you were mine all right, awkward, and stubborn, and fierce, and funny, and, yes, I can say it to *you* as I never could say to my stern young self all those years ago, just wonderfully loving, and kind, and good.

I wonder what your world will be like, great-great-granddaughter, sixty-some years from now? Will you travel everywhere in motor cars with wings instead of wheels and fly to the moon on rocket ships for weekends? Will the ladies dress like men, as seems to be the fashion now, and the men like ladies, for turnabout is fair play and I'd like to see some of *them* wrestling with stockings and girdles and garter belts morning after morning? Will all disease be cured and all war be banished and every single person equal to every other person, with no one poor or humble or looked down upon? I'd like to think it, but after a century spent living among these dear flawed creatures called men and women, I ain't betting the barn on it.

Have you been told about me, great-great-granddaughter? Did you know that I lived in Massachusetts, and was fifteen years old when the war to save the Union — what they now call the Civil War — was begun? Did you know that I loved horses and stories and longed to be a boy and once cut off all my hair to sell to send money to my father, sick in a hospital in Washington? Did you know that I was a writer and yearned to be famous for it, and for a few years was so (some fool of a fellow in Boston once wanted to put my letters into a book — I soon sent him packing) until the tastes changed with the new century, everyone forgot about me, and I found I didn't care a fig, for my family are more important to me by far than fame? Did you know that I had three sisters, that one was taken from me far too soon and never a day passed afterward that I didn't miss her and mourn her? All of my sisters are gone now, and so is my husband, but don't fret for me, dearie — I know I'll join them soon, along with my parents, and will rejoice to do so, for I'm growing tired at last.

Be a good girl, dear, and be happy. Find work that you love, for work is essential for a happy and independent life, and you and I can't live without some passion for what we do — I wonder what you *will* do? It don't matter, so long as you love it. Treasure your family, for, as important as work is, family is far more so. Love your sisters — I have the idea that you have a couple of them, and if so you're blessed, for a happy family is the most beautiful thing in the world. And love yourself, too — it weren't always easy for me to be kind to myself in my day, but I see that gentler days are coming, and I want you to remember always that you are very special and dear. Think of me sometimes, dearest child, and know that on this day I was thinking of you, and was more proud than I can say to know that I was one of the ones who helped to shape you.

With all my love, dearest great-great-granddaughter, from,

Grandma Jo.

P.S. to Cousin Henry. Quit snooping, Mister, this is between my girl and me.

Acknowledgements

Obviously, this book would not have been conceivable without Louisa May Alcott's extraordinary *Little Women*, which has entertained and inspired girls for generations, and to which my work must stand as most humble homage.

Back in the twenty-first century, I'd like to thank Lydia Newhouse, my wonderfully imaginative first editor, who had the idea in the first place and was kind enough to commission me to carry it out; Trish Todd of Touchstone Fireside and Mari Evans of Michael Joseph, who encouraged me to go the extra distance; Samantha Mackintosh, eagle-eyed copy-editor; and Felicity Blunt of Curtis Brown, who believes in me and makes me smile.

In London, I owe immense thanks to the Barber family: Patti, Richard, Edward, Grace and most particularly Harriet, whose unerring ear for contemporary London idiom has kept me on the straight and narrow throughout; as well as to Roger Tagholm for professional advice; to Frances Stevenson of Curtis Brown and to Joseph Thompson for advice about the theatre; to Sheila Ebbutt and John Raftery for inspiring the wedding venue; and, in Hastings, to Josephine Fairley of Judges Bakery for advice about wedding cakes.

In America, my thanks go to Deborah Kolar for professional help; to Geoffry D. White Ph.D., of Los Angeles and John Hargrove MD, of Eugene, Oregon, for psychological and physical medical background respectively; to Elizabeth Montez for inspiring Lulu's career choice; to Michael Tschetter for providing bachelor humour; to Candi Lira, Cynthia Medeiros and Kimberley Wells for unending moral support; and to Brian Letscher and the funny, sunny and wise women of the Penmar Park exercise class for helping me stay sane.

And at last, and of course, I salute my wonderful husband, Owen Bjørnstad, who has my love, always.

We do hope that you have enjoyed reading this large print book.

Did you know that all of our titles are available for purchase?

We publish a wide range of high quality large print books including:
Romances, Mysteries, Classics
General Fiction
Non Fiction and Westerns

Special interest titles available in large print are:
The Little Oxford Dictionary
Music Book
Song Book
Hymn Book
Service Book

Also available from us courtesy of Oxford University Press:
Young Readers' Dictionary
(large print edition)
Young Readers' Thesaurus
(large print edition)

For further information or a free brochure, please contact us at:
Ulverscroft Large Print Books Ltd.,
The Green, Bradgate Road, Anstey,
Leicester, LE7 7FU, England.
Tel: (00 44) **0116 236 4325**
Fax: (00 44) **0116 234 0205**

DON'T LET ME GO

Catherine Ryan Hyde

Ten-year-old Grace knows that her mom loves her, but her mom loves drugs too. There's only so long Grace can fend off the 'woman from the county' who is threatening to put her into care. Her only hope is Billy. Grown man Billy Shine hasn't left his apartment for years. People scare him. And so day in, day out, he lives a perfectly orchestrated, silent life within his four walls. Until now . . . Grace bursts into Billy's life with a loud voice and a plan to get her mom clean. But it won't be easy, because they will have to take away the one thing her mom needs most . . .

COME THIS WAY HOME

Liz Lyons

It's a stormy Irish summer, and the three Miller sisters are gathering at their beautiful, but shabby old family home, Tobar Lodge. Gina, middle sister and single mum, is doing her best to keep the country house afloat by playing host to summer visitors. Eldest, Lottie, is home to lick her wounds after her latest romantic adventure has ended in disaster once again. Rachel, the youngest, has led a more charmed life, but this time is bringing back a family who are struggling after the collapse of her husband's business. Family and strangers meet and collide, and as the holiday season draws to a close a long-hidden secret comes to light. All are forced to look at what home and family really mean to them.

THE KIRILOV STAR

Mary Nichols

November, 1920. After the Revolution, Russia suffers a brutal civil war and thousands flee for their lives. The Kirilov family, distant relatives of the Romanovs, are in danger. When tragedy strikes, four-year-old Lydia Kirillova is separated from her family. The only key to her identity is the opulent jewel concealed in her petticoat. The benevolent diplomat, Sir Eward Stoneleigh, brings her to England, where she grows up well educated, wealthy, and surrounded by a loving family. Yet Lydia, yearning to know the truth about her heritage, quickly accepts the charming Nikolay Andropov's invitation to join him on a trip to Russia. But with the Second World War looming, Lydia's situation becomes desperate. Will she ever find a place to finally think of as a home?

THE CAT'S TABLE

Michael Ondaatje

In the early 1950s, an eleven-year-old boy boards a huge liner bound for England — 'a castle that was to cross the sea'. At mealtimes, he is placed at the lowly 'Cat's Table' with an eccentric group of grown-ups and two other boys, Cassius and Ramadhin. As the ship makes its way across the Indian Ocean, through the Suez Canal and into the Mediterranean, the boys become involved in the worlds and stories of the adults around them, tumbling from one adventure and delicious discovery to another, 'bursting all over the place like freed mercury'. And at night, the boys spy on a shackled prisoner — his crime and fate a galvanising mystery that will haunt them forever . . .